WE CAN SAVE US ALL

US

A NOVEL

ADAM NEMETT

The Unnamed Press
Los Angeles, CA

AN UNNAMED PRESS BOOK

www.unnamedpress.com

Library of Congress Cataloging-in-Publication Data

Nemett, Adam, author.
We can save us all : a novel / by Adam Nemett.
Description: Los Angeles : Unnamed Press, 2018.
Identifiers: LCCN 2018021901 (print) | LCCN 2018023933 (ebook)

ISBN 9781944700775 | ISBN 9781944700768 (pbk. : alk. paper)
Classification: LCC PS3564.E47989 (ebook)

LCC PS3564.E47989 W4 2018 (print) | DDC 813/.54--dc23
LC record available at https://lccn.loc.gov/2018021901

Designed & typeset by Jaya Nicely

Distributed by Publishers Group West
Manufactured in the United States of America
First Edition

This book is for my kids, and for all the young people whose timeless mission is to remake an inherited world.

TABLE OF CONTENTS

EVIL SUPERMAN:
"Well I hope you don't expect me to save you, because I don't do that anymore."

LORELEI:
"Don't worry about me. I'm long past savin'..."

—*Superman III*

The Ten Assured Futures of the USV

1. *You will see the clock ticking.*

2. *You will discover your powers and weaknesses.*

3. *You are not mild-mannered.*

4. *You are not a nerd.*

5. *You are not entitled.*

6. *You are not yet free.*

7. *You will evolve or perish.*

8. *You will keep your mask on. Our mystery is our power.*

9. *You will zero in and emerge from the dark neck of time luminous without end.*

10. *We can save us all.*

WE CAN SAVE US ALL

I AM ANOTHER YOURSELF

Even Hitler was on meth. Google it. Every morning, Hitler's personal physician, Dr. Theo Morell, entered his bedroom to administer charisma intravenously: a cocktail injection of methamphetamines and morphine, plus cocaine eye drops. Adolf never asked what was in the needle and Theo never offered the secret. He simply upped the dosage until Hitler succumbed to something like Parkinson's, something like addiction, and drowned in his own sea.

For the record, David Fuffman never assumed Mathias Blue was real—real meaning unenhanced, unadulterated—only that Mathias's was an evolved consciousness. Though David would likely fail to comprehend the extent of Mathias's genius, he'd be among the tawdry heroes who faked greatness, who sat at the feet of Mathias's being and came to class. David only and infinitely *believed* in him. And now the power is going off and the light is leaving them, maybe forever. The tide is coming in.

They claim it'll be the biggest flood since Noah. David envisions a giant blue wave, an emblematic tsunami ripped from a Japanese woodcut, its many crests crashing and bouncing back like a cavalry charge, galloping hooves beneath gaunt horsemen. Something quick. But here on campus, from the roof of Spinoza Field House, David thinks it looks more like a bathtub slowly filling. He can see the swell on the horizon.

The sky is not falling; the ground is just rising up to meet it.

Toward the end of his freshman fall semester, whenever campus flooded, David would put on rubber boots and his grandpa László's blazer and explore campus. He'd lost most of his friends—or was "in between" friends—and these solitary treks offered David the kind of escape he once found in reading, reimagining Princeton as a book he could bind and annotate with pithy insights. It was after the snows of midterms that he sloshed his way to the Institute for Advanced Study—a think tank once inhabited by Einstein and Oppenheimer—which led to the infamous Institute Woods, where upperclassmen went to smoke things or burn things or grope things.

The grass was crispy. David loved being the first of the morning to crunch the blades, navigating treacherous goose shit. Up ahead, the institute grounds were littered with metallic forms from minimalist schools of sculpture, spread like sentries around a man-made pond. He spotted a middle-aged couple walking their Labradoodle by the edge of the Institute Woods. David smiled and waved as he tramped silently past them. The woods smelled like tea. David imagined Einstein traversing these paths, thinking great things, hoping one of them might save the world.

Up ahead the trail became a footbridge arcing across Stony Brook—larger than a stream but smaller than a river. Melting sleeves of ice had formed on branches overnight, and the morning thaw made for a wily current below. Beside the brook was a tower of flagstones, the kind you'd find in a garden path.

And then David saw Mathias Blue for the first time.

Maybe six feet four inches on flat feet, Mathias emerged from that water wearing a purple surfer's wetsuit, moving so slowly as to be almost invisible, sun blinking off his bald head. His whole body looked like the inside of a lip. Written across the chest of his wetsuit in melting yellow font it said: MUTANT.

As Mathias climbed from the brook onto muddy snow, his gaze was steady, aimed through David to somewhere far behind. Each foot was clad in black neoprene surfing boots, the reptilian big toe separated from the rest. His gait was absurdly slow, deliberately rising and then rolling each boot onto the ground as if leaving a precise ink print. It took a full minute for him to go ten feet.

What was happening? David felt like he should keep walking forward, but he didn't know whether he should walk at a normal speed or conform to the thick pace of this oddball. He decided to defer to the man in purple and proceeded in slo-mo. It felt strange at first, the slowness, David's body craving speed and motion against the cold. But soon he dropped into something of a rhythm, finding balance in each flamingo stance between steps. They were a reverse duel, pacing inward.

Once he got close enough, David whispered, "Are you a mime?"

"Yes, *shh.* You're forcing me to break character."

"A mime in a wetsuit."

"I'm a river mime."

A jogger in a pink running outfit bounced over the footbridge and shushed past them.

The guy in purple whispered, "*Man,* she's fast."

With that, he headed slowly toward the chest-high pile of flagstones. He introduced himself as Mathias Blue—first and last name—lifted a massive stone slab from the pile, muscles pulsing against the wetsuit, and began a slow pivot back toward the water.

"Pick up a rock and hop in if you wanna keep talking," Mathias said.

"Um."

"Warmer than it looks."

There was no way David was getting his grandfather's jacket wet. He clomped to the center of the bridge. Looking down into the water, he almost understood what Mathias was doing. In the center of the river, he'd built a tube of stones, like a hollow castle turret, about five feet in diameter. It was tall enough that the top layer of stone extruded from the water. Mathias reentered the stream and placed another brick on his wall.

"Looks like Andy Goldsworthy, the sculptor," David called down, remembering one of his parents' coffee-table art books.

"One thing you should know about me," Mathias replied, eyes still focused on his tower, "is that I'm *extremely* derivative."

From his perch on the bridge David scanned the forest. A few hundred yards downstream, he spotted three others mimicking Mathias's meditative walk, phantoms drifting through the trees. Disciples, clearly. David felt this should probably explain something, but he wasn't sure what.

"Are you like a performance artist?"

"Actually, I'm trying to build a hot tub," he said, "but I haven't figured out how I'm gonna get good *bubbles.*"

"You could make it into a little still pool instead," David offered.

"I like where your head's at. Stillness amid the rapids. Very Zen. But I'm afraid I'm wedded to the idea of hot bubbles."

David didn't know what to think. He wasn't sure if this Mathias Blue was funny or brilliant or an idiot. He obviously had some engineering acumen and a whole stockpile of will. Perhaps a bit too much time on his hands.

And just then, as Mathias rotated a slab into position, part of his wall began to cave in.

"LOOK OUT!" David screamed.

Mathias seemed unfazed. He pressed his weight down hard on the rock to lock it in place and the wall held, for the moment, with Mathias leaning into it.

"Listen," Mathias said, "I know you don't want to get that jacket wet, but I'm wondering if you'd mind bringing me a few rocks to balance this thing out. It's gonna fall if I take my weight off."

"The water must be freezing."

"It's purifying."

David pointed downstream at the phantoms and said, "Can't one of your friends do it?"

Mathias looked up at David. "Do this for me and you'll be my new best friend," he said.

So, okay. David tore off László's jacket, his sweater and jeans and socks and shoes, and piled them next to a tree and ran to the pile of stone and grabbed two slabs and eased into the river and Jesus fucking Christ. The air temperature was warm enough, but the river was biting cold. The shock hit David hard, and the stones got heavier with each wet trudge to Mathias's tower. His toes sunk into the riverbed. There was no whitewater, but the current was strong. When he reached the hot tub, David poised the slabs over the back of Mathias's pressing palm. Mathias said, "Now!" and removed his hand as David dropped the flagstones into place.

They froze. Waited for the fragile tower to collapse. But it stayed strong.

"You saved the day," Mathias told him, eyes shiny and thankful.

"Great. I'm a hero to site-specific sculptors everywhere. Can I get out now?"

"Wait," Mathias said, "would you like to see the tiniest two ducks ever?"

Mathias grabbed David's arms and turned him around to direct his gaze to the water's edge. They were the tiniest two ducks ever. David knew nothing about duck gestation, but he couldn't imagine what these animals were doing here, at the end of fall. They looked fresh from the egg. Furry things, heads like peanuts, no larger than a human thumb. They swam with the current, side by side, peanut heads darting. One in the lead and the other huddled carefully into her sister's cotton-ball flank. Two small miracles.

David wondered if they'd survive.

"Do you think they're brothers?" asked Mathias.

"Fuck, it's cold," David said. "Seriously, how are you doing this, even with the wetsuit?"

And then Mathias pulled a pill from god knows where.

"This'll fix the cold," he said. "Open up and lift your tongue and don't be afraid."

"What is it?"

"It'll come on fast and feel like forever. But I promise, it will end."

David didn't have time to think, to say no, but right then he would have shot heroin into his eyeball if someone told him it'd help with the cold. Mathias cracked the capsule's chalky contents directly under David's tongue, behind his bottom teeth. Almost immediately, David felt it working.

"The Mayans have this special greeting," Mathias said. "*In Lak'ech*: I am another yourself."

A wave of physical heat. Something heady, too.

"And then *you* respond *Ala K'in*, which means 'And I am you.' It's a perfect saying."

As long as they were talking religious nonsense, David said, "There's this Buddhist quote, I think: 'When you realize how perfect everything is, you will tilt your head back and laugh at the sky.'"

"Hey, new best friend," Mathias said, "the sky is nothing to be laughed at."

David saw Mathias staring through him, his gaze still focused on the distance, but he felt the drug working, coming on. Zero to 98.6 in three seconds.

"'Sometimes... when the ice was covered with shallow puddles,'" David quoted. "'I saw a double shadow of myself, one standing on the head of the other.' That's from Thoreau, which is actually pronounced like the word 'thorough,' but it sounds so pompous to say it like that and—hey, what's happening?"

"I promise, David. This will end. You will come back. Don't be afraid."

Mathias's soaring form began to shrink, but his eyes grew larger, alien, blacker. David felt fingers under his tongue where Mathias had dumped the pill. Then he felt a hand pressing into his mouth, then a wrist, then an entire arm and shoulder, and finally Mathias's head, all pouring down David's throat, his face coming unhinged like a python feeding, and his vision was gone, but he could still feel the rest of this foreign body shimmying its way in: Mathias's chest, his waist, his thighs, his neoprene reptilian feet—all diving into David. And then he was gone, the Mathiasness charging and saturating David's marrow like fingers stretching into an empty glove.

PART ONE

1
PRECIPITATION

i.

In December, David returned from exile back to Princeton, a complex feat of space-time navigation. The yearning for independence was strong, so he refused to rely on family for rides, opting instead for buses and trains. On his passage from Baltimore to Jersey, David marveled at the synchronization his travel demanded, mostly unseen. On the surface it was just a few short hours and a weird cheeseburger on Amtrak's Northeast Regional, but he knew invisible machinations were making it all happen behind the scenes. The technology, the communication. The steel and strength.

Trains, he'd read, birthed our modern universal time standard. Before interstate rails, each town had its own notion of noon, its own clocks, its own sun in the sky. From this chaos, they created a single, agreed-upon schedule. Humans once rooted in the animist present moment powered their way to a temporal iron godhead, or maybe a holy trinity of Early, Late, and On Time.

Time had been on David's mind, specifically the specter of chronostrictesis. It was increasingly dominating his news feed. Sure, the storms had gotten worse, stronger, more frequent, and he knew dozens of kids from college and high school whose houses got annihilated and who'd left school to help their parents deal with the fallout. David recognized that it was his youth and privilege and dumb luck that left the Time Crisis as the dominant freak-out in his world.

He'd lasted almost a semester at school before they forced him to vacate the dorms. Housing Services agreed to hold David's stuff in storage through mid-December, but today was the day, time was up. When David arrived back on campus, having completed his trip from Princeton Junction, it was freakishly quiet in Forbes Hall, the dorm cleared out for winter break. He wanted to move out when people were gone, so he wouldn't have to explain himself. Housing was kind enough to provide a hand truck, so David loaded up his wine boxes full of books and wheeled this sad stack of cardboard out with the rest of his belongings to Visitors' Parking. There, he'd wait for his ride to Mathias's place off-campus.

He rolled past a lone soul on the lawn—Tolu, a kid from the second floor, reading a Newtonian physics textbook propped atop a bike rack. Tolu was from Lagos and among the many international students who'd stayed on campus through winter break rather than risk leaving the country and being denied reentry.

"Sorry they are making you go," Tolu said to David, removing his knit cap as if offering condolences.

"I have a plan," David said awkwardly, embarrassed, realizing everyone probably knew about why they were making him go. "Don't have to go home, but I can't stay here, right?"

"I suppose my problem is the opposite," said Tolu.

He wondered if Tolu had a car, if he enjoyed trains.

Waiting by his tower of boxes, thankful it was only flurrying for a change, David again considered time. His own past, present, and future: there'd been his first embattled semester, but that was past. Now, winter break was the alive, present moment, full of potential. And laid before him, he hoped, was Mathias, who could hack the future.

He'd been home through Thanksgiving, sticking around for two more weeks to get his head straight. He tried hanging out back in Pikesville with his parents and sister and old high school crew home from school, but it was impossible, he had to be back here, doing something, before the world got any worse. When David had classes it was easy to ignore, but his trigger had been that viral video clip—an interview on Fox News with one J. Stuart Mott, Princeton professor of astrophysics, go figure. Mott was a sixty-something black man with salt-and-pepper temples. He was an odd duck, slightly unhinged. Initially, the host questioned him for his knowledge of weather patterns.

"As a teenager growing up in Oklahoma I considered myself a 'storm chaser,'" Mott said. "The air of a tornado takes on solidity. Especially close to the ground. The bottom tip is so dense, spinning so fast, it might as well be made of iron."

Mott held the bell of an orange plastic cone and traced a downward spiral along its insides to illustrate his point. The camera cut to a close-up. David could tell that Mott bit his fingernails.

"Modern physicists know," Mott said, "that four-dimensional space—3-D matter, plus the fourth dimension of time—is also shaped like a funnel, a Picard topology hyperspace, and—"

"Professor, we—"

"The Earth's energy spins around—see, like this—and down this vortex. The spiral gets tighter and tighter, see? And eventually we reach what's called the 'Null Point' at the bottom."

"And you're saying this is the cause of the strange weather we're having?"

"I have no idea, Tabitha. What I'm saying is that it's the *mechanism* of chronostrictesis—of the changing quality of time we're experiencing. It's why every second feels shorter than the one before it. Though, a change in the fourth dimension *has* to affect the third dimension, so—"

"Well, thank you, Doctor, this has been—"

"Now, what happens when we reach the Null Point is really—"

"We're just about out of time. Coming up next, we'll have—"

"Indeed we *are* just about *out of time*! When you consider the topology of time, the Null Point is the real question, and if you believe the shamans who say we're approaching the Pacha Cuti, then we're entering a new stage in—"

"Doctor, we're going to have to break."

"Yes! We must break our—"

"No! We need to *break* for commercial and—"

The report might've easily disappeared into the cable ether, but by the time Mott yanked off his lapel mic and sprinted toward the camera babbling about supercells, the newsroom was in full upheaval and the segment's YouTube immortality was confirmed. By week's end, all the comedy pundits and late-night hosts did bits on the viral video, and the casual viewer might've chalked it up to an admirable troll job of stupid Fox News.

But days later major news outlets ran stories on chronostrictesis and the Null Point. Legit science papers had been published, reinforcing the news. If natural disasters were ratings gold, cosmic doomsday scenarios were platinum.

The symbol of chronostrictesis became known as "Mott's Funnel," a vortex icon in the upper left corner of the screen beside an ever-increasing

"Time Crisis" graphic. Some tried to downplay the crisis, trading the funnel image for the swirl of a flushing toilet. But it was getting harder and harder to believe nothing was going on.

The temperature was dropping when two new faces—Fu Schroeder and Lee Popkin—arrived at Forbes. Their ancient powder-blue Buick would spirit David to his new home in Pennington, about ten miles away. They got on the road.

The trunk was bungee-cord full, and David sat in the backseat between two columns of duffel bags. Fu drove and Lee sat shotgun, smoking. Lee reminded David of a stork with a wallet chain. He had a small tuft of reddish hair holding out against a massive forehead. Black-rimmed glasses wrapped his ferret-like features; a downturned nose and protruding silver-dollar chin accentuated the pinch of his face. His legs were long taffied stalks ending in black Converse, propped against the dashboard. One skinny-jeaned knee poked out the passenger window and the other nearly nuzzled Fu's ear.

Fu was taller than Lee and more jacked. Male model handsome. His lips were full and unsmiling, but his eyes kept glancing eagerly at David in the rearview mirror. White wireless earbuds stuck out from a bowl of black hair. David couldn't tell if his music was on or if Fu was just nodding. He wore a nice scarf—Burberry, maybe—and generally, sartorially, looked like he came from money.

Move-in days were David's kryptonite. Always disorienting, and he far preferred being the guy who knew where everything was.

Back in August, his first day on campus had been no different. It had rained all morning, and his introduction to new hall mates would be from inside that waterlogged gray wool blazer that once belonged to his grandpa László (also a Tiger, class of '59). Beneath the blazer, David wore an orange Princeton hoodie, which Mom insisted he put on because otherwise he'd catch a cold. Under this hood sat a matted turban of auburn hair, a beard, and oversize Clark Kent glasses with nonprescription lenses. Riding the dorm elevator, David stared despondently at his reflection—a short, melting blur in the gunmetal doors.

When the doors parted, he strode past room 327, 325, 323, names, names, names, names and hometowns emblazoned on different pastel shades of construction paper taped over doorjambs, alongside Japanese calligraphy and magazine cutouts of pagodas. The hall theme was apparently "Asia." Freshman Zen.

David remembered thinking this was a strange choice. American attitude toward the East had dropped since China began cashing in its U.S. bonds, sending the dollar into free fall. On a dry-erase board in the hall, some eager kid had already written, "Vacate Afghanistan!! Invade China!!" in fiery lettering. David wondered if he'd be expected to understand global politics in college; if he'd have to take sides, become an activist, at least socially. This wasn't his power swing. He didn't know enough about Afghanistan. He knew we'd discovered vast mineral deposits there, especially lithium, which China wanted. He knew we'd left Iraq but were still kind of in Iraq. He knew we were never technically in Iran but were always kind of in Iran. And now Jordan and Bolivia and Chile. He knew we'd been in Afghanistan since the 1980s, when something happened there involving the Russians, and this thing had been adapted into a movie starring Tom Hanks. And David knew, generally, that he was against war—any war, most wars—and that he was, in all likelihood, against the ones in the Middle East. He'd resolved to do some googling, and until then, if anyone asked, he would agree that, hell yes, we should most definitely vacate Afghanistan.

Now, here was another disorienting ride to parts unknown, with two strangers in the front seat. As they'd pulled away from Forbes, David asked, "Are we headed straight to Mathias's house?"

"It's not a house," Lee answered, sounding annoyed. "It's The Egg."

Lee talked in an intentionally oblique way, constantly flicking his cigarette, prohibiting even a hint of ash to collect at its cherry. Fu, meanwhile, barely moved, save two fingers drumming an intricate beat on the steering wheel. When his phone rang, Fu picked it up without speaking. David heard a mumble on the other end, and Fu hung up without a word. He then deftly thumbed a text.

"Why does Blue always call *you* when you're the one who barely talks?" Lee asked. "And why do *you* always drive when you're the one who's Asian?"

"Why do I let you keep all of your teeth when they'd be so easy to knock out?" asked Fu. He flashed a text message for Lee to read from his phone.

"No, tell him we're not picking up this freshman *and* going to PQM. If he wants batteries he can send Owen. They're calling for like three inches."

"I only heard freezing rain," David offered.

"Well, I guess they upgraded it then, huh?" said Lee to the backseat. "You're lucky, Blue's actually in town for a change. No way we would've brought in someone new if he was traveling."

"Like a study-abroad thing?" David asked.

"No, like a trust-fund-out-his-ass thing," said Lee. "Like cash-just-falling-from-his-anus thing. The Egg—all of it—is paid by Blue."

They looked like pterodactyl elbows, Lee's knees. Or maybe bendy straws. Lee turned around deliberately, his eyes droopy.

"You know his mom was a *Bond girl*?" Lee asked, taking a slow drag. "Timothy Dalton era. The old guy from *Hot Fuzz*." Clearly a favorite piece of lore that Lee relished in telling. David couldn't picture Mathias springing from the loins of a 1980s sexpot. He had a wiry rock-star thing going, but his wasn't movie-star beauty. Sure, he had a well-defined bone structure—sharp angles under smooth skin—but piece by piece his features were unremarkable.

His mouth, however. His mouth was a nucleus of envy.

When the surge would happen midway through March and girls started living at The Egg, they'd scour the house for Mathias's used drinking glasses, coveting the quarter-moon of his bottom lip on the rim like detectives protecting a prized fingerprint. They'd press their own mouths to the same spot of the glass, less for the pseudo-sexual thrill than for the rush of being in the same exact spot as Mathias. David, too, would sheepishly place his winter boots in the footprints Mathias had left during a walking meditation through the backyard's fresh snow, hoping the energy that had passed between Mathias and the earth might still be lingering there and might accidentally pass into David's own soles.

"That's why you wanna move in, isn't it?" Lee asked the rearview mirror.

"Because of Mathias's mom?"

"No, his dad. His money and connections and whatever."

"Who's his dad?"

This time both of them turned around. Fu slowed the car, nearly pulled over.

"Um, probably our next secretary of defense," said Lee.

David nodded as if that answered everything, but before he could get them to elaborate, Fu's phone vibrated again and he showed it to Lee.

"Now they say *six* inches," Lee relayed.

"I didn't even know there was money," David admitted. "I just need a place to live."

Lee sighed. "You need to think of this shit like applying for a grant. Mathias is a foundation."

"I'll be honest," David said. "I've never been comfortable around superrich kids."

"You went to a good high school, right?"

"Public," David said, like it was a badge of honor.

"Your parents well-off?"

"The Fuffmans are solidly upper middle class," he said. "But I work a summer job."

The job, however, was running the snack bar at Bonnie View Country Club. Like David, most of his high school friends preferred to act as if they had *less* money than they actually had. Trust-fund kids like Mathias, unashamed of their station and willing to act as benefactors—it was not something he'd ever encountered before.

"Well, get comfortable with it," Lee said. "Gotta have an angle or else he'll never fund you."

"Fund me? No, I just met him at the Institute Woods," David said. "He was building a hot tub in that Stony Brook river and I helped him carry rocks until he drugged me and stole my grandfather's blazer. So..."

Lee blew a stream of smoke at him. "Mathias was right. You're more bishop than knight."

"Clearly," said David.

"Yeah, see, knights kinda plod along in this L shape, move by move, and you can basically see where they're headed. But bishops can fuckin' hide in the back row until they get an opening and then fly diagonally across the board to fuck your shit up. Don't even see them coming."

—Ø—

Though the snow picked up as Fu pulled into Pennington, the town still felt sunny and sweet. Fu's driving stayed solid, but the ice made him slow his speed, giving David ample time to scan the neighborhood. Lots of yuletide cheer and a distinct lack of corporate presence. All the storefronts on Main Street were mom-and-pops: NIFTY THRIFT, THREE DOG HARDWARE, RED, WHITE & BLOOMS. David felt giddy. He'd never lived in a town with an actual Main Street, this gently sloping road lined with sycamores and two-story houses and American flags shooting up from porches.

And just off Main Street, on a cul-de-sac called Woosamonsa Court, was The Egg.

Immediately, it was clear why they called it that. Instead of the typical colonial home—triangle on top of square—The Egg's facade was a near-perfect parabola. Like one of those Buckminster Fuller geodesic domes, but stretched, so that head-on, the home looked like a grocery egg protruding from its carton, or an Easter egg hiding in the grass, or a boob. It was pale yellow and, yes, eggs are white, but whatever, the name made sense. The place also had an attached garage—a kind of motorcycle sidecar—plus a big backyard fenced in by cypress trees. Only two other houses in the cul-de-sac, one of them empty looking with a sign in the yard that read, IN ESCROW. Lots of privacy.

On top of The Egg, wearing purple sweatpants and a purple hoodie, was Mathias Blue. With a small hand axe he was hacking away at a tree branch that had fallen on the roof, trying to break it into two pieces, making it easier to move.

Despite the snow, he looked much warmer up there than the first time they'd met at the Stony Brook and even more impressively tall, high atop The Egg. Yet there was something elfin about him, pointy ears and an angular chin punctuated with a pyramid of hair. David remembered thinking Mathias was a grad student when they first met and being surprised to learn he was only a sophomore. Mathias had taken at least a year off school to travel, so he was maybe two or even three years older, but they were basically the same age, which made David feel strangely jealous. Hearing the car arrive, Mathias tucked his axe into his sweatshirt pouch and climbed down a ladder.

Clearly, Mathias knew stuff about carpentry and other manly things David now felt a dire need to learn. Seeing that axe, it started to sink in that this was the reality of off-campus living: no school-sanctioned maintenance crews to fix things. David was okay at hanging shelves or assembling IKEA furniture, but he wanted to understand electricity and plumbing and other household guts no one ever taught him. The notion had been weighing on him: that there was something inherently more noble about knowing how to fell a tree or skin a fox or rebuild a carburetor compared with the high-minded skills that made one attractive to Ivy League admissions officers.

But still, what was he doing here, moving into this architectural relic with a bunch of crazy people? These guys were part of the scant 2 percent of students who lived off-campus. David had witnessed his roommate Owen's meltdown firsthand, but what tragedies had befallen the others?

He wondered if they'd been kicked out, too. He wondered if they, like him, could no longer conduct themselves in a manner befitting a Princeton Man. At least David wasn't the only one. He'd read that the fall semester had seen more dropouts and leaves of absence nationwide than the previous three years combined. Kids reclaiming their time before time was officially up.

David hadn't noticed the *quantitative* shortening, but the *qualitative* shift was real. Despite what clocks and scientists said about chronostrictesis, it simply *felt* as if there were fewer and fewer spare moments. Outside the Princeton bubble, futures markets speculated on the value of the minute. Unions picketed for wage increases, while CEOs threatened pay cuts for "shortened" workdays. A disorganized governmental agency began regulating calendrics and temporality, with some lobbying for a recalculation of the second and others wanting adjustments of the month or year. Plenty wrote it off as soft science. There was no truth, they claimed, to chronostrictesis.

A minute was a minute.

Shimmying down from the roof, Mathias grabbed a milk crate full of booze. He tossed a full bottle of vodka into a nearby garbage can. It smashed delightfully.

It was then that David got a better look at that fairly serious hatchet also sticking out of his sweatshirt. David was going to ask about it, but instead, he said, "Nice pants."

"Hey, thanks for thinking my pants are nice," Mathias said back.

"You wear a lot of purple, huh?"

"I'm a purple supremacist. Now, did you come for your grandpa's blazer or did you come for good?"

David pointed to the Buick, its trunk overflowing with his boxes of books. Fu began unloading them into the house, one balanced atop each shoulder, seemingly a welcome excuse for aerobic drills. Lee stood by, smoking, engrossed in his phone.

"Super," Mathias said.

David took a longer look at the axe. Black iron axe head and a cherry handle, straight out of the Middle Ages. He tried to stay cool. Mathias seemed to sense concern and held the blade gingerly for David to see.

"You told me your grandfather made jet engines," Mathias said. "*Mine* used to make weapons. Guns and knives and hatchets for Civil War reenactments. I think he was the main guy doing it at one point, so he was a big deal in certain circles. He's dead now, but he gave me this axe. I'd like to make it into a functional wood splitter, while still retaining its original integrity, like how you co-opted your grandpa's blazer. Hey, is there actual vino in those wine boxes?"

"Books," David said. "I hope you're not dumping alcohol on my account?" When they last spoke, David had mentioned, with no small sense of pride, his recent decision to quit drinking.

"Don't flatter yourself." Mathias winked. "Lee's been tinkering with the chemistry in these bottles and accidentally created poison. You know anything about distillation? Don't worry, you'll pick it up quick. It's a crazy useful trade skill for when shit hits the fan, regardless of whether or not you actually drink the stuff. Here"—he handed David a full bottle of brown liquor and pointed to a car across the cul-de-sac—"go ahead and chuck this at that Nissan Sentra."

Was he serious? David wondered if he should smash it, to prove that he could, or else decline, to prove that he could. Either way, he wanted Mathias to know whom he was dealing with.

"I'm concerned that you're hazing me prematurely." David was trying to say no.

"It's not hazing. More of a Buddhist koan. You don't know whether I want you to be the type of guy who will smash the bottle just because I asked or the type of guy who will tell me to go fuck myself. Maybe I'm not looking for either response, just a little creativity. Maybe you hand me an orange peel and yodel. Either way, it kinda comes down to imagination. And maybe balls."

David barked a single laugh. Mathias reminded him of a prince in disguise, possibly a bit psychic. In response to the liquor bottle koan, David decided to recite a favorite *Walden* quote:

"'Is it impossible to combine the hardiness of savages with the intellectualness of the civilized man?'"

"That's your response?"

"That's my response."

Mathias snatched the bottle from David's palm and, with a graceful hook shot, catapulted it end over end toward the middle of the cul-de-sac. It exploded dead center, splattering glass and froth across the snow-dusted pavement.

"The answer is yes," said Mathias. "Yes, it is possible."

It was then that David became aware of the next-door neighbor, a mustached middle-ager in a teal Miami Dolphins jacket. He was boarding up his windows. The guy looked at them, brow furrowed. David assumed they were in very big trouble.

Then the neighbor called out to Mathias, "That wasn't the good stuff, was it?"

"No, that was horse piss," Mathias yelled back. "I've got a box of good stuff all packed up for you, Fred. No worries!" With that, Fred went back to hammering.

"That's Fred," Mathias said. "Fred's the best."

"Sixteen inches," Lee relayed from his phone, and walked inside.

"What about the glass?" David asked.

"He's really just the best."

Lee poked his head back outside and yelled, "No, two feet. They're closing schools."

"They always overestimate snowstorms," David offered. "People go crazy for no reason."

Mathias looked taken aback. "Have you *seen* the weather lately? People have every reason to go crazy, yet somehow remain sane. It pays to be prepared. This place loses power if you sneeze wrong. I love it to death, but it's a bit dumb." He waved his axe around and said, "Nobody makes triangle-shaped plywood!"

"Can I case the joint?" David asked.

"First we need to batten down the hatches." From his kangaroo pouch Mathias pulled a printed list and a softball-sized wad of cash. He plucked off some bills. "You're new, so you're on grocery duty. Here's our list. And get the usual apocalyptic provisions, too. Water, batteries, canned soup, gasoline, pet immunization records, puzzles, whatever it is you like to eat and drink."

"Is this another koan?"

"No, this time I'm hazing you." The clump of twenties and a set of car keys dropped to David's hand. Mathias gave directions to the fancy supermarket up the street.

"Go," he said. "It's gonna get seriously dangerous to drive within an hour. We'll get you acclimated when you get back. You'll enjoy living here."

"Even though it's dumb?"

"Dumb and wonderful," Mathias said.

"Why *did* you pick this house?" David wondered aloud.

"It's not a house," Mathias said. "It is The Egg."

ii.

Blizzards hit fast. Something about warm air from the south meeting arctic air from the north. Two opposites form an offshore phenomenon. Then, powers combined, they attack.

"The Great White Death lasted seven weeks in 1949," said NPR. "To save livestock, the air force dropped tons of hay, but nearly a million head of cattle perished nonetheless."

Scare tactics, David thought. *That was a different century, before Doppler. Now, they just love to freak us out, make us go shopping. Impending doom is the best advertising.*

The Egg had two vehicles: a beige GMC Savana cargo van they called the "Rock-it-to-the-MaxMobile" and the 1992 Buick Roadmaster he'd arrived in, named "Christopher Walken." For this errand, his inaugural solo mission, David took the MaxMobile.

He liked riding up high, surveying his new town, but couldn't help conjuring images of his hometown—Pikesville, Maryland—wrecked by the fall weather. The record storm surge of Hurricane Jamie had leveled the shore and didn't spare the mid-Atlantic mainland, either, from Philadelphia to Richmond. Pikesville suffered 80 mph winds and heavy rains. Roofs ripped from houses. Trees and power lines down everywhere. Two dozen dead. David didn't know any of the deceased personally, but his little sister Beth's sixth grade science teacher lost both her boys, two and four years old, when the woman's SUV stalled in floodwaters. She tried to swim them to safety but lost her grip on her sons. To watch them float away like that, David couldn't even imagine.

The news went crazy for Hurricane Jamie. Waiting in University Medical Center for his parents to collect him, nursing the psychological wounds of his first semester, David stayed glued to the tube. He consumed cable news footage of pummeled gas stations, evacuees living in repurposed school gymnasiums, floating cars clustering in the flood like the last Cheerios in a cereal bowl.

When he left campus and arrived back home, he drove around his old, familiar town and saw how Hurricane Jamie had worn away at the fabric of Pikesville, once situated into manicured rows of street, sidewalk, lawn, house. Now everything spilled into everything else. Driveways were full of waterlogged cardboard, exploded sandbags in the street, remnants of flooded basements and attics tossed into the public space not to be quickly and quietly disposed of, but as a testimony, as if to say, *Look at this mess, would you?*

As he'd driven past his old high school, noticing government vehicles parked in its otherwise empty lot, David heard on the radio that Hostess Brands Inc. was going bankrupt. He thought of how Twinkies, legend had it, contained so many preservatives they could survive the apocalypse. Now even Twinkies were going extinct?

David decided to buy all the Hostess stuff he could find. Maybe he'd eat a thousand Twinkies before heading back to school, catalyzing a physical transformation to see what emotional, psychological, and spiritual powers might come along with it.

Or else he'd just become a fat guy.

—Ø—

David blinked himself back to the present moment.

Turning into the parking lot of the upscale Pennington Quality Market a mile from The Egg, David saw the citizens who made this town tick: moms in Lexuses and lawyers in minivans. Another upper-middle-class bubble like Pikesville.

David wondered if any crime occurred in a burg like this. Maybe he'd have an opportunity to thwart would-be attackers, become a local hero. David saw a grandmother load cans into her Cadillac. He kept an eye out lest someone try to swipe her purse.

The grocery list blew in the wind as David jogged through a parking lot teeming with beeps. The printout, with Mathias's handwritten edits, read like this:

PQM LIST OF DESTINY

Mathias:
4 lbs of lean, grass-fed shoulder roast
(beef or deer/caribou/moose if they have it!)
1 Giant Fucking Thing of Salsa (Hot!)

Blueberries
Winston Lights (3 cartons!)
Kitten faces (JK! LOL!)

Owen:
16 Lemons, Organic Grade B Maple Syrup, Cayenne Pepper, Girly Beer

Lee:
Mama Celeste Pizzas, big ole slab o' ribs, blue cheese, tissues,
cheddar cheese, cottage cheese, yogurt, tight slutty vagina,
turkey jerky, whatever else I eat

Fu:
Fresh nutmeg (NOT powder)
Arugula
Bouillon cubes
Arborio rice
Kools (NOT Newports; 2 cartons)
Pork butt (from butcher; NOT packaged!)
Sriracha (2 btls.)
Cremini mushrooms
Mountain Dew (1 case)
Lop chong (Chinese-style sausage; chorizo okay)
Large tail-on shrimp (2 or 4 lbs.)
All the tofu they have
Raw, unfiltered apple cider vinegar (with the "Mother")
Dry white wine (NOT for drinking!)
Saffron

Mathias's hundred bucks would maybe be fine for this list but definitely not enough when you factored in his "apocalyptic provisions." Luckily, David had his parents' credit card. As much as he'd usually downplay this convenient fact, even to his own ego, he was thankful to be carrying plastic at a time like this. There'd be a threshold where his parents would notice and inquire (the credit wasn't limitless, just unknown). But what if he really had only a hundred dollars? Like *to his name*. For those without a safety net, life must involve so much more math.

David entered the automatic doors of the supermarket with a mighty *whoosh*. Two massive product pyramids of bottled water and toilet paper stood by the entrance area like those guardian lion statues in front of Chinese restaurants. It was clear from the surrounding detritus that these stacks had been picked over and replenished, and stock girls were once again doing their best to accommodate the last-minute crush of shoppers stocking up. David realized he was stepping into battle, some kind of suburban ritual he'd been sheltered from during fall semester dorm living. Pre-storm supermarkets show the American veneer cracking, something animal peeking through.

David checked off pretty much everything on Mathias's list and was surprised that, with a few odd exceptions, it didn't include any of the usual storm stockpiling items. So David took it upon himself to grab what he could. He got water. He got one of almost every over-the-counter drug. He got peanut butter and jelly, and the bread was all gone so he got matzo, the unleavened apocalyptic carb of his forebears. And porn! If they lost internet, they'd need a substitute. David headed to the magazine aisle and picked two choice items, skipping the usual *Playboy* and *Penthouse* for sluttier-looking stuff with pouty girls suffocating beneath magazine plastic. Mustard, honey, Parmalat, candles, Chinese checkers, cartons of Kools. Asking a dreadlocked employee where to find organic grade B maple syrup felt absurd amid this bare-necessity spectacle, but the guy knew just what he was talking about and led him to a wall of Vermont-y jugs. Fu's saffron was insanely expensive. David made the executive decision to remove it from his cart.

When he finally found a spot at the end of a long checkout line, it was wild to see what this homogenous horde had in their carts, what they deemed vital and life-affirming at a time like this. Trail mix and antifreeze struck David as practical, and he shook his head, wishing he'd thought of that. Other goods were more curious: a priest with a cart comprising only coffee beans, as if this were the last time in history one could buy such a thing. Maybe he was stockpiling, preparing to barter. What was David forgetting? What could he not survive *without* if the End really came?

Before he could hide the skin mags between two boxes of Honey Nut Cheerios, the cashier began scanning them. Holding up *Hustler*, she said, "This is gross." Swiping *Swank* across the laser, she said, "This one's actually pretty hot, though."

Embarrassed, he glanced down at the waxed floor, and there he saw her. Blink.

This was happening more and more, this side effect of the pills. Owen had warned him about it back when they shared a dorm. Visual memories piling up on the present moment. Owen called it "superimposition."

David was trying to get used to it, and the simplest thing, he found, was to let the mental detours happen and try to think of it as a different kind of remembering...

—Ø—

Two weeks ago, back home, he'd shopped methodically at the Pikesville Giant, comforted by the fact that he knew his family's favorites. David enjoyed the aisles of color, the waxed floors reflecting fluorescence. *Say what you will about capitalist imperialism,* David considered, *but they don't enjoy such bounty in Tajikistan.*

Once the cart grew heavy, David used it as a dogsled, one foot on the lower rail and the other propelling him swiftly forward. He mushed to frozen foods, a space-aged flight deck. Two rows of frosted cases lay before him, each freezer door lit with vertical tubes.

There, he saw her, ponytailed, holding two tubs of ice cream.

He'd like to think of it as fate, that they'd find each other on winter break there in the frozen food section of the Pikesville Giant, that perhaps they'd been betrothed from the beginning and this synchronicity was another crease in their love's unfolding. But it's possible that aisle eleven was not predestined. Her parents lived nearby, and on that Monday maybe she just wanted ice cream.

David saw her neck before the rest of her. He recognized that light fuzz beneath a mane of dark blond wetness drying on her shoulders and jumped off his cart, letting it roll into oblivion, catching his balance behind Haley Roth.

Haley had graduated from McDonogh, a private high school near Pikesville, but even among public school kids like David, she'd been the area's best drug slinger, known for her daddy's bottomless bottles of pharmaceuticals as well as her formidable breasts. Between these two commodities—boobs and pills—the high school nickname committee had dubbed her the "*Rack*eteer." She tried her best to shrug off the snide comments, the double standard. She was smart and popular, had good parents and a bright future. Haley Roth knew who she was and realized if she were a man she'd be the Fucking Man. So why change?

That's how she used to feel.

Without thinking, David crept up behind her and placed his palms over her eyes. *Guess who?* No sooner had his palms touched Haley's brow than her body recoiled in knee-jerk reflex and she flung her elbow directly into his chest.

"Oof," he said.

"Oow," she said.

She caught him sharply. He doubled over while Haley clutched her arm. David now understood that *guess who?* was probably the very worst thing you could do to a girl who'd been through what she'd been through. David realized they had something in common: a disastrous first semester had sent them both back home to lick their wounds.

"I almost maced you in the fucking freezer aisle," she hissed, rubbing her elbow.

Straight from the gym, Haley wore a white V-neck over a black sports bra. Her pulled-back hair was a mess of sweat and flyaways. She was small like David, with intense eyebrows and perpetually glazed-looking eyes, like she was always stoned, and maybe she was. Dimples framed her insanely perfect teeth, and her tanned skin shone with that charmed smoothness David envied, given his early battles with acne. But there was a sunkenness to her eyes now, and he thought her head looked oddly big, or else her neck was tiny. In fact, her whole body seemed scrawnier than he recalled. He wanted to hug her, ask if she was okay, but he worried he might break her in half.

"Sorry if I stink," Haley said, sniffing her pits. "It's day ten of my twenty-one-day Fat Blast."

"You really don't need to blast any fat," David said, catching his breath.

They shared a silence. She smiled less than he remembered from back in high school, which he imagined was a side effect of strange men telling her to smile more.

David wondered if she knew he'd gotten kicked out of the dorms the prior week. Maybe they were on the same team. The Princeton Lepers. He reached for what to say next.

"What should I get?" she finally asked. "I've been staring at these two flavors for like an hour. I need someone else to make the decision for me."

She needed him. He took the tubs and spun them and tried to look cool but almost dropped the Breyers on his foot. He knew he was being awkward, trying to keep things light amid darkness.

"I'd go rocky road over crème caramel," he replied. "More stuff going on."

"Fine, great. Sold," she said, exasperated. He wondered how long she'd actually been standing there and why. She stared off at something behind him and snorted a giggle.

"How's, um, your break so far?" David asked, trying to make eye contact and failing.

"It's great, um, *really* nice to be home."

"Me, too," he lied.

"Actually? No, it's bizarro. The weather sucks and I apparently don't want to talk to *anyone*."

"Me, too!" he admitted. "I keep making excuses. Like 'Sorry we keep missing each other!'"

"Ships in the night!" she said.

"Rowboats in the morning," he said. She cocked an eyebrow. He prayed she didn't remember. "Yeah," he recovered. "I'm trying to go back to campus early."

"Not me. Maybe I'll go to art school? Like one of those people who goes to art school."

"No, you should stay!" It flew out of David without thinking. A genuine plea. He suddenly realized he meant it, that he very much wanted her to stay. Don't lepers need colonies? She glanced through him again, gaze distant. "I'll stay if you stay?" he said. Like a question or a deal.

"Are they gonna let you back in the dorms?" So she *had* heard. Wait, what had she heard?

"I'm, um, looking for an apartment," he admitted. "Off-campus."

"I know of a place in Pennington," Haley said. "I was gonna take it myself, but it's all dudes."

"Wait," said David. "You mean Owen's place in Pennington? Is it called, uh, *The Egg*?"

"I don't know any Owen, but yeah, it's this guy's place. The Egg. Ask your pal Owen."

"I'm pissed at him right now. I met this guy Mathias and he was building this hot tub and—"

"Yeah, that's the guy. Rather brilliant. And hot as shit, too."

David felt himself redden. Mathias was weird looking, wasn't he?

"He seems dangerous," David countered.

"Well," she said. "He's the one who ID'd my guy. And he teaches self-defense at Jadwin Gym on Thursdays. Druggies like you and me are more dangerous than Mathias."

He was about to ask a million questions when Haley opened the freezer door between them and began tracing lines into the frost. David thought they were hieroglyphics, but once she dropped that @ symbol he realized he was looking at a backward email address: hr1237@princeton.edu.

"I had to change my email," she whispered. "Holler if you need supplies."

"I can actually use a bag to get me through Reading Period and exams. Can't tell—is that an *S*?"

"Is that your shopping cart?" She pointed to the end of the aisle.

When he'd jumped off it, David's cart had smacked into a far-off freezer case so hard that it cracked the glass. A Lactaid-colored pool had formed beneath the wheels. Two teenage employees with red aprons were leaning on mops, their palms upturned like, *Look at this mess, would you?*

David wasn't sure whether to help them clean or quickly leave the scene of his crime.

"I'm on my way home"—Haley turned—"if you want to re-up now, I'm lousy with product."

He'd glanced at his mess and said, "Haley Roth, I'll follow you to the ends of the earth."

—Ø—

Back in high school, she'd shuttle David and his then girlfriend Madeline up to her room to conduct business. "Welcome to Waffle House, what'll it be?" Haley might say as David and Maddy entered to make an after-school purchase. She always had an opening quip like this. Once it was "Good afternoon! How may I recharge your superpowers?" which David liked very much. Haley would sit on her bedspread, pink and white striped like an after-dinner mint. He remembered her carpeting was mottled with a few stiff patches—maybe dried semen? He'd tried not to look.

This time, she asked David to wait in the kitchen, which he understood. After showering, she came downstairs wiggling a Ziploc bag of weed and a pill bottle in one hand, the other behind her back.

She said, "You're into superheroes, yeah? Or used to be? Your whole getup?"

It's true. In high school, David still thought of himself as a superhero that had yet to realize the fullness of his magic. As a weird affectation, David always wore László's blazer: his cape. A ubiquitous blue hoodie was his cowl. His hair and beard and glasses composed his mask. He'd even bought a belt off Etsy, a handsome black leather thing with a secret compartment in the buckle where David kept his Adderall. His utility belt. He'd toned it down since.

David admitted he was indeed still into superheroes, but you know, not in a weird way.

"Would you like to see my very favorite superhero book in the whole world?" she asked.

The question surprised him. He guessed the thing behind her back was some obscure graphic novel, but instead Haley introduced him to *Eloise*—she of New York's Plaza Hotel.

Haley snorted with delight even at the opening sentence: "I am Eloise I am six."

Paging through it at the kitchen table, Haley guided David along Eloise's madcap exploits through the hotel. The little heroine ripples with confidence, outwitting doormen, telling white lies to old ladies, stealing trinkets from the gift shop, pouring pitchers of water down the mail chute. She uses zero punctuation. She likes things and she hates things.

Eloise likes dandelions and her mother's lawyer likes martinis.

"She's marvelous," said Haley. "I used to dream of owning a hotel once I turned *six*. Ooh! And see how she always says 'rawther' instead of 'rather.' She is *rawther* brilliant."

Haley was especially fond of Eloise's particular brand of metaphorical repurposing.

"Look." She pointed. "'Kleenex makes a very good hat.'"

David glanced back up to find Haley wearing a cardboard tissue box on her head. She looked like a pirate captain.

"And I love how she's always sticking her belly out. That's all I want, really. To be the kind of girl who can stick her belly out like that and have it be okay."

David caught Haley squeezing handfuls of her taut stomach flesh underneath the table. And she saw his face, saw how he almost pitied her recently changing body. Haley considered how men like David—aware enough of her situation but hardly original—assumed she was working out and dropping weight because of some vendetta, some reflexive need to reclaim her body. But Haley was doing it because she was good at it. She'd always had endurance, she could run long. Sometimes she'd look around the gym and see elephantine middle-aged men huffing and puffing up stairs to nowhere. Haley would note her own minimal sweat, hardly darkening the top of her neckline, and she'd be secretly proud of this, like it was a vital skill to conserve one's own water.

"If I were a superhero," Haley said, "my power would be getting really tiny so I could hide or wiggle out of small spaces. That's a good skill for our pre-apocalyptic times: not taking up too much space. What would *your* superpower be?"

He considered lying, but his real answer had been the same forever.

"Visibility," David said.

"*In*visibility?"

"No," he said. "The opposite."

"It's honest," she said, after thinking a moment. "It's very *you*."

David liked Haley. He liked that she had some inkling of what he used to be, what he could be again, and felt he understood the same thing about her—that she wasn't permanently damaged. She was simply unrealized. In some way, maybe this was projection. He, too, was special yet hidden, wasn't he? A real mensch? But David felt jealous that Mathias had been the one to speak up and wondered how he'd known, and what else did he know?

"I don't think it's bad to want to make a mark," he said. "Isn't that why you're an artist?"

"I want to make things," Haley replied, "but not for fame and fortune."

"I just don't want to be a nothing." Trying to act cool, he added, "Call it ambition. Drive."

"Pride?" she offered. "Vanity? Lust?"

David smiled. He stared at Haley Roth's arms, her skinny arms, as she closed *Eloise*.

"That was you at my dorm room, right?" Haley asked, still staring at the book's cover. "You came by last week. I almost forgot with all the other... That *was* you, right?"

He went cold. Nodded. Tried not to say or do anything else stupid.

"When we were in the supermarket just now, when I wrote my email on the glass? You looked how you looked through my peephole that day. Total déjà fucking vu."

David laughed awkwardly. Was she testing him? He wanted to tell her everything.

"It's a shame no one else on campus believed me," she said. "They hate me."

He really wanted to tell her. But all he said was "Maybe no one will remember next year."

They heard a car pull up outside. Her dad, probably. "See you back at school," she said. His cue to leave. But as she closed the door after him, she added, "I'll meet you there, by the rowboats."

He'd agreed to this, as if it were a real plan.

—Ø—

Blink. Upon exiting Pennington Quality Market, David now faced a white swell of sideways snow, close to a foot already on the ground. How long had he been in there? There'd be no way to part this sea of stuck cars. Why did he not wear his good boots? Did he even *own* good boots?

He loaded up and the van started, mercifully, robustly, and David felt more okay about his chances of making it back to The Egg alive, with toilet paper. As he pulled through the obstacles of the parking lot, he spotted what appeared to be a snow blower, but then realized it was a Toyota Prius kicking up a jet stream of sleet from beneath its helplessly spinning back tires. David drove over.

The driver was an older guy. Nice suit, peacoat. He had a manicured silver haircut parted like a politician's or former NFL head coach Jimmy Johnson's, a perfect seam between slabs of marble. David registered the fact that he'd hoped it would be a woman—an exotic, handicapped beauty with eighteen kids, maybe, and blind—badly in need of saving. But he also recognized the inherent sketchiness of offering a stranded woman a ride in a van. This dude in distress, he'd do.

"Sir, do you need a jump?" David asked.

"The engine's fine," the guy said. "It's the rest of the car that's not going anywhere."

They negotiated. The guy, Martin, lived nearby, so David instructed him to ditch his car and load his stuff into the MaxMobile, and soon they were on their way. Martin stayed huddled in back, trying to prevent all the groceries from spilling and rolling around the empty cargo van.

"I froze in there," Martin said. His face was between the front seats near David's arm.

"It was pretty cold," David agreed.

"No." He shook his head. "I mean I *froze*, I blew it. My wife's sick and I was supposed to be picking up her prescriptions, plus a cake for my daughter's birthday, but then when I realized the weather was serious... I don't know. I got caught in the middle somehow. Look at this..."

He pulled open one of his own bags, revealing a Transformers-decorated sheet cake.

"That's nice," David offered. "Your daughter is into Transformers?"

"See, that's the thing," Martin said. "I bought about *twelve* cakes."

"Why?"

"I don't know! The prescriptions took so long! I was worried they'd run out and didn't want to go far from the pharmacy. The bakery was right there. Everyone was stocking up! Then I got flustered and instead of getting—I don't even remember; what the hell else was I supposed to get?—I just kept grabbing cakes from the fuckin' bakery." He hung his head. "My wife's gonna die."

The guy was genuinely panicked now, mortified at his own ineptitude.

"But another way to look at it," David said, "is that you're going home with *twelve* cakes!"

"I just said that. I've already admitted it."

"You think your daughter cares about first aid kits and propane? Your wife might be pissed, but to your kid? You'll be a hero! Twelve cakes!"

His body language softened. Together they rode in mostly silence. Martin directed David to his place on 88 North Main Street, and David said he was just off South Main on Woosamonsa, and Martin asked if David knew Fred Shuster on Woosamonsa, and David said he knew Fred, that Fred was the best. Otherwise, Martin stayed quiet and let David focus on the white roads.

When David dropped off Martin, he offered to donate a bag of his own rations—batteries and other essentials that might help the man avoid the doghouse—and the guy traded David a cake in return. Martin departed, saying, "Hey, I appreciate it. For sure." That was that.

And see, that's the problem with saving an adult male. He barely admits to it.

There's simply no substitute for a damsel in distress, David thought, but the MaxMobile screeching against the side of a parked car jolted him back to the snow-covered roads. Again, he'd been lost in thought. *Focus, man!*

Rather than stop and assess the damage, he decided to keep going. He'd done one good deed today, driving Martin home, which would cancel out this bad one. He was even with the world. The world was even with itself, a blank slate, perfect and pure. Plus, he *had* to keep going.

C'mon, just a straight shot down Main Street to Woosamonsa. Up ahead was a street sign that looked semicorrect, but David had to open the driver's-side door and squint in order to discern that this was the cul-de-sac he was looking for.

He made the turn, and from the whiteness came the specter of The Egg, a whale momentarily cresting. David tried to swing the ass of the MaxMobile around to back into the driveway, but he took the turn too fast and he felt the vehicle careen onto its passenger-side wheels and very nearly topple completely. But the van came to rest. David backed up carefully, and in the rearview the garage door rose and a team of parka-ed housemates swarmed the van like a Nordic pit crew. They chucked the stuff inside, and David tried to help, but he tripped and came to rest like a snow angel on the concrete floor. He watched the garage door clink down, metal meeting snow, north meeting south. It would be eleven days before they left The Egg again.

iii.

"Question on why you bought a Batman sheet cake," said Lee, sifting through the groceries.

David rose from the garage floor. Before he could explain, Owen emerged from a parka.

"Airplane!" Owen shouted.

"Yeah!" said David. He had no idea what this meant, but he was unimaginably happy to see Owen again.

His first face-to-face with Owen Surber, Jr., had been on Princeton move-in day, although Owen had arrived a week earlier for ROTC orientation. Opening the threshold of room 331, David had found this massive gentleman sitting cross-legged in the center of their shared residence. Arrayed around him were shrink-wrapped packages, maybe a hundred beige things strewn across the threadbare carpet: *Chicken in Thai Sauce, Chocolate Pudding, The HooAH! Bar*. Some packages were open, and Owen was spooning himself what might have been powdered hot cocoa mix. He looked like a fat kid gathering candy from a busted piñata.

For move-in day, his little sister, Beth, had wanted to wear her Batgirl costume, a tasteful black leotard with yellow insignia, covering wrists to ankles, plus a shin-length skirt and cape. She was eleven years old, on the outer edge of being able to pull this off, and her figuring was she'd be a walking conversation starter. Other freshmen would remember him and say, *You're Batgirl's brother*. And he had to admit: it wasn't a half bad idea. But ultimately, David felt embarrassed and nixed the idea, and they settled on her wearing a Wonder Woman T-shirt as a compromise.

"Yo!" Owen had pointed to David's piles of stuff. "You've got a lot of effing books, man!"

It was true. David had brought an insane number of books to school. Maybe a dozen wine boxes full. The multitude of reading material seemed a foreign concept to Owen, who looked equally strange to David in a khaki camo uniform, black boots, and a thick-billed patrol cap.

"Yo!" David countered. "You've got a lot of effing... what are these things, exactly?"

Owen did a little hop and hup-to, then scanned the floor, realizing his mess.

"Sarge gave us these MREs today. I'm testing them out." He held out a hand to shake. "So you're David the businessman!" David had mentioned via email his plan to major in economics.

"Well, my parents want me to be a writer." David shrugged. "Thoreau once wrote that authors, 'more than kings or emperors, exert an influence on mankind.' But I don't know, it seems to me that corporate leaders probably play a greater role in shaping the world these days, right?"

Owen nodded. "Yeah, you're definitely smarter than me."

David's face got hot. He reminded himself to tone it the fuck down. Owen was his roommate, not an admissions officer. And just as nervous as David. He was sweaty, built like a basement oil burner. David knew Owen had played high school football in Waco, Texas—left guard and occasionally fullback for the top-ranked Midway Panthers, which was kind of a big deal—until an injury sidelined him. But this was more bulk than he'd expected.

"Sorry," David said. "You must be Owen the, uh, the marine?!"

He saluted. "Actually, I'm Owen the *army* cadet."

"I'm Beth!" yipped David's sister, extending a hand. "The *Wonder Woman*!"

Since living in The Egg, Owen's hair appeared to have grown back from its weird skinhead phase, and a short beard complemented his close-cropped black hair, which formed an attractive widow's peak. He'd also lost weight, or turned fat into muscle, or changed somehow. He had the look of a former child star who'd survived a few rough years before pulling things back together. Owen dropped to the garage floor, faceup, and lifted his legs, positioning them near David's hips. Fu and Mathias removed their jackets and stood beside Owen's body as if coaxing a corpse in a séance.

"Go ahead," Owen said from below. "Do an airplane."

David looked back at Mathias and whispered, "This is... kinda..."

"I understand your trepidation. But this is a safe place," Mathias replied. "Try to smile."

"Dude bought like *so* much medicine," grumbled Lee. "And I don't see my yogurt, either."

Dropping his jacket, David leaned forward onto Owen's feet. They grasped hands. Owen's palms were waxy and massive. It was oddly intimate, this thing they were doing. David used to do airplanes with Madeline, back in the day, a little post-hookup ritual they shared. He couldn't help but taste the echo of heartache. Some stuff stays in the spine.

"Get your balance," said Owen. "Lock your core."

David wobbled at first.

Shifted his hips.

And then, just like that: equilibrium.

He held his arms out to the sides, fists clenched in a powerful overhead Superman pose.

Once David was stable, the fellas each grabbed a limb and hoisted him into the air, off the platform of Owen's feet and onto their shoulders, as if he were a pharaoh's sedan chair. On three, they extended upward, pressing David toward the ceiling. He hung up there like track lighting, noting the garage's piles of sporting goods and outdoor gear—football pads, whitewater raft, Super Soaker water gun, beach chairs—and they carried him like this into The Egg, flying.

The interior of The Egg was like the inside of a balloon with a magician's giant pin sticking through it: a living room, dining room, and kitchen were clustered around a central wood-burning stove—a forest-green Norwegian Jøtul—the stovepipe rising up through the center of the ceiling. There was a sunroom toward the rear of the house, where the big screen lived. The Egg was the product of a hippieish time of American history, but it looked cleaner than any college housing David had ever seen. A distinct lack of sidewalk salvages and porch crap. There was wainscoting.

"Our sound system is nasty," Owen claimed, "but Fu will castrate you if you max the tweeters."

They swooped David toward the kitchen, where the sink was filled with stagnant water.

Was it clogged, David wondered, or were they just stockpiling?

"Can you smell it? Yesterday Fu was making potato latkes in here," Lee said. "Tripped me out. Like if your Jewish ass was cooking up a wok full of fucking kimchi."

"Ceiling fan!" David yelled, ducking. They maneuvered him under the wooden blades.

"You don't make kimchi in a wok," mumbled Mathias.

"That door's the pantry," Lee said. "And *that* door goes to the basement."

"Where all the interesting stuff happens," added Owen.

Climbing a set of stairs that hugged the inner curve of the dome, they reached the upper floor, over the garage. Here, they navigated him past a bathroom (bathtub and sink both filled; yup, they were stockpiling), plus three bedrooms. David saw Lee's towers of chemistry books, Fu's army of laptops and an electronic drum kit, Owen's piles of languishing extracurricular uniforms. He liked that The Egg looked very lived in. This was a home.

They flew him everywhere. David marveled at his new housemates' shoulder endurance. Somewhere around the sunroom, with its purple velvet couch and impressive media library, he started to feel both more and less nervous. His muscles relaxed, surrendering themselves to the aerial tour. But he was astonished that they'd gotten to this point, that they'd convinced him to do *all this weird shit*, before settling on basic things like rent. David's parents warned him to ask questions in advance, but each minute of flight eliminated old queries (like "How do you divvy up utilities?") and brought new ones to mind instead.

Where do I sleep?

Why are you flying me around the house?

What's happening?

"This is the best way to see The Egg," Mathias lectured, as though reading his mind. "Through the power of flight. We'll help you fly this first time. After that, you're expected to fly on your own."

"Just so I'm clear," David asked down to them. "Did you all drop out of school?"

"Leaves of absence," said Lee. "But no, we don't plan on going to classes anymore."

This was news to David. He'd assured his parents that he'd maintain a full course load.

"Okay, but what do you *do* here?"

"Think of The Egg as a new eating club," said Mathias. "It's farther away from campus and our membership is currently all dudes. But we've still got three floors."

In his grandpa László's day, there were twelve such eating clubs. Similar to fraternity houses, these odd Princeton institutions each occupied a mansion on Prospect Avenue, which was for some reason dubbed "the Street." The functions of the clubs were delineated by their three floors: the main floor was the dining hall, where upperclassmen ate their meals; upstairs were the residences where seniors lived and worked and accustomed themselves to the amenities of the ruling class; the basements were the taprooms, where the interesting stuff happened.

Each step down the stairs to the basement of The Egg brought with it strained swears and the echo of feet on wood. David could tell their arms were getting tired and he wondered what staccato rhythms his body might make if they dropped him down this jagged slope of stairs. He felt the specificity of his conditions, the carefully orchestrated strangeness. All action was special now, all time sacred.

Reaching the bottom of the stairs, the guys finally set him down and shook out their arms. It smelled like spray adhesive, primer, old cold. Fu ran back upstairs to fetch grocery bags. David scanned and immediately found a fully stocked and impeccably ordered array of metal shelving units, a true prepper's pantry: cooking oil, salt, beans, powdered milk, sugar, honey, scary-looking bags that looked like landscaping mulch but were probably rice, a serious cache of canned goods, myriad backpacks, first aid kits, soap, vitamins, TP, massive blue barrels marked WATER. It was only four storage racks but might as well have been that infinite stockroom of weaponry from *The Matrix*. David suddenly realized Mathias had intentionally neglected to tell him about this supply. He'd been testing

David to see how well he'd do at the grocery store. And here David was with a fucking birthday cake.

He wondered if The Egg had weapons, too.

"I didn't figure you guys for right-wing, tinfoil-hat conspiracy types," David said. He was kidding around, but Mathias took it seriously.

"When you say 'right wing,' you're talking about American political parties that aren't going to exist in the same way after things break down. What you're *really* talking about is two kinds of people, what Fu would call a binary system, like ones and zeroes...

"Maybe the *Ones* are people who think humans are basically born bad and have to be *made good*—by religion, by law and order, what have you—and so these people are scared of everyone else, especially the different, the deviant ones, the Other, hence racism, xenophobia, homophobia, right?

"And then there are the *Zeroes*, people who think humans are basically born good and are tragically *made bad*—by socioeconomic pressures, by their parents—but that folks can generally be trusted or, at worst, turned around and rehabilitated...

"The Zeroes prevail when times are good. But it's easy for the Ones to take over when times are tough. The Egg is filled with Zeroes: *we* like to think people are pretty good. Yes, we have a pantry. With weather like this, if you don't have extra food and supplies on hand you're either stupid or lazy. But those're just basic necessities. We've got bigger projects, too."

Mathias pointed. Beside the stairwell sat a workbench with a metal vise hanging from the wood, ingrown like a barnacle. On top was a homemade radio setup, more wires. There were two recently built bedrooms down here, with uneven drywall and spackle like fresh cupcake icing. One of them, David learned, was vacant and would be his. The other belonged to Mathias. Its door was open. Inside, David spotted an antique refrigerator, padlocked shut.

"What's in that fridge?" David asked, pointing.

"My thesis," Mathias said.

"You keep your thesis in a *refrigerator*?" asked David.

"You keep your thesis in a *computer*?" asked Mathias.

"Well," David said after a moment, "I don't keep mine anywhere, because I don't have to write one until senior year, I thought. And at this rate I kinda doubt I'll last that long."

Mathias sighed. "Let me guess: You're dissatisfied with Princeton, right? You were expecting some magical Hogwarts utopia, but it's actually not, so you're dissatisfied, which, in turn, makes you feel like an ingrate. And at the end of it all, you're supposed to write a thesis, some long piece of critical theory that sits on a shelf for eternity. And who gives a fuck, right?"

Lee strolled over to the pantry shelves to help Owen stock cans; they'd heard this spiel before.

"Well, the thing is all you've got to do is drop out or go to a different school. Yes, of course, familial pressures, parents are paying good money. But honestly? My response to that is: wipe your ass like the rest of us and make a decision. It's daunting, but the things we desire *are* daunting."

"I'm not afraid of hard work," David insisted.

"Well, *that's what we're doing here*: high-concept hard work. The point of The Egg is for you to develop a thesis. I bet you've already got the kernel of an idea. Your Halloween thing was a debacle. We both know you can do better next time. At The Egg, you're always working on your project, your vision, your thesis—something only *you* can do. If it's viable, I'm happy to help fund it. Preferably something practical, not merely theoretical. Something that helps others."

"I'm still trying to figure out whether you're a good guy or a bad guy," David said.

Without blinking, Mathias uttered gently, "'I never knew, and never shall know, a worse man than myself.'"

Thoreau. That did it. David was in.

But this freaked him out, viscerally—this crossing over, this liminal space, whatever it was he was deciding to enter into—and that fear must have shown on his face, or else Mathias just sensed it.

"You're scared," he said to David, gripping his shoulders the way he did in the river when they first met. "We watch movies and assume the end of the world will be filled with bad guys, devolving into some sordid *Mad Max* hellscape. I'm betting our world is just going to become different. Smaller. It's going to be *our* job to make that smaller world into a close-knit community, starting with this container, The Egg. Supporting, educating, transforming, always improvising. If we don't succumb to fear or protectionism and—this one's big—if we don't assume our college pedigree somehow makes us elite or more important than anyone else... we can help create a generous, safe society. Our own small heaven on earth. *That's* what we're building."

"Honestly?" David finally said after taking this in. "I don't see why I can't go to classes *and* also do your thesis project. It's Princeton for chris-sakes! I like my classes."

"Fine, then do both." He shrugged. "You won't sleep much. But Lee can help with that."

Hearing his name, Lee took the cue to wander back from the shelves. Like a ship's captain spinning a helm, Owen turned the workbench vise, and David heard the rising whir of machinery purring to life—a furnace kicking on, he guessed.

But the sound grew and grew, a mechanical growl that wouldn't stop.

And then the stairs began to move.

Quaking and lifting like a jaw coming unhinged, a system of heavy-duty hydraulics elongated beneath the stairwell, tilting the steps up and back, opening wider and wider until they touched the ceiling. To look at the undercarriage of these stairs was unnatural, as if staring at the craggy roof of a dragon's mouth. A curtain now separated the basement from whatever mystery lay under the stairs. The rest of them stood with smug smiles on their faces, arms crossed like soldiers at ease.

All men become little boys when shown a cool machine.

Lee handed out a stack of surgical masks and placed one around his own snout. They walked under the curtain into the black mass. David assumed the stairs were recent retrofitting—the whim of Mathias, their trust-fund baby who'd maybe seen the movie *Clue* too many times. But Mathias told him the previous owner, a gun collector keeping his firearms locked away from his kids, had installed it. The presence of a hidden panic room was Mathias's primary criteria in looking for off-campus housing. It took him months to find this place.

Flipping a switch, Lee made the cave come alive with blinking fluorescence. David peered down the room, deep and thin like a walk-in closet, tubes forming graceful, calligraphic conduits between beakers and IV stands. Toward the back were vats and mixing bowls and foreign packages marked with Germanic umlauts and squiggly Spanish tildes. At the far end of the space was a tall gray gun safe, probably from the previous owner, though the Winchester logo looked reasonably new. He wasn't ready to ask if it was full or empty, so instead he asked, "What is this? A meth lab?"

Lee's shoulders deflated. "This is my thesis. I'm cheaply counterfeiting a few commercial pharmaceuticals but mainly experimenting with new hybrids."

"So... it *is* a drug lab, though," David clarified. In truth, he was disappointed. It could have been anything in that secret room—Narnia or a cryogenic freezer of unicorn brains or whatever—and a drug lab felt almost pedestrian at first. Regardless, Lee gave a short tour through his arsenal. Arranged in pristine rows sat a cornucopia of raw chemicals, labeled in meticulous block lettering. Along one wall were gleaming synthetics with labels like "HIn/phph" and "Hexamethyleneteramine." On the other wall, dusty brown bottles with organic names: "kava kava," "zizyphus seed."

David pointed to an older one. "What's yohimbe root?"

"Herbal Viagra," whispered Owen. "Careful, though. Makes your heart race like crazy."

Lee's demeanor had changed since entering his lab. He was professorial, calm, almost nice. Placing an arm around David, he said softly, "And we call this pill the 'Big Bang.'" He opened his palm, revealing a red gelcap, then pulled it away.

Mathias mimed an invisible ball exploding and whispered, "XplO..."

"I've got it in pill form, smokable wax, liquid. It's best intravenously, but the MAO inhibitor in my pill makes it orally active, like ayahuasca."

David suddenly felt a visceral memory of his first meeting with Mathias at Stony Brook and the consequential trip that had carried him down that waterway and ultimately into The Egg.

"What you got at the river was the high dose, what psychedelic pioneers like Terence McKenna called the *heroic* dose," Mathias said. "You rocket past the veil and it's hard to be an atheist ever again. Lee's pill is a more gradual, subtle experience."

Just then, the power went off. David panicked, fearing he was about to be beaten up or left in the dark. Some new initiation. But the guys were unfazed.

"We've got a generator," said Mathias. "And Fu will bring a flashlight in a sec, I'm sure."

"So that's me, that's what I know how to do," Lee said. "Your boy Owen is working on a new kind of power source. Fu—where *is* Fu?—he's into robots and radios and shit. Mathias is—"

"I get it," David said. The blizzard would provide an opportunity to hunker down and figure out his project. "Just give me a little time."

"If you need time," Lee said, unscrewing a mammoth GNC canister, "we've got plenty."

There must've been a thousand purple pills inside. Lee distributed a handful. David wondered if Lee's counterfeit version of Zeronal worked the same as the Pfizer version, which he'd read was nearing FDA approval. The pills halted the mechanism of melatonin production—usually based on light, time of day, season, whatever—like freezing time.

David recalled the feeling. Of not being worried about the past or the future. Of being *in it.* His first foray into Zeronal was responsible for hastening his removal from campus housing. He wasn't sure he was ready to experiment again.

"Kiss the pill," Mathias stated. He smooched his capsule, swallowed it.

They echoed back, "Kiss the pill," and brought the Zeronal to their lips.

On cue, Fu entered the lab, carrying Martin's donated Batman cake, now covered in candles. He sang the "Happy Birthday" song in a sweet, lilting tenor.

"Your voice!" Fu's tone was pitch perfect.

"I was gonna just light a random candle," Fu said. "But this seemed cooler."

"Make a wish," directed Mathias.

David made the same wish he'd been making since Halloween: to do better next time.

2

HALLOWEEN

i.

The black mask had smelled like a baby bottle, a mix of rubber and plastic. It fit perfectly. Wiggling into the massive chest padding, airbrushed to look like muscles poured into spandex, David watched himself slowly transform in the door mirror. There were black boots, a yellow utility belt (with real functional holsters!), a vinyl cape, and latex black gloves with gauntlets serrated on the sides. David made a few tight fists, pounded the bat insignia spread across his pecs. When he fit the codpiece in place, he gave a nod at the mirror, saluting his suddenly impressive-looking junk.

Look at you, David thought. *You are a demon of sexiness.*

So, yes, David was *that* guy. The kid with the overdone Batman costume. Because this was more than Halloween. It was his Princeton debut.

The Forbes guys were pre-drinking down the hall. During that early freshman moment, barely two months in, David's core foursome consisted of himself and Owen, plus another odd couple of roommates: Bob and Esteban. While David had spread himself around, making lots of acquaintances to deduce who might become true and lasting friends, Owen had swiftly chosen Roberto "Bob" Badalamenti, a soccer player from San Dimas, California, and devoted his hip to be conjoined forthwith. By default, David and Esteban became their co–third wheels.

Owen's bad knees made him unfit for college football and most other sports. So he busied himself to overcompensate for the leftover physical energy, but he clearly longed for the locker room camaraderie. Hence "Soccer Bob." Everyone said Bob would be captain someday. He was towering and chiseled and Italian and had bleached-blond hair and a ridiculous sound system, a billion-watt Bose behemoth. Guys on their hall nodded like disciples whenever he leaned on those chest-high speakers, running down specs like it was some juicy Trans Am.

Esteban was Tuscaloosan, Latino, gay, wore a cross around his neck. He was tall like Bob but skinnier, with a smile both genuine and constant and a head of tight dark curls. He was the kind of guy who might've been the lead counselor at a summer camp, trotted out to impress and calm nervous parents on drop-off day. To David, Esteban seemed eager to make an exit from this particular friend arrangement, yet simultaneously riveted or at least curious to experiment with what was clearly an uncommon social milieu—a closeness with two athletes who hadn't yet devolved into the overt or accidental bigotry that David assumed Esteban experienced in Alabama.

Maybe Owen and Bob found Esteban unthreatening. Maybe they appreciated that he attracted women. David played a similar role. His facial hair made him look like a guy who was dangerous and mature, and his shyness could be mistaken for the brooding intensity some girls go for. Either that, or he looked like a guy who had access to weed, and some girls go for that, too.

As a group they almost made sense. If they stood in a line, diminutive David bringing up the rear, then hefty Owen, then fun Esteban, with sexy Bob in front, anyone could see the upgrading trajectory of their height and attractiveness, an evolutionary timeline come to life. But the gap between David and Bob was considerable, and on the occasions when they'd find themselves as a duo, their other two links missing, they'd swiftly part ways and opt to roll solo. David was never the sidekick Bob wanted.

Another way of saying this: David was conspicuously a virgin.

He'd arrived late to both drugs and girls. When puberty mangled him, expanding his nose, ears, and teeth faster than the rest of his face, his dad used to say, "Count your blessings. The normal kids can go out and get popular. You can stay home and get brilliant." So David became a plodder, an academic workhorse. He read voraciously and his favorite was Thoreau, whom Hawthorne once called "ugly as sin." In solidarity, David grew a neck-beard during that middling era of high school when few boys could grow decent facial hair. So despite his five-foot-six stature, David was seen as something of a man. In his junior year, he'd started smoking pot and dating Madeline Cone.

David and Maddy fooled around a lot, but they never had full-on sex. Slowly, they tiptoed around bases, experimenting in cars, in fields and bathtubs and off-duty construction equipment, sometimes successfully. He bought flavored condoms, let her guess. She bought a candy bra and let him bite the sugary dextrose from her breasts.

She said it first, those three magic words: "You're my bitch."

Then the blush wore off. So they tried to summon it back. They drank, smoked. No hallucinogens, though, not ever. David's loving parents, Gil and Eileen Fuffman, never said much about cocaine or heroin—they figured there was plenty of negative propaganda already—but they'd staunchly warned David against the dangers of tripping. A single dose of LSD could fry his brain, they said. He'd be a pointless presence in the world, nothing, a zero. David had respected this rule. Hallucinogens were his kryptonite, he'd decided, and if he ever disobeyed, there'd surely be righteous punishment for hubristic defiance.

Even here in college.

David took it easy on drugs and alcohol but tried his best to get out and partake of the Princeton nightlife. The Street advertised its weekend slates of bands and DJs on lamppost flyers, and David and his hall mates endured many embarrassments before learning to differentiate band names from theme parties. Once, they showed up to the Terrace Club wearing homemade tunics and horned helmets, only to discover "Viking Night" was actually a five-piece emo band from Rahway.

The third weekend in September, they'd aimed for "Space Odyssey" at Cottage, one of the WASPier eating clubs, which Esteban referred to as "Snottage." David was hoping for a trippy, Kubrick-ian experience, but the space theme only meant purple black lights, glow-in-the-dark punch, and painted Styrofoam orbs (planets?) circling a disco ball (the sun?).

David, Esteban, Owen, and Bob pseudo-danced in a circle together, trying to entice at least one girl into their orbit so that they didn't look like four guys pseudo-dancing in a circle together. Owen and Esteban eventually got bored or uncomfortable and went to the taproom for a beer. Bob scanned the room and motioned David toward First-Floor Allie, a statuesque volleyball player in Forbes whom they all openly coveted. She was out of David's league, height-wise. And otherwise. Still, he worked up the nerve to waddle over and bounce his knees near hers, purse his lips into some kind of dude dance face, trying to keep a beat.

"I know you!" he screamed over the shrieking treble.

"You're in Forbes, right?" she said. "I am, too. Our fucking power is still off in the Annex."

"That sucks," David yelled. "Do you need anything? Candles or whatever? We have a bathroom in our room if you need to take a shower or anything."

He meant it innocently, just trying to help and make conversation, but Allie gave him a shady look. She yelled, "You're Soccer Bob's friend, right?! Tell me your name again."

"David!"

"Gabe, wait here a second!" She held up a finger and then ran off. David looked back and Bob was gone.

So, I'll just wait here then, David thought. *Rolling solo. She'll be back. Any minute now.*

Gathering the whole foursome usually took wild feats of social engineering. But tonight was Halloween. Tonight, they'd be a formidable crew. Grabbing his neon-green flyers, David strutted down to meet them all in Bob and Esteban's room.

The flyers read:

Engaged in a dispute over personal honor? A blood feud?
The favor of a lady? Want to prove you're a badass?
Without going to Afghanistan?
Forget fisticuffs!!

JOIN THE PRINCETON DUELING SOCIETY
Inaugural Midnight Series

- Challenge a rival or defend your honor!
- Settle your disputes in a more civilized manner, with paintball guns!
- *Don't* actually *die!*

HALLOWEEN – MIDNIGHT – POE FIELD
BE THERE.

Because why settle for a typical Halloween when
you can shoot someone in the face instead?
www.facebook.com/PDS

Word had spread quickly: a single visionary—a freshman—had stepped up and created this safe forum for bellicosity. He'd purchased two sleek paintball handguns and launched a successful social media campaign. The PDS Facebook page promised students vs. professors, roommate vs. roommate, ideological throw-downs. Swiftly, matchups formed. It was something to distract them, an ancient channel for modern anger; something pseudo-violent to stem the tide of slap fights on campus and jolt the students into reflecting on their lives of privilege and entitlement.

It was something different, something bold.

It was something David Fuffman had created.

Back in high school he'd run many a circus. He'd planned a blood drive for leukemia, a beef jerky sale for lupus. David was the dude behind the scenes, operationalizing the theoretical shit, giving it shape. He'd seen the documentary *Hands on a Hard Body,* about folks competing in an endurance contest to win a new Nissan truck. In the wake of global disasters, including the latest seismic activity in Port-au-Prince, David had staged his own fund-raiser stunt in the Pikesville High parking lot, which he called "Hands Across America on a Hyundai for Haitian Hematology." He found a leukemia society in the ravaged land and made it his cause. How could humans cope with cancer *and* earthquakes? His event and its social media campaign raised $52,000, which was nuts, and when it boiled down to sleep deprivation, David pulled a caffeine pill from his secret belt buckle and kept going, reaching 101 hours awake. The local NBC affiliate did a story on it, which made him a minor local celebrity and probably helped him get into Princeton.

This was more than an act, though.

Unlike Batman, the essence of Superman, David realized, was that he'd been born that way. His powers manifested only on Earth, making him an accidental god among men. He took his station in life seriously, using his powers for good, and David understood his own privileged station, that he'd been born a white guy in America with parents who hung his art on their fridge and bought him unnecessary sneakers. There was a solid chance he'd never ever starve or go to jail. He realized his luck. *Things could be so much worse.*

David planned to carry this sense of obligation to college, to a school whose motto was "Princeton in the nation's service and the service of humanity." Armed with a self-consciously retro Mead Trapper Keeper, David had arrived with the class of 2025 and poured himself into intellectual pursuits. Wordsworth, Machiavelli, Iacocca, he dove into the required reading, trying not to hate *The Faerie Queene*. He fed himself "world beat" from the Scheide Music Library and took campus tours, disseminating both official and unauthorized campus lore to other freshmen ("*Scheide* is the German word for vagina, you know"). And he dug his classes. Viral Marketing. Romanticism and Revolution. The Problem of Evil. And Oratory Leadership in Historical Perspective, which he hoped would boost his poor public speaking skills.

The posh suburbia of the town of Princeton hadn't offered much—a destination for yuppie shopping, with more high-end boutiques than head shops. The campus itself housed better secrets, David was sure, if approached scientifically.

He'd started at the perimeter and worked his way inward, as if circling a prey. Princeton's North Stars were a constellation of Firestone Library, the university chapel, and the stately Nassau Hall clock tower. In the south were the cogeneration and chilled water plants—the latter a bong-like smokestack surrounded by pipes and turbines—and Spinoza Field House, where hockey happened. To the east: the imposing black-cube Death Star of the Engineering Quad and the Peyton Observatory, a domed R2-D2. By the end of September, David had explored most of the campus's exterior. He liked having a good lay of the land before his workload got more intense. Next, he wanted to go deeper.

Someone famous once said, "Home is the place where you sleep and the place where you defecate." So David systematically went about both human activities in as many campus buildings as possible. It's nice to have attainable goals. He napped in the Whig and Clio debate halls, shat in the Lewis-Sigler Institute for Integrative Genomics. *Structure by structure,* he thought, *I'll take ownership of this place.*

David's favorite building, hands down, was the Sloan Center for Integrated Scientific Materials (SCISM), a research lab funded by corporations and government agencies. The walls were corrugated purple metal, shifting color in the sunlight. It looked like a ninja training facility.

But wouldn't you know it, the only place that wouldn't let him in for a snooze or to use the john, even when he faked an emergency, was SCISM. Reporters and corporate competitors had been caught spying, so only those with legit business were allowed in via photo swipe card.

Owen was planning on majoring in mechanical engineering or chemical engineering or electrical engineering, so he actually got to go inside and said SCISM was "*the* academic laboratory at the tip of the pharmaceutical spear." He sang the praises of SCISM's nuclear pharmacy, its cyclotron, its CGMP compliance, its Cray Gemini 14-petaflop supercomputer—words and numbers that guarded the possibility of an infinite and magical future, where David and his generation could give up praying to invisible gods and, through technology, create their own omnipotence.

Still, David's image of college—leggy coeds on bright lawns, frat boys flinging Frisbees, everyone laughing and reading and smooching in the sun—was demolished by the storms of September.

About two million people from South Carolina to New York without power for over a week, and about twenty lives claimed before rescue crews arrived from Tennessee. Parts of Forbes experienced rolling blackouts, but Princeton had good generators and fared fine. Still, it seemed more urgent than ever to unite the campus.

Inspired by Professor Wingfield's Oratory Leadership class, David decided to take a more active public role than he might have otherwise and launched the PDS in theatrical fashion. Here was the plan: during dinner, he'd wear a vintage suit and clink a glass and read aloud a speech and challenge none other than Bob Badalamenti to a duel and, by proxy, be respected and adored.

In practice, it went down like this:

"Gentlepersons of Forbes, your attention please!" Okay so far. David read from a shaky printout as sweat formed. "In the dawn of July 11, 1804, Aaron Burr and Alexander Hamilton rowed to Weehawken, with their 'seconds' in tow, to finally, fatally lay waste to their discord..."

By the time David finished this first sentence, he had indeed quieted the dining hall. But David's strong opening soon disintegrated into a list of obsolete concepts like "portmanteaus" (cases for dueling pistols), and David soon saw that he was sucking the life out of the room.

Luckily, Bob responded. Cartwheeling into the dining hall fresh from the soccer field and still wearing his shin guards (as David had instructed), he removed his sweaty shorts and slapped David across the face with them (this was improv), crying, "I challenge thee to a duel!"

He sauntered out wearing only his jock strap.

The crowd went wild. Guys barked at the dishonorable offense. Girls hooted at Bob's butt cheeks. Plastered by the smell of Bob's horrific sogginess, David waved genteelly, dabbed his face with a napkin, and announced the Facebook page and email address.

The gauntlet had been thrown down. It was so *on*.

David passed out his neon flyers and emails poured into PtonDueling-Society@gmail.com with requests to join the Halloween undercard (Bob vs. David would be the main event). As the lineup formed, David couldn't help fearing, from a showmanship standpoint, that he and Bob didn't have the obvious dichotomy of the other scheduled duels: battles of the sexes, political opposites, et cetera. The only clear-cut difference David could pinpoint was that he was East Coast and Bob was West Coast. Their real rivalry existed below the surface, unspoken, a biological, lizard-brain sort of competitiveness linked to the fairer sex. Bob was idiotic around girls but somehow bedded many of them; David could hold a solid conversation but never sealed the deal. His longing nights usually culminated in a meatball sub from Hoagie Haven, a bong rip, a conversation with lonely guys on a ratty couch in Bob's room (while Bob was likely or conspicuously in some girl's room), chest-high speakers blasting in protest. On the rare occasion Bob was actually there, he'd put on his Mexican wrestling mask and really rub it in.

"*El Oso Terrible* gets all the poon! Dave, you should ask more girls if they wanna shower with you, that's great game! Room 331, *tu es vales verga!* Loose translation: you are worth penis!"

He'd then perform a leaping jump kick from the top of his couch/turnbuckle.

"Why, Lord?" Owen would plead, head in his palms after yet another strikeout. "I mean, I told her she was *beautiful*."

Jesus, David thought. *At least I'm not the worst at this.*

Still, David slept alone, womanless and hoagie-full. He was jealous of Bob but could tell the feeling was mutual. *Maybe this is why Bob agreed to duel me,* David considered. *I'm someone he wants to beat.*

Regardless. With the less than obvious reasons for their enmity, David felt they needed to distinguish their Halloween rivalry through costuming. David's first pick was, of course, Batman.

"You should be the Joker!" he suggested to Bob. "Batman vs. Joker."

"You should be a pansy-ass bitch," Bob replied. "You should be fucking Robin."

"I'm Batman," David stated, trying to be firm. He'd already purchased the pricey costume.

"Well, I don't really care what *you* are. *I'm* getting laid. And creepy Joker lipstick is not going to get my dills wet. I need to accentuate my positives." Which meant he was going shirtless.

David tried another tactic. Fishing Frank Miller's *The Dark Knight Returns* off his bookshelf, he opened up to a spread of the Mutant Leader, the graphic novel's beastly villain. He was shirtless, with wraparound shades and aggressive nipples. Bob loved it.

So when David walked into Bob's room on Halloween, he was expecting a true nemesis. Instead, Bob was indeed shirtless, but on his head was that Mexican wrestling mask. A sequined blue-and-white thing with holes for his eyes, nose, and mouth.

"Holy shit!" said Owen, wearing his ROTC camo gear, sizing David up. Esteban, dressed as a foppish dandy with a frilly shirt and monocle, squeezed one of David's fake pecs.

Pointing at Bob's face, David asked, "What happened to the Mutant Leader?"

"I'm going as a Mexican wrestler: *El Oso Terrible*!" He zestfully rolled his *R*s.

"Dude, it makes no sense with the Batman costume and—"

"He could pass for Bane," offered Owen.

"Doesn't Bane wear some kind of gas mask?" David asked.

"You're thinking of the movie. The original comic book villain was a Mexican wrestler. For a guy who loves superheroes you don't really know comic books, huh?"

"My relationship to superheroes is mystical," David said. "Not fundamentalist."

"Nobody cares if our costumes match," Bob snapped. "Now, here, bump this line of yip and take this shot of Rumple Minze before I suplex you. And I'm bringing this little buddy for later," he said, waving a small vial. "This shit is my new favorite, it's like Molly plus booze, with no hangover." David had a hard time justifying the cocaine—a new drug added to his repertoire—but without much cajoling he put a rolled Wawa receipt to his nose and watched the powder disappear inside him. Tonight was his debut.

Within seconds, and at some length, David found himself elucidating to his hall mates: Why Batman? In high school, David had fallen hard for Batman. And why not? Bruce Wayne saw the world in human terms. He was a man of extraordinary intellect, blessed with cash and an infinite utility belt of ass-kicking toys. His alter ego was a bat, an honorable mirror of his fears, a demon exorcised nightly. What did sacrifice mean to Superman, a Man of Steel, able to stop bullets, turn back time, leap buildings in a single bound? No, it was Batman, the vulnerable Dark Knight, who understood life and anguish and stuff. Plus, Batman was the most capitalist-friendly superhero. A rich innovator, he could dream any vehicle, any weapon, any potion, and *poof!* It was his. Having money makes you almost invincible.

Meanwhile, say what you will about the privilege of alien Superman, but *he* worked a day job.

There are three types of superheroes, David continued, really feeling it now: the Supermen, Wonder Women, Thors, and X-Men mutants, with powers inborn; there are the Spider-Men, Hulks, Dr. Manhattans, and Deadpools, acquiring their powers accidentally, via science; and a third kind—the Batmen, Iron Men, Captain Americas, Black Panthers—those not content to stick to baseline mortal means, who proactively gain or enhance their powers. Even if they have to cheat.

Like a lapsed Catholic finding the Church again, David came back to Spider-Man and Superman in the summer before college and merged their spiritualities with that of Batman, godfather of the self-made superhero. David solidified this holy superhero trinity into three tenets:

1. *Be like Superman: Cultivate your God-given gifts, count your blessings, don't whine. Shit could be worse.*
2. *Be like Spider-Man: Surround yourself with radioactive arachnids and fall headlong into their webs.*
3. *Be like Batman: When destiny fails, use your smoke pellets.*

ii.

Midnight. They strutted onto Poe Field—a soldier, a dandy, a wrestler, and a Batman—joining some five hundred other costumed coeds. There were flappers, hippies, several Elvii. Sexy angels and devils, sassy Dorothys, sultry Cleopatras, fairies, nymphs, genies, cheerleaders, French maids, entire staffs of nurses in fishnet thigh-highs. Poe Field was a male fantasy. Barely bright enough to ogle. The guys got some stares of their own as they entered the mass. Bob with his barrel chest. David with his movie-quality supersuit. Esteban jauntily twirling his cane. Owen in fatigues. Men in uniform. It was unseasonably warm and only drizzling for a change. David sweated beneath his rubber bodysuit. He realized, with some ire, that Bob was positioned as the front man. Still, their collective swagger was in full effect. Did people know who they *were*? Who David was? Did they know *he* was responsible for all this? Should they strut even slower?

Tucked behind the mythical SCISM building, Poe Field was a manicured swatch of grass used by the varsity soccer team for practice. As they entered the scrum, Bob high-fived a pirate and said, "*Dónde* booze?"

The pirate pointed to a clump of costumed kids on the bleachers and droned, "Beer..." He then pointed to another huddle by the far soccer goal and giddily whispered, "*Absinthe...*"

In the netting of the far goal, a witch poured the absinthe, dropping sugar cubes into each Solo cup, turning the potion milky white. David had personally organized the keg delivery. The absinthe was a surprise. Owen and Esteban headed toward the kegs on the bleachers, but Bob grabbed David by the batcowl and dragged him toward the absinthe, saying, "Let's celebrate our creation, Dave."

Our?

David replied, "I don't really do hallucinogens."

"Forget that Van Gogh swirly shit," Bob said. "Absinthe won't make you trip. It's like very potent alcohol. I tried it last weekend. Dude, do you know what *happened* to me?"

"No, what happened?"

"No, see, I'm asking *you*," he said. "I have zero recollection. All I know is that I woke up wearing blue snow pants, a wifebeater, and a bowler hat!" They both laughed. Bob put his arm around David. Suddenly, they were totally comfortable. The best of friends. It felt pretty okay.

The absinthe witch beckoned them with long, warty fingers, fondling her bottle. "Catch the Green Fairy, my pretties," she cackled. Bob knocked David a cheers, and they bottomsed up. It tasted like frozen licorice and David wanted a chaser, but there was none in sight. Beside them, three retro cereal brand mascots—sorority sisters, David guessed—lifted their masks and tilted the absinthe into their hidden faces. When everyone finished, Bob snaked over and put his arm around one of them, gripping her against his naked chest with the crook of his elbow. She was dressed and labeled as CAP'N CRUNCH. Tight white yoga pants, a deep blue V-neck, a blue kerchief tied round her neck and down her back like a tiny cape, and a mask depicting the elder helmsman of breakfast. The other girls had BOO BERRY and HONEY SMACKS written across their shirts. David couldn't help but stare at their chests.

"Any of you ladies dueling?" asked Bob. "Because *we* are. We invented this thing. I'm El Oso Terrible. That's Davy Gravy."

"David Fuffman," clarified David. He was feeling superconfident, but as he bowed slightly in salutation, the point of his bat-ear jabbed Honey Smacks in her mask.

"Whoa! I totally emailed you to sign up my friends!" said Boo Berry. "I pictured you taller."

"So did I," David sniffed.

"Mr. Fuffman, this is NBC News," said the Cap'n Crunch girl, shoving an invisible microphone in his face. "You've launched the Princeton Dueling Society. Tell us, how do you feel?"

"Um, like getting wasted?" he replied into her fist, kind of confused.

"Excellent. And tell us, to reach this level, have you ever taken performance enhancers?"

"Plead the Fifth?"

"Excellent. And tell us, are you still diddling that mousy, flat-chested Pikesville chick?"

As Cap'n Crunch held her fist in David's face, his eyes instinctively dropped to her breasts, to the Sharpie'd *C* and *H* lettering delightfully warping along the contours of her V-neck.

"Haley?" He smiled. Slowly, Cap'n Crunch lifted her mask to reveal the familiar face. He'd assumed they would meet up immediately after arriving at Princeton, but tonight was actually the first time he'd seen her on campus. Haley Roth, the Racketeer, laughed and told David he had a nice costume. He said the same about hers, and they agreed that classes were okay and the weather was lousy and that it was great to see each other.

"I can't totally fucking believe I haven't run into you sooner," she said. "Ships in the night!"

"Yeah! Rowboats in the morning!" David replied. Like an idiot.

Boo and Honey whispered something, winked, and just like that they ran off, leaving Haley to catch up with David and fend for herself in Bob's elbow. Before David could say anything else stupid, Bob interrupted to ask how they knew each other.

"Same town," she said. "Different school."

"You guys used to bang and stuff?" he asked.

"Dude," said David.

"Nope, he never touched me," said Haley. "I wasn't his type."

"Well, we kinda *did* hook up once," David offered sheepishly, then immediately regretted it.

"Did we?" She shrugged and put her mask back on. "Who remembers?"

He was taken aback and about to offer details, but he held his coked-up tongue.

"O Cap'n! my Cap'n!" Bob belted, suddenly shoving his own microphone in *her* face. "Tell us, on a scale of one to ten, how much would you like to take a shower with Batman later tonight?"

"Dude," said David. He understood Bob was maybe trying to help, but... *dude*.

"I don't know," Haley said. "Solid six and a half?"

"Second question," Bob whispered, pulling from his pocket that vial, his little buddy. "On a scale of one to ten, how much would you like to do some liquid Ecstasy tonight? No strings attached."

"Perfect ten." She smiled. Bob turned his back and asked the Absinthe Witch for two refills. Just two. Bob emptied the vial into Haley's cup and they swallowed their shots. David saw her shudder and scan for a chaser.

"Jesus, it tastes like Windex," she moaned. Bob let her go for a moment, and, sensing her chance to get away, she pretended to spot her other cereal sisters, offered a half-assed goodbye to David, and ran off.

David felt cheated. As they walked back into the crowd, Bob took him by the shoulders again. He lifted off his mask, leaned in, and whispered, "Trust me, you didn't want any of that."

And at the time David thought he was just being nice, comforting him with a plenty-of-fish-in-the-sea platitude in response to Haley's apparent rejection. But that's not what Bob meant.

iii.

"Lads and lasses!" Esteban belted. "On this most hallowed of eves, we conform to Russian-style rules. Seconds shall inspect weaponry. Principals must state the nature of the offense. Stand back-to-back. Take ten paces. Turn. Fire. Three shots only. We are not, after all, barbarians..."

David had tapped Esteban, a theater nerd, as the emcee. Affecting a foppish British accent and with a top hat tilted most rakishly, he swung his rapier cane and called orders into the night.

"Mortality of wounds shall be judged in a civilized fashion, and honor shall be bestowed or forfeited accordingly." Then he dropped the accent and said, "Okay, let's *do* this fucker!"

Near midfield, a wide dueling circle formed, stretching out to the foot of the bleachers and the line of oak trees. Handles of booze got passed around. The hooting and hollering and wagering heated up. David abstained from more absinthe but got drunker on beer. The first duel—two roommates, Tommy O'Leary and Yan Shen, battled over the time-honored stereotype of Irish vs. Asian penis size. Incredibly, both duelists hit their below-the-belt targets; it was ruled a draw. Then, in a gorgeous display of marksmanship, Count Chocula knocked off the Trix Rabbit with a resounding single shot to the forehead. A heated bout between a red Republican elephant vs. a blue Democratic ass ended when the donkey mortally wounded his counterpart with a neon-yellow splotch to the chest, which felt like an orgasmically satisfying victory to most of the yipping crowd.

Things were going great. And then it was David's turn to duel.

He babbled to Owen, his second, "In the time of the ancients, before the human brain evolved, broke into its warring bicameral hemispheres, mated with itself, and begat consciousness, there was only the spirit and the vessel."

"Oh yeah?" Owen smiled, walking his nicely plastered roommate to the center of the circle.

"A human couldn't act of his own volition. It had no *I*. It could only be *imbued* with a spirit, with a tendency toward war or love or music or compassion, like Ares entering a human warrior right before battle. Dressed in suits of flesh, the gods found agency. I read that in a book."

"Neat," Owen said as David burped in his face. "Well, now you must evolve or perish."

Bob and David swayed back-to-back in the center of the circle. David heard Esteban's voice: "It's well nigh past midnight, gentlepersons, and this duel marks our last of this hallowed eve!"

A whoop of approval. The onlookers were drunk, entertained. It had been a successful night. David spotted Haley in the crowd, the sailor-girl's arm sprawled across Honey Smacks's shoulders. Whatever Bob had dropped in her drink, Haley was in fine form.

The barker continued. "In the blue wrestling mask and chiseled chest, I give you the swarthy, the excessively tall, the linchpin of our varsity soccer team... Roberrrrto Badalamenti!"

"El Oso Terrible, motherfucker!" Another whoop. It hadn't occurred to David that they were dueling on the *soccer* field, Bob's home turf. Was David already at a disadvantage?

"And in the overly elaborate costume, I give you the daddy of the Dueling Society..."

"I'm Batman," David rasped through the stuffy mask, trying to sound like Batman.

Fuck, he immediately thought. *I should have said, triumphantly, "David Fuffman!"* He'd intended the moment to be his public debut, his name resounding brilliantly across the crowd, worming its way into their ears and latching on to their brains forever, so that by the time he was a senior and had fully exerted his influence, people would remember Halloween as the first time they heard about the man who was David Fuffman. But his cheeks were sticking to the rubber mask and sweat had begun to drip into his eyes, and he tried poking a gloved finger in there but that only made it worse, and dammit, he really wasn't thinking straight.

"Gentlemen, may you fire upon each other with honor!"

David's stomach sank a little. He was nervous. And so it happened that standing spine to spine with sweaty Bob Badalamenti, at the crux of this human wheel of Halloweeners, he found himself whispering to unseen deities.

Here I am, wearing this supersuit, he prayed. *Everyone's watching. Give me some sign. Make me super.*

The dandy duel master backed away. He held his cane aloft. He screamed, "ONE!"

Bob's body stopped supporting David. He lunged into his initial step forward, the other foot following like a practiced wedding processional.

"Two!" David lunged again.

If Bob hits me, if I emerge from this duel splotched with paint, if my cape and cowl are soiled, then I'll take it as a sign to give up this silly dream of campus superherodom. I'll prepare myself for a career in operations and management, like the world wants me to, I promise. Something with a 401(k) bouncing on its horizon.

"Three!"

But if I hit Bob, and emerge unsplotched, this will be my sign that the path of heroics is long and winding. That I may still greatly influence humankind yet, the way I've always dreamed. That I must simply be patient.

"Five!"

"Five?" David yelled. "What happened to four?"

"Whatever!" Esteban yelled back. "Seven! Eight!"

It was on eight that David's faith flagged: *My god, I'm wearing the wrong costume,* he realized. *How can I make my own name when I'm in someone else's clothes? And how can Haley not remember we hooked up?*

"Nine!"

Shit, he thought. He tried to revise his covenant, and quickly.

Okay, if I get hit, then... no... if he hits me first, or if we both hit, that means, wait... do we fire on ten, or do we wait for Esteban to scream "Fire"? He glanced around for Owen, his rock, but couldn't spot him.

"TEN!"

David turned. He lifted his gun from his hip, straight-armed, a firm gatepost. His eyes found a Mexican wrestling mask. His finger found the trigger. His heart found a moment of silence.

He fucking *had* him.

And then David's answer came. From above.

It was hard to comprehend at first. Like an earthquake. A surge of typewriter clacks, the aural activity in some 1950s newsroom. A torrent of yellow spears rained down from above. David thought perhaps his visual cortex was melting and that these sparks were the by-product of a cracked bicameral brain. Too many shots of absinthe.

Yellow splats bounced off David's shoulders, his chest, his cowl. And then it hit David: an entire bucket of yellow paint. The pail smacked off his back and its contents latched on to his cape like a vicious octopus. He was dripping yellow. The whole circle of students was under fire! Across the field, Bob aimlessly fired his pistol into the air.

They'd been ambushed by semiautomatic paintball technology. Someone had pulled a delicious prank. Taking cover, David pulled his own gun into his cape and tried to save his costume, beating a hasty retreat to the bushes near the side of SCISM. He dropped his gun by the bushes and hid under his cape, playing dead. When David finally poked out his pointy head, he looked up to find three ghostly shadows flitting across the roof of SCISM, their gun barrels piercing the dark sky. Bounding over that peaked horizon, they disappeared into the night.

Paint cans hung from branches, dripping their remains like gutted animals.

iv.

A few kids were nursing semiserious welts, but overall, the mood was jovial. There was some cleanup, and then a movement to hit the Street to keep the party going. Delegating like a boss, David convinced two juniors (juniors!) to return the kegs for him. He couldn't locate Bob, but he found Owen and Esteban and prepared to join them for the after-party.

"Where's Bob?" David asked. "Already went home with someone?"

"What an asshole," hissed Owen.

"Shit," David said when they were halfway to the Street, "I left my gun by the bushes!"

"What an asshole," they all chimed.

"It's expensive." He saluted and jogged toward Poe, his cape undulating in the moonlight.

They'd been gotten good by that group of ne'er-do-wells on the roof. But to David, the night felt perfect, epic. He realized the Princeton Dueling Society could be great, and him along with it. He'd plan a follow-up, and quick! Would people recognize him at the Street tonight?

He strolled back across Poe Field, rolling solo, playing kick the can with a crushed Milwaukee's Best, feeling kinda special. Reaching the foot of the tree, David crouched and felt around for his gun. It was right where he'd left it, splattered with paint but otherwise in fine shape. Faintly, he smelled the acrid odor of fresh vomit. And then, twenty yards away, David saw movement.

The path from the lawn out to the Street did not bring the crowd past the glass windows of SCISM. If it had, the entire crowd might have seen what only David saw: there on the grass, below the line of bushes, beneath a breathtaking glass backdrop, he saw a girl. She was down on all fours. White yoga pants bunched around her ankles. Blue shirt pulled up. Her smiling mask was still on, pressed into the dirt: Cap'n Crunch.

For a second David was pleased. Kids were getting lucky at his event. A Halloween fantasy becoming a reality. Godspeed. And then the jealousy. This was Haley Roth, on the shortlist of girls he'd seen partially naked and was hoping to see again. Why had someone else gotten her?

Then his stomach turned.

He saw her forearms and knees were on the ground. But her balance was off. She kept drifting to one side, tilting like a rhombus.

And her silence. The man behind her was plenty noisy, grunts exploding from his mask. But there was nothing from *her*. No breathy exhales. No moaning. No audible pleasure or pain, either. Considering the extraordinary force of the pounding—the loud smacks of his abs into her ass—the girl's silence wasn't normal.

Something was wrong.

The man behind her was up on his toes, his knees splayed out around her bare bottom like pasty demon wings. His grunts sounded like *"Hey, hey, hey, hey..."* David saw sweat on his torso, the kind of chest that didn't need to be augmented by a molded costume.

"Fuck off, Davy Gravy!" growled the man in the mask. "El Oso Terrible works alone!"

He didn't stop pumping. David didn't know what to do. He wanted to leave, and he wanted to stay and ask a dozen questions that he didn't know how to ask in that moment, or what the questions even were, but he wanted to confirm or deny what he was seeing, that this person could do this, and he wanted to fight, and he didn't want to fight, and he wanted to flash back to the warning signs or flash forward to visit punishment on the guilty, but he was stuck in that one endless present moment with nothing but paralyzing fear, and so he just stood there. And then, from above, someone aimed and fired.

A pellet exploded on David's forehead and yellow goop ran down his rubber nose. His head darted, searching for the source of this new firing. Looking up, he found a silhouette on the roof, saw it point the shadow of a gun barrel at him, as if tapping him on the shoulder from afar.

David looked down at his hands: he was still holding his paintball gun. There should still be three pellets in its chamber.

Okay, hero, if someone has bestowed you with powers, he thought, *now is the time to unleash them.*

David raised the gun, aimed high at Bob's head, waited for something to happen.

The force of the first shot took him by surprise and his hand recoiled, sending a small projectile sailing wide right into the darkness.

Using both hands, David steadied the stock of the gun, closed an eye, and trained the gun's sight on Bob's blue mask. He fired and heard the audible flick of a pellet against skin. Bob cried out as the shot stung him in the shoulder. It halted his thrusting. He looked down at his chest, dripping paint like egg yolk, and his face flew up to meet David's. He whispered, "...the fuck?"

David still had one shot left, and he tried to think back to every cartoon he'd ever seen, every man vs. monster scene, remembering *The Dark Knight Returns* when Batman fights the Mutant Leader and nearly gets his ass handed to him until Robin shows up and goes for the villain's eyes. David looked back to the roof, hoping the silent assassin up there would heed his tacit call to arms, give him a nod, help him take down this behemoth. But the man was gone. David was alone.

And David understood then, for a sickening second, that he was not actually a superhero.

He was just a kid witnessing something terrible, and this would not end well for anyone.

Bob was still staring at him, but had begun slowly pumping again, his face fixed on David's in warning. David thought harder and came upon the plan that every David employs when facing a Goliath: aim for the sensitive parts. He'd have to hit Bob in the mouth, the jugular. Any vulnerability available. Aiming again, this time at a small black eyehole in Bob's mask, David lined up his shot.

Squeezed. Fired.

He watched the bullet speed through the air, a yellow trail through the darkness.

So tiny and so huge.

When it flicked off the glass behind Bob's head with an unceremonious *plonk,* the pane didn't even shatter.

David had missed.

Bob turned, looked back at David. He growled. Now he pushed Haley away from him. She was stable for a moment, and David wondered if he'd made a mistake and ruined a perfectly sexy moment. Then her body crumpled forward into the dirt, arms twisting unnaturally beneath her, and David knew for certain this was not *sex* he'd witnessed. Bob took his cock in his hand, and with muffled moans he unloaded his own shots onto the girl's lifeless thigh. Slowly, his body slumped, exhausted. His head bowed to her.

"You're dead," Bob whispered, loud enough for David to hear. "I'm going to bury you."

Haley lay still in the dirt, the creepy eyes from her mustachioed mask staring at David.

Bob leaped to his feet, pushing his dick back inside his pants and sprinting forward. Turning to run, David saw no one was left on the field. And then, without knowing why, he was throwing his paintball gun at Bob coming up fast behind him, then he yanked off his rubber gloves and threw them, too, the first gauntlet landing with a splat on the ground and the second one connecting with Bob's mask as he finally caught up, lifted and dragged David across the field, all the way to the dirt behind the bleachers. One of David's boots fell off.

"Hey, hey," Bob whispered, as he ripped off David's cape, tearing it loudly along a seam. "Hey, let's duel! Hey," he said. "No, hey, c'mon, hey." He tore the batcowl off, rubber stretching and pulling at David's hair beneath it. He pulled off the arm sleeves, biceps and shoulders, and ripped them open, exposing foam rubber. He pulled off David's other boot and he punched David in the ribs, finding a soft spot between the folds of the molded chest plate, and then he pummeled him again in the side and then in the jaw, and before the pain set in and blinded David fully, he felt his dark blood mix with sweat and paint and dirt from the ground and it all ran into his mouth and gagged him with the particular taste of being so easily vanquished.

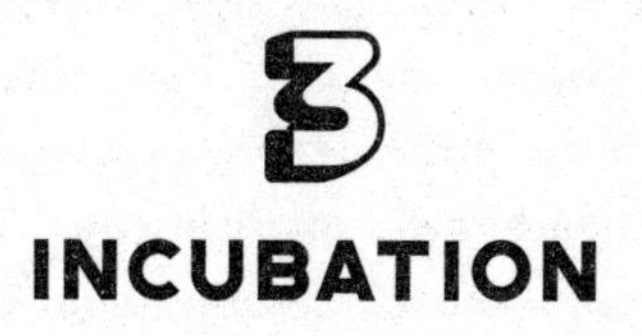

INCUBATION

i.

Whiteout is when the sky and land are the same color. The horizon disappears. Footsteps vanish immediately and you can't figure out where things end or begin. The blizzard had dumped snow for three days, trapping them in The Egg, and as David watched the wind whip off the ground's new, higher, whiter surface he thought of deserts, of *Lawrence of Arabia,* of vast expanses of sand where you peered deep into the wiggly distance and wondered, *Is that someone?*

He popped a Zeronal and thought about his thesis project.

He would call his parents back tomorrow.

—Ø—

"Five feet is a shitload of snow," Lee mumbled. "The patio looks like an igloo village."

David poured coffee, tried to wake up. Fu nodded, grinding pepper into a panful of eggs.

Pointing at the cross section of snow against the sliding glass door, David played along.

"And *that* looks kinda like an ant farm," he said.

Lee glanced, shrugged. "Yeah, maybe if all the ants had died."

"Death toll is at 114," Mathias yelled from the sunroom, closing his laptop. Internet had been spotty at best. Same with their cellular signals. It was getting harder to function without internet, but also easier, because what choice did they have? Still, when the internet worked, they consumed greedily, stockpiling news and data and social media, checking NJ Power's interactive outage map to see where crews were working and when power might be restored. Estimates remained unavailable. Meanwhile, the death tally now included two charter flights, plus some elderly folks in Virginia. But most of the dead were the restless ones, the brave yet stupid who'd left their homes, got disoriented, and kept walking into whiteout. David thought it must be odd to panic and freeze at the same time.

"Always tie a rope so you can winch your way back," Lee said, like he'd done this before.

—Ø—

Blackout, on the other hand, is when everything shushes. You can't see, but forgotten senses come alive. New opportunities abound for the creative minded. David remembered a bus tour through Manhattan when he was eight. The guide told them of the Blackout of 1977, in the infancy of hip-hop, when hi-fi stores were looted. "The next day, we had a thousand new DJs," she'd said.

So blackouts were apparently the midwife of innovation. But they also made it hard to see.

—Ø—

The news called it Snowmageddon, Snowpocalypse, Snowtastrophe, the Big Dump, Snow-Man's-Land, Snowtel California, Blizzard King, Blizzkrieg, and David's favorite, the White Curtain.

"Jesus! Fuck my balls with a wood chipper!" Mathias finally screamed at the television, during an hour of regained power. "Okay! We get it! It's *a lot* of fucking snow! Heavens to Betsy."

Fu flipped the channel. And there was Mott again. The other all-pervasive storm plastered on the twenty-four-hour news cycle. Mathias left the room, the visage of Mott on screens somehow making him boil even more. David knew why.

Back in Baltimore, David researched Mott. Getting lost in a Google rabbit hole, he'd eventually bumped into Mathias Blue. He found an article from the National Institute of Standards and Technology. Mathias had participated in the NIST summer fellowship program a couple years back, and the article's photo showed him standing between an elder physicist—none other than J. Stuart Mott—and a massive machine straight out of *Willy Wonka*. This machine, David learned, was the most accurate clock in the world. All networked computers and electronics used it to tell humans the precise time, to the nanosecond. The physics were beyond David's understanding, but it sounded like a complex molecular version of watching the sun rise and set a billion times per second. David got wrapped up in these sites, trying his best to decipher optical frequency combs and UV lasers. If Mathias was into this stuff, David wanted to do his homework.

The power outage was another good time for research. The Egg had tons of books, aside from the cache David brought. Once he got settled, he got deep into a tome on World War II, especially the chapters on the London Blitz. It lasted more than eight months, and at one point Hitler's Luftwaffe pummeled that city for fifty-seven days straight, a relentless barrage of bombs. They strategized that the sheer consistency of mayhem would eventually take its toll. But he underestimated British ability to manage emotion. Maybe humans in general were made to be resilient and positive in the face of calamity. Londoners took care of one another, built underground communes in the subway tubes. They kept calm and carried on.

But fifty-seven days? And when you don't know if it's ever going to end?

When David needed a hit of the outside world, he rationed his cell battery and stalked Haley Roth on social media.

Haley Roth is trapped.

Haley Roth is getting really into krav maga.

Haley Roth is searching for a new 1BR in Princeton. Open to suggestions.

David thought about this last one. He remembered the last time they'd talked, at her house after running into her at the supermarket back in Pikesville. He knew she knew about The Egg and decided this status update of hers was meant for him: a sign, a test, a fish for an invite. He commented:

Live with us in Pennington!

He typed this, then deleted it, then typed, then deleted. Then typed. Hit Enter.

Then he swallowed another of Lee's Zeronal pills and got back to work.

Haley was in Baltimore, at her parents' house, which she still thought of as *her* house, where she could pretend she was back in high school or middle school or some other invincible time.

She got bored, though, stuck in this relic. When she fully exhausted their collection of board games, throwing Mouse Trap angrily across the living room, she unearthed her old sewing case from the summer before eighth grade at Camp Louise and discovered a dozen skeins of colored thread. The muscle memory was strong. Soon she was tying knot after knot, crafting a friendship bracelet of blue and lighter blue. She had no particular friend in mind for this bracelet. It was just something to do.

She was seeing a therapist, Dr. Hittson, and her parents were doing all the right things—giving her space and not giving her space, knowing when to do one rather than the other. As an only child, she got all their attention. Even when she was being left alone, she knew they were thinking about her. Haley's mom confided stories of lesser but similar evils from her own past. Not trying to compete, just trying to normalize. It only made Haley more sad and furious for womanhood—the commonness of this particular villainy. She cried softly often. When she needed to cry louder, she found solace in her walk-in closet, burying herself beneath old winter coats and letting loose. Get it out. All of it. Get it out.

Haley remembered back in the summer, rolling her eyes when Dad gave her pepper spray. Part of their off-to-college care package. During those first months at Princeton, she hated when Mom inquired about security escorts, not wanting her to walk back to her dorm alone if she was out late studying. Haley never wanted to believe the worst about strange people. She was perfectly capable, and people weren't dangerous, were generally good, she believed. It's one of the things she hated most: that Bob took that from her. She was determined to claw her way back.

She completed six friendship bracelets, patterns of increasing difficulty—stripes, chevrons, diamonds—before she thought, *What am I even doing?* It was therapeutic, though, she couldn't deny. So she found her father's old Boy Scout book on knot tying and began practicing with two lengths of rock-climbing paracord stashed in their garage. The square knot, the slipknot, the bowline, the half hitch, the noose. Knots could be useful, she imagined, if this frigid wilderness continued indefinitely, or if some final flood forced everyone to become sailors. She practiced knots for trapping, for restraining, for joining one thing to another.

She felt herself getting faster, the rope growing taut, able to hold more and more and more.

—Ø—

Ever since Halloween, David had become fascinated by his Problem of Evil seminar. Professor Hague started each class with the theoretical rundown: since evil exists, that means God is not particularly benevolent, or else not particularly powerful, or else not particularly real. Maybe he's all-powerful but sadistic as hell. Maybe he's kind but lacks the capacity to keep all his children happy. Or maybe he's an invention, something produced in a secret lab millennia ago.

David wondered, Wasn't there another option? What if God was powerful and good but had a secret Kryptonite-y weakness, exploited by the powerful and evil?

Like Superman.

—Ø—

David was surprised to find how cagey the guys were about their respective expertise, their theses. He'd been hoping to learn some doomsday-scenario skills and instead found his new housemates miserly hoarding their knowledge. He confronted Lee about this.

"Well, obviously, right?" said Lee. "Your skills are your insurance policy. I can make drugs, so in an extended grid-down scenario I'll probably have snipers protecting me. Hold your formula close to the chest."

It was Fu who first extended the olive branch.

"Hey, man," he'd whispered in the kitchen one morning. "If you're interested in radio communications, I'd be very glad to walk you through what I'm working on. But only if you want."

David wanted.

Fu had apparently set up a backup comms center in their outdoor shed, with a separate, secure landline and modem, but the snow made it impossible to get out there. His main project was now anchored by some kind of ham radio apparatus.

"It's valuable for news, but I'm *listening* more than talking," he said. "We don't want people to know where we are or what provisions we might have. We don't want to amplify our position."

Fu had his ham radio operator general license and briefly explained to David the importance of their BaoFeng UV-5R handhelds for short-range VHF communications. They looked like orange walkie-talkies to David, but he soon learned they were more powerful and important.

Still, above everything, all tasks relied on a power source, and as The Egg's resident electrical engineer, power was Owen's purview. He was kind of a hoss, even though he didn't fully realize it and hadn't succeeded much. He had a few different projects, each in a state of initiation but hardly functional—a single 250-watt solar panel, not yet out of its packaging; a bank of golf cart batteries daisy-chained together but not hooked up to anything else; plans for some kind of wood-powered gasifier that could run their generator if they got desperate. But Owen's big idea had to do with piezoelectricity, using force to generate a charge, which David wasn't prepared to learn from scratch.

He wished Owen would focus. Pick a project and make it happen.

After twelve hours without the power blinking back on, they gathered in the basement to get the generator working. For smaller stuff they had a hand-crank emergency radio—AM/FM with a flashlight and USB input for charging. You couldn't run anything big, but a few minutes of cranking created enough juice to make a phone call or send an email, assuming you could get a cell signal.

"How does a generator even work?" asked David. He was embarrassed, but...

"Propane," said Mathias. "We've got a good week's worth."

"And then what?"

Mathias squeezed David's biceps and said, "Self-power!"

Until a next-generation power source could be found, they still needed heat, and the woodstove was the obvious default. Stocking the stove was everyone's job. Owen especially liked dude stuff. The how-to tasks that show up in men's magazines. He loved chopping wood, but when it came to technique he was a novice, just hacking away at cold logs.

"You *are* the Brute Squad," David said.

Mathias was more methodical. "It's like deconstructing the tree," he said, "piecing it apart in the opposite way it grows." He'd start along the perimeter, slicing off the bark. "Then you look for natural cracks that can be exploited as starting points. Drive in a few wedges. Lop off the outer layers. Once it's exposed, you take its heart, the centermost ring. Everything after that is super easy.

"All of this is probably a metaphor for something," he said.

—Ø—

David soon learned what it was a metaphor for. At nights, after they'd exhausted all other options—books, games, home improvements, basic necessity management, whatever thesis-ing they could undertake with the lights off—they'd talk. Sometimes it was organic, and sometimes it was structured, a particular question asked and then they'd go around the horn answering, telling stories.

They covered hometowns and high schools and paths to Princeton. They did top fives: movies, novels, starlets. Sometimes they invented outlandish apocalypse scenarios, trying to outdo one another with weirdness and carnage. One night, it was siblings.

Fu was the only only child. Lee had a sister who was transgender and estranged from everyone in the family besides him. Owen had two older brothers, both of them in the service, one somewhere in Africa, going after warlords, and the other in Afghanistan, ostensibly working for the Red Cross but probably this meant he was in the CIA, though Owen wasn't sure. David talked about Beth, her boldness, the goofy games they used to play together, his hopes for her.

And Mathias told them about Edison, his twin brother. When they were nine, and their dad was stationed at the National Ground Intelligence Center near Charlottesville, there'd been a massive summer windstorm called the Derecho. It came on fast and without much warning. Mathias and Edison were outside playing, just five more minutes, when one of the first big gusts caught hold of a pine tree, its roots shallower than other trees, and sent it toppling toward Edison.

"I saw it happen," Mathias said. "We were there, just playing, and suddenly this massive trunk was coming down, like it had singled him out or been choreographed. It wasn't a direct hit, but we were little, and a branch caught him on the head with enough force. We got him to University of Virginia hospital, but the storm ended up taking out the power there, too, so there were generators, those yellow emergency lights, but people were coming in from all over the county, and I guess the doctors were just stretched too damn thin. He died the next morning. I'd say that was pretty much the last time I trusted any system or agency intended to keep us safe. They didn't. They won't."

Just then, also as if choreographed, The Egg's power came back. The TV popped on. And there was J. Stuart Mott again, ranting. As soon as that feeling of relief came on them—the comforting hum of electricity in the walls—it popped off again. And everything was dark and silent once more.

"*They* won't keep us safe," Mathias repeated. "But *we* can."

—Ø—

The storm got worse. It had been fun for a while, but once the snow reached their peephole, David got scared. With their sporadic internet, the guys monitored the Emergency Relief Agency's Twitter feed on new areas affected, new deaths, new travesties.

Then, with America already buried under snow, China struck abroad.

China had bribed the Afghan government to win control of its lithium deposits, not to mention untapped stores of cobalt, iron, and natural gas. But lithium. *That* was the real prize. Laptop and cell phone batteries were only the beginning. With the auto market making a push into electric cars with Li-ion batteries and more houses relying on rechargeable battery banks for emergency power, speculators said lithium might soon be more valuable than oil. China could now mine those Afghan mountains.

After decades of American occupation and general dickishness, the Asian propaganda machine convinced the Kabul government it was time to expel the infidels from their holy lands. China hacked the U.S. Command and Control Centers in Afghanistan, rendering the troops blind and deaf. CNN called it the "Cyber Pearl Harbor."

What that meant was "We're going to war."

—Ø—

They lay there on the garage floor like cousins at a sleepover, shoes in a box.

David vs. Mathias.

Here's how it goes. A second of *savasana*: corpse pose. Then a whistle: *tweet*.

David pops up to find his paintball pistol. He spots Mathias. There's an inflatable Intex raft in the corner of the garage and David grabs it, too, uses it as a shield. They fire. They duck.

The gun safe in Lee's chem lab held no real firearms, Mathias said. But David brought to The Egg his two paintball pistols and the remainder of his bag of yellow ammo, like jumbo M&M's. Mathias offered to stash it all in the gun safe, that he had the code, and said doing some opposing forces exercises in the garage might be good practice. But Mathias was against guns, even in the event of total societal breakdown. "Once one side has guns, the other side needs to have guns," he'd say. "And if both sides have guns, the tendency is to use them."

Lee gets bored and scuttles across the battlefield like a Wimbledon ball boy. He heads for a giant pump-action Super Soaker water cannon, the kind with a huge tank you wear like a backpack. It's understood this means open season on Lee. A brief moment to exact revenge for all his assholery. David feels some invisible energy lock himself and Mathias as teammates as they form an unspoken treaty to pelt Lee instead of each other. But he's wrong about this.

Mathias likes to win.

—Ø—

The last step is boiling. First, you have to filter it.

They had a cone-bottom tank in the garage already set up: a layer of gravel, a layer of sand, a layer of charcoal—briquettes or pulled straight from the woodstove. Then another layer of each—gravel, sand, charcoal—like a parfait. It came out the bottom spigot reasonably safe. But boiling is what made it pure.

They gathered round the woodstove, the pipe rising up through the home like a central artery, vital and life-giving.

David knew about superimposition: how when you're not on Zeronal, memories pile up on each other and get more visual. He stared at his hands. He'd just used some of the unpurified tank water in the garage to shampoo for the first time in a week. Now, standing over the runoff bucket, he couldn't help but notice that his fingers were loaded with hair. His own.

"Hey, Lee!" he yelled into The Egg. "Is hair loss another side effect of Zeronal?"

"Why?" Lee screamed at the garage. "Are you losing your hair?"

"No," David said. "Just asking." Blink.

ii.

Before Zeronal there were other substances and side effects, and they all orbited around Haley Roth. Maddy was a year older, and by the time she was about to leave for the University of Maryland, they'd graduated from weed to pills and powders, mostly painkillers purchased from the Racketeer.

"You're in luck," Haley once told them. "I got a bunch of acid I'm trying to unload."

"David doesn't do hallucinogens," said Madeline with a dose of condescension.

"Mkay, then I've got Lortab, which is kinda orthodontist-y. I have Valium and Xanax and also a little E, but that's thirty bucks per."

"Ecstasy could be fun," David suggested under his breath. He then excused himself, realizing he'd left his wallet in the car. He wanted to pay for their drugs, like this was a date.

"Chivalry is not dead after all!" Haley yelled after David as he bounded down the stairs.

Left alone with Haley, who'd begun sorting pills, Madeline strolled the bedroom perimeter. From Haley's nightstand, she lifted a picture frame exhibiting Haley with her arms around three olive-skinned, dark-haired boys, all of them incredibly cute, mugging for the camera. One wore a yarmulke. Madeline realized the photo was from a recent teen tour or birthright trip to Israel, a kind of taxidermy mount showing off some of Haley's exotic kills.

"It was a truly spiritual experience," Haley said, deadpan.

Madeline responded by swiping a finger across the glass of the frame, collecting the residue of white powder she'd noticed there. She conspicuously rubbed this stuff into her gums.

Haley told Madeline she liked her, which wasn't totally a lie, but what she meant was that she liked David and, for the moment, approved of Madeline *for* him.

She made a recommendation: Ecstasy.

"It's great for couples," Haley said. "Tell you what: you're both so cute how you always come here together, like you're picking out furniture. I'll give you two for fifty bucks, how 'bout that?"

She opened a wooden box and began sifting through different Ziploc bags. Bending over her wares, her pink tank top revealed a tunnel of cleavage. Madeline shook off a pang of jealousy.

"Look at me," Haley said, "just *slashing* prices!"

"Thanks, but honestly, I don't know how long we'll be a couple, what with me going away to school in the fall," Madeline confided for some reason. "You get it."

Haley stopped what she was doing and looked up.

"As your dealer," she said, "I'll stick with my recommendation. You need truth serum."

"How'd you get into dealing?" asked Madeline, trying to change the subject.

"Is this Career Day?" said Haley.

"You just don't strike me as the kind of girl who needs to do this," Madeline said.

"I enjoy it, providing a service for the community." Haley shrugged. Then she stared hard at Madeline. "And I enjoy doing something that people like you think I shouldn't be doing."

It had hurt David when Maddy left for college, and he soon figured out she was cheating on him. He could've turned to painkillers, but instead, he drowned himself in work. Even after getting into Princeton, when senioritis was supposed to set in, David frequented Haley Roth's house, but now to score study drugs. He'd never really needed them before, but withdrawal from caffeine pills made him mopey and unfocused.

"Study drugs?" Haley said, taken aback. "Cheater, cheater, pumpkin eater."

"Adderall. Caffeine. What's the difference?"

"Amphetamines is the difference," she said. "You don't have ADD, right? 'Cause if you do these'll even you out. But if not, Adderall's like speed with tunnel vision. A performance enhancer."

"Will it make me a superhero?" David asked, eyebrow cocked.

"Put it this way: random fuckups could probably run all of New Zealand when they're on the stuff. *You're* a smarty-pants, so you could probably take over the world."

"Isn't that more like being a super*villain*?" he said.

"Depends on your vision for the world." She laughed this totally sexy laugh. She threw her head back, lips parted, perfect rows of teeth on show, eyes droopy.

David bought ten Adderall pills and ate one immediately. When she slipped him a baggie, David felt her fingers and found himself telling her, "Maddy's enjoying college too much."

"Speaking of which," she said, nodding across the room, "look who's *also* a smarty-pants."

Taped to Haley's vanity mirror was a college acceptance letter. From Princeton.

David looked stunned, and Haley quietly reveled in his shock. Granted, she went to private school and he'd never shared a class with her and had no frame of reference, but she realized that in his arrogance he never thought they might be applying to the same schools. They talked about how they found out, their hopes for the fall, their visions for the world.

Something welled up inside him, the pill beginning to work, maybe. He saw her room anew and became aware of a ballpoint pen drawing on her vanity. She said it was only a doodle. But in fact she'd crafted an army of characters—cartoonish, lifelike, lanky, fat—swimming through some calligraphic text. The page had the air of a religious fresco, a mad Hindu gathering. Bustled Victorian beauties floated next to tattooed cyberpunks. David was impressed and shook her hand.

"So are we going to be friends at school?" he asked.

Haley shrugged. Then she took David's hand and pulled it to her chest, smirking, feeling powerful. David didn't resist. Her nipple was hard, poking against her bra.

"Cheater, cheater," she mumbled, bowing her head against his arm. Her own pill was kicking in, too, her bones going melty.

David stared down at Haley's neck. It was even hairier than his. Not something he usually found compelling, but something about *that hair*. The V of blond fluff cradled her neck, and David knew it was the type of downiness that continued along her spine like the wake of some powerboat, down to the parts where the hair grows darker, denser. Her skin was smooth and tan, the color of stained hickory. Wedging his hand down her shirt, he grazed her satiny pink bra.

"You can be rougher with those," she'd said, and smiled. "I'm on Xanax so I can barely feel that."

She lazily took off her jeans and underwear, and David noticed she had much more hair than Madeline, who'd gotten into creative shaving. Haley was more natural. She lay back and opened a drawer in her nightstand. David recognized this to be some universal modern-animal signal that meant there were condoms in there, that he should grab one, that she wanted him to fuck her or that she'd let him, that the concept of fucking her was on the table. And it was around now that David realized he wasn't actually hard.

This, for all intents and purposes, was the moment he'd been waiting for. He'd have preferred to lose his virginity to Maddy, but here was this girl, and she was hot, she was smart, apparently, and talented, and a shrewd businesswoman, and all the things his brain said were good, and she was naked from the waist down, waiting. *He* was waiting, too, for his body to respond, for the blood to rush to his proverbial underground lair. But some circuit was disconnected—the tributary that normally bore his teenage hunger diverted or dammed. What was happening? Was it the Adderall? To stall, David decided to go down on her. For a while. With each moan he felt the false drug-baron swagger leave her body, float out her window, and soon it was like she wasn't there anymore, only watching from outside. She made little sighs. But David was accustomed to a *growing* intensity of sound, and she seemed to be trailing off.

"Is this okay?" he mumbled into her lap. She said nothing. He peeked up at her face.

Her eyes were closed. She was still. Passed out. Paralyzed.

Meanwhile, back at the Batcave, cruel fate had finally blessed him with a belated boner. David realized that he could still have Haley. She'd never said no—had kinda said yes—and they were naked, and he was sad and ready now and full of vengeance for she who'd left him behind.

Then David shuddered and thought, *I'm a bad person.*

When he looked at Haley again, she was no longer a sexual being. More a deadweight toddler, ready to be carried to bed. He gathered Haley's clothes and tried his best to put them back on her limp limbs. Her bra was unwieldy and her jeans were nearly impossible, but he yanked and maneuvered them back on to her legs and over her butt and even got the fly back up. He covered her with her peppermint bedspread and turned off her light. As he slowly shut her bedroom door, he waited for Haley's voice to tell him the thing he most wanted to hear:

Wow. Thanks, David, she might say. *You're a really good guy.*

He waited by the closing door for this queen to anoint him. He waited. Any minute now.

iii.

Bob had been careful not to leave many marks. The day after Halloween, when David had woken from Poe Field, he had no shiner, no broken nose. Only a sore jaw and some breathing trouble, possibly a broken rib or two. And a trashed costume.

He took to bed, too raw and horrified to see anyone. David knew he'd failed but told himself he'd wait till he was feeling better physically before punishing himself psychologically.

He slept or pretended to sleep through most of the next two days. Thankfully, Owen wasn't around much, and when he did pop in David hid in the bathroom. By mid-week, David was still nursing his wounds, still reading the same damn Hume sentence for the fourteenth time, when down the hall he heard Owen screaming. At first David thought he was kidding around, but as the sound got closer, he realized Owen was actually crying.

David went to the door and poked his head out. A few other heads were out their doors, hanging in the air like wall sconces. Owen strode down the hall, arms swinging, ripping down flyers taped to the walls. He looked drunk and violent; and it was a Wednesday evening, which wasn't a typical time for such things. Following behind him at a good distance, Esteban supervised.

David ventured up the hall to Whitney Garfunkle's room. She was a rower on the lightweight crew team, tall, fair-skinned, with hair always ponytailed. David didn't know her too well. But she stood in her doorway, arms crossed, and looked like she knew something.

"What's happening?" David asked.

"You haven't heard?"

"I guess not."

"Soccer Bob got arrested for sexually assaulting someone at your fucking soiree."

"*Soccer* Bob?" David was doing his best to sound surprised, but the news *had* strangely shocked him. For David, it was as if the events of Halloween happened in a parallel dimension, never to incur any real retribution in this realm.

"Who did he assault?" asked David, hating himself harder and harder.

Whitney sighed long, lips pursed, and then said, "Maya Angelou. Does it matter? The victim's identity is nobody's business."

Whitney speedily lectured David on how it's hard enough for a woman to come forward and deal with people questioning her character, wondering if she's telling the truth, calling her a cocktease, and how the best she can hope for is to remain anonymous, so even if Whitney knew, she wouldn't tell him, but she didn't know anyways so fuck off.

"What's going to happen to Bob?" he asked.

"I'm going to sodomize him with a fucking skateboard," she answered. "I don't know, David, your special buddy will probably have to leave school. Jail, maybe?"

"But that's crazy. Bob wouldn't do that." Where were these lies coming from? David could only guess that maybe he was scared Bob might find him and hit him again.

This was David at his most pathetic, begging for retroactive mercy.

"And why *wouldn't* he do that?" she asked. "Because, oh, 'he has sex with girls all the time'? How about this, how about I twist your nuts off and we call it a hand job, okay? How 'bout I smack you in the face with a frying pan and call it cooking? You're a typical—"

"HE DIDN'T DO ANYTHING!" This was Owen's voice. He rounded the corner and came back into view. David could see his face, red and swollen like a catcher's mitt. Without breaking stride, Owen grabbed a plastic recycling bin and slammed it against a wall, exploding empty Gatorades and Red Bulls in all directions. The sound cleared the hallway, heads darting back into their rooms to avoid his wrath.

David knew he should get out of the way, but he inched toward the center of the hallway, trying to cut off his roommate's path. The boy's speed continued. He passed a hanging Exit sign and volleyball spiked it with an open palm, taking it clean off the wall. Sparks shot from the red lightbulb popping inside it.

The sign hung from its now frayed wire like an eyeball dangling from its socket.

Owen continued back and forth down the hall, trapped, angry at a nameless girl for coming forward, angry at Bob for being guilty, angry at himself for choosing the wrong new best friend, and angry at a red Exit sign for being so easily shattered.

But the victim didn't stay nameless for long. The rumor mill churned, and students discussed who was who and how they'd put what into where. Two days after the hallway meltdown, Esteban was hiding in David and Owen's room while Bob Badalamenti's relatives were clearing out his room, carrying his monstrous speakers down the Forbes stairs. David kept hearing the dull thud of them dropping, but no one wanted to help carry anything of Soccer Bob's. The prevailing rumor was that Bob was taking some time off, and he'd probably be back next semester or next year, maybe, once they sorted this mess out. But when the *Daily Princetonian* got delivered to each door that morning, there it was. Front page above the fold: "Freshman Arrested on Sexual Assault Charges."

It didn't offer a ton of detail, but the basics were: during an unsanctioned campus paintball event, a student-athlete plied the victim—dressed as Cap'n Crunch—with the date-rape drug GHB, attempted to lure her to his dorm, and, when she resisted and ultimately lost consciousness, forced her into an undisclosed outdoor space and committed aggravated sexual assault, a charge usually filed when penetration is alleged to have occurred.

It named names. First Bob's, and then, much worse, the victim's.

David couldn't believe the newspaper had printed Haley's name. Was that even legal? He wondered if she *wanted* it to use her name, to make a statement of some kind. He wondered if she had to leave school now, too. He wondered if she had the kind of friends who would help carry her speakers.

Actually, Haley did tell the *Princetonian* to print her name and mention her costume, betting on the universally acknowledged asexuality of Cap'n Crunch. She wanted people to see she'd chosen a reasonably prude outfit, knowing full well this would be part of the public's judgment, the decision-making on whether she'd been asking for it. Still, she imagined the speculation: What choice of accessories had visited this trouble upon Haley Roth, they'd wonder, and how could she have been so stupid, so naive, to wear those boots, that neckerchief? Didn't she *know?* For men, neckerchiefs are like sex-catnip in a bucket of get-out-of-jail-free cards! She should've dressed as an exploding garbage bag, a Hefty Cinch Sak maybe, but not the sexy kind!

She told the newspaper to print her name because she wasn't at fault. And because she mistakenly believed everyone would understand and agree on that.

Owen sat on his lower bunk looking fat and bloated. "They're making an example of him," he said. "Fuffman knew her in high school. You said she was a slut then, too!"

"That's not what I said, asshole. I said before any of this happened that I *kind of* hooked up with her once and that she had a lot of pubic hair and phenomenal teeth. That's all I said."

"Give me the campus directory," he barked. "I'm gonna call Haley fucking Roth, Cap'n *Cunt,* and tell her she needs to drop the charges."

"Dude," David said.

"That's *completely* illegal," claimed Esteban. "You're talking coercion, obstruction of justice. You'd absolutely get arrested, too, no question."

"Jesus," said Owen, pointing to David with a nod of his head. "Here we've got a Jew in the room and it's the gay Mexican who knows all the legal shit."

"I'm prelaw," Esteban said, "and I'm Dominican, you fuck."

"She might not be lying," David muttered.

"What?" barked Owen. "What did you say?"

And David said, "Nothing."

"What an asshole," Owen muttered. David couldn't be sure whom he was referring to.

On page 2 of the *Princetonian* the next day was another noteworthy column, a public statement from university president Diane Graynor, linking sexual assault to campus binge drinking. It talked of a crackdown on alcoholism, a task force, radical approaches, statistics, et cetera. The upshot was an end of the salad days. Eating clubs would go dry for an indefinite period. Stricter suspensions and fees were meted out for intoxicated students. There would be a re-visioning of the blind eye. And, of course (as David learned from a brief but forceful email from Graynor herself), it meant the end of PDS. Take down the website. Put the pistols in their portmanteaus. Pack it in.

Since Bob was now gone from campus, it also meant Haley Roth received the brunt of the blame for the new, strict partying policy. Students speculated, calling her a liar behind her back. And to her face. Haley became the campus villain, the destroyer of fun. David heard guys speak her name with disgust. Even girls distanced themselves, not wanting to be labeled as man-haters, killjoys. All who openly came to Haley's defense were dragged into screaming matches or else met with silent disdain. Haley went into hiding. Meanwhile, the story was told and retold.

Cap'n Cunt's infamy grew.

For David's crew, it meant they weren't going to be friends anymore. One of their own was gone, a very dishonorable discharge. It was time to disband, exit friendships quietly, and start over. Esteban checked out entirely. A distance grew between Owen and David. They were now roommates in name only, their schedules and time in the room growing ever more staggered.

Just before Halloween, Owen had lost his heart, his dignity, and his Catholic virginity to a cruel senior residential adviser playing Fuck-a-Freshman before buckling down to write her thesis. They'd gone on a few dates. Then she popped his sacred cherry and promptly threw his clothes from her third-floor window, placing him nude and sweating in her hallway like a pair of wet sneakers. David thought Owen was over it, but after Halloween, Owen Bic-ed his head clean. He threw himself scalp-first into many extracurriculars. He got ordained in the campus Agape Christian Fellowship, then quit, then joined again, then quit again and began waking up at four A.M. to train for a vaguely nonexistent marathon along the wooded trails of the nearby Institute for Advanced Study.

And for David, it meant awareness. If we are forever judged on our performance in clutch moments, he'd missed the big shot. Each moment since, he was missing the big shot. His silence was his failure. David began to understand why the gods never saw fit to bestow real superpowers upon him. He clearly wouldn't know what to do with them.

Guilt and remorse metamorphosed into anger. He kept replaying Halloween in his head. Each daydream brought some new regret, but also some new justification or self-acquittal or fury. He hated himself, but he'd grow mad at Boo Berry and Honey Smacks for abandoning Haley. Shouldn't they have taken better care of their friend? And didn't *someone* see Bob and Haley walking off together and wonder why poor Cap'n Crunch was so obliterated? Wasn't that enough to cause concern, to spur action? Was being a cockblock worse than being a coward? Or was it really Haley's fault for drinking that spiked absinthe without being sure what substances Bob had mixed into it?

No, it was Bob's fault. David knew that. *Bob* was the one on trial. But that's the thing. The investigation was under way—teammates and professors were being called in as character witnesses—and David realized his own eyes could provide accurate and damning testimony.

But he was too scared to speak up.

And so David was a bad guy.

The next Friday on the phone with his parents he admitted he was losing it, burning out.

"Remember how Superman crushed coal into diamonds?" Mom said. Yeah, he remembered. *Superman III*. "Well, you're creating a diamond soul. And the only way is through intense pressure!"

Dad put it a different way. "You think they have these problems in Afghanistan? Sure, it's tough. You're at Princeton, for chrissakes. You were expecting, what, a footbath?"

Sometimes there's nothing wrong but the world, David wanted to say.

"Tell us what you're learning," asked David's father.

"*Scheide* is German for vagina," David said.

—Ø—

from: dfuffman@princeton.edu
to: bhague@princeton.edu
date: November 12, 2021
subject: Help Please

Dear Professor Hague,

I am a freshman in your REL 202 class, The Problem of Evil. With the final paper, I'm stuck on the subtleties of Pascal's Wager and William James (super reading list, by the way) and on how to rationalize their views with my own current state. I can understand an unmerciful or indifferent God who sees the plight of his children but does nothing to alleviate their pain, but my freshman existence feels closer to this view: that God wants to do good but doesn't have enough *time* to be everywhere at once.

Basically, what I'm saying is that I would very much appreciate an extension on the midterm. And more deeply, I'm asking for help, as I am presently struggling with concerns greater than just my paper. Surely you were once a freshman like me, with your own questions about the world, and I would greatly appreciate the benefit of your wisdom and experience. Please write back. Thank you in advance.

—David

The professor replied:

No problem. You can turn it in next Monday. Write with purpose. —BH

—Ø—

November 13 was registration day for the spring term. For most, classes began taking a backseat to more pressing concerns like war and natural disasters. Surprising himself, David signed up for two courses in the religion department, plus Environmental Studies 215: Risk, Rescue, and Resilience. His only economics course was Entrepreneurial Leadership, typically reserved for upperclassmen (he'd sent a persuasive email). On the way back from the registrar's office, he bought three reading list books and was distractedly skimming them when he reached the door to his dorm room and found it uncharacteristically locked.

This was weird. For one, he'd barely seen Owen for about a week, and David assumed he'd been pulling long nights at SCISM or else doing top secret ERA war prep stuff—moving battalion pieces across table-sized maps, sharpening knives against whetstones, strutting in slow motion against backdrops of flames, kissing his dog tags, so why on earth would Owen deign to slum it with regular folk in Forbes? Second, their room was up three flights of stairs, last room on the hall, and a significant number of urinary close calls had led Owen and David to a no-top-lock policy. They had a special signal—Mardi Gras beads hanging on the door handle—that meant, *Go away, I'm with somebody and/or yanking it*. Today, no beads.

David pumped a fist on the door and called his roommate's name.

"Dude, if you're rubbing one out, please expedite." Nobody answered. Finally, David dug around in the second-smallest pocket of his backpack, deep down next to a disfigured Nutri-Grain bar he didn't know he still had, until he found his key ring.

The room was full of steam. The shower was on. Its sound was steady, void of the intermittent splashings that mean someone's moving in there.

David called Owen's name again: "Dude?"

Nothing. It was the middle of the day. David did a quick mental inventory of the bathroom. There were pipes over the shower, probably sturdy enough to hang from. And Owen owned an old-fashioned shaving kit, a gift from his grandfather, the kind where you can remove the razor blade. David set his backpack down and opened the bathroom door.

Peeking out from the bottom of the shower curtain were the soles of Owen's bare feet. David walked through the shower fog, and softly this time, he said, "Dude?"

When David pushed back the curtain, Owen was slumped on the shower floor, back stacked into a corner, his chin against his chest. His legs were splayed and his wrists rested against his hairy thighs, framing his belly and withered penis, palms curled up and opened as if in meditation.

David scanned his wrists for blood.

Then Owen picked his head up. His eyes met David's. Two flushed stripes ran down his face where tears had left their mark. Owen looked back to the floor.

"I'm sorry," Owen whispered. "It just feels better down here."

He pulled himself up, sloshed past David, and climbed naked into his top bunk without drying himself. David turned off the shower and took a merciful piss, spending it strategizing. David was no stranger to heartbreak, but he had little experience consoling massive dudes. He tiptoed to the bunk bed. Owen was huddled under the covers, already darkened with his moisture. Only his bare wet scalp stuck out.

"I wanted to go through it with her," Owen mumbled into his mattress. "Girls are evil."

"Well. You know. So are men," David said, thinking of himself.

"But it's different. Girls pretend like they're not evil, and by the time you figure it out they've already ripped your heart out and shat on it. At least we're honest about what we're like."

What were men like? David thought back to the TV dads of his formative years. The Peter Griffins and Phil Dunphys. He thought of what they were like.

"I guess we're just supposed to be *stupid,*" David said. "And it's tough, because we're *not.*"

"*You're* not," Owen said. "*I'm* a fucking idiot."

David stared at Owen's head, the recently shaved flesh pale like a plucked chicken. He stared at thin lumps of veins and arteries pulsing softly.

"Neither of us are idiots," David said. "We're just... I don't know. Breakable?"

Owen sniffed once. "I'm not," he said. "I'm no snowflake."

"That's right!" agreed David. "You're a fucking soldier!"

And then Owen's body began hiccupping under the covers. He sobbed into his arms, scalp turning red. David reached out his hand and placed it on Owen's bald head, lightly tapping the hard bone of his skull and the cold, soft skin that covered it.

"I'm sorry I said all that terrible shit to you and to Esteban and that stuff about Haley. That was pure evil, I'm sorry," Owen sniveled. "There's evil, and there's war, and there's disaster. You know where it is?" He poked his head from under the covers. He pointed downward.

"The first floor?" David asked.

"Underground!" Owen hissed. "And up there"—he raised his eyes—"in the actual sky."

Owen looked beyond David, his eyes filled with fear, like there was some monster sneaking up on them. His face disappeared again beneath the covers.

Owen was beyond David's abilities.

"Dude, should I call someone?" David offered.

"Probably," Owen said. "You should call everyone."

Owen didn't want to be a soldier. The next day, he went down to the ROTC office and quit. They implored—wouldn't he rather join the ERA and lend a hand? He told them that there was no time to help anyone, that the Time Crisis was real. Everything was too late. There was work to be done right here and now.

Owen left school.

He packed his things and David helped truck them downstairs to his parents' car and tried to talk to them like everything was normal. David assured them Owen never got violent, suicidal. He was just confused. He missed the people who knew him. *Owen doesn't need more school right now,* David thought. *He's learned enough for one semester.*

David was surprised to learn that Owen wasn't moving back home, but to a friend's house in nearby Pennington. His parents claimed it'd be good for him, that he always did well in smaller settings, that he was committed to finishing out the semester. This was all for the best.

As he said goodbye, David thought Owen looked marginally better. Still worried, but with some kind of resigned peace, like a parent watching a child put something into its mouth that probably won't hurt all that much. As David gave his roommate a solid bro-hug, Owen palmed him an orange plastic bottle. They were pills. His Zeronal.

"Here, take one capsule every day," he whispered. "They'll keep you sane in an insane time."

"Well, kind of," offered David. "They also kind of made you flip out, didn't they?"

Owen shook his head. "They're the perfect merger of impulse and rationality. An amygdala hijacking. There's no fight or flight. There's just..." He tapped the pill vial and said, very plainly, "These prepare you to fly."

And with that, Owen and his family were gone. And though he didn't realize it yet, David was holding in his hand the drug that would define a revolution and catalyze his heroes.

iv.

David could still remember the first time he saw Superman. Smack dab on the comic book cover. Ripping open a bland button-down shirt, exposing his insignia. That same giant *S* over the title. *The Man of Steel #1*. Behind him, a doomed planet bursts with blue flames, popping like a firework.

David was five, curled into the couch beside his mom, getting lost in the folds of her kaftan. They watched *Smallville*, his mom's favorite show. Season 7, episode 18. The plot of this one was about Jor-El showing his son what the world would've been like if he'd never existed or come to Earth, a superhero version of *It's a Wonderful Life*. David glanced from the television to the comic book in his lap, then back again. He couldn't understand why this TV Man of Steel looked so different from the illustrated one. He demanded an explanation.

"Well, see, superheroes never die." Eileen Fuffman pointed at the TV, at his hero sweeping Lois Lane off her feet. "*This* Superman is named Tom Welling, and there's another Superman in the movies named Brandon or Ansel, I think, and back when I was a little girl, Superman was named Christopher, and before him was a Superman named George Reeves. And someday? Maybe Superman will be *you*. David Fuffman!"

David was doomed from the start.

As a kid, he trained endlessly to take Superman's place once this latest incarnation passed on to whatever afterlife is afforded alien sons of Krypton. His first exercise was climbing up the floor: lying facedown, David clawed hand over hand across the living room, pulling his stomach along that scratchy sky-blue carpet, pretending it was vertical—a steep, jagged cliff face covered in ice and monsters. Invisible obstacles occasionally impeded his progress. Grunting and straining to maintain his grip, he'd dangle from two uncertain fingertips, stuck halfway between the den and kitchen. He spent entire days like this, facedown on the carpet, scaling Floor Mountain.

When his little sister was an infant, he let her climb, too.

"Hang on tight. We'll climb to Disneyland," he'd say, as little Beth dutifully pawed the shag. If David could not yet be a superhero, at least he could be her Sherpa.

Once he'd mastered climbing the floor, David trained himself to fly. He executed flips off his parents' wooden headboard, using the mattress as a trampoline and landing pad—*jump, bounce, flip, land. Repeat*. But the first time David's mother saw him somersaulting through the air and onto his back, her screams put a stop to his training.

"It's for your own good," she said. "You're going to kill yourself."

She crossed her arms and made David cross his heart and promise never to fly again.

But prophecy is something he always took seriously, and after Mom divined that David was next in line for Superman's throne, David did his homework. He ran through the greatest hits: Netflix sent DVDs of the 1980s Christopher Reeve stuff; his parents pulled up choppy episodes of vintage animated *Super Friends* on YouTube; Mom kept including David in her weekly *Smallville* sessions, and they even tried a few episodes of *Lois & Clark*, which David didn't care for.

Once he was up to speed, David begged his dad to take him to *Superman Returns*, the one from a couple years ago, the one with the Superman named Brandon. It'd be his first live-action movie in a real theater. David was thrilled at the idea that, ever since that god-awful *Superman IV: The Quest for Peace*, the Man of Steel had been gone for nearly twenty years, an eternity of a hiatus, like he'd never really existed or come to Earth. But now, here he was again! Returning!

Dad found an art house screening an all-day series of recent superhero flicks, and Gil and Eileen agreed that *The Incredible Hulk, Hancock, Iron Man, The Dark Knight*, and *Watchmen* would be far too intense for young David. But *Superman Returns*? It was doable.

The theater was huge. Nearly empty. Initially, the scale and sound were scary, and Gil Fuffman talked his son through it.

"Why's Lex Luthor so *mean*?" David asked.

"Because he's too smart for his own good," Dad explained. But then Dad wouldn't shut up. He kept whispering asides, his breath hot and buttery in David's ear. He was quick to cover his son's eyes, to assure him all blood was ketchup. He loved it when Superman's dead father appeared.

"See, that's the Fortress of Solitude, and all the books and scientific facts from dozens of other worlds is contained in those crystals," David's dad whispered, "and now the ghost of Superman's father is helping him understand it all!"

"I know," David hissed. "They just *said* that." David was *trying* to listen to Jor-El explain how human beings could be great—because of their capacity for good—if only Superman could show them the way. But Dad continued, his beard scratching David's cheek.

"I took his picture once, you know. The one hanging over my desk."

"Superman?"

"No, Marlon Brando. Superman's dad, Jor-El. The guy talking. He was pretty old, and—"

David watched Superman remember himself as a younger man, discovering his powers, running crazy fast through all that corn. He held his breath as Superman snatched that flaming plane out of midair and set it down gently in the middle of a baseball diamond, the most American thing possible. And he fought back tears as Superman saw his home of Krypton bursting into flames, transforming this Kal-El into the last man of a dead world.

"And don't worry," Dad said. "Planets don't really explode like that. It's just special effects."

"Shh," David said. "We're missing the point of everything."

David remembered the Christopher Reeve version where Lois Lane perished in an earthquake, and Superman flies faster and faster around Earth, reversing its spin, reversing time, erasing his beloved's death. Those old special effects were pretty bad, and by comparison *Superman Returns* was magic on screen, a spectacle like he'd never seen. David sat shell-shocked through half the credits—*wow*—until Dad said it was time to leave that dark mystical theater. On the ride home, David tried to ask questions about Lex Luthor and the annihilation of Krypton, but his dad kept coming back to the scene where Brando explains Superman's origins.

"It's nice when dads tell stories to their sons like that, huh? Like when I tell *you* stories."

"Did your dad tell stories?"

David's dad thought for a moment, then signaled left and cut someone off.

"Grandpa would tell me that a fish jumped in his car window, and I'd tell my friends at school and they'd laugh at me for making stuff up." Dad snorted, chewing a hunk of ice from his movie theater soda cup. "My father wasn't really a storyteller so much as a liar."

"Where is he now?"

"Your grandpa László is dead. You know that."

"Like Jor-El."

"Mmm, not like Jor-El."

"Do you still talk to each other like Superman and Jor-El?"

"Nope."

"How come?"

"I guess he's busy," Dad said. Then he grew suddenly concerned. "I'm not too busy for you, am I buddy? I'm around and my time is free enough, you'd say? Because, you know, I'll always be here for you, whatever you need, even when you get older and too cool for me, I'll still be around. Even if for some reason I wasn't around in person, you can always call, or even just close your eyes and pretend to talk to me and I'd be right there."

"Like Jor-El!" David said, getting it now. "He was a great actor, right, Dad?"

Gil Fuffman smiled. "When Brando was younger he was in an acting class and the teacher told everyone to act like chickens. So everyone's clucking around, pecking at the floor. Then the teacher goes, 'Okay, now pretend there's a nuclear bomb headed right for the henhouse!'"

"What's a nucular—"

"A big, *big* bomb. So everyone in the class starts going crazy, all these chickens running in circles, squawking like mad, like 'Ah, it's the end of the world!' Except for Brando. He squats down, pretends to lay an egg, and then goes about his business, slowly clucking and pecking at the floor."

David was confused. "Why? I thought you just said he was a great actor."

"Well, he was acting like a *chicken*," Dad said. "What do chickens know about bombs?"

V.

David was still drawing a blank. He had kind of an idea for his Egg thesis, but it seemed silly to focus on that with all the work that had to be done in the house to keep them warm and fed. Or maybe, with the world in shambles, his thesis was more important than anything?

Mathias funded Lee's chemicals because sure. From antibiotics to painkillers to recreational drugs, pharmaceuticals were a solid investment, a potential postapocalyptic gold mine.

Fu told David his dream was to figure out how to make robots play improvisational music, thus opening the possibility for AI to create art and maybe *have a soul* and be responsible sentient beings, and if you believed in reincarnation and the transmigration of souls, as he did, it was basically engineering our collective evolution. Pie-in-the-sky stuff. But during the blackout he shifted gears and focused on his ham radio project. Basic communication. More immediately practical.

Mathias, meanwhile, knew carpentry and cars and kept dangling that tease about teaching liquor distillation, even though David never saw a still, only the by-product. Mathias knew these things, but more important, he understood time. And time was becoming everything.

At first it was probably an imperceptible shift, they said, a few tenths of a millisecond every year. After Mott, studies were showing they were losing a minute every week. A solid cadre of fancy-sounding scientist-pundits—folks other than Mott with all their credibility still intact—all concurred on calculating that the so-called Time Crisis would hit absolute zero, the Null Point, on June 6, give or take a couple days. None of them could agree on what that meant.

"Mott still doesn't get it," Mathias said on day eight trapped in The Egg, more to himself than to the room. "His hypothesis is still based on the presumption that the hypersphere is a funnel, but that implies there's nothing at the bottom, and we just go down the tubes into nothingness. But actually? It doesn't *end* at the Null Point. The shape is more like an inner tube. Here, picture a bagel!" This was how he talked. Science was his thing. Theoretical physics.

David still didn't get it. He chalked up the phenomenon to a misplaced decimal point. A cosmic anomaly. A false alarm. And yet, he pictured those graphs from biology class. The fat horizontal bars chronicling billions of years from the Big Bang to the amoebas, slimming down to hair-thin slices—births of human interaction, industry, internet, the twenty-four-hour news cycle. Evolution is always collapsing. December might bring whole new leaps. Who knew how long January would be? The blink of an eye? Before David spent his parents' modest savings and took on a mountain of student loan debt for Ivy League tuition, he wondered if chronostrictesis meant the end of the future for which his parents had endlessly prepared him. He hoped he was doing okay by them.

"Dude!" said Mathias.

Blink. David snapped back.

"I said picture a bagel," Mathias barked. "Are you picturing a bagel?"

David pictured a bagel.

Mathias instructed: "With your finger, trace a spiral down the inside of the hole. *Now,* imagine you don't just fall through the hole. You *stick* to the bagel. Each time we pass through the proverbial bagel hole, a new era of humanity emerges. The next species is called *Homo luminous.*"

"Is that Light Man?"

"No," he corrected. "Light *Men*. Which means there will be many of us."

"Luminosity would be super helpful right now," David said, noting the darkness. Owen was working on ways to harvest sustainable energy, at least enough to power some lightbulbs and a space heater. David was pulling for him. They could see their breath down there.

The temperature was actually becoming a serious problem. László's blazer helped with the cold, but more layers limited mobility. So David went to his new basement bedroom and grabbed a red fleece blanket from the bed. He tied it around his neck and let it drape down his back, so he could move freely or warmly bundle himself as needed.

"Good idea," said the others, and soon all five of them were wearing their blankets.

Blankets make good capes, David thought. And amid the blackout, a lightbulb went on.

— Ø —

from: dfuffman@princeton.edu
to: hr78546@princeton.edu
date: December 21, 2021
subject: Rocky Road

hey haley,

no idea if you have power. you didn't respond about your housing plans, but I wanted to get in touch about a project I'm working on at The Egg.

I need an illustrator. If I provide written descriptions (see attached) could you translate these into images?

lemme know,
DF

—Ø—

But seriously, David wondered out loud, where was the government in all of this?

"What?" said Lee. "You want them to swoop in on snowmobiles, delivering soup?"

David thought about this. "Yes, actually."

Or *something*. Wasn't that the point of ERA? Who saves the day when *everyone* needs saving?

"That's the danger of being in the spread-out suburbs," said Mathias, clipping his toenails.

Mathias was the one who picked the suburbs. During last year's tuition strikes, he found himself on the front lines of student activism—at first just a fuck you to his dad. "Then the cops broke my arm, burned my eyes," he said. "So I stopped going to class and started educating myself."

His standoff with the riot cops ended up on YouTube. This would have been around the same time David Fuffman reached regional notoriety by placing his palms upon a Hyundai.

"Yes, I googled you," Mathias admitted. "Like I said: I am another yourself. *In Lak'ech*—"

David responded, *"Ala K'in."*

Their breath clouds met in the middle and hung there.

—Ø—

A minute of cranking yielded two minutes of laptop time, five minutes of phone, or ten minutes of flashlight. That was life during the blizzard: furious cranking, then a dwindling to darkness.

Finally, after sitting in his phone's outbox for like nine hours, the email sent. David stupidly assumed Haley might get it immediately and respond even more immediately, with gusto. But her response time lagged. Two more days passed, and David tried to reassure himself that maybe be her technology and connectivity were also a crapshoot, that she was equally stranded. David's email became a message in a bottle, thrown to sea. He realized his odds were not good.

He still had her number, from back when he occasionally texted her for drugs in high school, but his run-in at the grocery store had been by chance, and he'd already reached out over social media and it would be weird if he texted her now, wouldn't it, regardless of the email but *especially* after the email and no response. He clicked her name in his phone, still listed as "The Racketeer," embarrassingly. He changed it to "Haley Roth." Literally the least he could do.

In reality she'd received the email just fine. She was always planning to respond. She just hadn't been ready yet. She was thinking.

A few times, she came close to texting him. She had his number saved from high school, too. But this time, she saw that little series of dots on his side of the screen, the ones that meant he was in the process of writing something, thinking about her, right this second.

She'd caught him in the act. Or maybe he'd caught her?

Either way, she decided to beat him to the punch.

"I get it," Haley texted him, blowing up his functioning phone. "It's like a social network?"

"No, it's real!" David texted back, after a suitable amount of time. "It's more an autonomous system of economic, social, and spiritual self-improvement tools to help us survive a major catastrophe," he clarified. "Or at least prepare for it."

"Sure, swell," she wrote. "But you only have engineers so far. Chemical, mechanical, electrical. If it's Armageddon you'll need food and water specialists, obvi. And doctors, defenders, other good guys."

"Good point."

"So who's the bad guy? The villain?"

David was having trouble figuring this one out. He'd hoped she wouldn't ask yet.

"The president, obviously, but maybe China, too? Or the military-industrial complex? Man vs. society? Or climate change and environmental collapse as a whole? Man vs. nature?"

"Not the president, but you need a singular symbol or figurehead," she wrote. "Some character to embody whatever you're fighting against. In order to recruit for *this* you need *anti*-this."

"I'll keep thinking," he wrote after a bit.

"I'll start drawing," she wrote back immediately.

But Haley had tough associations with costuming.

She remembered part of Halloween night, or maybe it was the morning, waking up on the edge of Poe Field. She'd staggered back across all that strewn detritus of seasonal plastic—the cracked tiaras, lopped-off pirate hooks, lone surgeon gloves, and Batman gauntlets—entire costumes ripped to shreds and half buried in the festering muck—feeling what had happened to her.

She told her roommate immediately that she'd been raped. Poor Jessica was tragically immature when it came to these kinds of things—Haley wondered if she'd ever kissed anyone—and once referred to second base as "the whole breastfeeding thing." So telling Jessica was almost like telling no one, an awful admission yelled down a well.

Visual details came back to Haley in horrifying flashes. Blink. His chest, hairless. Blink. His mask, a blue *lucha libre* thing with silver flames around the eyes. It didn't take long to piece it together. To ask around and be sure who it was. Haley took two days, and then came forward. After that was the blur of politically correct administration meetings and empty apologies and lawyers and not-exactly-lawyers and things to sign and tricks to hide her growing rage.

She wondered if David could understand her feelings about masks. Maybe he was just as oblivious as her roommate? Or maybe he was all too aware. Maybe he was giving her this assignment as a rogue, uninvited form of exposure therapy. Regardless, she went for it.

What else was there to do?

—Ø—

Haley had mentioned Mathias back at the Giant supermarket in Pikesville, David knew they knew each other, and he'd been waiting to see if Mathias ever brought her up. Finally, two days before Christmas, when the two of them were digging through the kitchen trash to see what might be salvageable, David broached the subject, told him she was helping with his thesis.

"You mean Cap'n Cunt?" Mathias asked.

"Yeah, ha! Exactly! She told me she knew you."

"Are you friends with her?"

"Yeah, we kinda hooked up in high school and—"

"If you're her friend, why would you reinforce that nickname, David?"

"What?"

"Why not tell me she's a really nice person and that I shouldn't *ever* call her that?"

David was taken aback. Immediately embarrassed. He didn't mean anything by it, just...

"Yeah, I know her," said Mathias. "Excellent roundhouse kick. You find your thesis yet?"

"Not yet."

"Try to elevate," he said. "Halloween was basic, safe. Didn't work out so well, did it?"

David fell asleep with this on his mind. He slept fitfully. Dreams of stapled cats. Rape and mutilation. Your worst nightmare. Mutants descend. The Mutant Leader promises: *We are damned.*

But wait. Searchlights in the night sky. Yellow and black.

Brilliantly pathological. Fierce survivor. Pure warrior. The Batman.

David woke in the middle of the night, went to the kitchen, ate the last piece of Martin's donated Batman cake. He swallowed the fast, cheap, sugary energy. He wondered how long it'd last.

4

THE BIG BANG

i.

A few hours after Owen had vacated their dorm room, David took Zeronal for the first time. With Owen gone, the room was now all David's. But the commotion surrounding Owen's recent exit meant that if David had any inclinations toward suicide or nervous breakdown, he'd have to shelve them for the remainder of freshman year. Once roommate A loses it, roommate B can't very well follow suit. Better to be alive and miserable than dead and derivative.

CAUTION: FEDERAL LAW PROHIBITS THE TRANSFER OF THIS DRUG TO ANY PERSON OTHER THAN THE PATIENT FOR WHOM IT WAS PRESCRIBED.

Of course, David would absolutely not take these Zeronal pills, these things that played such havoc with his roommate's mental state and sense of identity and ability to shower properly. He would return them to SCISM. Or flush 'em.

DO NOT DRINK ALCOHOL WHILE TAKING THIS MEDICATION.

David googled "amygdala hijacking," that weird term Owen had mentioned during his move-out, which turned out to be awesome. The example: a guy walking along a canal sees a woman staring at the water, intense fear on her face. Without knowing why, the man dives into the water, clothes on. Only then does he realize the woman had been staring at a little girl who'd fallen into the canal and was drowning. The man swims to her, drags her to shore.

A positive hijacking. Pure gut. The will to save.

Owen's final tease repeated itself over and over in David's brain: *These prepare you to fly.*

TO OPEN, HOLD TAB DOWN & TURN.

They were smooth purple capsules, black code on the side. Inside, a bunch of teeny white beads. David considered their chemical majesty. *So small, and so much potential. Little eggs waiting to hatch.*

David took the pills for two days, to no discernible effect. He noticed a piqued interest in schoolwork, a renewed appetite for reading. But not much else.

And then.

David's regimen of Zeronal left much of the next few days an amnesiac blur. Amid his blackout David remembered buying provisions from the Wawa. Apples. Gummy salamanders. Easy Cheese. He remembered trying to cook things on his hotplate. He remembered becoming jealous of his air ducts and water pipes, how they carried heat, water, everything vital, and you turn a knob and warmth magically shoots from the wall! Amazing! He spent hours balancing on the arms of a desk chair, prying out little boogers wedged between the crown molding and ceiling, sifting through them like a prospector searching for gold. *How did they get up here? Where is the booger catapult?*

Mercifully, after days and nights of this nonsense, Owen called.

David hadn't spoken to anyone in who knows how long. Words felt weird. Owen asked if he'd been taking the Zeronal and David confirmed. They made small talk about the erratic weather and medium talk about Bob Badalamenti. Owen said he'd been released on $8,000 bail and had settled out of court with the Roth family and was now gone from Princeton. David imagined Bob exiled like General Zod in the beginning of *Superman II*, trapped in some weird diamond-shaped mirror-prison, spinning endlessly through the cosmos.

"It's called the Phantom Zone," said Owen. "Invented by Superman's dad, Jor-El."

Wait, had David been imagining out loud?

"Just think about it, David."

"Think about what?"

"Think about getting out of there. It's good here. At The Egg. Think about it. We'll be at Stony Brook again tonight if you want to—"

David agreed to think about it but had to hang up, because he'd just discovered a document open on his laptop that contained a term paper, a ten-pager, for Hague's Problem of Evil class, somehow already drafted. He had vague memories of frenzied writing, but that felt like months ago. Nice. What a positive side effect!

His paper was apparently about the Iranian prophet Zoroaster, a.k.a. Zarathustra, and it wasn't too shabby. In Zoroaster's version of Earth's origin story, the god of Time—named Zurvan—was pining for a son. Instead, he was impregnated with twins: the Destroyer, conceived from doubt, and the Wise Lord, created from the merits of sacrifice. In Zurvan's androgynous womb, these twins wrestled to see who'd be born first and create the world in his own image.

David's paper was about how this battle birthed monotheism, a new view of man's active role in the fight between good and evil. Suddenly, we were accountable for our own actions. And wasn't accountability the essence of being a hero, or at least an adult? And can one be accountable after the moment has passed? Do you just try harder next time, or is sacrifice the only redemption?

Spell check. Page numbers. Attach. Send.

He headed toward Nassau Street. Just after taking another Zeronal.

Shortly after the pill kicked in, David found himself taking a long detour. To Hamilton Hall. To the dorm room of Haley Roth. What would he say? He had no idea but knew he needed to knock on her door. He felt like he was about to ask someone to prom, except he was confident.

When her roommate answered, David boldly asked if he could talk to Haley.

"What about?"

"Sexual assault," he said. The roommate bristled, made herself larger in the doorway.

"You mean *rape*?" The word sounded foreign. David grasped with awful horror that *rape* was something happening to people he knew, people his age, not just people on TV. *Rape* did not only occur in the dark ages, when Mongols conquered new territories, or on the evening news. Right now, men everywhere were enforcing their will on others.

Haley's roommate closed the door on David. He heard her socks thudding through the room, her muffled explanation to Haley. David's finger traced the grain of their wooden door.

"Who is it," said a familiar voice behind the door, not *asking* so much as *warning*.

"Sorry to bother you," he said. "It's David." No response. "Fuffman."

"I know you think I was a whore in high school," she said. "But believe it or not—"

"Can you give me like three minutes of your time?" David asked.

"I don't have any time. None of us have any time anymore. You have three words."

He took a breath and offered her all he knew how to offer:

"I believe you."

David said it like a question, rising at the end. It wasn't an apology or a confession. It wasn't very much. But in three words, it was the least stupid thing he could think to say.

"Super," she said, quieter this time. "Bye, David."

Feeling semi-accomplished, David jogged to a bar on Nassau Street called the Ivy Inn where he'd heard they didn't card. Alone, he got drunk on Scotch—shot after shot—which he'd never done before, but it seemed the sort of thing a guy in the process of exorcising demons might do. The Ivy Inn was at the northeast corner of his world, and he was sure he could make it to the far southwest boundary in record time, a personal best, sure, let's do it. He hadn't worked out in ages, but let's just fucking do it, right? He started in a jog and soon broke into a sprint, arms chugging faster and faster, legs whirring like the Flash, and whenever he needed to change directions he did so in ninety-degree angles, also like the Flash, faster and faster past the Wawa, past Forbes, back to the Institute for Advanced Study.

When he arrived at this familiar, unfamiliar place, David strolled to the lip of the pond and stared down at his reflection. Out of many pages of fall semester reading, one thing David retained was the story of Narcissus. Everyone knows he died because of vanity, but it turns out the river nearly died as well. It missed Narcissus too much. Not for his beauty, but because the river had fallen in love with its *own* twinkling reflection found in the gloss of Narcissus's eyes. David began to cry. It came on suddenly, powerfully, like a sneeze. David crouched and hung his head and wept so the tears ran inward, onto the bridge of his nose, freezing there to build over time like stalactites. He wept for Owen and for Haley, and he wept like the river when it realized its mirror was gone.

And now the sprinting caught up with him. He struggled to his knees and vomited, *Exorcist*-style. He slumped, stared at his orange mess. Running across campus was fine, he decided, but what David really wanted was to fly above it. Over the Gothic spires of campus, toward the future, where time might someday stop and cycle back on itself. Pretend it never happened.

But he had none of those powers. So he lay stomach-down on the crispy grass, once more scaling the treacherous crag of Floor Mountain, hand over hand, ice and monsters.

ii.

Helicopters were in the sky the day before Christmas. ERA, maybe, but it sure took them long enough. And they didn't do much, didn't relieve anything on the ground that David could see. They only sat up there, searchlights on, like ominous dragonflies. David imagined them shooting Santa Claus from the air: reindeer plummeting, sleigh trailing fire. A once-in-a-lifetime comet.

The next time David self-powered his iPhone to call his parents, the hand-crank thing fried his phone instead. Now, everything was gone. All his numbers, all his notes, all his delightful apps.

And Haley.

"Welcome to the Buddhist doctrine of nonattachment," Lee said.

"Nobody likes you," David said.

But Lee was right. The blizzard taught them sacrifice. Can't get one thing without losing another. No electricity without gas. David knew this when the generator finally ran out of fuel.

After ten days, with the power still out, the thaw began. Next came the plows, with their massive light bars and thunderousness. They pulled into Woosamonsa, forging a path down the center, even though this meant slamming snow to the sides and blocking all the driveways even worse.

But then, something awful. As the plows cleared the court, they uncovered Fred.

Fred Shuster who was once the best.

From the window, Mathias saw the plow rolling his body around the court, frozen into an awful frostbitten log. At first, Mathias fell apart. But soon he was back in charge.

Bundling up, they got the front door open. Snow poured into the foyer, but they dealt with this and carved a kind of staircase and scaled the snowdrift onto the pristine surface, still a good four feet high. Owen tied tennis rackets to his boots—makeshift snowshoes. The others piled into the Intex raft and Owen pulled them from the front door to the court, where they could now see pavement. Six hours later an ambulance arrived to load up the body. EMTs figured Fred got stuck during the whiteout, dropped a glove, and never regained his bearings. Or maybe a heart attack. Said there'd been similar tragedies everywhere. Mathias believed Fred had been heading to The Egg for help.

David shivered at the sight of the poor kind man, frantically groping for a landmark amid the White Curtain. Screaming until his voice went numb. Praying. He thought of Lee's idea—*always tie a rope so you can winch your way back*—but some people just don't own that much rope.

Their Jøtul stove kicked out a good amount of heat. As long as you packed it full of wood at night, there'd still be some good embers in the morning that could be reignited pretty easily. The wood made them warm twice—splitting it and burning it—and they took turns chopping. But the log rack on the covered porch ran low, and then it was gone, their central stove eating up the last of it like that final gallon in the gas tank that always goes too damn fast.

When Mathias took his axe out to the porch and began hacking away at the wooden posts, David thought he'd lost it. But it's just that burning the porch was better than burning books. It was hard to pinpoint the moment they'd crossed over, but they were now in true survival mode.

David's dad said the toll had reached 450. His mom heard 500. David told them about Fred. Princeton sent out a list of its deceased. Barry Hague, his Problem of Evil professor, was on it.

"Unbelievable," David's mom said. "And do you remember the Hachenbergs?"

"Like *Tracy* Hachenberg?"

"Roof caved in on them," said his father. "Her sister died. Unbelievable."

"But you sure *you're* fine?" That was suddenly all that mattered to David.

"Fine," his mom said. "Plenty of food. Warm enough. Beth is teaching herself mandolin."

"Mandarin?" David asked. "You're breaking up."

"No, the mandolin. Although Mandarin would make more sense these days."

David didn't care about China. Jersey was a closer war zone.

"I just can't stop picturing Fred," he said.

"Nothing you could have done, buddy," said his father. "I'm sorry you had to see it."

"I'm not. I just wish I saw him *earlier*. I would've..."

"Would've what?" they asked, after a suitable amount of time.

With cell service more reliable again, the others also phoned home. Families reconnecting. Once, Owen came upstairs with a confused and frazzled face. He stared at Mathias.

"*Your father* is on my phone," he said.

Mathias stopped patching a leaking roof panel. He glanced down from the ladder.

"Tell him I went out for cigarettes," Mathias said loudly.

"Your father says that he can hear you and that he knows you didn't go out for cigarettes because there's five feet of snow and you're smart enough to have stocked up before the storm and... hold on... and that he just wanted to make sure you're alive and that your mom is worried and he'll tell her you're fine. And he says to stay warm. Okay. Okay, yes, sir, okay bye now."

Owen hung up. Mathias went back to hammering and said, "He spoils me with affection."

—Ø—

Haley thought of paper dolls, those booklets she used to love with half-naked male and female figures and pages of outfits, hats, accessories, ready to be cut out and hooked with little white flaps onto blank-slate bodies. One minute, they're policemen. Next, rodeo clowns. It's amazing what costuming could do. When she was little she got obsessed with beauty pageants, briefly, and ended up drawing fake contestants with evening gowns and sashes and gave each a unique name and age and state and talent. She didn't like drawing hands and feet, so Haley rendered them as footless, handless women. They were ridiculous looking.

David's assignment was the first time she'd done any real work—the friendship bracelets and knots didn't count—since Halloween. She was rusty, she knew that, but it felt good to be roughing something out on paper again. She told herself it was work for hire, something she didn't have to strap her soul on to. Just a commission. But she wasn't going to take any money from David.

Fearless Infrared, she thought, *here are my sketches for an as yet Unnamed Supersquadron of Vigilantes (USV?). I had fun drawing them. I'm a big dork, too.*

She tried to stick to his instructions but took some creative liberties.

She was pleased with how Infrared—David's character and costume—came out. She made his goggles more steampunk than futuristic. His Mohawk idea was nice, but Haley flipped it sideways, ear to ear, so that it looked more like a halo or infrared aura. He'd mentioned his grandpa's blazer, but she expanded the look into a sharp three-piece suit.

For Peacemaker, the ROTC-defender character, she went with standard-issue army camo gear and just added football shoulder pads underneath.

Golden Echo, she made him techie like David said, with yellow-gold body armor and lots of computer-y circuits attached. He got a motorcycle and helmet, like Akira. Haley worried his jacket was too robotic looking but reminded herself this was just a sketch, a beginning.

For the Dr. Ugs chemist character—*I get it,* she thought, *hardy har har*—David was exceedingly clear that the figure have very thin legs. Instead of the typical white lab coat she painted it black. Gave him black Converse, except they were tall like big-ass Goth boots that laced all the way to his knees because why not have some fun.

And finally, Ultraviolet. It took Haley a while to mix the skin color and find the right purple. It was way too lavender froufrou at first. But his jacket turned out awesome. She designed it so his hands could stick out of holes in the sleeves, which were abnormally long, hanging like the extra lengths of an unstrapped hospital straitjacket. She gave him purple parachute pants and silver John Lennon glasses. On his forehead, a "third eye" tattoo.

David had spouted something about ones and zeroes, so each of the superhero characters got a Ø insignia on the center of his chest, but she'd rework the logo at some point.

When she was finally happy enough with the work, she took phone photos, zipped them tight, and sent them into space, through the cellular sphere or whatever it was called.

Her accompanying message was simple:

You thinking of incorporating any ladies, or is this just a pure sausagefest?

—Ø—

Mathias shrugged listlessly. He was listening, but he was also still torn up about Fred.

"ERA is clearly insufficient," said David. "If you're right and things continue to get worse, we'll need more people to learn practical skills to deal with basic needs, but also how to stay civil and not deteriorate into some bleak, violent nightmare. Combining the heartiness of savages with the intellectualness of civilized man, right?"

"But why the silly outfits?"

"I'm trying to *package* what you've been doing here. Superheroes are ubiquitous these days, but they're always fighting alien monsters instead of dealing with real shit like hurricane evacuation. This way, we become elevated versions of ourselves. It's collective branding mixed with radical individualism—best of both worlds. And costumes allow for anonymous protest."

"It's true," said Owen. "The origin stories are the most interesting. Once superheroes are already powerful and battling aliens and stuff, it's just watching fight choreography. But seeing *how* they go from being ordinary to being superheroes... ?"

"I hate my name," said Lee. "Dr. Ugs? People will think it's about those stupid girl boots."

"Okay, how about this." Mathias rubbed his eyes, warming to the idea but also hangry. "If *we're* the superheroes, who's the super*villain*? Who or what are we fighting against?"

David still wasn't sure about that. He suggested the weather: man vs. nature!

"Too faceless, there's *real* lives to be saved"—Mathias motioned toward the cul-de-sac—"but keep going."

Watch this, David thought.

The next morning, David lay on his bed, arms flopped over his head like a sleepy Superman preparing for liftoff. He didn't stir while the guys paged through his folder marked "USV."

The power was still out, but what had transpired over the past twenty or so dark hours was a mad, focused feat of electric effort. In the endless back and forth between popping Zeronal and hand-cranking and typing until the batteries ran down, David had fleshed out five core superheroes and solidified each persona—each backstory, costume, accessories, strength, and weakness—in a way that supported their individual theses in progress. He drew a floor plan of The Egg, outlining a room-by-room training experience to guide new recruits from origin story to completed persona. He developed a ninety-day schedule of public "spectacles," as well as an elaborate chart detailing the USV's short-term recruiting targets—food / water specialists, doctors—all the all-stars a pre-apocalyptic commune might need to survive the end of time. He even added an appendix of financials. He bound his treatise with speaker wire. He would show them Haley's drawings just as soon as she finished them, as soon as she sent them through. She was due to send them yesterday. It'd be soon. Any minute now.

As for whom they were fighting, the USV's bad guys were not evil corporations, nor hordes of paramilitary personnel, nor cackling madmen bent on world destruction, not even the fucking president. The villains were *themselves* at their worst. The shadow side.

Just as each mythological deity and demigod in the Greek pantheon was capable of both good and evil, the USV did not need one single devil, because it had no single god. Each evil was part of the good. Each USV hero had his own private fiend to battle.

Man vs. his own nature.

Along with this proposal, David had drafted an initial set of "tenets" for this collective:

The Code of the USV

1. *Our clock is ticking. Discover your powers and weaknesses, your persona and shadow.*
2. *You are not mild-mannered. Be like Superman: a bulletproof alien, a fucking god.*
3. *You are not a nerd. Be like Spider-Man: a hunter of radioactive arachnids, falling headlong into their webs.*
4. *You are not entitled. Be like Batman: flawed—mortally—and willing to work like mad. If destiny fails, use your smoke pellets.*
5. *We must evolve or perish. Doomsday prep the spirit, shore up this house.*
6. *It's not a house. It is The Egg.*

When David woke the next morning, Mathias had scrawled an additional entry:

7. *WE CAN SAVE US ALL.*

iii.

Before he became David's grandfather, László Ffodor was a scientist. He was also one of the two hundred thousand Hungarians who marched through Budapest in October 1956 to proclaim their unrest to the free world. The rebellion was crushed. Thousands of unarmed students were massacred at the foot of the parliament building. But László and his wife, Rivkah, were among those who escaped, preferring exile to incarceration or death.

Layered in three woolen blazers, László carried suitcases of personal effects and engineering textbooks through a fifteen-mile border expanse the Soviets had flattened into wasteland. Machine-gun turrets were installed every mile. Here was László's plan: hope no one was manning the turrets.

So László began his plod, shielding Rivkah, wondering if it would ever end, wondering which step forward onto the tundra might be met by the distant popcorn sound of gunfire come to claim them. Exhaustion and hallucination eventually took hold, and when three distant spires finally broke the horizon, he assumed they were dead, and here was Lucifer's pitchfork heralding their arrival in Hell.

As it turns out, it was Austria.

David inherited one of László's storied wool blazers, an honorable cape, and liked to think he inherited his grandfather's work ethic as well, that he came from good stock, that if shit truly hit the fan, David could be counted on to suck it up, steel himself, and survive.

In 1957, several Ivy League schools offered scholarships for Hungarian refugees. Grandpa László did well at Princeton, was among the top two or three engineering students in his class. But the fact remained: he was not among the two or three thousand students killed in the massacre. And for that, he never forgave himself. László took to the bottle and to new intravenous poisons. He died of a morphine overdose, when he was fifty-two. David's dad never failed to mention that he died the same week and at the same age as yippie revolutionary Abbie Hoffman, as if these two unrelated suicides somehow conflated the scientist with the activist.

Before he became Spider-Man, Peter Parker was a scientist. Sure, that radioactive spider bite was lucky, but the bite occurred only because Peter was poking around a science fair one day. And the powers of that spider bite were unleashed only because of Peter's tinkering know-how, installing those cool web-blaster things on his wrists. *Knowledge is power,* David realized. *When it's organized and systematically tested and applied, that knowledge can become a superpower.*

David wasn't a scientist, but he liked to experiment.

Blink. A power surge rolled through his body and David remembered that moment in Stony Brook, when he first tasted that Big Bang pill under his tongue.

A synthetic smell of garbage bags. Dots of warmth tickled his back like bubbles rushing to the water's surface. He fell backward, body paralyzed, and David recognized he was afraid, that this was what feeling really afraid felt like. His eyes shut, and from the chestnut warmth behind his lids came layers of tracing paper scrawled with penciled animation. His ears went blank underwater, but his vision stayed strong. His eyes homed in on a star—one nameless pinprick of light above him. He fastened on and wouldn't let go. But *David* had not chosen that star. The star had chosen *him*. He felt watched. Like some disembodied head reading David's thoughts and being displeased. Maybe it was László.

With the oomph of a nuclear cannon, David shot from the water, and now he was flying or falling or flying, yes, flying down a tunnel, with the star at the center drawing him in, and everything else was periphery and the periphery danced red. The star opened its tiny aperture in the blue sky, and from its center the star began to flower. A circle of fingers spewed from its center—over and over again—petals blossoming and wilting and re-blossoming and curling back like gas fire.

It was microscopic and it took up the entire sky, all at once.

David was *watching* a supernova. He was sure of it. Billions of years ago this star exploded and the visual news was just reaching Earth. He was Hubble. Privy to the swan song of a world.

Beautiful. Perfect.

But then the aftermath. The chain reaction.

Earth spins faster and begets the flood, which begets the power outages, the food shortages, and then money is gone, electricity gone, water gone, all the hours gone, but still there is this star.

There was no room for interpretation, disbelief or suspension thereof. He'd stumbled into a vision. Was this what his parents warned him about? Was that a sky-snake feeding or just a line of birds?

David reached for a single rational thought: *I am a man floating down a river. Gently down the stream.* Flying forward, he broke through the brilliant flower membrane to the sound of Saran Wrap crinkling. As if stepping into a new room, there before David were small, clownish beings. Their faces were masks, like those cheap Halloween things for kids. Without words, David asked if they'd take them off, they were scaring him. And so they did. Clothes and costumes fell away, too, and underneath were reptilian bodies, part organic, part machine; part sweet, part sinister.

"This will end," they said, over and over. *"This will end."*

iv.

When Christmas came and went with still no power and no ERA, they realized most residents of Pennington—especially those with fewer provisions than The Egg—were out of time. So the Unnamed Supersquadron of Vigilantes would provide their power. Four hours was all it took for the five of them to get the MaxMobile unstuck and the driveway clear enough. An hour later they got the Intex raft situated on top, with a hundred feet of rope tied to each end, for pulling.

David unclicked his belt buckle and plucked out a Zeronal. The rest of his Infrared costume he'd have to pull together, but the belt and blazer were Infrared's now, they stayed. Up top, he'd shaved a sideways Mohawk, ear to ear, spikes like the Liberty crown. It was a bold call, maybe a mistake, but also a preemptive strike on his impending hair loss. Zeronal was worth its side effects.

Owen / Peacemaker wore his camo and football shoulder pads, just like Haley's drawings, which had finally arrived in David's inbox after their time at sea. Lee / Dr. Ugs had a white lab coat. It would suffice until he could find a black one. Mathias / Ultraviolet didn't have time to make his whole straitjacket getup, but he was still a piece of work: purple hoodie, purple beret, purple-tinted aviator shades. As a last touch, he'd fashioned a Santa beard out of cotton balls. White beards provide comfort in dark times.

Lee's Super Soaker flamethrower was the accessory that made David nervous, the thing most likely to win them a dubious Darwin Award. He'd filled the backpack-mounted water tank with tiki torch / kerosene mix, added the CO_2 tank from their SodaStream along with a bunch of valves and fittings and a diesel nozzle, and positioned a pilot flame directly in front of the nozzle.

"CO_2 is inert and the pump-action mechanism has valves that prevent the flame from shooting back through the gun and making the whole damn thing explode," Lee assured David. "Do you *get* that?"

David didn't. Anyone else, he would've vetoed the idea outright. But this was Lee's thing and it likely wouldn't work, and he'd be way out in front of the van anyway should it backfire, and so fuck him.

"You've all been good children this year," said Santa-bearded Mathias, divvying out Zeronal.

"Kiss the pill," they said, swallowed. David didn't want to be rude so he swallowed another.

When you're on Zeronal, complex movements seem preordained. Fu/Golden Echo had rigged an amplification system in the van, and to watch him slink from the passenger seat through the cargo space of the Max-Mobile, tweak his sound system, climb onto the roof, deliver the mic to Mathias in the Intex raft, tie Owen's snowshoes tight, then scurry back down again through the passenger-side window... it was like watching a practiced soldier dismantle a rifle. Moves tight and fast like *pow!* He was the Michael Jackson of everything.

"You're like totally fieldstripping *life* right now," David said to Fu from the driver's seat, adjusting the rearview. Fu reached over and honked David's horn twice. On cue, Lee fired up his flamethrower and a thin plume of orange excellence shot forth into Main Street's remaining sheet of snow. It was slow as hell to melt anything, but it looked pretty badass. Meanwhile, Fu wielded two iPhones like six-shooters, mixing music on the fly. Overtop this wild audiovisual experience, Mathias spoke.

"Good people of Pennington!" poured his voice from Fu's speakers. "Don't be afraid. Our fiery Rudolph makes way for a sleigh full of food, fuel, firewood, first aid, blankets, batteries, a partridge in a pear tree. We're here to help. Give us a signal and a life raft will deploy to your door!"

With Lee in the lead, firing his fire thing at the ground, David pressed the gas and inched forward onto this trench between two walls of snow. The top of the van was level with the snow-shelf that stretched from Main Street across the lawns to the houses on either side. Neighborhood roofs peeked out from this pristine whiteness like kids hiding under covers. When the guys caught sight of a flashlight shivering frantically inside a split-level on the west side of the street, David parked as close to the snowdrift as possible. Owen-in-snowshoes hopped off the roof onto the snow. He'd transformed his football shoulder pads into a kind of harness attached to a rope, which was attached to the Intex, and he pulled Mathias-in-life-raft toward this door of citizens in need. Owen was really strong. The bottom of the raft was smooth. And they were on performance-enhancing drugs. So the whole operation happened efficiently.

David was not privy to the conversation or physical maneuvering that occurred once his heroes reached this first house. Maybe Owen was patching holes in ceilings and accepting bartered survival tools. *Here, take this sheet cake,* the homeowners might say. *We have thousands of them.* Soon, Fu got a message from Mathias on his BaoFeng radio and sprang into action, gathering requested materials from the cargo space. He climbed to the roof and used a separate rope to winch back the now-empty raft, filling it with supplies like a tree-house bucket for Owen to pull back to the house. While David waited for this whole thing to play itself out, he thought of that silver-haired guy—Martin, was it?—who lived on 88 North Main Street and hadn't adequately shopped for the last two isolated weeks. David wondered if the MaxMobile could make it all the way to his place. Would Martin's family still be okay? Would Martin remember him? Would his wife be grateful? Beautiful?

They must make it there, David decided. At all costs.

In time, Owen and Mathias returned with reinforcements: newspapers (kindling?), an armful of tennis rackets (more snowshoes?), and two additional humans, a balding guy and his teenage son (they crossed themselves and hugged David in thanks).

"These guys are here to help!" announced Owen. He made the introductions, but David immediately forgot their names. He had a job to do. He put the MaxMobile back into drive.

"Owen!" David yelled into the back. "Is everyone settled on the roof again?"

Owen clamored to the front, his eyes embarrassed. "Dude!" he hissed. "Call me *Peacemaker*."

—Ø—

They continued like this—for hours? days? moments?—until they passed the barely visible HADDIE'S HABERDASHERY sign that marked the crossover from South to North Main Street. At each stop they deployed tools for survival. And at each stop they picked up new consumables and human resources alike. The MaxMobile was filled with people and a dozen more joined on foot, helping Dr. Ugs clear snow, taking turns dragging and pulling the raft ropes back and forth to citizens in distress. Their small but growing army consisted of only a few women. One was a surgeon, Maria, dispatched to a dozen doors to check vitals and, in one case, dress a grizzly shin wound.

Medicine is the best way to be a hero, David decided. He might've liked to be a doctor. He certainly had the sleeplessness gene; if only he could've handled the math and blood and lifestyle and pressure and science. Oh well. As David drove through that fiery white trench, he couldn't help but think of Moses parting the waves, leading his followers through the Red Sea. He imagined that bearded Jew, that iconic movie poster of Charlton Heston raising his staff and guiding the Hebrews to the Promised Land. Here in blizzarded Pennington were citizens trapped on the wrong sides of frozen waves. Now it was David who orchestrated their transport from isolation to fellowship, their conversion to the middle way. And it was easy! Find an inflatable rowboat. Tie a rope to both ends. Use it to convey people and stuff back and forth. And in the process, achieve saviorhood.

But that's not what he was! No, he wasn't even really doing anything, was he? He was just driving a van. Slowly. David shivered. He felt so stupid, so embarrassed, to catch himself equating himself with the likes of Moses and even Charlton Heston, these icons with their own Wikipedia pages, and here was dorky David Fuffman with a stupid haircut and some determined friends, shoveling suburbanites out of the snow a few months before the world would end anyway, and so who really gave a fuck? But they *did* give fucks, didn't they? These scared folks with nowhere else to turn? And maybe Owen—no, *Peacemaker!*—was the brawn, and Dr. Ugs's flamethrower was the most visually spectacular, and Ultraviolet was the vocal leader, and Golden Echo was a stone-cold ninja, but wasn't David/ Infrared something, too? Wasn't he both literally and figuratively driving this whole thing forward?

David shivered at the thought: what he was creating—his thesis—was not merely his latest entrepreneurial circus but rather the beginnings of *an organized religion*, the finest and most lucrative business known to humanity. What else do you call something that captures the zeitgeist of a world on the edge, provides comfort in times of need? This moment might be the creation myth that future biographers would biograph about—*Lo, and it was the Great Blizzard of 2021*—followed by the introduction of mythological figures—*and from The Egg birthed five heroes, the Light Men*—and then a liturgy of rituals, beliefs, instructions for psychotropic meetings with whatever lay beyond the end of time—*And thus spake Ultraviolet: "Kiss-the-pill."* It felt right, yes. The way it felt right when he got accepted to Princeton (his congregation) and when he met Mathias (his prophet) and when he fell in love with Haley Roth (his...). Good god, was he *in love* with Haley Roth? Fuck it. Yes. Yes. To all of it. Yes. Let's do this. All rivers lead to oceans! All plagues to salvation! To clear an area, you must build barriers and incite people to claw their way through them like mad and yes I said yes I will *yes!*

David glanced at the rearview mirror and saw a dozen silhouettes pointed toward him. Had he been thinking out loud? What had he said? What was happening right now?

"Everyone okay?" David mumbled at this assortment of faceless spectators.

"You were chanting, '*Yes, yes, yes,*'" said one of them. "We were hoping *you* were okay."

"Fine," said David. "I'm good. Really, really good. Everyone else good? You good?"

The word hung in the air: David was *good*. Was David capital-*G* Good? He was certainly juiced up by this whole search-and-rescue stuff. His eyes shot again to the dark figures in the rearview. These were his shadow: the Anointed. If Infrared was a hero of seeing and doing, the Anointed was a villain with eyes averted, body paralyzed with performance anxiety, seated in an unearned throne. The Anointed was the delusional boy-king, an entitled cheater. Power-hungry yet powerless. Stupid! He'd fallen right into its trap. Evil is good in costume.

"What's his name?"

It didn't matter what you called them, David thought, *so long as you knew which was the bad guy.*

"David, what was his name?"

"I call him the Anointed," said David. "But I am Infrared, and—"

"No. The guy. The guy with the birthday cakes." Fu was grabbing David's head, shaking him. Fu forced eye contact with David and spoke in slow, low tones. "What. Was. His. Name?"

Fu/Golden Echo pointed out a house, nearly buried, with its mailbox unearthed: 88 North Main Street. "I think we're here, right?" said Echo.

"Oh," said David, coming back to earth. "I thought we were somewhere else."

—Ø—

Outside was another world where humans moved like zombies and nobody spoke. The cold hit David hard. He turned up László's collar and sat in the rear of the raft, hunkering behind the mountain of Ultraviolet's back whenever the wind picked up. Five neighbors pulled them forward, their bodies and faces hidden under parkas and ski goggles. David figured, *Here are more superheroes who just haven't figured out their costumes yet.*

Martin wore pajamas when he greeted the Unnamed Supersquadron of Vigilantes at the door, candle in hand, like some eighteenth-century nursery rhyme character. David shook his hand.

"You cut your hair." Martin pointed at David's head. "It's just awful."

Martin looked awful, too. Circles under his eyes and silver hair going everywhere.

"Is your family okay?" David asked.

"Our daughter is sleeping. But my wife's in the bedroom," Martin said, smiling oddly out of one side of his face. "She, um... she thinks you're here to kill her."

"No, tell her not to be afraid! Our fiery Rudolph makes way for a sleigh full of food, fuel—"

"Come in," Martin said. "Tell her yourself." And he walked them up a set of stairs.

The house smelled like shit. Not *gross,* in a general way, but actual feces—human and animal, old and new, a throat-stinging mix of life and decay. Ultraviolet covertly radioed for Golden Echo to load the raft with trash bags and kitty litter so they could dispose of any biohazard inside.

When they reached the upstairs, Martin led them into what might've been a den or office or guest room in its previous life. One wall was covered in books—a library surrounding a dark TV—with a mandala-like rug at the center of the room. David saw the machines before he saw the human. A stack of electronics stood dormant beside an IV stand, twinkling with reflected candlelight from the doorway. When David peeked over Ultraviolet's shoulder, he found a tiny person in an adjustable hospital bed, propped against a dozen pillows. David thought it must've been Martin's daughter, that he'd mixed up their bedrooms. But as the candle shed light on her face, David saw it was indeed an adult woman, emaciated and bald. Her shoulders were sweaty or polished looking. Two painted-on eyebrows added stripes to her gray face. Deep half-moons cradled her eyes. David thought she looked like an alien, some otherworldly being with skinny limbs, and inside him something jumped when he imagined stepping into her extraterrestrial craft, the sort of voluntary abductions southwesterners never fully remember yet can't possibly forget.

"Oh thank god," she rasped. Her voice made David's eye twitch. "I knew you'd come."

"We are here to help, ma'am," offered David. "How are you doing today?"

"My rectum is on fire," she said. "How are you?"

Martin explained his wife had stage four cancer. It started as a tumor in her breast, he said, and then metastasized to her liver and lung. Now, doctors were pretty sure she had throat cancer, too, but they obviously hadn't followed up once the storm started.

"I can get by without most of my parts," she heaved. "But they can't take my voice. I told them let the angels of death come take me! And now"—she smiled, calming—"now you've come."

David began backing out of the room, but Ultraviolet grabbed him by László's lapel.

"Tell Peacemaker and Echo to join us," he instructed. "And tell Dr. Ugs to bring medicine." Ultraviolet asked the sick woman's name—it was Barbara, but she said to call her Barbie—and took a knee at her bedside. After David radioed for reinforcements, Martin pinned him in the doorway.

"She *begs* me." He, too, dug his fingers into the blazer. "Someone else has to do it."

Martin had that same frantic, mortal whisper David remembered from their drive home from the grocery store. David suddenly understood. But he couldn't stomach what the man was asking. He feared what might happen if he refused, and how could he do anything but refuse? The USV was here to help. He was happy to deliver food, sure, but this was a distant moral hinterland David was not prepared to venture into.

"Do you boys have power?" Barbie interrupted Ultraviolet.

"No, ma'am, I think everyone's power is off," Ultraviolet replied.

"When your power goes off, at first it's a relief, isn't it? You don't have to work. Everyone gathers together. You thank god for technology, television, heat, and even when the batteries run out it's not the end of the world. You've got card games, books. You tell ghost stories. When the plumbing goes, though? When you start living in your own filth? That's when it's enough."

David piped up. "We have a real doctor back in the van, actually. Her name's Maria and—"

"No!" Barbie said. "I've taken every medication. And they've taken half my body. Only thing they ever gave me was sixteen weeks to live."

"How long ago was that?" Ultraviolet asked her.

"Two years ago," she coughed out.

"So you're a fighter," Ultraviolet said, nodding. "My brother was, too. After his accident doctors said he wouldn't last the night. But Eddie fought, for four months—"

"Can't fight anymore, honey. But can't do it myself, either. I don't know where I'm going next, but if I kill myself that pretty much clinches that it ain't Heaven. No, I'm ready. I'm scared, but I'm ready."

As Barbie reached out to her husband, Golden Echo, Peacemaker, and Dr. Ugs arrived in the bedroom doorway.

"Smells rough in here," said Dr. Ugs.

Ultraviolet gave him a look. Ugs apologized and handed over a Ziploc baggie.

"We can't offer you an end." Ultraviolet took her bony hand. "But we can offer medicine."

"I told you, honey. I've taken every pain med—"

"It's not for pain. This is plant medicine. Ancient. Very powerful."

David hadn't attempted another Big Bang since Stony Brook. But this was the time.

"You fear the horizontal," Ultraviolet continued. "Life and death along a flat timeline. The Big Bang provides the vertical experience, communicating above and below. With Heaven, I guess, and the opposite. You exist at that intersection of the vertical and horizontal, where there's no time. If you want to swim in that truth, Barbie, we can create the vessel for you."

Barbie giggled. "You cute boys all make me feel so young!" she said. "And so fucking old."

"I am Ultraviolet," said Ultraviolet. "And I will be your shaman—a safety rope tied from this world to the other. And this here? This is the all-seeing Infrared. He will join you on your journey."

Mathias passed a pill to David—no, Infrared—and the other he held to Barbie's lips. He pulled her blanket up around her back, tying it loosely around her neck like a cape.

"Repeat this chant," Ultraviolet whispered. "Kisszapill... Kezapel... Kezapel..."

"It'll come on fast and feel like forever," Infrared said. "But I promise, it will end."

Soon, that synthetic smell of garbage bags. A swarm of tracing paper. A Good Witch with white hair. He recognized he was afraid, that this was what feeling afraid felt like.

He shot into the air, his eyes fixed up in the blue sky, blue like Superman spandex above, wait, so blue, wading down until the sky opens and an army forged in blue light pours down from the heavens hundreds thousands millions billions of bubbles blue like whitewater warriors of light to quench the world beneath red underground coming up to meet blue crashing down till the earth opens and swallows evil into itself and the water spreads like water and everything is okay again.

"Are you afraid?" David heard Mathias whisper.

"No," he heard Barbie say.

"Were you afraid before?"

"Before when?" she said.

"Good," Mathias said. "You're good. You're really, really good."

V.

The ground shed more layers. Soon the muddy field was strewn with bodies. David and Mathias huddled beneath the bleachers of the Pennington High School baseball field while late-arriving SUVs parked and parents rushed their kids to catch the first blast of Pennington's annual New Year's Eve Fireworks Extravaganza. It was a warm evening and the air still smelled like the holidays. A stack of outdoor speakers played James Brown's "Living in America," and middle-aged white people did their best to boogie down. Life was kind of good again.

While the others smoked menthol Kools, Fu twirled a motorcycle helmet around his fist and puffed one of those twig-colored cigarillos, the kind Colombian dictators might smoke while overseeing interrogations. Owen stood guard outside Mathias and David's hideout under the bleachers. Good thing, because every time they showed their faces, they got mobbed.

Ever since their rescue mission, the boys from The Egg were regional superstars. CBS's WNJ24 featured them in a segment called "Superheroes of the Superstorm." The details got distorted, but plenty of neighborhood folks joyously offered televised testimonials on the strange yet brave costumed youngsters who'd arrived at their front door in a snowbound life raft, just in the nick of time. And none was more thankful than the mayor of Pennington, Martin Rosse.

He'd never divulged his job to David, neither in the MaxMobile from the grocery store nor during the ordeal with his wife—and nobody'd cared to ask what the man did for a living—but Mayor Rosse was now forever in spiritual debt to the USV. His brave Barbie passed away two days after Christmas, but hers was a welcome end, peaceful and pure. When David parted ways with Barbie after their DMT trip, she and death were ready for each other.

During the town's year-end parade, David got to drive the convertible while Mathias / Ultraviolet and Mayor Rosse sat on the drop-top, waving. Martin wore his suit and the guys all wore their costumes. It was festive, but there was something bigger afoot than annual community spirit. As a town, they'd *escaped* something, and David's crew had served as shepherds.

The Godfather of Soul faded out and in came the subtle strings of an orchestral prelude.

"Ahh, the *Eroica*!" Mathias said, nodding his head toward the parking lot where the music was coming from. "Tasteful. Refreshing. Goddamn *1812 Overture* has been done to death."

They scanned the ball field. Some folks were passing bottles of wine. Others ate sausages from a grill manned by Pennington Quality Market's butcher. Mathias and David hung back while Dr. Ugs wheeled a cooler around. He was handing out his homemade ayahuasca tea. News of the USV's trip with the mayor's wife had slipped through the grapevine, and David knew at least a dozen moms and dads in the neighborhood now very curious about trying DMT.

During David's last trip and its aftermath with Barbie, the value of the Big Bang had become exceptionally clear to him: a glimpse behind reality offered assurances of something more, something beyond this world. As a result, the idea of death became less final and frightening. This was an important revelation in pre-apocalyptic times, not only for the terminally ill, but for the countless millions scared shitless. You emerged from the Big Bang not feeling abandoned or doomed, but supported by unseen gods. It was a new era. And it belonged to the cooperative evolved who'd rather defer to death than rip each other apart for the last can of SpaghettiOs.

Still, David knew it was crucial not to ascribe too much power to the drug. It was a peek, a jump start, nothing more. If all they wanted was to do psychedelics, they could just do them in dorm rooms like normal college kids. The goal of the USV wasn't some drug-addled counterculture.

Real heroes remain good in the face of catastrophe, David decided. *That's the whole point of everything.*

Twin orange dots popped into the sky, faded, burst. Red tendrils curled down toward them like sea anemones. David found it fascinating to watch this refuse, these ashes, and wondered if this was the reality of the Big Bang: trillions of years ago, all that far-flung carbon was merely a worthless by-product of an infinitely pretty explosion; now, they were all merely star farts.

"The wind's blowing in," David noticed. "Don't they worry about ash falling on the crowd?"

"What's weird is that it looks like the fireworks are only falling toward *us,*" Mathias said. "But in point of fact, those things explode as a *sphere,* in all directions." He let his palms cup an invisible ball and mimed its explosion, whispering, *"XplO!"*

"Then how come it looks like it's headed right toward me?" David asked.

"Because you're a self-centered prick," said Mathias.

Under the bleachers, the slats laid horizontal shadows across Mathias's painted face. When the fireworks popped, muted stripes of color lit up his eyes. David thought this was what jungle soldiers must feel like when the sky is alive with enemy fire—when they look at each other before rushing into battle and wonder if this is the last other person they'll ever see.

"It's going well," David offered, a bit proud of himself.

"You're great at organizing," Mathias mused. "Like the Halloween thing. You were *Batman*."

"Y'know, I always thought there was potential there, too, but—"

"And that was you that got beaten up, too," Mathias said. "By the wrestler."

David was suddenly speechless.

"I remember shooting you."

Wait. What?

His neck got cold. Of course it was Mathias who shot him that night, who saw him. He'd almost forgotten. He tried to talk but could only say, "The man on the roof."

"Lots and lots of shadows," Mathias replied.

"Okay, fine, so what about your shadow then?" David shot back. "Your brother? You told me he died the morning after the tree fell on him, and you told Barbie it was four months later. You keep something locked in that fridge in your bedroom, and I know you worked with the Mott's Funnel guy, I saw pictures online, but you've never once mentioned—"

"That's no secret, dude. I'm legally *not allowed* to talk about Mott until our issues are resolved. He recruited me to Princeton but now he's too concerned with celebrity, and so okay, what else? My brother? Okay, he got paralyzed. I watched him die. I literally walked out of the situation without a scratch. I thought I was invincible. Not like how little kids think they're invincible until they break a leg—I mean I really thought I was invincible for real. I got a little weird so they put me in inpatient, but I could see what was going to happen. I saw time running out. And I set out to prove it. That's chronostrictesis."

"Wait. So. *What?*"

"You want to know what's in the fridge?"

"Jesus, I don't know. Do I?"

"Come, I'll show you. Enough public self-congratulation anyway. It's bad for the ego."

David followed Mathias to the high school parking lot. On his way out, David scanned the field. One by one, David saw people going off like popcorn, those who'd taken the ayahuasca tea. Mothers and teenagers and old people vomiting into pure snow, lying back, finding something holy. They'd be fine. Blinking, David watched the mass baptism, the infinitely pretty explosion.

—Ø—

A long, weird bunch of hours. It was close to midnight when they returned to The Egg. Mathias told David to leave Christopher Walken idling in the driveway, which David found strange. But in the foyer were Mathias's frame backpack and stacked boxes and coolers. Mathias barely entered. He grabbed a large insulated cooler in each hand like dual suitcases. Mathias turned to David and said, "Grab one, will you?"

David grabbed two and followed Mathias to his car.

"What's in those coolers?"

Without turning back, Mathias lifted up the one in his left hand and said, "Blood." He lifted the one in his right hand and said, "Semen."

Was Mathias leaving? For a second, David was scared to death he was leaving forever.

"Where..." he stammered. "Where are you going?"

Mathias arranged boxes inside Walken's trunk, then took his pointer finger and poked it into the space in front of him, connecting invisible dots on an invisible map.

"First, Altoona, to see my lawyer," he said. "Mott is settling. I need to sign papers. Then Atlanta"—his finger curled—"Oglethorpe University. Crypt of civilization. I'll be gone a week, maybe two, if there is such a thing anymore."

He said this like it was normal. David had so many more questions but, closing the trunk, Mathias climbed into Walken and turned on the radio, which was preparing listeners for the New Year's countdown. David chased him to the driver's-side door.

"No, dude, you need to stay. We're in this together."

"We're getting close to the Null Point, David. I can *feel* it. Now, we're ready to *prove* it. Mott will make the announcement and it'll be corroborated and nothing will be the same. Plus, we'll have more money. The settlement is sizable, but I can't talk about it until the *T*s are crossed."

"Let me go with you?" David asked, so pathetically confused.

"You need to be here. I'm leaving you in control."

"What am I in control *of?*"

"You know how to organize. You are... *the Marketer!* That's your superhero name."

"Fuck that. That's a stupid, terrible name."

"Okay, then how about... *Sales*man! Like Bat*man*, Super*man*. Hey, FUFF-*man*!" Mathias was getting excited. "I never caught that before!"

"I am *Infrared,*" David said.

"Okay fine, so you're Infrared. You're still in control. There's always the chosen ones. The survivors. The USV, your thesis, is about gathering them. Saving the chosen. Or put it this way, you're in control of building the ark, and I'll like help you get everyone on board before the flood comes, right? We're mixing metaphors, but whatever, the point is we keep going."

"I don't think I want to be in control of all that." David was trying not to cry.

"Sure you do. But you're *Infrared,* so you want to be in *remote* control. Get it?"

David got it.

"So own it!" Mathias said. "Ultraviolet is supposed to be the mad prophet, so I'll just wear the straitjacket and own all that crazy. You can continue to operationalize what we're doing at The Egg, sharpen it to a point. But we do this together. We evolve or perish together. We both need to *commit* if we're going to sell this USV thing on campus and beyond. I'm the front man. You're my mysterious number two. But you're secretly the puppet master. That's how it's gonna work."

David started to argue, but Mathias was kind of right. David did want to be in control, but behind the scenes. He wanted to exert influence on mankind, but he didn't want all the responsibility, you know? He was ready to chart their course forward and lead everyone to the Promised Land, but he didn't want to be the guy out in front with the staff. Ultimately, he knew it was selfish and sexist, but he still wanted to save the day, the way superheroes do. But saving *the day* is so impersonal.

Saving *the girl*, though?

Superman had Lois. Spider-Man had Mary Jane. Batman had Rachel. Black Panther and Thor and Wonder Woman all had their mortal beloveds. It was an old but true trope. David had been faced before with damsels in distress and failed to save them. The USV was his next best shot.

"Ten... nine... eight..." chanted the radio DJ. David wished Haley were here right now, standing next to him, maybe willing to kiss him as "Auld Lang Syne" played. As he thought this, he realized he was leaning in the car window, awkwardly close to Mathias, and the countdown was hitting its own Null Point. David wondered if Mathias might try to kiss him. And it's not like he'd be *into* that, but they were sharing something special, weren't they? Wasn't this a moment to honor?

"...three... two... one..."

Mathias looked at David, raised his arm, and from below lifted a pistol. He pulled the trigger.

Something bit David's shoulder and he flew back, thinking, *This is it.* But his life did not flash before his eyes. He looked down to find himself covered in neon-yellow paint goo.

"Smile!" Mathias said. "Smile at your collarbone, for it still works and you are still alive!"

As he drove away, Mathias tossed David an orange pill bottle. David watched the brake lights disappear out of Woosamonsa Court and then, unscrewing the pill bottle's cap, David poured its contents into his palm. He found himself holding a pile of shavings.

It was hair. Stubble. Hundreds of millimeters of hair, a mound of short follicles.

They were soft and sharp all at once.

vi.

The first time David failed to save a woman's life was in elementary school. Her name was Claire Shiller and red curls somersaulted off her head onto her neck and shoulders. Their mothers met in a Jazzercise class. Occasionally the kids were brought along and put in a kind of drop-in class at the bowling alley next door. They were shy around each other until, on lane six, Claire approached him as if dealing illicit goods and whispered, "How do you make yourself shrink?"

Ashamed, David admitted he had no such power.

"Yes, you *can* make yourself shrink," Claire insisted. She explained how he shrunk every time they said goodbye and her parents led her away from him. Claire was fascinated by this special property of David's. She didn't want to hear that things simply look smaller when they're farther away, until they disappear at the horizon. She asked whether David could feel it happening, the shrinking, and she vowed right then never to do it, to only grow bigger and bigger and bigger. David never thought to ask her why she believed only *he* had the power to shrink. Even in first grade, you don't question logic when a wonderful girl thinks you're special, too. She asked David what the shrinking felt like, if it felt weird, and he said yes, it felt weird but, you know, no big deal.

Back when Claire Shiller came to play at his house, Dr. Seuss was part of their sweet routine. They'd make a tent together, draping a blanket over the tops of two armchairs and hunkering in the white cave made between them. Their fortress. Inside, he read aloud the tale of Morris McGurk's wild plans made real, reciting *If I Ran the Circus* rhymes while Claire studied illustrations of old Mr. Sneelock's vacant lot evolving into a glorious big top spectacle. Reading was his favorite.

And when David went to play at Claire's house, they did *her* favorite thing. She'd wait until the sun was setting and then take his hand and lead him outside. The flagstones winding through her backyard were still hot from the day, and Claire removed her shoes and stepped onto each flat polygon, showing David how to soak in the delicious heat through the soles of one's feet. He followed, staring at her bare toes, staring at the red curls falling down her back. The stones were cooler by the time he reached them, having given their gifts to Claire. But he didn't mind at all. They'd reach the end of the hardscaping, and then Claire would ease into the soft backyard grass.

"C'mon," she'd say. "We're making tea."

Claire was a sensory being. She craved the fuzzy feel of pajamas and wore them always. Her parents kept a small garden of vegetables and herbs, but she could never make it there directly. Stopping every few feet, she'd crouch down to gather rocks, sticks, and daffodils like wispy babies into the cradle of her pajama shirt. At the yard's lone tree, her fingers picked at the trunk and came away with bugs or hunks of bark, more savory ingredients. David worried he didn't have the same instinct for collecting. He gathered what he could: some grass, some dirt. On a particularly inspired afternoon, he might wade into the pachysandra and grab a pristine leaf to add to her brew.

"Is this one poisonous?" he'd ask her.

"No, that one's good," she confirmed. "It makes you strong. But find more red. Like the berries from last time. Red is really good for your hair and eyes!"

David ran off thinking, *Okay, red, red, red, red*. And the garden! Parsley, bell peppers, red(!) Indian clay from the earth below and fallen seedpods from branches above. They gathered them all. But mainly, David watched Claire. She'd point. Wide-eyed, she'd pick out her favorite finds and tell him why she liked them so much. She smelled positively everything, so he did also. And even then, he thought, *I don't care, Claire, what they think little kids don't understand. I'm so very in love with you.*

When her mother called them back inside, they'd pour their plunder onto the kitchen table and ask, very nicely, if she would cook the tea. Mrs.

Shiller always obliged. She told them to run along upstairs while she prepped and brewed. At nightfall they'd drink. It was delicious. Their palates became increasingly sensitive to the individual ingredients.

"You can really taste the Indian clay," Claire would say, twirling a ringlet of her hair. "See?"

When his mother came to collect David, he'd tell her all about their fun.

"Be careful," she'd say, "you know, some of those plants might be poisonous. Make sure you know what you're drinking."

"No, you don't understand," David told his mother. "Claire knows *everything*."

But then Claire Shiller began to grow.

Not her whole body. Just her skull. It started in the forehead.

During naptime, when the world was horizontal, David asked her the secret of how she made her forehead grow. She told him it was because of someone named Luke Hemia.

David was destroyed. She'd made a vow, promised him and promised herself, that she'd never shrink, only get bigger and bigger and bigger, and now someone else, not David, had unlocked her ability to grow. He'd been replaced. Had Luke forced his huge-brained powers on Claire? And Claire had fresh bruises. Was this Luke a bully?

A distance grew between them. For several weeks David experienced his grief privately, until Claire stopped coming to school altogether, and then he could take no more. During dinner one night he began to cry and his parents asked why and David told them the truth.

Claire had grown and gone away without him.

Mom made a phone call and then sat David down in the living room. His dad paced and picked at his beard. Eileen twisted her long hair into a bun. She pressed her knees up against David's and rubbed her thumb over his eyebrow.

"Claire isn't gone," his mom said. "But she's very sick. She has something called leukemia."

David scrunched his face and shot bull-snorts through his nostrils. He wanted to kill him.

"I know," he said, sulking. "She told me about him."

"No, honey, it's not a *him*. It's a *sickness* that some people get, even children."

"Is it bad?"

"It can be bad. But we hope not," she said. "See, our bodies are made of tiny little cells, and there are good cells who fight the bad cells that make us sick. It's *really* rare, but with leukemia a bad thing happens to the good cells and they get confused and they just keep making more and more of themselves until there's no more room. They don't know how to stop. And they're still good cells, but they just get so crowded and confused that they can't fight off the bad cells anymore. And that's why Claire is feeling sick."

David wanted to help. And he was confused. How could he save a girl whose attacker was invisible, hidden inside her body? How do you fight something so tiny, so huge?

"I think it would help if you went to visit her," his parents said. And the next day they kept him out of school and made the drive to Mercy Medical Center in downtown Baltimore.

The pediatrics ward was another planet where everyone existed in slow motion and the machines all sounded like lonely pianos. The ammonia smell made David's eyes water, and he didn't want it to look like he was crying. He shadowed his mother through the hallways, burying his face in the towering trunk of her thigh whenever it became too much. Adults gathered around children in beds, children whose heads had grown into enormous bald globes and whose faces had lost their color. David figured, *This is where they bring all the children who've figured out how to grow their heads.*

He saw Claire's parents before he saw Claire. When he looked out from behind his mother's leg, David found that Claire had not only figured out how to grow her skull, but the roots and sinews of some living, breathing machine were flourishing from her tiny form. She was bald. It was all gone. Without hair, David thought she looked just like a little baby, like his sister, Beth, when she first came home from the hospital, and inside him something jumped when he imagined he could see Claire like that; like he'd known her since she was born.

But despite Gil and Eileen's assurances, David couldn't shake his guilt.

"Look, Claire. Look who's here!" Claire's mom, who looked really bad, draped a blue blanket over her daughter's bald head. David's father picked him up, and suddenly David was looking down at Claire in her hospital bed. She looked even smaller now.

Maybe she was shrinking, too.

"Hi, David," she said, and smiled the way she used to. "Do you still make the tea?"

"No," he said. Not without her.

"They have me on chemo," she said. "My lymphoids are up."

"You look like a baby," he said.

Her eyes sank away from David, retreating into puddles that shook and spilled down to her mouth. David couldn't understand. What had he said? His parents had warned him to be nice. Claire, in her new body and bare head, had helped him travel back through time, allowed him to see her at her most pure. She was a baby again. A teeny pristine thing full of only good.

In that moment, it was the nicest thing he could think to say.

The parents covered up David's blunder. They tried laughing, diverting her attention back to the lymphoids. Meanwhile, David waited for the world to suspend its animation or cycle back on itself, for Spider-Man to make hair sprout from her head. But that never happened. Time kept moving forward. Claire kept being bald. Before they left the hospital, David asked Dad to pick him up so he could look at Claire again. There was one more thing he needed to tell her.

"I'm sorry I was so bad," he whispered.

He was bad because he could not fight some evil genius or hunt down clues that would save her life. He was bad for being so bad. He was bad because, one night, months ago, he'd forgotten to ask her if his leaves were poisonous, and he'd sat silently by and watched as she drank the fatal tea that was now making her shrink and shrink and shrink back to an invisible beginning.

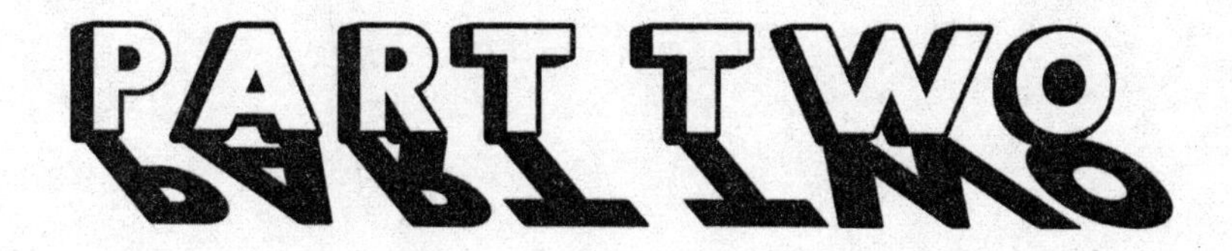
PART TWO

5
JANUARY

i.

Two big things happened in January. First, Pfizer officially unleashed Zeronal on the global marketplace. The commercials were nonstop, and the pill soon became the most successful product launch in pharmaceutical history, reaching the coveted $1 billion "blockbuster" status in only a month. This was no surprise to David or anyone else in The Egg. The general public needed Zeronal to extend their shortening days. And though David understood that enlightenment was not achieved via magic bullets, he also believed zero was a window, a supercharger, pointing at where humanity needed to go. And so was the USV.

The second thing. In January the lawyers representing J. Stuart Mott announced a settlement: his publication in the journal *Science* establishing the now famous notion of chronostrictesis would heretofore be shared with its rightful coauthor, a Princeton undergrad credited as "Ultraviolet," who contributed the kernel of the discovery as well as quantitative data analysis establishing the possible Null Point date of June 6. Ultraviolet released a statement, against his lawyer's advice, that soon took on the dubious gravity associated with all crackpot prophets:

> The gods grow sick of our noise. The Big Bang explodes upon the universe and sweeps us toward the supercell like waves pulled to the moon. The world will spin and shake us off. Rivers will run backward. But for the vigilant, the heroic and evolved, we will pass through the dark neck of time, zero in, and emerge luminous without end.

Eye-rolling ensued. But some saw the recent hurricanes and blizzards as proof of this prophecy, speculating on the coded meaning of "the dark neck." Others went so far as to suggest that this so-called Ultraviolet might be placed in the pantheon of revolutionary theoretical physicists, alongside names like Newton and Einstein. The scientific blogosphere went nuts.

"A supermassive black hole is causing erratic celestial orbits," said the astrophysicists.

"New atmospheric reagents will be formed and their unforeseen molecular-level interactions with mechanical and biological processes will ultimately destroy us," posited the chemical engineers.

"It's all hooey," said the Republicans.

David would have loved to connect with Mathias—to transform his glory into action, strike while the iron was hot—but their leader was still nowhere to be found. He'd be back soon, though.

Any minute now.

—Ø—

Haley sat on the steps of Foulke Hall, off to the side, allowing students to travel past her as they loaded back into their rooms. Fresh from winter break, they carried furnishings and books from the U-Store. They carried cases of AA, AAA, C, and D batteries, cell phone batteries, lithium ion batteries for laptops. You had to have at least a dozen charged backups for when the power went off for days at a time, which just *happened* now.

The sky looked strange to Haley. Uniform cloud cover glowing with backlight. It was a decent day, though, and Princeton had seen fit to move its event outside, to the lawn below that toweringly photogenic Blair Arch. Haley watched as kids stood in lines. Bought merch. Signed their names on clipboards galore at the Activities Fair. No time to lose.

She wished she smoked cigarettes, or felt like looking at her phone, or had something to make her look busy. A pang of self-consciousness ran through her as she glanced at semifamiliar faces passing her for the fifth time, offering closed-lip smiles and half-averted eyes. Haley wondered or worried, or maybe she was just curious, if they knew who she was, if she was recognizable in that way. As her mind closed in on itself, Haley bounded from the stairs and jogged off toward the Activities Fair below Blair Arch, hoping to get lost in a crowd.

Instead, as she browsed the arrays of 2022 calendars and fuzzy black light posters, the throw pillows and leather goods embossed and emblazoned with the orange-and-black Princeton seal, she felt more conspicuous than ever. She hadn't worn the right thing, for starters. Typically, she would've agonized over an outfit, something new she'd copped during break and was ready to debut. Today she was wearing a boxy yellow sweater and sweatpants that weren't the cute kind of sweatpants. She plucked a black hooded sweatshirt off a table and decided it fit.

Haley caught two girls looking at her, pretending to browse the sterling silver mugs. One looked away and the other held her gaze, briefly, and nodded. Haley understood the look to mean something like: *I know what you're going through, because it also happened to me*. Haley wondered if she *really* knew, or if she'd just experienced an unwanted kiss or grope or something brief and disgusting while she was sleeping. *You were not raped the way I was raped*, she caught herself thinking. *Stop trying to combine your story with mine*. And then she immediately hated herself for thinking this.

Because maybe this girl really did know.

Either way, Haley looked away sharply and spotted David and his crew, sans Mathias, standing there under Blair Arch. Haley booked it toward that grand flight of steps leading to David Fuffman, feeling just fine about stealing the sweatshirt.

From his perch overlooking the Princeton campus, David didn't immediately spot Haley Roth. He was considering the mass, not the individuals. He laughed, watching them all scurry. Only a few months ago, this had been him.

In light of new belief systems nurtured by the Big Bang—namely, their impending doom and/or evolution—this hullabaloo seemed so futile. Even China and the escalating hostilities there seemed small and distant in comparison.

They'd agreed none of them would register for classes. What would be the point? They each had their passions and projects. Extraneous busywork would only get in the way, and a degree was meaningless. David tried not to hate his parents and teachers for all those hours he'd spent memorizing SAT flash cards. Months and years wasted, sweating the small stuff. Nevertheless, David had already registered for his religion, entrepreneurship, and environmental studies classes. He didn't see the need to drop them outright like the others had. He could just *not do the work*. And it couldn't hurt to have a fallback in case apocalypse didn't work out.

It was then he spotted Haley, shrouded in a black hood, striding two stairs at a time up to Blair Arch, headed right for him. David stepped away from Lee, Owen, and Fu, asked them to give him a minute. He watched Haley's performance, her leaps feminine and athletic like a figure skater's. When she got to the top, she held her fists in the air.

"Not bad, Rocky," David said.

"Who's Rocky?" she asked. "Just kidding, I've seen it. Seriously, you should see the old-school movie posters down there. They're from another time and place, I swear."

"Do they still sell that John Belushi *Animal House* poster where he's wearing the sweatshirt that just says COLLEGE?"

"Who's John Belushi?" she asked. "Sorry, I'll stop. But yeah, it's like: yup, college in the 2020s is just one long, sweet-ass keg party. With flooding and blizzards."

"I like your new hoodie, that's a nice score," David offered, pointing at the hanging price tag. "I feel like every time I see you, there's commerce involved."

"Bitches be shopping." Haley shrugged, ripping off the tag. "But *this*? A dorm room poster sale? Really? Now?"

They smiled at each other. They'd both graduated to something beyond and recognized each other as Other enough to be familiar.

Haley asked if the trio of guys by the bike rack were indeed the USV she'd costumed.

"Nah," David said. "Just buddies from Forbes."

"Really?" she asked. "That skinny guy is exactly how I pictured Lee."

"Nope." David shook his head, not knowing where to put his hands.

"I saw you all on YouTube, moron," she said, folding her arms. "Introduce me."

"Not yet," he said. "I'll explain later, but it's not a good time. And Mathias isn't here, he's still away, so... it'd be best to wait until he's back and then you can meet the whole crew at once."

"I know Mathias, but whatever, that's fine," she said. She didn't want to give him the satisfaction of seeing she was hurt, so she just cocked an eyebrow, pulled out her phone, and said, "Sorry, I have to take this, it's Jesus Christ." With that, she turned and pattered back down the stairs.

David did feel like a moron. He turned back to his brethren. The sun was setting behind them, and David looked down at their elongated shadows stretching far and thin along the concrete. Owen was making shadow puppets with his hands. Fu was crouching and jumping, his shadow peaking and fading like a stereo's equalizer bar. Lee smoked.

"Who was that?" Lee asked. "That the girl who drew our outfits?"

"Man, I told you, the artwork was by a sophomore dude in my marketing class," David lied.

"Why don't you just introduce us, dude?" asked Fu.

"Okay, whatever," said Owen, changing the subject. "How does it happen?"

David was happy to take his cue. "I say gravity stops working and we all go floating up into the sky like balloons," he said.

Fu: "Gozer the Traveler will come in one of the pre-chosen forms. Like in *Ghostbusters*."

Lee: "What if there's a collective orgasm and everyone on the whole planet cums at the exact same time, and it's so crazy that your brain just fucking melts."

They tried to be light about it, but underneath their cloying, speculative banter was more than blind trust. The future opened and shut during David's Big Bang, the same as it had for them all. The world was going to end, and soon.

David was hoping for a warning sign—a nice, clear buildup to the grand finale—but then again, the idea of it all going down quite suddenly today or tomorrow didn't seem far-fetched at all.

"Mathias says," said Owen, "that time is going to be the first thing to die, but it's the lack of potable water that will kill the most people. That's why he's so into filtration and stuff."

"I wonder if every era believes the end is nigh," David speculated. "Maybe it's intrinsic to being human: fearing our collective destruction and doing whatever it takes to avoid it."

The guys nodded. They were now part of a noble lineage of the scared and ambitious. Their job was to gather other such overachievers. Initiate and protect them. Train them to be good in the face of apocalypse. And maybe, with enough preparation and devotion, the gods might let them be.

Time to buck up, David thought. *There is life to be living, and precious little left.*

Owen craned back his head, squinting at the sun. "Does the sky look weird to any of you?"

ii.

Everyone popped a Zeronal so they could hit the ground running. Their New Year's resolutions—each geared toward their individual thesis and, now, aligning with David's broader plans for the USV—were a point of focus since Mathias had left. When they had a task to accomplish, they aimed to get shit done as quickly as possible so they could get back to The Egg. They alternated as needed, cultivating both the animal and the automaton within themselves.

Sometimes a man needs to be a machine. And sometimes he needs to be a beast.

David chauffeured the MaxMobile, tracing the I-295 corridor beside the Delaware River that separates Pennsylvania from Jersey. They each had a different destination.

Peacemaker/Owen was learning to fight, frequenting a Bordentown krav maga school taught by a former Israeli Defense Forces field officer. This training complemented his cardio regimen at The Egg, which had reached exciting heights. While Owen continued to research solar, he'd jettisoned other power projects—the piezoelectricity, for one, which was just too complicated. He'd instead purchased a stationary exercise bike and hooked it up to a simple generator, a DC/AC inverter, and then their battery bank—he dubbed it the Electrocycle—where a single workout could produce about forty watt-hours, enough to power a phone for a few days. It was meager, and a person could only pedal for so long, but if they were really going to scale the USV and buy more bikes, and if enough human hamsters contributed, Owen said, they'd eventually have enough wattage to power the whole darn Egg.

Dr. Ugs/Lee jumped out of the car in Trenton to meet with paranoid underworldians at a music venue called Conduit. Lee's main contact was a DJ named Derek who also worked at a hospital. Fu somehow decided this dealer was an anesthesiologist and referred to him as "DJ Dirkesthesiologist," which annoyed Lee in all the best ways. Lee was trying to create a new strain of the Big Bang DMT experience—a low-dose alternative that was more manageable and had the mainstream allure of a party drug.

One of his earlier iterations didn't work and instead paralyzed the user for about thirty minutes. He held on to this formula, a potent varietal they called "Liquid Zero," in case they ever needed to incapacitate anyone on purpose.

David then dropped off Golden Echo / Fu in New Brunswick at Ivan's Audio-Visual, where they knew his name. What began as a sensible yellow-and-black North Face parka became bejeweled with six-inch speakers, woofers, tweeters, and artery-like webs of speaker wire. He called it the "RacketJacket." The final touch was a gold motorcycle helmet outfitted with a wireless headset microphone. He bought four more mics and routed them to the jacket, making a mobile amplification system, a super-megaphone—the perfect thing to disseminate the voice of a leader.

If their leader ever returned.

And the RacketJacket worked. Mostly. It was going to work. It was all going to work.

As for Infrared / David, he kept his laptop in the van, using the engine to keep it charged. In the gaps of this meticulously crafted carpool schedule, he'd lean back in the driver's seat and work: Establishing strategic objectives. Identifying target demographics. Figuring out finances. Plotting specific activations to move the needle on all their key performance indicators.

Phase one was to establish the USV brand.

Phase two was about boosting membership.

Phase three was education and training.

Phase four was disaster deployment: mass do-gooding when the shit hits.

And phase five was sustaining this new heaven on earth.

He thus expanded his initial USV outline into a pretty comprehensive business plan for a growing, scalable member-based organization. And since it was so damn good, he decided he'd simply change any names and incriminating details and enter the annual Princeton Entrepreneurs' Network Startup Competition, which had a history of launching major tech startups and other successful ventures David might've applied to if the world wasn't ending. Ted Zhou, the professor of David's Entrepreneurial Leadership class, was judging the PEN competition this year. Last year's winner had landed $5 million in VC funding, he'd heard, so why not submit?

David smacked the laptop screen down reflexively as Fu banged open the MaxMobile door and jumped into the passenger seat. They had an hour to kill before picking up Owen, so Fu asked if they could hit a comics or costume shop. David made one more stop, picking up Mathias's grandfather's axe from a guy he found on Yelp who did side work restoring old weapons—he thought it'd make a nice welcome home gift for when Mathias ever returned. Then they GPS'd a vintage clothing shop called Incogneeto in Somerville, around the corner from a joint called Comic Fortress.

Fu was quiet in the car. Something was up with him, David was sure of it. Fu hadn't quite *found* his persona yet, and while he was fun as hell once you got to know him, he was a shy soul, and the USV's increasing publicity was freaking him out.

"That's where Paul Robeson went to high school," said Fu, pointing to an oppressive Somerville building. "Robeson was a lawyer, a player in the NFL, a Shakespearean actor on Broadway—sang opera in like twenty-five languages—a huge civil rights activist. *That* dude was a superhero."

David loved going places with Fu. He was smart as shit, but not in an annoying way. David assumed he didn't know Paul Robeson trivia off the top of his head, but Fu was the kind of person who'd research the cool stuff about an obscure Jersey town during the ride there, because it was more interesting to know a town's historical context than simply pass through to do some shopping. He wasn't a great student, per se. As the only Korean kid in a white Connecticut suburb, he had a hard time in high school, and the PTSD manifested in his focus on solitary bodybuilding as well as an aversion to classrooms. Before The Egg, he'd skip every class and then, a week before the final exam, he'd drag his textbooks and a sleeping bag to a computer cluster and teach himself the entire semester. And it worked. It was always one detail that made a whole course make sense, he claimed. He loved focusing in on one single circuit, and through this specificity he'd discover an entire system.

When they got to Comic Fortress, Fu browsed quietly at first, flipping through back issues and examining action figures in their plastic packaging.

"Help me understand," said Fu. "Are we joking or like dead serious about this, the USV?" He dusted off a Deadpool action figure, which included lots of guns and knives but also a taco and a bazooka with a boxing glove affixed to the end. "It's like when you're a kid, you want to build a fort and you've got these ideas for how awesome it's going to be, with rocket blasters and a drawbridge and stuff. But it's never that cool in real life. It's like a pile of branches and bungee cords."

David considered this. Fu was right.

"I want to make sure we keep a sense of humor, but... it's true," David admitted out loud for the first time. "We're trying to fight something much bigger than we are. And we're faking it."

"If it's going to be a real fort it should at least be *weird*. It shouldn't look like anything else."

David thought of Mathias by the river, building that hot tub.

"One thing you should know about me," David said, "is that I'm extremely derivative."

"No, you *know* yourself. You're the chief operating officer. Lee makes the drugs—"

"Shh!"

"Owen is like the bodyguard. And Mathias? He's just... the guru. What am I? Nothing!"

Fu turned and left the store quickly. When David caught up with him on the sidewalk, Fu was already engulfed in headphones. His lacquered hair shone in the sun.

"C'mon," David said. "You're amazing with machines and computers, first of all."

"Awesome," he said. "The Asian kid can be tech support for when the power dies."

"Fuck that. You're *the party*, the musical soundtrack and gateway drug for the USV."

"But I'm stockpiling all this A/V equipment that needs *power*. What happens when the grid goes down? I can't just bust out an acoustic guitar. How do I create a soundtrack without instruments or amps? No, I think maybe I'm just a nerd. I'm going to die a nerd. And a virgin."

David sighed, perhaps too audibly. "Me, too."

"You are not a nerd." Fu smiled. "The USV's third commandment, or whatever, right?"

"Debatable that I'm not a nerd," David said. "I am a virgin, though. Part of my shadow."

They both let their truths hang in the air as they turned the corner and entered Incogneeto, which looked like every other Goodwill shop pretending to be a "vintage clothing" store.

"Humans are so dang messy," Fu said. "There's something so beautiful and, I don't know, *poetic* about our messiness, but there's something dark and destructive and just *evil*. That's why I was all about AI. If we could engineer the robotics, and then teach robots to make music and create *beauty*, that would have been creating the next step. Forget the Luminous Ones, or the Terminator shit, we'd just create artful machines and let our souls evolve. That's what I was going to do, that's what Mathias got excited about and why he agreed to fund me. I was the first one to join The Egg. But then, when I saw it all crashing? Once the electricity is gone? That's the end of machine learning, and it haunts me... what I could've done with just another decade or two."

"If you're haunted by one image," David said, "maybe you need to replace it with another."

"What does that mean?"

"You're haunted by what could have been, so replace it with what is."

So they bought Fu vintage clothes with buckles and straps and futuristic flare straight out of *Blade Runner 2049*. They stole Fu's haircut from the Sandman but had the stylist next door at Jade Salon dye it gold, a blond version of the Cure's Robert Smith. When their inhibitions were just low enough, they popped into Artisanal Tattoo and let two smelly Hell's Angels ink zero insignias—Ø—right on the centers of their chests, which was painful as fuck. And then they headed to Delilah's Den, a depressing gentleman's club with no gentlemen, where David paid a pair of brunettes to tattoo a new, enduring image on Fu's sexual psyche.

As they headed west to collect Owen and Lee, Fu smoked a Kool.

"How do I look?" asked the Golden Echo, who was no longer Fu.

And David said, "Loud."

On the drive back to Pennington there was an excited spirit in the car. The others were impressed with Fu's new Golden Echo look.

David was pulling off the turnpike when Lee said, "What about you, Dave? If Golden Echo is the music, what's the point of you?" It hurt, but David tried to take it as a healthy challenge. Lee was helping David figure himself out. Clearing his throat, David answered as confidently as possible.

"I am Infrared," David claimed. "I see through the bullshit and—"

"You should be something else," Lee said. "Something business-y. Like ManagerMan!"

"What about my Mohawk?"

"Then add something Native American," said Lee. "But let's face it, you're just appropriating superficial details. There's nothing authentic. I mean, I guess you could be the Mohawk Manager."

"That's stupid. I'm Infrared."

"You could be the Boy Named Sioux." Fu spelled it, cocked an eyebrow.

"I'm Infrared," David said.

But maybe, after all his talk, he didn't know what he was, either.

When they pulled onto Main Street a familiar pang hit David. Each time they turned onto Woosamonsa Court, he wondered if this would be the moment they found Mathias's car back in the driveway. As they turned into the cul-de-sac and The Egg came into view, the van always went silent. They tried not to crane their necks. They tried not to look crushed when his car wasn't there. They parked and pretended to be as big as their shadows had been at Blair Arch.

Until today, when they found Mathias tending a small fire in the center of the cul-de-sac.

They parked and exchanged greetings, asking all the natural questions about his last few weeks. Mathias never gave any straight answers but seemed incredibly excited to share some news.

"We got you a little welcome home present," David said, presenting Mathias with the rejiggered axe. The original wood handle had been inlaid into a gleaming purple fiberglass handle.

He looked pleased. "I got you guys something as well," Mathias said. He reached into his pockets and then rocketed his arms out straight, fingers pointing to the houses on either side of The Egg. Dangling from each pointer finger was a set of keys.

"We closed on Fred's place this morning. And as of last week we're out of escrow on that lovely pink stucco rancher," Mathias said. "Happy housewarming!"

"Shit, dude," said Lee. "What in god's name are we supposed to do with two more houses?"

Mathias shrugged and said, "Ask David."

iii.

We love to place frames on the world. Frames help us figure out what's important by helping us figure out what to exclude. Frames help us focus.

We create boxes and then check them off, one by one. These boxes, they even help us escape. We love them, until they're taken away.

David shuddered at the thought of the power going again. He closed his eyes and suddenly he wasn't inside the MaxMobile, he was conjuring the illustrations of Haley's debut comic book, *Tales of the USV #1*, printed and delivered, the ink still fresh.

The opening spread: flying through the air, looking down on the Annex of Forbes Hall, four cinder block buildings creating a rectangular frame around a courtyard. It's nighttime, five minutes to midnight. Dorm room window frames pop with the glow from desk lamps and laptop screens. Students stare at their computers, separate and stressed.

It was a Thursday and students were settling in for all-nighters, prepping essays for Friday delivery. David remembered himself in this same state. He remembered comparing lengthy to-do lists with Owen and Bob and Esteban, identifying action items like lunch and sleep as if they weren't obvious.

He almost felt guilty for what the USV was about to do.

Here was David's plan, originally:

First, they'd interrupt business as usual at Forbes Hall. They'd gather the students and give them a glimpse of the future they'd all now seen. They'd launch the USV, as individuals and as a collective. They'd support Ultraviolet and let him lead. They'd begin their recruiting.

And yes, a few dozen students might lose a couple hours of work, but tonight they were providing a vital service, he was sure of it. Between the Halloween failure, the unpredictable weather, and, now, a few publicized run-ins between Princeton students and a cadre of semi-militant religious fundamentalists taken to proselytizing in front of the Wa, the town and school had collaborated on an onerous curfew, announced a week ago via official, student-wide email:

...due to Borough mandates caused by the past semester's binge drinking and resulting hospitalizations, no alcohol, loud music, or unsanctioned gatherings will be permitted in or around campus dormitories after midnight until further notice. Breach of this mandate will result in academic probation for the spring semester...

It blew. And it begged for disruption.

Time to get into character.

David / Infrared sat behind the wheel of the MaxMobile, strategically parked at the courtyard's only means of egress. It was warm, but still he shivered inside László's blazer, adjusting his wireless earpiece and headset mic, an impressive sideways Mohawk glowing red from ear to ear. He checked his watch. The day's final minute was rising toward midnight.

"Clock's ticking," he spoke into the headset. "Get ready."

Squinting through a pair of dark welding goggles—his "infrared specs"—he surveyed the scene: To his left, Owen / Peacemaker was positioned by the Annex's electrical fuse box, which they'd found to be almost stupidly accessible. To his right, Fu / Golden Echo sat on his Vespa, idling in the nearby loading dock. Up in one of the courtyard's oak trees, Lee / Dr. Ugs held the barrel of that giant Super Soaker cannon-gun. Mathias's silhouette was perched on a limb of another tree, straitjacket sleeves dangling between its gnarled branches.

Infrared's watch buzzed. "Cut it," he said, thinking he sounded pretty damn cool.

And Jesus, it actually worked! Lights in all the windows blinked off, leaving the dull blue glow of laptops and tablets switching over to battery. A collective groan-gasm rumbled.

"You're live in five seconds," said Echo into Infrared's earpiece, having patched into the dorm intercom. Infrared cleared his throat and affected his best authoritarian baritone.

"Attention Forbes students," he purred. "This is the Princeton Bureau of Fire Safety and Housing Inspection. After yesterday's weather event we're experiencing power outages campus-wide. Due to a security threat inside Forbes, we do apologize for the inconvenience but ask that all residents evacuate to the Annex Courtyard quickly and quietly."

Like clockwork, Infrared spotted students groping in the dark, droves of them beginning to exit Forbes into the night air. Soon, he was convinced the entire dorm was outside. The phrase "security threat" had considerable power these days.

"Go," he said into his mic. "Lock it down now!"

And that right there was the last moment when things went according to plan.

As the students evacuated Forbes, the exterior doors slammed and locked, trapping them in the courtyard. From above in the tree limbs, Lee planned to spray the Forbes crowd with a fine mist of water from his backpack-mounted cannon: a simulated rainstorm.

They'd set up two large field tents, a makeshift soup kitchen for students to cluster under, avoiding Lee's fake rain. In each tent was a clear cone-bottom tank: the first demonstrated their water filtration rig—layers of pebbles, sand, and charcoal—and the second tank was meant to offer similar hydration, but with small amounts of Zeronal and orally active DMT added, like a spiked punch bowl. Set and setting—the proper intentional frame of mind, as well as the appropriate physical location and companions—were essential to the Big Bang experience, and David didn't want to unleash that kind of thunder on unsuspecting kids. So the vats were clearly marked, and Owen, David, and Mathias had their talking points, meant to educate and excite them on the both practical and pleasurable end-times endeavors.

In truth, the whole night was a mess. The MaxMobile's headlights were to provide light for an impromptu party, with Golden Echo riding circles around the gathered throng, music pouring from his RacketJacket. Instead, Fu's Vespa wheels had skidded in the mud of the quad, throwing him headfirst from the bike. Mercifully, he'd landed in a mound of dirty snow left over from the blizzard, but he got a nasty gash along his calf. Lee, meanwhile, had apparently upped the dose of the spiked batch, and for good measure, he'd apparently also filled his water cannon with the same formula. Once it seeped into everyone's skin, many kids reacted as if they'd received the heroic dose of DMT, and the vast majority spent the evening puking and then paralyzed in what looked like a mass cuddle puddle on the wet lawn of the Forbes courtyard.

David tried to manage the crisis. But Mathias ended up tripping or else completely committed to his character, climbing into a tree beside Lee to orate about how winter break proved a harsh truth: dependence on outmoded systems and institutions, on book learning and liberal arts education, all fails when survival is at stake.

"When the darkness comes and the power leaves, *we* must be the power," he'd screamed. "We're here because someone decided we're gifted, or hardworking, or simply know how to play the game, but none of us is here by grades and test scores alone. Each of us boasts skills outside the ordinary. All your extracurriculars that wooed the admissions officers: someone in this mass knows how to restore engines. One of you is an Olympic biathlete, can traverse blizzard conditions while shooting a rifle. There are at least three beekeepers among us. Soon, we will ask you to tap your unique power and build a powerful persona around it. We, the Unnamed Supersquadron of Vigilantes, have begun the process. Allow me to introduce them now, my USV brothers..."

He named them and their roles: Peacemaker, the Muscle. Golden Echo, the Music. Dr. Ugs, the Mad Scientist. Infrared, the Manager. And he himself, Ultraviolet, was the Mouth.

"Be warned," his voice crescendoed. "This drug acts as a finger pointing to the moon. But *it's not the moon...*" He pointed to the full white orb in the sky and said, "*That's* the fucking moon!"

The oration was solid. But otherwise, the night was disaster. When Lee hosed everyone down, Owen accidentally took a shot in the mouth, leaving him blissfully paralyzed in the back of the MaxMobile, and a bleeding Fu soon joined him. As campus police arrived, the MaxMobile peeled out, headed to Trenton's Capital Health Regional Medical Center. Mathias and David abandoned their vats and scattered in opposite directions, toward backup rendezvous points.

Bolting around a dorm corner, David tried to pull his welding goggles off his head, but the strap got caught in his hair. *Costumes and accessories are a pain in the ass,* he decided. Real superheroes should be unadorned. Less of a hassle. And never, ever a cape. Pure suicide. He matted down his Mohawk, trying to look as unheroic as possible.

Just then, David spotted Haley Roth under a streetlamp a hundred yards ahead. He'd asked her to photograph and video the whole thing with her DSLR, so he knew she couldn't be far from the action. And now here she was, waving a flashlight over her head like an air-traffic controller. *She's offering me a hiding place,* David thought, *beckoning me to follow.* So he did, all the way to Prospect Gardens, the center of campus.

They'd been communicating over email and text, but he hadn't seen her since that day at Blair Arch. He sprinted fast but tried to steady himself and be cool. As he got close, Haley halted. She smiled. Then she roundhouse-kicked him in the gut.

David dropped to her feet.

"Wait!" he gasped, winded. "I'm a good guy!"

"I know," she said. "That's why I brought you here."

He lifted his gaze. Haley was a vision. White jeans tucked into black knee-high boots. Puffy blue jacket rimmed around the hood with white animal fur, mixing with her curly halo of blond hair, unshampooed, wild. It was night, but she had on giant black sunglasses, the lenses twinkling with flashlight flame.

She looked like a goddamn superhero.

"Are you from the future?" David asked, catching his breath.

"No, I'm your fucking conscience. That was terrible. You can't *paralyze* people, David. That liquid stuff is a nightmare. When I illustrated your comic book I didn't think it'd actually work!"

"I swear, that wasn't the plan!" he implored. "Something went wrong. I would never give someone that drug against their will. It's too intense. Lee must've got the formula wrong or—"

In the distance, he spotted the fumbling flashlights of campus police.

"Help me," he said. "Please."

"Promise you won't use Liquid Zero in these spectacles anymore," she said.

"Yes, I promise."

"And you need me. I'll raise your credibility. Otherwise, you're just dorks in costumes, which also need work. Bring me into the tent, David."

David tried his best to regain composure, but her kick was spot-on and his breath was gone.

"I already have my persona worked out," she said. "And I can help you guys with self-defense stuff. Look at you! Besides Peacemaker and Ultraviolet, USV combat skills are piss-poor."

"Fine," he hissed. "Now help me hide."

She turned off her flashlight. "Get on your back," she whispered.

Huh?

There on the cold grass, she climbed onto David(!), shielding him with her soft blue body.

Her elbow found a pressure point in his forearm and she pressed down hard enough for him to feel it in his teeth. In case he didn't understand, she slid her leg between David's thighs.

"Do you want to have kids someday?" she asked.

"Yes!" He beamed. "Definitely. Actually, I'm pretty good with kids and—"

"Then don't try anything stupid." She pressed her knee slowly into his balls. "I don't make out with colleagues."

"Understood," he said. But blood now drained from his face and made its way south. It was a race against the clock.

They lay in silence. David knew this moment would come. Truth was he didn't want Haley to join the USV. He was happy with the status quo. She was his silent collaborator, his illustrator. He was the puppeteer, but she was the woman tugging *his* strings.

"Where's your three-piece suit?" she asked. He'd taken liberties with her costume design.

"I'm Infrared." David pointed to his head. "The goggles? And the hair? See?"

"You should be... Business-Man!" she hissed. "Like Aquaman or Spider-Man."

"I want to be Infrared."

"Bummer," she said. "I'd like you in a three-piece suit. Maybe a pocket watch? Super hot."

He thought for a second and said, "I could be Business-Man."

Flashlights danced on Haley's hood. The campus police crunched through the garden, looking for the ones who'd started the thing at Forbes. But they only found themselves embarrassed by the anonymous couple snogging on the grass, girl on top.

"Whoops," one of them said. "You okay, ma'am?"

"Oh, OMG, uh, just fine, officer!" She lilted it sweetly, adding a little giggle at the end.

"Well... take it indoors, will you?"

And the flashlights jogged off to find the real culprits.

"You saved me," David said. He wanted to bestow on Haley a superhero name. "I think... you are... the White Rabbit. Enticing, enigmatic, always late for an important date. Never enough time."

"Bushy tail," she said, wiggling against him. Oh god.

"Cute whiskers," he said, and he grazed her upper lip with his finger. Like an asshole. She had a hint of a mustache, and David realized from her face that he'd landed on one of her self-conscious sore spots, left over from high school, perhaps. *Stupid.* He stammered, tried to cover: "I just mean... your costume... you could wear whiskers. You could be... the White Rabbit."

And just before she kneed him in the balls and left him writhing in the grass, she lifted her sunglasses, lowered her lips to David's ear, and whispered, "I know who I am, buckaroo."

iv.

When you hear the sordid histories of much-loved rock bands—the kinds with lengthy discographies and stadium-filling world tours—there's inevitably the tale of that lackluster first gig. A paltry, disinterested audience, or maybe the drummer took a thrown Budweiser to the face. The USV's first campus caper would go down in a similar book of history, in a chapter somewhere between "Humble Beginnings" and "Booming Success." But it heralded a coming out. It's the one that started everything. After all, the USV would someday fill stadiums.

The sun was already rising when David and Haley pulled Christopher Walken into the visitors' parking lot of Capital Health Regional Medical Center. David couldn't tell whether his experience of the last bunch of hours—the flying time and pangs of déjà vu—were due to drugs or a new progressive leap of chronostrictesis, or maybe they'd simply driven the same stretch of road back and forth a million times that night.

Haley had played her preordained role of getaway driver, having stashed Christopher Walken at the secluded arts building on the north side of campus. Mathias, riding Fu's Vespa, followed Lee, Owen, and Fu in the MaxMobile at a suitable distance.

It was Haley's idea to stop by The Egg first, to grab fresh clothes and toiletries for the rest of the guys. David was smart enough to know that this wasn't Haley offering a coy excuse to "go home with him." He knew she had some ulterior motive, but he probably didn't realize the extent to which this trip was pure reconnaissance.

Like David's first trip to The Egg, Haley, too, wanted to case the joint.

David found himself happy to oblige. He steered her to Pennington, to Woosamonsa Court, to their space age buckyball domicile. As she pulled into the cul-de-sac and he saw Haley's face light up, David suddenly realized what a chick magnet The Egg might be under different circumstances, for the right kind of chick. They parked and entered. He knew he was probably breaking some kind of bro code, but he took it upon himself to offer her a tour—the open globe of the living room, the reasonably well-appointed kitchen, a genteel wave toward the sunroom in the back, a quick spin through each of the upstairs bedrooms (none of them in an embarrassing state), where they tossed clothes into a duffel bag. The Egg showed well. Especially after she'd kneed him in the crotch and insulted the USV's credibility—the "dorks in costumes" crack—David wanted to prove they were better than that: more sophisticated and serious. He felt their living quarters were reliable yet visionary, safe yet funky as hell.

"How many people did you say live here?"

"Just the five of us you illustrated," David said. "Including me."

"You could fit at least twice that, comfortably," she said, leaning toward the kitchen window, cupping her face against it to view the backyard.

"We own the other two houses on the cul-de-sac," David said. "They're empty. We have plenty of room to spread out."

"Is that lawn as flat and private as it seems?"

"Flatter!" David said, realizing she was getting it, seeing what he saw. "Private-er!"

She smiled warily at him. "You're weird," she said.

Haley was trying to keep a good poker face as she assessed each room, eyes darting to inspect the floorboards and trim, furtively running a fingertip along the speakers to measure dust, playing with paint colors in her mind. They had lots of books, which Haley respected, and zero video game consoles. The level of filth was reasonable for a house of guys, although the couches were a problem. They were mismatched and stained, and she had a visceral fear of old couches, specifically all the disgusting scraps of food and hair and sloughed-off human history hiding in the cracks of their cushions. They'd be the first things she'd replace.

And the lighting. They had all these terrible battery-powered LED touch lights everywhere, with austere blue-white bulbs that hurt her eyes. Candles would be better. Tall ones and votive ones.

She sensed David doing his best to stay professional, acting the part of unemotional real estate broker, in part to make it very clear that she was in no danger of him making an ill-advised move on her, given that they were alone in his house. And she appreciated this kindness. But she could sense his urgency, his need to impress her, so she decided to press her luck.

"And *that* door goes to the basement," said David on his way back to the car, adding, "That's where all the interesting stuff happens."

"Great," Haley shot back. "Show me."

She'd stopped in her tracks by the basement door. She showed no intention of leaving until David showed her. So he did. How could he help himself? Everything was so damn cool.

On the way downstairs he felt his lips loosening, all of his dams busting open. He told her about how they'd carried him—"flown him"—down those stairs on his first tour of The Egg. He showed her their Electrocycle generator and battery bank, their shelving units full of apocalyptic provisions that came in so handy during winter break, offering small asides on how his time there influenced his grand, brilliant vision for founding the USV. Yes, compared with Haley's, David's poker face was for shit, and all the while as he pointed out his bedroom, and Mathias's across the way, and Mathias's mysterious refrigerator, and all the things that had intrigued *him* about The Egg on his first visit, he couldn't hide a smug smirk of knowingness—the grand secret of Lee's laboratory under the stairs—and Haley picked up on it and needed only a minute of pressing—"What else are you hiding in this underground lair?" she asked, looking him in the eyes, knowing him too well—and of course he broke, of course he spun the damn vise and stood there arms crossed as the hydraulics raised the stairwell, unearthing that hidden room, The Egg's soul laid bare.

Of course he showed her. Obviously, right? She was once a drug baron, too.

"Give me the rundown," she said, trying hard not to seem impressed and thrilled.

David walked her through their core arsenal:

- There was their stash of counterfeit Zeronal, gazillions of pills exactly like the Pfizer performance enhancer, totally safe, great for getting shit done. When taken alone.
- There was the Liquid Zero, this paralyzing stuff they'd promised to never use again. Zeronal mixed with low-dose DMT and a muscle relaxer, but clearly they needed to dial back the neuromuscular agents.
- And... there was the Big Bang pill, these red gelcaps that could change everything: Zeronal mixed with heroic-dose DMT—creating an extended trip to hyperspace.

David unscrewed a gold canister, bringing the red pills close as if appraising diamonds.

"You've never done DMT?" he asked, aware he might be mansplaining. She hadn't. He'd assumed Haley had tried it all, and David liked that he had one rarity in his repertoire.

Without asking, she plucked two gelcaps from the dish, pocketed them in her white jeans.

"Hey, seriously, slow your roll," he said, curter than he'd intended. "I'm sorry, it's just... I don't know much and probably don't have the same kind of experience you do, but... this stuff takes you deep. It's not... recreational. I don't think it's strictly *safe*, psychologically speaking."

She nodded silently, as if truly internalizing this information.

"You can hold those, but don't do it alone, don't do it when you're doing *anything* else..."

"I understand," she said.

"No, you don't," he said. "Not yet."

—Ø—

"HOLY NOISE COMPLAINT! COSTUME CRUSADERS PULL OFF PARTY PRANK!"

Hot off the early-morning presses, the USV's first vigilante orchestration on campus had received prominent below-the-fold billing on the front page of the *Daily Princetonian.* According to the article, a group of masked mischief-makers did little more than lock students out from their rooms—causing several to miss assignment deadlines—while disseminating a sleep aid. The phrase "mass drowsiness" was used more than once. It mentioned the vats of filtered and spiked liquid, but there was no mention of Ultraviolet's inspired speech, very little description of individual superhero personas or costumes, and no allusion to the deeper unrest the USV aimed to uncover.

The epilogue to the evening was good news, however. Miraculously, no one had required medical attention for overdoses of the mysterious liquid, and after the guys had slunk away, the students adapted. Once they regained mobility and electricity, they placed speakers in their windows and blasted music into the courtyard. A Forbes party continued for an hour—a small act of defiance—until university proctors shut it down to take statements. One *Princetonian* photo depicted two students, both tongues out, index fingers and pinkies raised in the devil-horn rock salute, their eyes wide as the Nile.

Haley reached into her laptop case and tossed him a copy of her comic book, *Tales of the USV #1*, a propagandized version of how things might've gone down.

"Study what you'd intended it to be," she instructed, and he did, all the way to the hospital.

As he flipped through the comic for like the hundredth time, he marveled at Haley's artwork, which was sketchy yet sure, full of motion. He thought she made them look pretty damn awesome, actually. Her drawings carried a surprising amount of information, but she'd promised to include more detail on the next go-round, if David could give her more time. For this first one, though, he'd felt they needed to move quickly to make sure the publication was ready in time for the morning after. Sure, there'd be discrepancies with the reality of their stunt, but he knew an aspirational piece of press was essential.

As they parked and headed to the hospital entrance, Haley gave counsel.

"Okay," she said, "when you get up there with them, be the first to speak. Don't cast tonight as a failure, talk about it as a successful trial balloon. Be compassionate to the kid who got hurt, but then get out of the room quickly, like you've got somewhere very important to be. Don't be rude, just be serious. And walk quicker. C'mon."

David jogged to catch up with her. The emergency department's automatic doors opened before them. For a second, David imagined she'd magically parted them with her mind.

David spoke as instructed when they got to Fu's sterile room, shared with a curtained-off septuagenarian and his vases of flowers. Doctors had just finished stitching up Fu's calf, leaving a long, scythe-like scar like a smiling purple mouth.

"Fuck that dinky Vespa," Fu said, laughing. "I need a dirt bike, or something that can handle mud. Kawasakis! Maicos! Pursangs! Swedish Fireballs!"

Lee and Owen were huddled in the corner, munching dry cereal from the hospital cafeteria. Owen read the *Daily Princetonian* aloud, while the others pored over the comic. Mathias was apparently downstairs in a waiting room, being lookout.

Keeping his spiel short and constructive, David finished by introducing Haley Roth. They all knew who she was. Owen looked especially conflicted, realizing she was the one who got Bob expelled, but he stayed silent. They also all knew full well that she was the illustrator behind the comic book. Lee took the opportunity to be a dick.

"You guys boyfriend and girlfriend now?" he asked, giggling to himself.

"We're colleagues," David shot back. "She's our marketing and communications specialist."

"I'm also the motherfucker that's going to make sure you never paralyze anyone ever again," she said, shaking his hand. "Pleased to meet you."

Lee glanced at Owen.

"Yeah, uh, Mathias already scolded me," said Lee. "Completely unacceptable, but honestly it was just a mix-up—I accidentally pulled from the spiked—"

"What's done is done," said Haley. "Just don't do it again. It's illegal. We have to be smarter than this going forward. Now, if you'll excuse us."

She motioned for David to exit. So David did.

—Ø—

It was seven something o'clock when David and Haley found Mathias. He was still in the hospital waiting room, still awake, still partially in costume, still rereading Haley's comic, and he'd tried to wash the purple paint from his face and body but streaks of violet were still caked around his ears and nostrils. David, too, realized he was looking filthy and still had a tremendous amount of hair gel in his mussed red Mohawk and neck-beard.

They sat down beside him, David putting himself between Haley and Mathias. He looked around the waiting room at all the normal folks skimming their *Consumer Reports* while he and Mathias hunkered behind dual copies of the same comic book, its cover plastered with cartoony action figures bearing striking resemblances to the half-cracked college freaks sitting just behind them. They must have been a sight.

Mathias flipped to the last page. He closed the comic and laid it atop a *Family Circle*.

"Didn't exactly go as you planned, huh?" Mathias said, staring down an old man on the other side of the waiting room.

"Minor casualties," David said. "The goal was student engagement. That goal was realized."

"No one died, I hope."

"So I'm Haley," said Haley, leaning over David to eyeball Mathias. "Do you remember me?"

"Of course," he said, bowing slightly. "The killer roundhouse. How've you been feeling?"

"I thought *you* did quite well last night," she said. "Oratorically speaking."

He opened a *Newsweek* and pretended to read. Didn't even shrug off her compliment.

"I showed her The Egg," David admitted. "All of it."

"And?" Mathias said, clearly pissed at this breach of protocol.

"And I'd like you both to explain the Big Bang to me, to the extent possible," she said, eyes front, now staring down the same old man.

"Dimethyltryptamine is a Schedule I narcotic," Mathias explained, putting down the *Newsweek*. "But it's also made in the human brain. Like melatonin, serotonin. It's released during birth, death, near death... even sex." He somehow resisted the urge to make this sound creepy or flirty, which only made him more suave and irresistible.

"It's the most powerful psychedelic in the world, but very short acting," David added, trying not so subtly to insert himself. "So we use the Zeronal to prolong the feel. That's the Big Bang."

"I'm no stranger to hallucinogens," she said. "How is this different?"

Mathias held out a hand toward David, inviting him to comment. For his part, David hadn't been able to stop thinking about his first experience in the Institute Woods. The memory swam in his mental soup, slippery, barely visible, covered with glutinous ooze. He recalled imagery and the overarching message, but he still couldn't parse what parts were true revelation vs. just drugs.

"To be fair," David began, "my experience was probably unusual. I got dosed without knowing what I was getting into, so the set and setting could've been better."

"So you dosed a complete stranger with something that simulates a near-death experience?" she asked Mathias. "Did you dose everyone in the courtyard on purpose tonight, too?"

"What stranger? David's famous! He stayed awake for a hundred hours touching that Hyundai!"

"And without his consent?" she continued, now visibly perturbed.

"I instructed Lee to add trace amounts of DMT to the water cannon, but clearly we overdid it. In the dusty days of America, Indians used to do a litmus test with Caucasian traders: they'd pump the white man full of peyote, and if he eased himself into the trip with dignity, they'd do business. If not, they'd take his scalp. When I dosed David, he stayed calm; he was totally safe."

"I don't remember *calm*," David said. "I remember *crazy*. Though I don't remember much."

"What *do* you remember?" she asked, temporarily moving past the triggering details.

David took a breath. "The first thing was my grandfather. His disembodied head. Like Marlon Brando as Jor-El in *Superman Returns*. He got really smug about how *he* used to make jet engines for GE and was like, 'So what do *you* make?' He said I was like the sawdust they sprinkle on factory floors to soak up moisture. That I don't *produce* anything, I just sit there and absorb runoff."

"Ouch," said Haley.

"*Then* things got weird," David said. He closed his eyes. He started to relay his memory of flying up that tube, the DNA double helix, but when he got to the far-off star and the self-dribbling basketball elf thingies with Halloween masks, Mathias stopped him.

"At this point, David's going to start sounding insane," he said to Haley. "But that's good, you saw the Masks, good," Mathias said. "Excellent. What else? We never fully processed."

"There was an explosion, and then this giant red ball of fire, I think. Or a massive heart?"

Mathias said, "That's the red-blue core of meaning, basically."

David laughed at his use of the word "basically."

"I'm sorry"—Mathias laughed, too—"it's just... hyperspace is a huge room with a million doors. We've all seen the same room, but from the POV of a different doorway."

"And, yeah, but, do you know what was happening inside the room?" David asked.

"Do *you* want to say it?"

David didn't even want to *think* it. But he couldn't think of anything else. His voice got tight.

"I feel like it's the End," David said. "I saw the chain of events. The Earth spins. The ice melts. Floods. Then the power fails and order breaks down and... and there's only one natural end."

"Or there's two."

"I see one: we all die."

"Or two: *some* of us die. Others evolve and survive."

They were all quiet for a moment. David figured Haley would be out the door, but her attention was rapt. He worried she was idealizing something she didn't understand.

"Normally, I'd probably just let you see for yourself, unprompted," David said to Haley. "But... I feel I need to warn you: it's not fun and games in there. There are dark, nefarious entities."

"Demons, basically," Mathias confirmed.

"Is that what was coming out of my body in the river?" David asked him.

"Shit, did you *become* the Null Point? That doesn't happen to many people, dude."

"I was a flat portal, they were shooting out of me, flying into the sky like I was their factory. They were dueling this other force coming from the sky. I don't know if they were good or evil."

"So, okay," Mathias said, forgetting Haley and just speaking to David. "Go back to your grandfather/Marlon Brando head thing, asking what you make. Now I'll ask, *what do you produce*?"

"I'm still not sure," David admitted. But he had an idea.

"But you have an idea," Mathias confirmed. "What *could* you make?"

David shrugged. "The evolved ones," he said. "Spiritual warriors."

Mathias smiled.

"How long does it last?" asked Haley, after a reasonable amount of time.

"Only five minutes or so," David said. "But it feels like longer."

"I can do five minutes," she said, more to herself.

"Okay, that's enough," Mathias said to Haley. "If you want to do it, we'll just do it. We'll establish a safe space at The Egg, ensure your mind is clear of obligations, doubt, regret—"

"Now," she said. "Let's do it now. Here. Somewhere in this hospital. A public space will make me feel safer than a private one, I'm sure of that. And..." She dug in her pocket and pulled out a pill she'd pilfered from The Egg. "We've got what we need. You'll talk me through it."

Mathias scrunched his face. David tried to echo the silent sentiment, shaking his head no.

"Forgive me, Haley, if this is insensitive," Mathias said. "But I'll just say it: Doesn't the idea of taking an unknown, *incapacitating* psychedelic with two strange men make you feel somewhat..."

"Terrified?!" she yelled. Then looking around, much quieter: "Yes, obviously. Since Halloween, I know all the best spots on campus to secretly cry. I used to draw *every single day*, since I was eleven, and the only work I've done since Halloween is this silly comic book. I'm in therapy, and I need more, but I had a good experience with EMDR—eye movement desensitization and reprocessing—and—"

"Maybe contact your therapist then first?" offered David.

"We both know what she'll say," Haley said. "This is *my* call, not anyone else's. *I'm* in control of this decision. *I'm* not going to leave campus or let that evil shithead and all the other shitheads win. *He* gets to leave and be scared for the rest of his life. Not me." Her voice began to crack but she breathed through it. "So I'm building my mask, right? My superhero mask, day by day, and part of that is maybe going toe to toe with your nefarious mind demons in a way that'll make my *human* demons seem less scary. And part of it is allying myself with people I feel like I can trust. Call me crazy: I think I can trust you two."

"Why?" asked Mathias. "I mean, thanks, but why?"

"Truth? *This* guy"—pointing at David—"was hooking up with me back in high school and I was on painkillers and felt myself passing out, and you know what he did?"

Oh god, David thought.

"He fucking *stopped.* Okay? He stopped and he even put my goddamn clothes back on me. He thinks I don't remember that, but I do. And it means he's not a complete and total disaster of a person. So I'm experimenting with saying this out loud: I trust you, David."

David stared at the diamond-patterned carpet—his way of accepting this compliment.

"And you?" she whispered, looking to Mathias. "I'm not totally kosher with you just yet. But you did me a solid in identifying my attacker, and there's something spiritually interesting about you and you've got a sweet fucking house, and besides"—she pointed back to David—"*this* numbnuts told me to film your little Forbes spectacle. Which I did. And it was probably really illegal in a dozen ways, so as an insurance policy I've loaded the footage on to Facebook, tagged you both, added the address of The Egg, and scheduled it to post about four hours from now. So! We're going to find a nice, safe space in this hospital, shoot me into hyperspace, and you guys are going to take extra great care of me so that I can be sure to cancel that post before it goes live and you all go to prison."

She took a deep, powerful inhale.

"I really, really like her," said Mathias to David.

He bolted from the waiting room chair, and before David could argue he was following Haley and Mathias down the bright white corridors of Capital Health. Mathias tugged a few locked doors, with signs that read ELECTRICAL ROOM, JANITOR, 00237, but nothing opened and also nothing felt right. Some of the rooms were unlocked and empty, but they felt too risky. Someone would surely come in right at the height of things. It was clear, they needed better access.

"Idea!" said David. He grabbed an abandoned wheelchair near an elevator bank.

"Idea!" said Haley. She sat down in it and stuffed her duffel bag under her shirt, forming it into a false pregnant belly-mound. "Nobody fucks with a pregnant woman," she said.

They wheeled Haley around the floor, every turn around every corner pushing deeper into a maze of sterile linoleum. And then they turned one corner and Mathias stopped. He was staring at a directory, a way-finding list of departments and divisions. His finger shot to one particular line that read: AQUATIC THERAPY & REHABILITATION BIONICS: FLOOR BB.

Getting access to the subbasement was easier than expected. After wheeling Haley into a crowded elevator, they simply asked a nurse standing next to the buttons, "Can you hit BB, please?" She didn't even glance at them. Just swiped her card across the scanner and hit BB.

"B-B," mouthed Haley. "Big. Bang."

Together, they reached the hospital's subbasement. They navigated down a quiet hallway to the aquatic therapy door, which was unlocked and open. Inside, a still swimming pool, maybe twenty feet wide by forty feet long. Aside from the therapeutic chair lift at one end, probably meant for lowering paraplegics and other disabled folks into the water, the pool reminded David of a Holiday Inn. Basic, with that ubiquitous over-chlorinated waft. The deck sported a trio of brown benches and artificial potted palms. A single blue-and-white racing rope traversed the length of the pool on one side, and on the other sat a staircase with metal handrails, providing entry into the shallow end. The entirety of the pool was marked as only four feet deep.

"Does water help?" Haley asked, rising from her wheelchair and shedding the duffel bag from beneath her black long-sleeved T-shirt.

"I've always felt buoyancy as a positive," said Mathias. "But I'm kinda Neptune-y like that."

She removed her puffy blue jacket and began pulling off her boots but announced, "I'm not taking my clothes off, obviously." She pulled off her socks and wiggled her toes.

"Obviously," Mathias answered. "But do I have your permission to get in the water with you? I'm going to suggest that I join you on your journey, for various reasons, not least of all so that you're totally clear that I wouldn't give you a drug I wouldn't take myself. We'll be on equal planes."

She cleared this internally and nodded. "Makes sense."

"And we should say again: this is just a stepping-stone, a means to an end. This isn't the whole point of the USV, just to do drugs or—"

"I get it," Haley said. "Let's just see how she flies."

Mathias kicked off his shoes and pulled out his cell phone, keys, wallet. "Do you like music?" he asked.

"That's a stupid question," she said.

"This is one of ours," Mathias said. "Golden Echo's music, made with neural synthesizers that use machine learning to combine sounds from different—"

"Whatever, is it chill?"

"It's chill."

He pressed Play. Quiet, clean bass faded up from his tinny iPhone speaker, followed by the subtle wash of cymbals. Mathias grabbed three folded white towels off a stack by the chaise longue and carried these down the stairs as subtle whirlpools of purple paint curled off his body onto the skin of the water. "It's quite warm," he said, and motioned for David to get in also. So David did.

"This is Infrared," said Mathias.

"Business-Man," David corrected. Haley smiled. "That's my name. From now on."

Mathias shrugged. "Okay then, this is *Business*-Man, and he will be our shaman—a rope tied from this world to the other. In other words, he'll be sober and will protect us both. Won't he?"

Mathias tied one of the towels around David's neck like a cape.

"I am Ultraviolet." Mathias smiled. "And though I will be equally shitrocked in about sixty seconds, I, too, will do my best to keep you safe." He tied a towel around his own neck.

Haley shook out her hands, like an Olympic diver stepping to the edge of a platform, and glided down the submerged stairs, gingerly tracing the railing with a single finger. As her white jeans hit the water, she looked down to make sure they weren't turning translucent (they weren't). She took one more step, then jumped back with a start, as if some snake had just swam by. She shook her head in disbelief and laughed, then shoved a hand in her pocket to pull out the two pills. She'd been one step away from submerging her waist, dunking the pills, and ruining the whole thing.

"That would've been a massive buzzkill," she said, and held the pills aloft as she waded over to Mathias and David. She looked David in the eyes and smiled nervously. He tried not to think about how amazing she was. He tried to stay stoic and professional and mentally monastic —aware of the weight of the moment and the asexuality he was to be maintaining.

But she was just so lovely.

Mathias tied a towel cape around her neck. She passed him a gelcap and the other she held to her lips. "We'll figure out your superhero name soon enough," he said. "But here's your cape."

"Repeat this chant," David whispered. "Kisszapill... Kezapel... Kezapel..."

They synced their chant to Fu's music, some kind of digital snare-flute going *rat-a-tat*.

Ke-za-pel. Ke-za-pel.

Mathias smiled at Haley, her face awkward with self-consciousness, but dropping into the music nonetheless. He said, "You're safe with us. You'll stay safe. Swear on my brother's grave."

Before she could blink, Mathias opened his mouth and pointed under his tongue. He tilted his head back, cracked open the gelcap, and poured the contents into that pool of membrane.

"It'll come on fast and feel like forever," he said, swirling it. "But I promise, it will end."

She followed. Her eyes went wide. Either the trip had already begun, or it was fear.

"Are you afraid?" David whispered.

"No," Haley said. "I don't think so."

"Were you afraid before?"

"Before when?"

"Good."

And it was good. Or he hoped it was good. He assumed it would be good. He assumed the scent of chlorine was being overtaken by that synthetic smell of garbage bags. That crinkling sound of them breaking through the membrane. But he had no way of knowing where they were or how it was, whether Haley was experiencing that sensation he'd felt that first time: of being saturated and charged and filled by Mathias. They were gone elsewhere together now, and it was just David, a sober fetter bobbing beside them in the water, making sure they kept afloat as together they plunged down deeper and deeper and deeper into this secret well. He tried to focus on Echo's music...

David listened to a whistle, the loneliest and loveliest human instrument. It joined that bass drone and the snare grew. He closed his eyes, tried to zero in.

—Ø—

Bleep. Bleep. Bleep. Blink.

And there's the sound of a lonely piano.

That's the feeling of clean sheets.

Wow.

David remembered his last time in a hospital, back in the fall semester toward the end of his post-Halloween breakdown, just before Thanksgiving break. He'd popped up from a dreamless sleep and immediately decided it was time to go. There was no need to call anyone.

Escaping from University Medical Center was easier than you'd think, David recalled. Just keep walking calmly and don't make eye contact. In no time, you're wandering down Witherspoon Street, past the ordered rows of bodies at Princeton Cemetery, toward the familiar yuppie bustle of Nassau Street, back to school.

He'd tried to piece back the puzzle of what had happened the day he got officially kicked out of Forbes housing. Tried to focus. Yes, he remembered now: DO NOT DRINK ALCOHOL WHILE TAKING THIS MEDICATION. He'd taken Owen's Zeronal, then gone to Haley's room to offer some pathetic apology, and then he'd sprinted across campus and ended up projectile vomiting and passing out near the pond of the Institute for Advanced Study. Some Good Samaritan must've called the police or ambulance to come collect this idiot freshman before he got frostbite. Thank god.

One thing was clear, he'd stop drinking. There was no magic left for him to discover in beer or bourbon. It was his kryptonite. Zeronal and DMT, that's where it was at. Without booze, he could fly. David had escaped from University Medical Center and arrived back at Forbes with a new sense of purpose, a lightness and freedom that came with making one of those adult decisions to put away childish things. He felt ecstatic.

When David reached his dorm room doorway, two cops—not the beige campus security guards but actual midnight-blue police—were sifting through the wreckage. Esteban was there, pointing like some museum docent.

David's room was a shitshow.

The first thing he noticed was the smell. He'd been living in his own stink since Owen vacated, and furniture sat diagonally in the center of the room. A few hundred books were collapsed on the floor, and the phrase BOOGER CATAPULT was scrawled on the wall in tomato ketchup.

The cops looked kind of amused.

"We thought someone was dead in here," said Esteban.

"Son, you can't just up and walk out of a hospital," said the larger cop.

"I didn't!" David implored.

The cop wiggled a finger at David. "You've got a bunch of those suction cup sensors still attached to your chest. The wires are hanging out the bottom of your shirt."

How embarrassing. The cops put their hands on David's arms, told him it was time to go.

Up till then, he'd never had what people refer to as an out-of-body experience. They seemed to occur only in hospital birthing rooms, sports arenas, churches, DMT rituals.

David's happened in a dormitory hallway. While he was sober.

Like a cell at the moment of conception, David's body split in two. While David kept walking down that hallway with the policemen, one foot in front of the other, another David stayed just outside his dorm room door, pinned to the spot, watching his twin drift into the distance. Flanked by cops, the back of his brother danced. Neck fuzz. Broad shoulders. Skinny waist. Calves.

He heard the whisper of a countdown.

Ten.

Part of him tracked down the hallway, past the open doors of his hall mates, their heads and shoulders leaning out into the corridor and forming for David a soft gauntlet of sorrowful eyes.

Nine.

Some reached out to give his shoulder a loving squeeze. Some recoiled into their rooms.

Eight.

Goodbye, construction-paper names I will never remember.

Seven.

Goodbye, Whitney Garfunkle. I will forever fear the wrath of your nonconsensual skateboard.

Six.

Goodbye, Esteban. You are prelaw. You are Dominican. You are a good man.

Five.

As David reached the bank of elevators and turned around for a last farewell, it was not the audience of students that caught his eye, but the boy at the end of the hallway, waving.

Four.

Look at you. So fragile down there in the distance. Shrink any smaller, and you'll vanish to nothing.

Three.

Goodbye, dignity. This is what failing at adulthood feels like.

Two.

They entered the elevator and a finger pressed L«. Once more, the gun-metal doors blurred his reflection. Staring back was a brilliant swatch of white between two bigger blobs of blue. It was David between two cops, but to him it looked like something with wings.

One.

They elevated down.

Zero.

—Ø—

Blink. David snapped back to the hospital pool, a quick splash startling him, as if waking from dream-falling. Fu's whistle traveled all over, with banjo-ish computer bleeps plucking the background. Against this melody, a series of oscillating drones rose and fell. David didn't know Fu could whistle like that or play the banjo—had never seen a banjo in his room and assumed he'd simply built these layers, recording himself wherever certain instruments lived, adding synthesizers and 808 drum machines and however it all worked. That sense of nostalgia that comes with good music, it came over David—the feeling reminding him of the best and worst high school nights, or maybe it was nostalgia that stretched back to the womb or to time immemorial—he grew sad and happy thinking of Fu alone with computers, a one-man band, rolling solo.

Fu was incredibly talented. They all were. He needed a band; he deserved one. David sunk into Echo's layers, a lush harmony now forming from three or five voices stacked atop one another. He imagined Fu making this track, starting so stark but feeling the song slowly grow around him like friends entering the room one by one, falling into conversation. Horns now. Or maybe that was a falsetto tweaked through some crazy processor. David listened to the bell curve volume, the gentle lapping of water on the plastic tub of the pool filter, almost rhythmic but not quite, but wouldn't it be amazing if the pool around them actually fell into time, too?

His thoughts turned to his studies, to remembrances from religion classes of his first semester. He made an inward list of gods and prophets transformed by water: Krishna was baptized in the Ganges. Some say Horus, too. Jesus was baptized by John in the Jordan. Zoroaster also was baptized, while prepping a psychedelic plant for ritual. There was Moses in the reeds, a different kind of thing. And even Superman, who never went into water per se, but that vast gulf of space his parents sent him into as Krypton exploded? Think about it, he's basically Moses.

Thoreau had Walden Pond. He moved there because he "wished to live deliberately, to front only the essential facts of life." These were sweet intentions. David would love to claim them for himself and say that he moved to The Egg to dive deeper into the dark pond of his Self, to join a powder keg of revolution, to follow a leader whose shadow would soon follow him forever.

But in truth, David's motivations were much less lofty. He'd simply needed a place to live.

Haley's reasoning, David realized, was more profound. She was processing a horror he couldn't imagine. So this was either the worst idea possible or the best. The Big Bang might push her deeper into trauma—a dysfunctional reaction by a girl living through a broken time of life—or...

Or it might bring meaning to that brokenness. Paint a path out of that hole. David knew it could really go either way. Haley understood this, he figured, and she was a gambler, banking on the upside rather than worrying about the risk. He had to respect that.

Yes, this was *her* decision. And she trusted him.

So it was now his job to protect her. To deserve her trust. To earn some heroism.

But there in the water, he felt Haley and Mathias floating away from him, farther and farther.

He would stay put. Rolling solo. But maybe not anymore.

They would come back soon. Any minute now.

FEBRUARY

i.

How the Unnamed Supersquadron of Vigilantes drove a critical mass to collect and launch the ballast of their lives into the flames, Business-Man couldn't be certain. He was late. And by the time he arrived at the lawn of Nassau Hall, toting garbage bags full of masks and capes, a swarm was already bounding from the dorms, carrying boxes of belongings as if the campus were under attack and an evacuation was under way.

A week earlier, an earthquake had hit St. Louis. Lakes sank into underground sinkholes. The Mississippi River reversed its course, just as Ultraviolet predicted.

Business-Man could feel the heat from a quarter mile away. The USV had taken charge of the annual spring homecoming bonfire, and its leader was sending Princeton's student body to gather obsolete and unworthy objects, return them to the bonfire, and convert them to ash once and for all. At least a thousand were present. No, two thousand! Looking at the eyes of those gathered, Business-Man saw students already under the influence of the USV's drug. David had resolved, with Dr. Ugs, to stay sober and shepherd the situation.

A husky dude carrying a cardboard box sliced a path into the onlookers and Business-Man followed, using him as a blocker, making his way to the epicenter. When they reached the innermost ring, the behemoth in front of him began pulling trophies and medals from his box. He unceremoniously underhanded each one into the fire. To Business-Man's left, a girl destroyed a scrapbook filled with report cards, certificates, and acceptance letters that bore her name and proved its worth. Others had come straight from Princeton's homecoming basketball game, and David saw spirited arena garb—Princeton sweatshirts and foam fingers—thrown into the fire, along with other school-specific kindling. Business-Man marveled as the fire grew, fifteen feet high at least, and was relieved to find a fire truck parked at the edge of the lawn.

Who was directing this show? Scanning, Business-Man found Dr. Ugs with his long black lab coat and exterminator-like cannon; Golden Echo was perched atop a metal awning, pumping lively tunes from his Racket-Jacket (it was finally working!); and dancing on the limb of an oak tree was Ultraviolet with his purple skin and undone straitjacket, bathed in a fierce firelight, swooping his arms like an orchestra conductor, elephant-trunk sleeves fanning the flames.

"Look up there!" spat some freshman, and Business-Man assumed he was referring to Ultraviolet on high but instead found him pointing toward a banner-like message projected onto the exterior brick of Nassau Hall. It read: RELINQUISH YOUR PAST. DIVORCE YOUR FUTURE. ZERO IN. Over this message ran a slideshow of images, including the kinds of personal memorabilia—trophies and SAT scores and such—now being bequeathed to Hephaestus. Business-Man smiled. He'd created this PowerPoint. He was the ringleader of this foolishness. This was all part of his plan.

And it was only wave one.

Next in the projected slideshow came a pictorial series of pills, powders, liquors, cigarettes, stalks of cannabis, et cetera, alongside the motto: CURE THE CURES THAT AIL YOU. A new wave of students soon threw in prescription bottles, their tops coming loose and spurting pills like New Year's confetti. Bottles of booze were tossed into the fire, cocktails suddenly made Molotov. Even bags of coffee grounds, the roasted aroma mixing heartily with the skunk stench of someone's weed, lofted in amid moans of disappointment. Business-Man traipsed a slow lap along the inner ring of gatherers. He had to stay vigilant against souls in the throes of catharsis, chucking larger and sharper possessions into the hub of this emblazoned wheel.

Business-Man grabbed Dr. Ugs for a quick aside. "Everything cool?" he asked.

"Ready and waiting," Ugs replied. As plastic and metal melted, the air took on a chemical potpourri. It made Business-Man light-headed, loopy. He reached into his garbage bag, put on a gray mask.

"Does that mask block these fumes?" asked Dr. Ugs.

"Who?" Business-Man giggled. Yes, he was definitely feeling it now.

"Fuck, never mind." He began backing away from the bonfire and Business-Man joined him.

And now another wave was cresting. Another series in the slideshow. This one called for a ban on technology: UNPLUG! WE HAVE BECOME THE MACHINES OF OUR MACHINES. Laptops, printers, tablets, cell phones, even the hot plates and electric kettles of modern-day dorm living—soon these, too, were gathered and added to the harvest. Peacemaker arrived in a golf cart and unloaded ROTC uniforms, rifles, combat boots, and other military implements into the flames. Business-Man wondered why the firemen weren't stopping this spectacle. Maybe they were high, too?

"What a fucking waste," said Dr. Ugs, still standing by Business-Man's side.

But next came a new equalizer. The projection flashed dollar signs, piles of greenbacks, fanned-out credit cards, with the slogan: YOU'VE GOT MONEY TO BURN. By this point, the students could be compelled to raze just about anything. And with modern electronic finances, Business-Man knew that any major financial strokes could be undone with a call to the credit card company the next day. Symbolic sacrifice was made nonetheless. A collective fumbling for wallets ensued.

Perhaps a shift of wind occurred then, because suddenly Business-Man found the smoke billowing around him, choking his throat. Dr. Ugs covered his face and sprinted away, every man for himself. Hacking, Business-Man wormed his way out into the fresher air of the circle's circumference. He regained his sight and breath. But his attention was grabbed back as the once thunderous crowd now simmered down to a murmur. Something was up.

The wall of Nassau Hall went blank. Everyone in the USV went still, even Ultraviolet.

Business-Man knew this was the cue.

He froze stiff.

Took a deep breath.

When the projector light popped back on, it was now a spotlight aimed up toward the zenith of Nassau Hall, and in this spotlight stood a singular figure, balanced on the roof's peak, decked in the unmistakable attire of a USV superhero.

Dark pirate boots. Formfitting white leggings. A royal-blue captain's jacket, its high collar embroidered with yellow trim and long tuxedo tails. On top, a wide blue Napoleon-style hat with the USV's trademark Ø insignia at its center. Her long hair was dyed white. It crisscrossed along her upper lip, hanging down off her face like a handlebar mustache.

Beneath her, projected on the peak of the wall, was her name.

And the crowd went silent. The name needed no elucidation.

CAP'N CUNT.

David saw her breathing up there, poised on the brink of that building. Flames danced shadows on her body. She held a plastic scabbard in one hand, pointed to the heavens as if preparing to give a signal to charge; in the other hand, an oversized Flavor Flav clock. Amid the silence and the crackling of the fire, Cap'n Cunt let loose a screech so prolonged and agonized and triumphant that one might have mistaken her for a witch being burned at the stake and enjoying it.

David always knew she had this fire in her belly.

And then the infamous Cap'n Cunt took a step off the ledge and jumped to her legend.

The gathering gasped as her body tipped off the apex, leaning headfirst toward the flames.

David shuddered as her body contorted, a marionette caught in its own strings.

He held his breath as she flew across empty sky between the Nassau roof and Ultraviolet's oak tree on the opposite end of the blaze.

He rose up as her body grazed the flames and she cast down the huge clock into its inferno.

And when Cap'n Cunt landed in the limbs of the oak, gobbled up into Ultraviolet's straitjacket, the collective exhale was so palpable that David worried they'd blown out the bonfire like a birthday cake, for he had closed his eyes and made a wish and it had inexplicably come true.

A double take revealed the near-invisible zip line strung from the roof of Nassau Hall to the trunk of the oak tree. After Cap'n Cunt flew along this wire, Ultraviolet tamped out the minor flames that had singed her coattails. He unfastened the harness camouflaged across her ample chest. The crowd did not linger long on this intimate groping—though David kept a close eye—because a surge of sound and imagery brought everyone's attention back to the projection. Clocks chiming, ringing, beeping, clanging. At breakneck speed, digital and analog timepieces shuffled through. And finally, Ultraviolet's NIST atomic clock, running rapid-fire beside the phrase: LET'S KILL SOME TIME.

Wristwatches and cell phones were shed. Alarm clocks and calendars burned to cinders. Could they have ripped the sun and moon and constellations whereby the ancients judged their eras, David was certain the heavens, too, would have been emptied, left blank and black.

Orange flames suddenly mixed with flickering red and blue. Police. But they didn't get far. As the mechanics of time were being thrown off, so were the students' clothes.

As Ultraviolet and newly anointed Cap'n Cunt descended from their perch in the treetop via a painter's ladder, three girls scurried up it, breasts exposed, arms cradling what appeared to be laundry. Edging themselves out on the same wide tree branch that Cap'n Cunt had just made famous, these girls flung their clothing into the blaze, catalyzing the horde to do the same. Shirts and pants were easily strewn, and the bravest stripped down to their barest essence. They danced.

It was a perfect moment. David got back to business.

He sprinted to his garbage bags by the base of the tree and dumped out hundreds of gray masks with eye- and nostril-holes, but no mouth, and the USV divvied out this bulk buy. Pulling elastic straps over their heads, the students transformed into a homogeneous horde, hiding their faces as they exposed their bodies. With Echo's music blasting, the gathering realized its tribalism. Business-Man, too, was ready to bare some flesh. But he feared for the safety of László's blazer and, anyway, the firemen began to unleash. They made liberal use of water cannons, aiming at the fire but allowing their stream to smack many Princeton student bodies. The scalding cold shocked Business-Man into something approaching sobriety. He ran with the others into the night, a smile on his face.

He felt amazing! He felt like Mathias probably felt all the time. Somehow, Business-Man ended up huddled behind a statue of Albert Einstein. He was giddy with laughter when he discovered Ugs, slumped against a tree trunk, smoking and shaking, clearly in a very unhappy place.

Business-Man cried something like: "All our earthly possessions are burned! We're free to bask in the unencumbered nowness! Isn't that great?"

And Ugs said, "Um, no." Business-Man sat down beside him. "Tomorrow morning," he explained, "you're gonna see a couple hundred kids sifting through these ashes, trying to find whatever it is they've burned. And when they don't find it, they'll just buy new fucking shit."

"But everything's lost, gone, razed to the ground! It's a new era!"

"Sometimes when you burn a good thing," said Ugs, "an evil thing rises from the ashes."

"Like a phoenix!" Business-Man cried triumphantly, not really listening.

"No," said Dr. Ugs, poking at the eyeholes of his mask. "Like religion."

ii.

Six nipples danced in Christopher Walken's rearview. Three girls in the backseat wearing blindfolds beneath those blank gray USV masks. Topless, with capes. David had on his infrared goggles, and though they made things dark they also made it easier to stare. Haley drove, tearing away from campus at forceful yet inconspicuous speed. David was crammed and balanced in the middle of the front seat, next to Haley, his arm pressed snug against her velvety blue Cap'n Cunt shoulder pads, his eyes pulled to her hair, dyed white, so sexy and severe against her super-red lips.

On the other side, sitting shotgun, was Mathias. He hunched. Thumbed his temple. Stared out the window. David could almost hear him thinking.

"Take those goggles off," Haley muttered at David. "I don't want to get stopped." She signaled and sped into a turn. "And see if you can find a towel or something for the titty trio."

David offered the girls his grandpa László's blazer. They draped it over themselves, huddling beneath it together, stifling giggles.

Unlike the USV's misfire at Forbes, this homecoming bonfire spectacle reached a massive, organic, orgiastic crescendo and they'd tapped out before things went bad. They'd achieved something collective and, he'd dare say, pure.

When the firemen started hosing, the core USVers had run to their cars. Haley, Mathias, and David in the Buick. Lee, Owen, and Fu in the van with the gear. It was a rash decision to include the three new girls. They'd swarmed the car like rabid groupies, half naked and fresh from the fire hose.

"Haley, oh my god, you are a fucking amazon," said one of them, a petite girl full of energy and compliments, her breasts small and areolas large. "I swear, I've never seen anything—"

David recognized them as the girls from the oak tree, sorority sisters who took the initiative to climb up there and burn their clothes, spurring the whole crowd to nudify themselves. He loved their moxie immediately, as well as other things, and realized that they were still feeling the effects of the drug gumbo vaporized in the pyre.

"Wait!" A lilting blonde jogged up to the car. "You guys! I can't find my shoes. Or pants!"

"You burned them!" said the short one. "Just get in!"

"Let's go!" screamed Owen, honking and starting the MaxMobile ignition behind them.

"Hold!" said Mathias. "Tell me your majors. Or what you want to be when you grow up."

They answered in order: architecture, psychology, premed. These were solid gaps to fill. But Mathias's vetting process had certainly been streamlined compared with a few months ago.

"Okay, girls, two rules," David shouted out the door. "First, give me your cell phones."

"Dude," said the blonde. "We *burned* them."

"Good, great. Second, we have to blindfold you." Seemed like a good idea. Probably pointless, but no sense in disclosing The Egg's location yet.

"Fine!" they screamed, clamoring into the back.

"Third," barked Mathias. Then softer, "If you come back with us... you don't go home tonight. No rides anywhere. Once we're in, we're all in for good. Got me?"

"Fourth," Haley shot at the guys. "Nobody's hooking up with anyone. Got *me*?"

Mathias shrugged. The girls had gotten in. And they never really got out again.

— Ø —

The psych major, Britt Childress, looked like she was on springs. When they got into the living room, she put on Fu's tank top and motorcycle helmet, obscuring her moon-shaped face and gathering up a wavy mane of blond hair mixed with streaks of pink. She struck David as a girl who expected someone else's drugs to be laid out for her everywhere she went. Hers wasn't an air of entitlement, he decided, so much as an unspoken agreement to repay such kindness with enthusiasm. She'd always keep the party going if there was someone to stay up with her.

Nyla White, a black girl with long braids, was more wary. There was an air of wholesomeness about her, as if this was maybe the first time she'd ever been to a boy's house without supervision. She had the kind of eyes that could be sweet and squinty when smiling, steely when serious. She graciously accepted Owen's oversized camo jacket and focused on browsing the guys' bookshelves, eventually plucking out a fat photography tome two-handed and curling into the couch next to Owen.

Zoe Olivares had a prominent, angular nose that took up a good portion of her face but was somehow still cute. She looked like the sorcerer's apprentice in Lee's lab coat as she rushed around the kitchen, laying out food, lighting candles, adjusting curtains—swiftly making herself indispensable. Before anyone could stop her, she'd done all their dishes. She talked a lot and made bad jokes that weren't really jokes—"That's a lot of soap suds, buds!"—and did this thing with her head as if constantly dancing to a song only she could hear. When she started pulling out drink-making implements and asking about limes, David decided alcohol was the wrong vibe. Instead, he suggested Mathias prepare the Big Bang initiation.

"Whose house is this?" asked Nyla, the architecture major.

"It's not a house," said Owen. "It is The Egg."

iii.

Haley stood over the bathroom sink of The Egg, looking down at the tiny hair shavings littered around the faucet and balancing on the edge of the drain. The shower was much the same, small curly hairs and longer ones peppering the tub and collecting in corners. Their bathroom was gross, like all boys' bathrooms. It would have to change. Lots would have to change.

She was changing, she realized. She heard their voices outside the bathroom door—these new girls, somewhat familiar, mostly strange—who'd inevitably look to her for guidance in this space, especially if they were truly down for the ritual drug experience Mathias was prepping. The old Haley might have respectfully bowed out, or else overdone it, insisting on being the most fucked-up person in the room—a different sort of bowing out—but no, goodbye, old Haley. New Haley'd be expected to play certain roles now. The earth mother, the caretaker. The queen, maybe.

The boys' roles were clearer. Mathias was the tip of the spear, and of course he was interesting and volatile and pretty and tall, and all the things her teenage self would've gone for. But David was solid and strong, and for her right now? Solid had its own mystery.

Blink. In her house during winter break, after running into him at the Giant, they'd talked about superpowers. David said he dreamed of being visible. And here he was, behind the scenes again. Maybe he liked it that way. Maybe it was safer. She understood safety. But still.

Haley remembered being around seven years old, watching that horrible earthquake in Haiti, people trapped under rubble for days and days. The best magic skill, she thought back then, would be to make yourself as small as possible, down to almost nothing, and crawl out through the cracks. She'd never given it much thought before, all this superhero stuff; she wasn't particularly well versed in that genre. She'd seen *Wonder Woman* the summer between middle school and high school and loved the *idea* of Wonder Woman, but the movies never totally did it for her.

After her first Big Bang, she shared this with David.

"I know about comic books as much as I know about, say, Islam," Haley said. She liked the compelling concept of the USV, and the acronym itself would make a cool logo—like USA, but with the last letter flipped upside down—but she needed to get smart on superherodom quickly.

The timing was perfect: February 4 was opening night for the much-anticipated Marvel-DC crossover *Krona: Justice League vs. Avengers*, an outsized blockbuster funded by two major studios, by far the largest budget in Hollywood history (maybe they also anticipated the end times and figured they might as well blow the bank). With a panoply of stars representing nearly all the big-time heroes—anchored by Justice League's core team of Superman, Batman, Wonder Woman, Aquaman, the Flash, and Cyborg and the Avengers' Captain America, Iron Man, Thor, Hawkeye, Hulk, and Black Widow, plus turns by the X-Men, Spider-Man, Black Panther, Ant-Man, Doctor Strange (Mathias's favorite), Deadpool, the Fantastic Four, and the Guardians of the Galaxy—it was completely absurd, but nonetheless served as a fitting 180-minute crash course for Haley.

She could tell David initially wanted it to be a kind of date—and she was up for it, sure—but it was time for Haley to get to know the rest of the guys, so it morphed into a group hang. Haley and the USV piled into the MaxMobile and headed for the AMC Hamilton multiplex, where every single screen was showing *Krona* that opening night. The release amounted to a cultural event, a nationwide, decentralized Comic-Con of sorts. Here in Hamilton, hundreds of moviegoers stood in lines and milled around the parking lot in full cosplay. Not just superheroes, either. Haley was disturbed by the middle-aged men in Harry Potter garb, the pre-teen girls in hypersexualized anime outfits, all the fat dudes in faded T-shirts referencing Jedi knights and Sith lords.

"Promise me just one thing, David," she whispered as they made their way into the theater.

"I know what you're going to say," he said. "I promise, none of us will grow a ponytail."

"That's all I ask."

The movie was insane, and Haley didn't care much for the cartoony CGI fight scenes, but the plot itself was oddly transfixing. She was stoned, so maybe it was all in her head, but it seemed to map perfectly onto their lives: I mean, Krona(!) is destroying all these universes(!) in his quest to understand the mystery of creation and agrees not to destroy Earth if the heroes fight and best each other in a kind of cross-dimensional scavenger hunt, and they eventually stop fighting and join forces and capture Krona in a damn "cosmic egg"(!).

After the movie, Haley joined the boys at the nearby Grounds for Sculpture, an outdoor museum seemingly designed for people on drugs. They all took a low dose, bonding them for life.

During this more cogent and manageable trip, Haley considered the appeal of superheroes. The flawed characters reaching for their idealized selves. The fun visual phenomenon. The subtle commentary on the end of American empire. The apocalyptic danger posed by an outside force, a villainous Other. All of those alien villains were just the climate apocalypse personified, maybe. And from a commercial standpoint, she'd just never understood the insane popularity and ubiquity until she saw it in person. Cosplay was different from Halloween. It was a way of summoning something, of presenting yourself differently to the world. A secret wish made public. It was playful. It was communal. And, it should be said, with the right body, it was kinda sexy.

The *Krona* movie stars were all easy on the eyes, and Haley had taken copious notes on costuming, hair, and makeup. Muscly dudes like Thor, Aquaman, and Black Panther were objectively hot, but her favorite was Ant-Man, the silly, size-shifting comic relief. Shrinking would be a great superpower, Haley maintained. But after you've flown across a bonfire on a zip line above a couple thousand tripping people while wearing a pirate outfit? It would be hard for Haley to make herself small ever again.

She was Cap'n Cunt now. From here on, the only thing to be was larger than life. Blink.

She left the bathroom and slowly descended the curved set of stairs leading to the living room, where the guys had already lowered the lights and laid out yoga mats and buckets for the girls. This was good.

"So how does this work?" asked Nyla. "Do we all just like shit our brains out?"

"Depends," said Haley. "With the Big Bang, some lie like quiet Buddhas with their eyes open, some strip naked, some scream and yell about seeing Satan and then immediately afterward describe blissful, angelic forms. And some people are barfers."

"Oh, I'm definitely going to be a barfer," said Britt.

"You're in a safe space here," Haley continued. "I'm here to make absolutely sure of that."

They asked if Haley was going to join them, and Haley told them she'd take a microdose to accompany them on their journey and bear witness and be a lifeline back, a bridge between worlds.

Cap'n Cunt passed out the pills. As resident shaman, Ultraviolet launched into a brief speech, towering over the girls who already looked up at him with disciple eyes. The guys bowed their heads respectfully and allowed him to say his peace. Something about respecting The Egg and keeping its mission firmly in mind: *The Big Bang explodes upon the universe and sweeps us toward the supercell. Only the heroic pass through the dark neck. Kezepel.*

The Big Bang took the girls over, asserting the power of that plant medicine. Nyla and Britt both puked (Britt missed her bucket), but not Zoe. In time, Haley saw them all reach that shared space she knew well by now—past the ego veil to the vast expanse where, despite the abyss, the human certainty of death, it's clear everything's gonna be okay.

"There's beauty coming together," Haley said once they were all back on Earth again. "You are gorgeous, badass women. Brilliant and skilled. We're all trying to remain heady in this space, while at the same time internally grappling with this new energy, of what you just came out of. And of them. And each other. So, brutal honesty time."

Haley sat beside the woodstove, feeling its radiant warmth, too much but just enough. At her feet, Nyla, Zoe, and Britt lay on yoga mats spread diagonally across one another, grounded again.

"This is an amazing space," Nyla said, scanning the domed ceiling, its intricate arrangement of chestnut triangles and octagons. "It's like a big sweat lodge."

"I didn't like that," said Zoe. "Not at all. Don't make me do that again, please."

"I was feeling it," Nyla said. "Maybe the thing is it's too easy to have that difficult an experience. And too easy to come back from it. Like, I don't know if I *earned* that."

"I thought it was wild," said Britt, shrugging. "Y'all are too uptight."

"You know, every time I'm with a group of girls," said Zoe, "we all inevitably talk of supporting and protecting each other, and the whole time we're just *triggering* each other—usually unintentionally, sometimes on purpose—because that's what we do. That's just what we do."

Haley pointed toward the backyard, where she'd exiled the boys. "That's what *they* do also; they just do it differently."

Britt piped up, stretching her arms and legs skyward like a cat after a nap. She crawled over to Zoe and hugged her. "I'm sorry if I said the wrong thing there. I'm just not easily triggered," she said. "I am already infinitely impressed with the women that we are and whatever we are becoming inside this really intense moment of history."

"Well, I'm terrified as fuck," said Nyla. "Of all of you. All this. Whatever *that* was."

"I'm also scared," Zoe concurred, sitting up now and hugging her knees to her chest. "Y'all are insanely beautiful, and if you're here that means you're smart, too. I'm used to being the only cool, smart girl in my school. I used to be the unicorn. Is that how you feel, Nyla?"

"Hell no," she said. "I wasn't cool at my prep school. And I was the only black girl. Different kind of unicorn. *Black* unicorn."

"That's a kickass superhero name," said Britt.

"Maybe for someone else," said Nyla. "Not for me. I know what I am."

"I see all of you and you see me," said Haley. "I am another yourself. And I saw from this side of hyperspace where you all have decided to go next. You're right, Nyla, you're no unicorn. I believe you're some kind of soldier."

Nyla's eyes widened and she turned to Haley. She asked if Haley had seen the same thing she'd seen. Haley wouldn't say yes or no, but she was beginning to think of this as one of Cap'n Cunt's special powers: under even the slightest bit of DMT, she received visions of those around her. Sometimes it was as vague as a color or aura, sometimes she heard a sound or phrase or incantation, and sometimes she saw a fully formed persona. She didn't want to overpower or prescribe something that didn't come from a place of truth for each person—she could be wrong, she realized—but she also wanted to share what she saw in hopes that it would validate the outcome of each person's Big Bang explosion. One by one, Haley called the girls up to the fire for individual blessings. They shared what they felt, what they remembered, what they saw, and Haley asked the right questions, guiding them back through the foggy details of a fever dream.

"Close your eyes," Haley said to Nyla, who went first. "Start with the feet."

This trick was drawn from Haley's stint in high school drama club. Find the right footwear and you'll discover your character, Mrs. Klassel told them. Haley liked this. She'd built up Cap'n Cunt starting at the bottom, with those rad over-the-knee pirate boots.

Nyla described a different kind of boot, the steel-toed variety, something meant for construction or combat. Her legs and torso, she said, were also clad in something thick and protective. She described something around her waist, something utilitarian, holding lots of stuff, and eventually came to the phrase "tool belt."

"What's on your face or head?" asked Haley.

"I don't know, I don't want to talk about that," Nyla said, eyes still closed. "I want to talk about what's in my hand." Nyla's pointer finger curled at something invisible.

"At the risk of *triggering* you," said Haley, "what kind of trigger are you squeezing?"

Nyla sighed and smiled. "Whyyyyy did the black girl's trip need to have a *gun* in it?"

"Was it a handgun?" asked Haley. "Or was it something else with a similar shape, like a power drill, maybe?"

"Maybe it was a drill," said Nyla, opening her eyes now, a new seriousness taking over. "But since we're on the subject, what do you do for security around here?"

"It's a supersafe neighborhood," Haley said. "We're talking about installing an alarm but—"

"No," Nyla said. "Not asking what *y'all* do for security"—she waved her hand toward the boys outside—"I'm asking what do *you* do? Do you have a sidearm? Or has the thought not occurred to you that one of these boys might..."

Of course it had occurred to her. She said as much, wiping sweat from her neck. Sometimes she felt like the trick was you just had to put out the vibe that you're not worth the trouble. Like in prison. Do something bat-shit crazy or beat up the scariest bitch in the room on the first day and then nobody will fuck with you. Or will *everyone* fuck with you then? Being the alpha was weird. And as a woman, she had to be the alpha but also the beta and everything else she'd already taken on.

Still, Nyla was right: knowing how to handle a gun might be important.

"Did you learn to shoot on the streets?" asked Britt.

"Thanks," said Nyla, sighing, "but no. I mostly grew up in Portsmouth, New Hampshire. Navy brat. They've got no 'streets' in Portsmouth—I learned on the base, at the shooting range, which was pretty much the only way I got to see my dad when he wasn't shipping me off to school. And after the Exeter shooting? You'd think I'd never want to touch a gun again. I felt that way for a while, for sure, and I'm not about that 'the only thing that stops a bad guy with a gun is a good guy with a gun' NRA bullshit. I mean, the NRA used to *love* gun control back when it was Black Panthers arming themselves in self-defense. I hate assault weapons and crazy assholes being able to buy a gun like it's a pair of pumps, but it's not the worst idea for a group like y'all to know how to carry and clean firearms. You think police won't mess with this because it's Princeton kids? Or because most of you are white? I guess this is the place to be, though, because when disasters hit, black folks are the last people they save. I could be carrying my grandma through floodwaters and still get shot because someone thinks I stole her." She turned back to Haley. "When you do this drug, do you usually get some set of lessons? Like one, two, three, this is what you have to do next?"

"In my very limited experience," said Haley. "Yes. It's different from mushrooms or acid. I've only done it twice. First, with just Mathias and David, and the second time with all of them."

Britt propped up on her elbows. "Brutal honesty time: Are you fucking both of them?"

"Who?" Haley said, feigning surprise.

Zoe and Nyla and Britt all cocked their heads to the side as if to say, *C'mon.*

"Are you joking?" Haley felt her face getting flushed despite herself. "I couldn't do that! Everyone's already calling me a slut and a fucking stupid cunt."

"First of all, you're *Cap'n* Cunt!" said Britt. "You flew through fire! And second of all, cunts are not stupid. They're fucking magic."

With that, something happened. Something triggered Haley, and the tears came. Not deep, full-body sobs, just water from her eyes. She'd been sweating by that woodstove, and maybe it wasn't sweat at all but pent-up tears finding an alternate exit. But that dam had now broken and it poured forth from her, and she curled onto the floor, and the women circled her, kept her hidden from any prying eyes outside. Nobody talked; they just let her cry. Shoulder to shoulder, they built a shell around Haley, bowing their heads over her, their hair falling down around her curled form like the tendrils of the backyard weeping willow tree she used to hide beneath as a child. After so long gone, Haley was home again, back in her body, in this container of women, in The Egg, in the womb of the world.

iv.

Mathias took David to the backyard. He wanted them to smoke a cigarette together, which made David feel special. Mathias was still jumpy, eyes scanning the trees for signs of flashing police lights. David smoked. With each exhale he felt the satisfied, melty feeling of something having gone exceedingly right. And with each inhale his stomach warmed as he wondered if this was *the night*—his best shot—the night he might try to kiss Haley Roth.

His confidence couldn't have been higher. After all, the bonfire had been *his* finely orchestrated freak-out. Sure, he'd pulled the concept from a Hawthorne short story and he'd let Mathias play the role of head honcho. But those on the inside? They knew who was really in charge.

Haley knew. Since her own Big Bang initiation at the hospital, she'd been a fixture at The Egg. She'd seen David in action—plotting it on paper, gathering images for the slideshow, rehearsing with the group. And then calling on *her* to be the main event. The Divine Resurrection of Cap'n Cunt. She didn't know why, but she knew he wanted it for her, that validation.

He wanted her to be a superhero.

David marveled at how far he'd come. A few months ago he was crying into midnight meatball subs over his dearth of nookie. And look at him now: the aloof cool guy, hanging with an even cooler guy, plus a harem of hotties. He'd devised a collective spiritual experience and was now hosting the most exclusive after-party of the semester. What a night what a night what a night.

"What a night!" Mathias said, and David again wondered if he'd just read his mind.

Mathias took a drag, smiled, and hugged David, strong and long. David craved these rare moments when Mathias allowed him to believe he was the favorite.

"We're going to be pretty huge, I think," David said.

"Careful," Mathias said. "Substance over celebrity."

He took David by the shoulders, and for a second David thought Mathias was going to kiss him, and David realized he didn't know what he'd do if Mathias *did* lean in. Dodge and weave? Curl into a ball? Kiss back? Surely, it would be another of his koans...

Instead, Mathias turned David around so he was facing the windows. A celebration was under way. Fu was taking the rest of them through his latest musical innovation:

Gather the group in a circle. Start a basic beat or "pulse" with your feet, swaying back and forth. Fu steps into the center of the circle and leads the group in a looped musical pattern, using only voice and body percussion. *Keep it going.* Then he splits the circle into segments, leading each in a call-and-response of a new musical idea or layer. *Think in terms of instrumentation: drums, bass, guitar, horns.* After four or five layers are added, he chooses another to take his place in the center. *Eye contact and body motions model dynamic changes. Raise or lower your arms to adjust volume and achieve a balanced mix.*

This was the "Human DJ," as taught by Golden Echo.

Orchestrated voices had taken the place of Fu's digital music-making machines, pouring a deep and dirty beat into The Egg. And Golden Echo was working on a way to expand it by modifying wireless earbuds with radio receivers and fixing a microphone in the center of the circle to amplify the sound. It was becoming democratic and participatory, with a much lower power draw than amplifying lots of individual instruments and voices.

"Look," Mathias said. "Look what you've created."

"Fu created that. And *you* created all this," David said. "I'm just along for the ride."

"Ha!" He stomped out his cigarette, opened his pack and lit two more. "I can be the queen, moving anywhere on the board I need to. But you, my friend, you are the king. And we'll protect you. Make no mistake." He ruffled David's hair. "Those bulk face masks were a stroke of genius. I balked when you bought a thousand, but seriously? Cat's pajamas."

"Seriously?"

"Perfect way for us to be anonymous, to strip away individuality and bring everyone into the fold. It's classless, collective. Fucking genius."

"It's Branding 101." David shrugged. "Best practices."

"Fuck branding. I know what I just said about celebrity, but we have to think on a larger scale." His gaze locked on the boisterous living room. "There's evolution in the offing. I get it: the superhero outfits mean everyone gets to have a secret identity. All these overachievers don't want to throw away their futures because they still think there's a future to be had. But if everyone's disguised? And if the future's up for grabs? If we zero in with enough heroes—a critical mass—these last months will be a collective paradigm shift we haven't seen since..." He trailed off, gazing into The Egg. And then Mathias Blue said, out of nowhere, "What do you think of Haley?"

David almost vomited on his own shoes.

"What..." David said. "No."

"No what?"

"I mean. No. I was gonna ask you what do *you* think of Haley?"

Mathias cocked an eyebrow.

"Stop."

"What?"

"Just stop." David tried to catch himself. "She said... she doesn't make out with colleagues."

Mathias took a drag and looked sidelong at David. "*I see,* said the blind man."

"You see nothing, dude."

"I see just about everything, Infrared. Make no mistake."

"I am Business-Man."

Mathias took another long unblinking drag, smoking the rest of his butt in one single inhale. David could hear the cigarette paper crackling.

"Or should I call you... *Bat*man?" Mathias stared through David as he said this. "Did you ever tell her about Halloween, Batman? About what you saw?"

David had wondered if and when Mathias would bring this up again. He hadn't wanted to press the issue if it was all in his head. But now? Shit.

"You shot me from the roof," David retorted. "You were there, too, asshole."

"I know," he said. "And Haley knows. My iPhone video was how they knew who to arrest."

"What video? Does... does she know I was there, too? Wait, am I *in* the video?"

Mathias stomped his cigarette and placed a hand on David's heart. Held it there.

"I have no idea what you are talking about," he said. Then, laughing through his nose, he walked inside. Directly to Haley Roth. David watched him whisper in her ear, and when he was done she looked up incredulously and then promptly looked outside and gave David the finger.

Oh, please no.

David wasn't sure what to do. So he found himself flipping the bird back at her for no particular reason. She headed outside. To David. She closed the sliding patio door behind her.

"It's cold out here," she said.

"What the fuck did Mathias just say to you?"

"He told me to look outside and give you the finger. Why?"

"Here, please steal my jacket for a while," David said, momentarily relieved.

"Only if I can steal your cigarette, too."

If I hadn't burned it all, David thought, *you could steal everything I own.* With a silent prayer to his forebear, David swung László's blazer over Haley Roth's shivery shoulders. It *was* cold. David wondered how long he could last before he started shivering, too.

Inside, Mathias asked, "Who wants the tour?" And right on cue, Owen dropped to his back and put his feet into the air. As the crew disappeared up the stairs with a newly airborne Britt Childress, David realized that he and Haley were alone. Outside. Together.

Had Mathias orchestrated this moment for him? To what end?

Haley took a drag and looked up into David's eyes. She looked tired and skinny. She was still dropping weight. Small brown circles had formed under her eyes, or else it was makeup.

They hopped off the porch and went strolling in the grass. She'd performed beautifully, stepped effortlessly into her new larger-than-life persona. David marveled aloud at this.

"Being in costume is being hidden," she said, shrugging. "Dealing with people as myself? *That* scares the shit out of me."

"Same," he said. "I should've chosen a more disguising costume."

"The suit suits you," she said. "You're the overseer, pacing in the background."

"I'm more of an arm-crosser," he said, affecting an administrative stance of calm dismay.

She got serious, eyes wide. "I could see *everything* tonight!" Haley whispered, nodding to The Egg. "When Nyla came up I saw her arms puff up, with this camouflage everywhere on her body, and she said she had the same vision of growing stronger like one of the warriors from Black Panther, or building huge houses with a massive tool belt. And Britt? I saw this beautiful yellowish light on her throat, but her body kept changing colors, so I think her persona is this constant chameleon changing costumes all the time. Zoe didn't feel it as much, she got really scared, but *I* knew and *she* knew that she had to walk into the basement, in the dark, by herself, until she wasn't scared anymore, and—"

Haley caught herself on this rant and looked at David, who was beaming. He loved seeing her like this. She was strong again. Respected. Respectable. Powerful. A powerhouse.

She smiled and smoked and said, "It was nice of you to transform me into a superhero."

"You transformed me first," David said. "Have you figured out your shadow yet?"

"I don't know what it's called yet, but there's a piece of me that thinks I need to be everything for everyone. It's exhausting."

David nodded. He understood.

"Are you still feeling it?" she said after a little while.

David couldn't be sure exactly what she was referring to, but he said, "Yeah."

"Me, too. I feel like Wonder Woman."

"Where's your Lasso of Truth?" he joked. Haley pantomimed her best cowgirl impression and swung an invisible lasso. David pulled his arms to his sides, pretending to be nabbed.

"There," she said. "Now you have to tell me some truth."

"Um, my hands are cold?"

"Here, you pansy," she said, turning her back to him. "Put your hands in these pockets." And lo and behold, she backed into him and let him slip his hands into László's blazer, curling his fingers around hers. They were warm, and David was embarrassed at how cold and clammy his must have felt, but she didn't say anything about it. Her spine pressed into his chest. He pressed back.

"Wow," she said. "Your heart is beating *really* hard."

"See what you do to me?" As the smoke from Haley's cigarette curled around her head, David allowed his nose to subtly burrow into her new white locks. "You have. Really. Nice. Hair." He knew this was lame but meant it so completely. "It's like cake icing. I want to eat it," he said.

"Go ahead." She turned, made a poker face. "Let's do this."

She bent downward slightly, letting her eyes come to the tops of themselves. It was time.

Go. Go. Go! XplO!

He closed his eyes and bowed down and leaned in and did not see that she had just lifted her cigarette to her lips to take a drag, and when David's mouth met the burning cherry of her Camel Light and he yelped and jolted backward, he thought maybe Haley Roth was so damned powerful that she'd sent fire through his face. But no. He was the dog that had pressed his luck too far and come upon the business end of an electric fence, reminding him to stay in his fucking place.

"Ow," David said.

As he nursed his upper lip, Haley said, "You are such a numbskull." She grabbed David by the back of the neck and said, "C'mere." And she kissed him. And it was a good kiss, the way you *know* it's a good kiss for both of you. She took his mouth inside hers, sucking his lips, and though he'd burned himself like an idiot and could barely feel it, she was kissing him. *She* was kissing *him.*

"Get on your back," she whispered.

Huh?

She dragged him to the edge of the yard, into the pachysandra, underneath a cypress tree, and pushed him to the ground. Her white hair hung around him. She unfastened the buttons of her naval frock and David took the cue and clawed off his tie and dress shirt.

She climbed on top of him, as she had in Prospect Gardens. This time her thighs clutched the sides of his waist. Her ass grinded down on him and he worried he was about to cum, but a wave ran through him like he'd just eaten a gorgeous piece of fruit, and all he knew was that she was there and awake and he was ready and *oh my god this is happening right now*.

"Are you sure this is okay?" David asked. "I thought you said nobody's having sex tonight."

"You're a good guy," she said. "But you need to be bad now or I'll lose my fucking mind."

With her pants at her thighs, she pulled her underwear to the side, unearthing the mound of blond hair he'd seen once before. She pulled out his cock from his pants, stroked it deftly, and guided it inside of her, and holy shit. The cold weather was no match for his craving. She rode him fast. David tried to slow them down, but she was going for broke, sprinting to the finish, so he reached to his sides and gripped the ground and tried his best to hold on. For the first time, David heard Haley's moan, her particular moan he'd missed those other terrible unconscious times, something guttural and surprised, and then she pressed her palms to the sides of his head and her moans stopped. For a moment David thought something was wrong, that he'd hurt her, or that she'd just seen a ghost or something, but then he saw her mouth open, eyes wide, breath held, face red, red, red, thighs shaking, twitching, and it was too much to bear.

From her silent seizing, she exploded, and so did he, waves pouring from him.

There in the dirt, in the yard, in the garden, in the grasses, covered in leaves and digging at roots with their fingers, David caught his breath. It had happened. With her. This was real.

They'd be together now, superheroes flying through the air.

They'd be the wind that made the trees shed their leaves, and they'd be the leaves falling to the ground, and they'd be the ground soaking it all up. They'd gather them all, forever.

She crumpled and then rolled onto her side, so they were both staring at the sky.

"Sorry," David finally said, pulling himself together. "If that was too quick, I mean."

"Don't be," she said, totally unfazed. "We both came, didn't we? Although I'm admittedly an easy cum. I'm like a bumpy-bus-ride cum. Still, you have a supernice cock."

David played a furious lick of air guitar. She laughed at him.

"Seriously, don't apologize. It's been a while for me, too, obvi. Have you fucked anyone at school since breaking up with that Madeline chick? I only ask because we didn't use a condom just now and I usually do," she said, "but I basically know where you've been, don't I? And I got tested after Halloween so I know I'm clean. And, also, the world's going to end, so..."

"Um, I never actually had sex with Maddy," David admitted.

First a shock of fear, and then a slow smile crept across her face.

"Oh wow. Oh my god. Did I just pop Business-Man's cherry?"

He nodded yes.

"Oh god! And here your first time is on top of a bunch of weeds and fucking flagstones!"

"It was perfect."

"I'm so sorry."

"A perfect night."

She smiled. "You brought me back tonight," she said. "In more than one way."

She smooched his chin. For the first time maybe ever, David felt like the exact kind of superhero he wanted to be.

"Don't mention it," he said. "It's the least I could do after fucking up on Halloween."

Stop.

"What are you talking about?"

"Talking... what?" he babbled, like a guilty, guilty man.

Stop, stupid. Stay still. Maybe you'll turn invisible and XplO into nothing.

"How did *you* fuck up on Halloween?"

"Nothing. I..." *Well... shit.* "I saw him. I saw Bob. And you."

She went speechless.

"I tried to help," David babbled. "I swear. I shot at him with my paint-ball gun but I missed."

Her arms crossed. She began nodding very slowly. "You shot at him. *With your paintball gun.*"

David realized it was the single stupidest thing to say.

"He kicked the shit out of me. I didn't know what to do. He was too strong."

"Yeah, David! *I know* he was too strong that night. But if you *saw*? If you *knew*!" She started tearing up and whispered, "Why didn't you ever say anything?"

"But I told you, see, that night—"

"The next *day*?! The next *week*?! Why didn't you EVER say anything?!"

He was suddenly scorching hot.

"Oh my god," she continued, holding her head in her hands now. "I fucking remember now. By the soccer goal. I saw you. I *talked* to you, David. You were *there* when he gave me—"

"Well, why did *you* let him do that to you?!" David fired back. "What, you just take any drug someone puts in front of you, drink any cup of whatever, without asking what's in it?"

"Wow. You think I'm some high school whore." She deflated. "Don't you get it?"

David stopped. He did get it. But she explained it anyway:

"David... I'm *Cap'n Cunt* now."

And with that, she tore off László's jacket and punched David square in his burned lip.

"You're a weak man," she said, and stormed inside.

That night could have been a triumph. A victory for youth. The night that the famed Britt Childress, Nyla White, and Zoe Olivares joined the USV and transformed The Egg from a glorified frat house into a full-blown revolutionary commune. The night David came into his own power and Haley Roth came into hers. The night he became a man.

But that night was the first night of many, many others to follow that Haley Roth sought refuge in the basement bedroom of Mathias Blue, just steps away from David's door.

V.

David had watched her run for the basement and decided to give her some space. He spent thirty minutes walking contemplative laps around Woosamonsa, racked by the powerful emotional pendulum swing between reveling in his loss of virginity to a woman he objectively loved and reviling himself for how badly he'd fucked things up. Once he got cold enough he went inside and tiptoed downstairs, mistakenly believing a long, apologetic conversation might smooth things over. He crept to Mathias's bedroom door. It was closed. But he could make out muffled voices.

"Keep going," he heard Mathias say. "Faster."

Inside, in response, Haley sounded breathy. David was seconds away from either busting through the door like a ferocious Kool-Aid Man or else slinking to his bedroom, broken like Charlie Brown, assuming they were fucking in there. But then David realized what was happening.

"Over and over," Mathias whispered. "Don't think too much."

"It's hard to remember," said Haley. "It's faded. Tell me again."

"Once there lived a little girl who was afraid of nothing at all," said Mathias. "Everyone knew she would grow up to be a good and important woman who would take on the world and never be afraid of anyone or anything. Then, one night, something scared her. And each night after, just before bedtime, the girl got scared, again and again, until she was no longer merely afraid of the thing that scared her. She was *haunted* by it. You remember the first movie that scared you, Haley?"

"*Monster House*," she said. "That demonic haunted mansion that devours kids—"

"The little girl was haunted until one day her father brought her paper and crayons and said, *'Draw it.'* At first she couldn't draw the monster house in her mind. It was too terrifying. But soon she began drawing it, again and again. The monster house grew less frightening, more silly. One day, the girl looked down at her paper, and staring back at her was just... a harmless little house..."

David heard Haley scribbling in there. He sat down quietly against the outside of Mathias's door, straining to hear her: crying quiet and pretty at first, then loud and ugly, then sniffling, then laughing, breathing, exhale, exhale. Mathias went quiet. For a while Haley was silent, too, and David soon felt like the three of them had slipped into some kind of linked meditative state, though he was fairly certain they had no idea he was there outside. All David could hear were the marks she was making on paper, a soft Morse code language defined by long, whittled strokes and the brisk, sandpaper rhythms of something being shaded in. He eventually heard a body rise from bedsprings.

"What's that one?" Mathias said.

"Nyla's daytime ensemble. I could *see it* during her Big Bang. Cotton gabardine lace-up camo jacket, army-style, plus camo twill hot pants. A leather-canvas tool belt covered in metal washers. *She'll* need to find her persona, but as a placeholder I'm calling her 'Sergeant Drill,' and hey, do you have any camo stuff in here? Because I'd like to rip off a swatch and make this a proper collection board like we're a haute couture atelier, Maison du Cap'n Cunt, and also, hey, while you're at it, can I snag just one more Zeronal, *s'il vous plaît*?"

"Have as many as you want, dear," he said. "You're on a roll."

"Check this one." She turned a page so loudly it almost ripped. "Zoe Olivares is our medical 'SuperVisor,' so she's got a teal rayon scrubs-pantsuit with matching belt, plus an ivory lab coat with gathered pleating, see, and this insane surgical mask—might be too much, but fuck it...

"And Britt is the 'It Girl.' Ideally I'd put her in a kind of electronic unitard made of flexible HD displays, something we could shift constantly like that shit they wear in Philip K. Dick's *A Scanner Darkly*, but with budget an issue, I may need to design her like fourteen different looks out of lightweight jersey fabric so she can tote them around easily."

"Budget ain't an issue, dearest," Mathias said. "Don't stifle. Keep going."

"Do you have more paper?" she asked, pen sounds growing louder. "Graph paper, ideally?"

"Bien sûr," Mathias said.

It happened quickly. A loud pounce inside the room, and David lifted his head away from the doorframe and recoiled from the bedroom just as the door flung open, Mathias standing there bare-chested, the entryway ajar, and Haley seated at his desk. She was wearing one of those creepy gray masks from earlier in the evening. Just then, Haley glanced out the door at David. She was too deep into her Zeronal-fueled genius to remember her rage, but before returning to her work, she casually dropped a phrase that would haunt David till the end of time.

From behind her blank, mouthless mask: "When a woman loses her mystery, she is finished forever."

MARCH

i.

Dissent in the Age of Flibberflibbergaboobieism
By Nina Samaras, *The Atlantic*
March 11, 2022

Last week I asked Mathias Blue if he would let me spend a day at his house in Pennington, New Jersey, and initiate me into a secret society known as the Unnamed Supersquadron of Vigilantes (USV). He agreed to grant me access and observation privileges only—adding that it wasn't "his house" but rather "The Egg"—and promised if my impetus were to turn spiritual rather than journalistic, an invitation to train might be extended. He passed the phone to a charming associate calling herself It Girl, who told me where and how to meet the world's newest and realest superhero.

Blue is the recognized ringleader of the USV, a flamboyant troupe of student activists who undergo a rigorous training regimen to support their drug-fueled, flash-mob spectacles. It sounds silly, until one recalls the secret societies of centuries ago, which helped birth modern science, democracy, and religion and which counted Voltaire, Ben Franklin, and George Washington as members. Until recently, Mathias Blue was an enrolled undergraduate at Princeton University. While many in the USV—including several top officers—were arrested and hit with yearlong suspensions for their transgressive activities in late February, Blue was singled out as the figurehead and fully expelled. He's now a full-time oracle, a magnet for confused youth who line up outside his bedroom door to hear their futures.

When I arrive at The Egg I expect theatrics. It's a geodesic dome, for starters. Stationed on the front lawn of this literal suburban bubble are a nineteen-year-old boy—introducing himself as "Peacemaker"—and his burly team of ex-athlete bouncer types. The USV's security detail eschews the sunglasses-and-shotgun goon routine. The key to proper security, Peacemaker explains, is *neutralizing* rather than *escalating* threats. Indeed, the group has the support of Pennington's mayor, Martin Rosse, and interfaces pleasantly with local law enforcement (state authorities are growing less patient, and the USV is on the FBI's radar). Peacemaker leads me to the front door, holding it open for me.

Once inside, an intense young woman (Sergeant Drill) takes over, rippling through The Egg in a black tank top and crew cut, camo pants, circular sunglasses, and an indecipherable clipboard. She is in charge of keeping the training schedules straight, molding an ever-growing influx of naive wannabes into a stream of worthy superheroes. I struggle to keep up as she leads me to the kitchen.

"After our Big Bang initiation," she explains, "paradigms get shifted. It takes a few days for my kids to complete the conversion from student to superhero." She allows me to glance at their self-published training manual, entitled *The Superhero's Journey*, which guides initiates through ascending levels of:

1) physical improvement (lifting weights, yoga, home improvement projects),
2) intellectual action (researching and developing a useful "thesis" project),
3) emotional understanding (exercises in interpersonal connection), and
4) spiritual self-evolution (contemplative awareness practices such as meditation).

The Egg is now a full-time training facility, initiating dozens each day with fresh superhero "personas," costumes, and transformed outlooks on what they believe are their dwindling days on Earth. One of the nerve centers of The Egg is the costuming workshop, located in what was once the home's master bedroom and managed by a heroine who goes by the handle "Cap'n Cunt." The room is lined with fashion boards, fabric swatches, and a mini-sweatshop of workers. Cap'n Cunt is the couturier: examining models, bunching or pinning fabrics, calling out direction to a team of assistants led by her right-hand hero (Stockman). It's prolific work. During spring break alone, more than five hundred new members joined, including dozens of non-Princeton students, a tenured professor of philosophy, and someone's mom.

Next, I'm received by a dynamic duo: the spandexed blonde with whom I spoke on the phone is a bubbly PR rep (It Girl) and her cohort in surgeon's scrubs and a stethoscope is the resident medical expert (SuperVisor!—she sings her name the way you'd sing *Su*-per-*man!*). Both are giftedly type A. It Girl talks incessantly as they lead me down a frightening set of basement stairs. They are taking me to their leader.

I'm met by a reasonably normal-looking guy, all of twenty years old, in a purple hooded sweatshirt. Blue has boyish good looks—the beginnings of a blond beard over a chiseled chin, a pair of eyes that shift from the sparkly softness of a poet to the piercing gaze of a soldier. I stare at his face and wonder if it might contain a zeitgeist. He removes his shades and shakes my hand—a perfect gentleman.

Mathias Blue—also known by his alter ego, Ultraviolet—is the brain behind the now-ubiquitous concept of "chronostrictesis," or time devaluation. While skeptics still exist within the scientific, religious, and mainstream communities, the theory has gained a considerable foothold with the youth demographic; and as we feel the rapid shortening of days grow all but undeniable, Ultraviolet's theories have shed their hokum label and now verge on prophecy. Academic papers emerge on a daily basis, crediting chronostrictesis with everything from California's seismic spike to the retreat of the Larsen B ice shelf.

I ask if the USV's flash mobs serve to spread Mathias's gospel of chronostrictesis far and wide. The goal, he tells me, "is not to spread science but rather to transcend it. We're fighting the end of time by preparing to subvert the countdown." The main target of this student's ire, therefore, is not an evil dean, as one might find in a cheesy college movie, nor is it an imperialist government or military authority. Blue's enemy is nebulous. His rhetoric is impassioned, if a bit juvenile and condescending.

He laments how "busy" we are forced to make ourselves, just to keep pace with the quickening of life. "You're a writer," he says. "Look up synonyms for 'busy.' They're all positive words. Then look up the antonyms." Indeed I do, fiddling with my iPhone. According to *Roget's*, synonyms include "active," "diligent," "engaged," "full," "lively." And the antonyms of "busy"? I find terms like "empty," "idle," "purposeless," "unfulfilled."

The Time Crisis does call into question our current higher education system, as well as our progression through life beyond college. Students are trained to play the game. Considering the current job market, crushing student loan debt, and increased natural disasters, the "game" may have less of a point these days. Maybe the USV's mission is to overthrow the existing educational paradigm and institute a more practical, trade-oriented curriculum and, generally, a more deliberate mode of being in the world—characterized by calm and silence, yet still *active,* still *engaged.*

The question remains, what methods of effective protest are left to the modern student radical? Does the War on Terror demand a nonviolent approach? Does the phenomenon of chronostrictesis require quick and decisive action? I can hear the rally cry now:

What do we want?!
SPIRITUAL EVOLUTION!!
When do we want it?!
TIME IS AN ILLUSION!!

But the USV doesn't go in much for marches. This isn't your grandpa's rebellion. Sure, they have their communiqués and samizdat literature (in the form of *Tales of the USV* comic books). But the methods employed by the USV are more affected, kitschy, and, at times, disruptive (isn't that a central goal of all protest?). I get my first taste of it right there in the basement. I'm halfway through a question when I hear a gong sound reverberate through The Egg. Blue halts in his tracks and says, "Stop."

I turn and find him frozen like a statue. I try to join him, but when I adjust myself into a similar statue pose he yells at me, "No, don't *prepare* to stop! Just *stop*!" I'm taken aback. But then Mathias affects a charming smile and says, "Pretend I'm painting you." I am uncomfortable. I can't help but feel self-conscious, and a bit excited, when I meet his young eyes.

This is the Seventh-Minute Stop: a chime rings—*tonggg!*—and all movement ceases. For sixty seconds all bodies shut down, stiffen, and hold a statuesque gesture. During this minute you can hear breathing. You can watch the world neutralize and reset. Eye contact is discouraged. This is quiet time. Alone time. Six minutes on, one minute off, 6:1, a ratio as natural and ancient as the week of creation itself. And, yes, my initial thoughts cycle through all the action items on my to-do list—all the things

I should be dealing with instead of standing in a basement with a conceited Peter Pan. My mind wanders...

Blue is not an atypical modern college student, I think. In some ways, he is no different from many affluent white members of the young intelligentsia. He strikes me as driven, capable, spoiled, and hopelessly disillusioned. And his restlessness has roots.

As a boy, Mathias was an acolyte in the Episcopal church and went to the prestigious Deerfield Academy boarding school, where he excelled in academics and athletics alike. As a sophomore he was captain of the school debate team and varsity wrestling state champion (182 lb. weight class). "They didn't have a boxing team," he said to me almost apologetically. And he was the star of the National Institute of Standards and Technology's Summer Undergraduate Research Fellowship (SURF) program.

That's one history. It aptly describes the mild-mannered front cultivated by this boy wonder. But like most superheroes, there exists a shadowy origin story, universally known by USVers: his father, Colonel Nathan Blue (ret.), directs the heavily expensed Defense Advanced Research Projects Agency (DARPA), a think tank for the next generation of warfare, IT, and other innovations heralding the future of the future.

Mathias described his relationship with his parents as "embattled" (they couldn't be reached for comment). At age eleven, Mathias's twin brother, Edison, was killed in a freak accident during a summer storm, crushed by a falling tree. As I stand in this basement thinking of the forces that conspired to create this young man, my mind oddly starts to relax. My body follows. My eyes blur, and suddenly I can make out other statuesque figures frozen in the shadows. I hadn't noticed them before this moment. I can see they are in costume. When the *tonggg* chimes again, one of them lies on the ground by my feet and tells me, "It's time to fly."

They lift me into the air, my arms outstretched like Supergirl. Soon we are in their garage and I'm placed in the back of a van, which should be horrifying but somehow feels safe. Here, I get a look at the so-called League of Nine USV superheroes: several scantily clad ladies and armor-bodied boys. There's Peacemaker, Sergeant Drill, It Girl, SuperVisor!, a techno kid straight out of Japanese anime films, and a short one in a three-piece suit.

As they systematically undress Mathias and help him into his superhero garb, I realize Mathias is not an altogether likable person. He is arrogant, like a Bruce Wayne playboy mixed with a less worldly version of

Brando's Colonel Kurtz from *Apocalypse Now*. But as he begins his transformation into Ultraviolet—a modified straitjacket, purple body paint, colored contact lenses—something childlike takes him over.

He whips around the van with Mad Hatter energy. There is something *invincible* about him. I ask if he's afraid of going to prison. After all, the school administration and federal law enforcement agencies alike have labeled the USV a "threat to the safety of our children and community." Some have lost their place in school and now face the very real possibility of going to jail and losing their personal freedoms as well.

Cap'n Cunt is undoubtedly the female leader, the Bonnie to Mathias's Clyde. She answers: "They think we're dangerous because they think we have nothing to lose. And in some ways they're right. We don't believe the future *exists*. So why waste time fearing its consequences?" The boy in the three-piece suit (Business-Man) continues: "But in some ways, this means we have *everything* to lose. The *present* is now much more precious."

So despite their ostentatiousness, the point of the USV is not to have the coolest outfit. The point is to evolve. When I ask if they have Marxist sympathies—as did many of their 1960s forebears—Business-Man takes offense: "We believe in utopian communities of mutual aid, so people call us communists or socialists, but really we're acting out of pure self-interest. Capitalist corporate cogs, *they're* the ones dressing the same and acting the same and doing the same work for the good of the larger unit. Look at us! Each costume represents something personal and entrepreneurial. This is 'super-individualism.' Print that, if you like."

"Actually, no, don't call it that!" yells Ultraviolet. "That's a term that'll get demonized. Call it like *flibberflibbergaboobieism*. I can spell that if you want [he spells it]. And the name of our movement is [makes a noise like a donkey and a spaceship]. Print *that*. Any other term and I'll sue for libel."

I can't tell if I'm witnessing a collective nervous breakdown—overachievers cracking under lifelong pressure—or whether this is overachieving taken to its logical, final step of saviorhood. Either way, these are overachievers on the edge. I ask if they've considered violent forms of protest, something besides civil disobedience. Ultraviolet says he's "an equal opportunity nutjob," and so long as the protest is effective, it's fair game. The looks on the faces around Ultraviolet belie this comment.

If this sounds like moral flexibility, it is. Despite its pacifist rhetoric the USV has become increasingly bold. Early pranks—including the famous nude homecoming bonfire resulting in twenty-four arrests—have evolved into disruption, disorder, and destruction. Just before spring break, the USV defaced the campus registrar's office, pouring duck blood on ERA recruiting paperwork. During a corporate employer's info session, the USV locked the doors of the career services building, caulking them tight, and flooding the lobby with a fire hose. Corporate HR reps and the few attendees were evacuated with only minor injuries.

The water theme continues as we exit the van and arrive at the Institute for Advanced Study near the Princeton campus, where more than two hundred students are lined up in the Institute Woods to be dosed by Ultraviolet's psychedelic drug and set adrift in the Stony Brook.

This is the Big Bang. Experiencing this ceremonial vision is the core prerequisite for joining the USV. I admit, I'm not up for it: my fear of losing control is, to a shameful degree, more powerful than my commitment to investigative journalism. I observe from a nearby rock and wonder what I'm missing.

A female initiate explains to me that DMT "supercharges the undergraduate experience. In five minutes, you see your path forward. You see what the Buddhists call your 'right livelihood.'" I ask her what's the point of finding your purpose in the world if the world will soon be gone.

"At the end," she says, "I need to know I'm still a good person. If I die, I want to die good. If I live, I want to live good. Survival of the fittest and dystopian hellscapes only happen if we lose our humanity. But if we stay good through the dark neck of time? We evolve the species. For the better."

I watch Ultraviolet deliver his medicine. Midlevel initiates are stationed in the current, guiding each body gently down the stream. Students float finally to Cap'n Cunt, the soothsayer who witnesses and validates their experience with vague yet interpretable visions of each one's superhero persona and its villainous shadow. The recruits are then fitted with blank masks and wrapped in purple "evolution capes." On the Stony Brook shore, they come to, baptized, ready to do some good.

Toward the end of this ritual, I ask Mathias what he sees as the USV's ultimate endgame. He answers quickly: "The purification of the world." The reply unnerves me. Specifically that word: "purification." But before I can follow up, a different word comes dancing into my brain.

"'*Stopped*'!" I scream. "That's the antonym of 'busy.' To be *busy* versus to be *stopped*!"

"No," Mathias says. "Someone asks if you're *busy* for lunch. You say, 'No, I'm not busy. I'm *free*.'"

Correspondent **Nina Samaras** is the author of the forthcoming *Time in a Bottle: Notes on the New Famine*.

ii.

There's tilapia swimming in the tank below. Seeds in the grow bed above. Bacteria convert fish waste into nitrates, and a solar-powered pump brings that nutrient-rich water to the grow bed. Plant roots feast and filter, purifying the water to cycle back to the fish below. They'd start small but expand fast. A good system could yield leafy greens and herbs for now—tomatoes, broccoli, and other fruiting plants once it's more established—plus plenty of pounds of fish meat.

This was Aquaponics 101, taught by a superhero called Owl Qween.

Clocks were becoming less reliable, but when the sun was in the sky, the USV went to school. David branded these breakout classes Savage Innovation Training Sessions (SITS). They were less formal than he made it sound. Members could drop into workshops on power generation, food production, paramedic training, chemical and herbal medicines, cordage and textiles, basic machine and engine repair, welding, scavenging, hunting, candle / soap / deodorant-making.

Commodity nouns became learnable verbs.

For instance, there was *gathering* and then there was *scavenging*. *Scavenging* was collecting what's been abandoned or taking what's locked up. Don't call it *looting*, that dog-whistle word meaning black or brown people are trying to survive. Scavenging was a different course of study from the one focused on edible plants, dumpster diving, and repurposing everyday household items. That one was Gathering 101, taught by superheroes named Foragette and Todd Everything.

Nobody was an expert, really. They were in college, and most had logged way more time considering nineteenth-century romanticism and student loan debt as opposed to trade skills. So practical and physical coursework was a focus for many, but cultural enrichment and spiritual practices still had their place. The world was getting tougher, and the USV had to match this turmoil with the kind of soft fortitude found only in the mystic's toolkit. Meditation 101, for instance, taught by a superhero named Janelle Monáe.

There was only one structured meal per day at The Egg, and even that was fairly improvised. A kind of potluck, plus whatever the cooking team in Fred's House could produce in mass quantities—usually pasta, pemmican, or something granola-based. Any other eating was DIY, catch as catch can.

The meal was relaxed and social—"Hey, I'm Lola Rolla. Majoring in power. Minoring in food. Nice to meet you!"—but every seventh minute, the chime rang out through Woosamonsa Court, a basic doorbell from Lowe's that Fu/Golden Echo put on a timer and wired to their new indoor/outdoor speaker array, added some reverb. Soon, the regularly scheduled chime became a powerfully resonant *TONGGG* that rang out religiously, calling them to a halting silent stillness every seven minutes, like a constant Sabbath waiting at the end of every six minutes of action.

They called it the Seventh-Minute Stop. And it became one of their few key rules: when you hear the *tonggg*, freeze in place. Don't talk. Don't move. Experience the moment.

It could break the proverbial flow, but it also defined the higher order of their movement.

—Ø—

David waited out the latest *tonggg*, finished his business, and dropped *The Atlantic* piece about the USV beside the toilet. He liked the *Time* magazine article better. It was more balanced and inclusive, he felt, focusing on the entire movement rather than only its figurehead. *The Atlantic* barely even mentioned SITS. On the cover above the headline "The Last Saviors?" was a Cap'n Cunt illustration taken from the splash page of *Tales from the USV #9*, an homage to *The Last Supper* with the League of Nine seated in their superhero garb around Ultraviolet.

Haley's illustrative style had grown more painterly, less campy, depicting a world of chiaroscuro contrasts and brooding close-ups that made them all look increasingly heroic. She'd handed over the comic work to her underlings and now either focused on the costuming vision of the USV or obscured herself with the black eye of a video lens. Mostly fly-on-the-wall documentary stuff. None of that wave-at-the-camera crap.

Somewhere along their collective journey, the spiritual partnership forged between Mathias and Haley (their Big Bang depths in the hospital swimming pool) had expanded to an emotional and intellectual connection (his artistic mentorship vis-à-vis her costume design and video work) and inevitably completed the cycle into physical union (they began fucking, reasonably loudly).

Haley still wasn't talking to David. When they'd cross paths she'd puff out her cheeks awkwardly and pretend to fiddle with her camera and pass by as quickly as possible. Rowboats in the morning. David made half-assed apology attempts. She offered equally half-assed acceptances. They both understood: the USV was now bigger than their petty personal issues. But she wasn't ready to forgive him. And, you know, ever since she'd started up with Mathias, David wasn't particularly ready to forgive her, either. So they shelved their respective love and hate.

They went back downstairs and did their jobs.

In the rare moments David was forced to resurface onto the main floor of The Egg, he felt like he'd stepped out of a cave and into a carnival. Once, popping upstairs to make a Hot Pocket, David bumped into an unfamiliar Gigantor. He wore athletic shoulder pads and wielded a lacrosse stick. As David pressed Start on the microwave, the guy whispered, "You're Business-Man, right?"

"Yup," said David.

"I thought you'd be taller."

David sighed. "Are you supposed to be Casey Jones? Like from the *Ninja Turtles*?"

"I'm LAX Luthor," he said with a practiced sneer. "I was a pretty decent midfielder but I'm done with sports. Now, I'm a USV defender. This is exactly what I should be doing right now."

"Looks like you're aping Peacemaker's costume." David scanned the living room. There were at least two dozen unfamiliar people in various stages of outfitting. He spotted a guy in a blazer and dyed red hair holding court. Seeing obvious echoes of his own Business-Man costuming, David became incensed at the blabbermouth, whom he knew to be named "the Red Ruminator," a neoliberal politics major whose superpower was filibustering (for his thesis he aimed to infiltrate Congress and pull a *Mr. Smith Goes to Washington*, though David was unclear of his legislative cause).

Behind him, cooking ramen on the woodstove, was "the Flop," a Harlequin-y girl covered in playing cards (she was an online poker champ, her thesis on game theory and war tactics, but her real value was generating gambling revenue for the USV kitty).

In the sunroom, with a healthy crowd gathered around him, was "Pop-N-Lock Popinjay," a break-dancer sporting an Afro and a top hat (he'd recently started an after-school hip-hop dance class for kids in Newark).

The androgynous kid huddled in the corner by the laptop and laser jet, wearing a purple crushed velvet jumpsuit, was a superhero named "Prints," whose thesis was about building a hard copy archive, printing out thousands of pertinent pages of the internet before it inevitably ceased to work and they had to resort to paper. He focused on the most postapocalyptically relevant sites—prepper/DIY tutorials, Wikipedia entries, how-to guides, medical texts, the Great Books series—and was on the short list of practically minded superheroes whom David was grooming to join him in the operational corps of the USV.

In fact, he began working with Prints to create the USV's Living Library, a ten-volume series of massive binders, constantly updated and organized around food (animal and vegetable), drink (water and booze), fire (for heat and community building), construction (for land and floodwater), medical (herbal and chemical), machines, security, communications, culture, and power (finite and renewable). Compressed print-on-demand versions of the library—plus *The Superhero's Journey*—were driven and hand-delivered to all known USV chapters, ensuring the whole survival network was aligned.

The full Living Library resided in the basement of Fred's House and would be one of the key things saved and transported in the event of emergency exodus. They also downloaded billions of bytes of YouTube videos to local hard drives and even rented an old 16mm film camera from the Princeton video department's equipment cage (they'd never returned it) to capture physical footage of the most important online videos—first aid and such—so they could always pass these reels through a hand-crank projector if the future got truly desperate.

Blink. The trio of women leaders, bounding through The Egg.

They often traveled as a pack, discussing the particulars of new recruits: Nyla/Sergeant Drill judging their overall training progress; Zoe/SuperVisor asking after their physical well-being; Britt/It Girl communicating their mental health. They swung through the kitchen, deep in conversation, all busyness, barely giving David a nod.

David looked back to LAX Luthor. "Why do you look familiar?"

"We were in Problem of Evil together. I thought you were nuts. All that Zoroastrianism stuff."

"Oh."

"But Ultraviolet helped me see," LAX continued. "You're a transformative figure." He shook David's hand. The microwave mercifully beeped and David removed his puff pastry.

With every new Big Bang initiate they had a new believer—one who'd seen the End with his or her own psychedelic eyes and could now think of nothing else but how to prepare for it.

David knew he might not be able to stem the tide of Ultraviolet's June 6 doomsday date, but national USV expansion seemed the obvious next step to prepare as many kids as possible for it. Per their volume on communications, they'd divided the country into five distinct regions and created a hub-and-spoke distribution model—the USV home office would disseminate information to each region hub, via radio or physical travel, and the hubs would communicate to their local USV chapters. They accounted for sea-level rise and future flooding, and David admittedly got a little nostalgic and romantic when it came to picking the college towns that served as region heads, selecting campus-based chapters with a history of activism. The world was crumbling around them, but here in The Egg was a countrywide ecosystem solidifying, coming together.

And so it was at about this time that David was forced to ask himself the question that all the articles were asking: Was the USV a *cult*? Is this what David had accidentally started? He told himself it was a social movement, practical with a slight overtone of spirituality. This was his work, his ultimate circus. And it was the positive thing he was doing, the thing they were all doing, to keep fear at bay and distract themselves from that annoying, nonstop ticking of the world's clock. *Maybe this is just a phase,* he thought. *We're past denial but not yet arrived at acceptance. We're busying ourselves to leave a final mark while there's still time. We're still too far away from the End. It's not real yet.* Maybe in another month or two it would be time for bucket-list craziness. For goodbyes. For now, this was his job.

David didn't anticipate a sudden painless flash on June 6 vaporizing them all. What if it happened a week earlier or later? Either way, this was a slower, less concrete demise, like Barbie, like Claire. The world had an invisible degenerative disease, impossible to touch; a villain that didn't fight fair. You couldn't just crack your knuckles, wind up, and take a swing at it, or imprison it in some Phantom Zone and send it spinning back into outer space like General Zod. Chronostrictesis was cancer. Luke Hemia cometh. They could only control what they could control and then wait and be wide-awake, unafraid. Hope it might not end after all.

David felt proud of the growing nuisance he'd caused. But he couldn't help but feel ill prepared to handle all these new recruits. Newbies were close to David's heart, but the League of Nine he'd grown to love like blood. David thought they were the smartest, strongest, most vibrant people he'd ever known. He felt honored to count them as contemporaries and comrades.

Fu/Golden Echo kept everyone fed and kept everything fun. His music was shared and became well known across the USV network. Despite serious plans and seriouser consequences, David wanted to make sure they didn't fall into the trap of losing their sense of humor, as these social movements tended to do, so Echo kept the music coming. And Britt/It Girl, their would-be psych major, counseled and listened to them all. Especially Fu, who was her favorite to flirt with. She spoke a mile a minute, touching his shoulder often, and though Fu never said much in return, after an onslaught of attention he'd pull David aside and whisper something like "That was like the best conversation with a girl I've *ever* had..." David wanted to kiss him on the head, because Fu was the best, and Fu was falling in love, and this was a wonderful thing to watch, but then David would realize it might actually *work out for him*. David's own jealousy would take hold. As Fu stopped wearing his headphones altogether, David began wearing his infrared goggles around the house so he didn't have to make eye contact. Heading outside he—

Tonggg!

...

...

Tonggg!

Outside, The Egg's backyard initially resembled a quilt of tents surrounding a central ceremonial clearing. But Sergeant Drill had since put her carpentry and construction know-how to use, working with teams to build three tin-roofed structures: The Shed was for woodworking and fabrication. The Studio was for writers, designers, video editors—anyone Ultraviolet referred to as the "quiet creatives." And The Shack was for music, liquor distilling, and general after-hours carrying on.

Late at night, the toast repeatedly rang out from The Shack: "To evil!"

Many new initiates now lived back there in tents full-time, and when he wasn't cooking in the basement, Dr. Ugs used the central clearing to facilitate Big Bangs, working with a few former acidheads to shepherd kids through the experience. Otherwise, Dr. Ugs stayed solo in his basement lab, making magic beans, always tweaking the recipe. Like David's, Lee's was a solitary existence.

"Ever feel self-marooned down here?" David once asked Lee, watching him titrate something into something else. "Like Thoreau at Walden Pond?"

"Stop talking like that," Lee said. "Thoreau was an *anarchist*. If he'd lived in the days of chemical terrorism, he'd have been the fucking Unabomber. Both smart, ugly bearded dudes, living in cabins. Thoreau burns down the forest and Kaczynski mails anthrax to civil servants. It's just fucking time and media that says one is a hero and the other a villain. Makes it hard for me to know whether Dr. Ugs is what I should be striving for, or whether my shadow is the real fucking ideal."

Lee's shadow character was called, very plainly, Mrs. Ruth Popkin. His mom's name. She was a lonely alcoholic who popped pills until she popped too many and her heart stopped.

"I revived her," Lee remembered. "But her brain was never as good."

"So then you saved her. You're a hero."

"I did it more for me than for her, though. It was ultimately a selfish action. Sometimes I think it might be better to let something die. Like it's unnatural to stop the inevitable. Maybe God knows that, too. Maybe he's fucking pissed at us for meddling with the order of things. It's humanity's turn to die and we're trying to revive our species, but maybe it's better to just let go."

David supposed he had a point. But he wasn't about to concede anything to Lee, not ever. In the basement of The Egg, hatching new and nobler spectacles, David tried to regain the good.

Haley and Mathias, too, stayed downstairs most of the time. They'd probably prefer to have emerged more often, but—on David's insistence—they paid only twice-daily visits upstairs. The growing status of Mathias Blue and Haley Roth—King Shit and Queen Bee—demanded they ration their appearances, doling them out sparingly like Christmas gifts to orphan children.

They'd rise from the cellar together, unhurried and regal, and then they'd break apart, separately surveying their kingdom. Mathias sauntered slowly but rarely stayed still. Sometimes he'd shake hands and make small talk like a good politician; other times he'd evade all contact, teasing everyone with his very presence and returning downstairs without doing much of anything (this was all carefully orchestrated). But if you were lucky enough to stand beside him as the chime went *tonggg*, spending a full minute in his energy field, it was like you'd just won a game of musical chairs.

Haley was more generous. She always looked like she'd just awoken from some delicious nap. David would watch from the patio, smoking, as she moved through the house, crouching down and offering design advice to a girl sewing sequins onto a costume. She was royalty passing through an elementary school classroom, bestowing blessings. He tried not to stare.

The only time she lost her cool was when some unwitting freshman donned a Mexican wrestling mask as part of his persona. Haley kicked him in the chin and clawed her fingers through his eyeholes as she ripped the mask off his stupid head and threw it in the woodstove. That made the USV's one and only dress code violation fairly clear for all would-be initiates. Haley had power.

It would've been easier to exist in the basement without the ecstasies of David's two loves intermittently finding his ear. And honestly? It's not like they were assholes about it. Mathias knew he'd hurt him and did his best to assure David he was still the favorite, the most important person in the house, the true leader, the secret king. And Haley? David liked to think she cared enough not to rub his face in it on purpose. Theirs was simply Olympic-caliber intercourse. They did it four, six times a day. Whenever the chime *tonggg*ed, David tried not to listen to them catching their breaths.

Except once. He could hear Haley whispering something breathy to Mathias, something like a chant. Creeping out of his own bedroom across the basement concrete, David saw their drywall shifting with each thrust. He stepped up to Mathias's door and pressed his ear against the frame. And he couldn't be sure, but he could swear Haley was grunting, *"Please quench me."*

Good god.

Why couldn't he hate them? It was hard to blame them for being the perfectly marketable power couple. But David—nay, Business-Man—wasn't he kind of famous, too? Didn't he deserve some recognition? So with Mathias and Haley always banging their brains out, David took it upon himself to get seduced, letting young ladies prey on his celebrity and insecurity.

Once, while in the garage taking inventory of a truckload of wholesale fabric, David got cornered by two opportunistic heroines. As he was leaning over the bolts of material, they flanked him from behind. The short one pressed her breasts against David's elbow, subtly at first, and then not so subtly. The other was at least a foot taller than David, jet-black hair pulled into a ponytail, and engulfed him with long, muscular limbs. He didn't recognize her at first.

"You're a little workhorse, aren't you?" said the tall one, massaging his neck. She wore a sumptuous Druid-like cloak rimmed in animal fur. "Do you remember me? From Forbes?"

"First-Floor Allie!" said David, taken aback.

"I'm Skyfox now," she said. "And this is Honey Mustard."

Honey wore yellow yoga pants and a tank top covered in mustardy puffy paint. She wasted no time, her hands already coasting along David's belt buckle. "I'm sweet and spicy," she said.

David turned his eyes back up to the towering Skyfox, who was running her fingers through David's Mohawk, tickling his bare scalp. "You never could remember my name," he reminded her.

"Well, I know who you are now, Business-Man," she said. "Can we get into it, or what?"

Honey Mustard had removed his belt and was working on the button of his shorts.

"That's quite an offer," David said. "But communal living is not simply about open, um, pleasures of the flesh. What I'm doing here is bigger, purer. I see the clock ticking. You're discovering your powers, giving something to the world as it faces collapse, receiving grace from—"

"We're going to receive *you* in our pretty little mouths," said Honey Mustard.

David resisted as they tried to guide him down to the pile of fabric bolts, but as they continued to whisper sweet nothings in regards to the fellating of his pecker, their vapid willingness and ulterior motives on full display, David couldn't help but get aroused. He wasn't comfortable, though, wasn't used to being the coveted one, handled and groped unexpectedly. He realized this was what women must deal with constantly and how annoying and uncomfortable it must be.

He tried to save himself.

"It's difficult to give myself over to this without a true connection," David said. "You see, I'm *in love*, is what I'm saying, I guess, and, oh wow, and the heart wants what the heart wants, and—and I feel like I would just be taking advantage of you both, which is not fair to you, or to our moral code, because no man has a right to enforce his will, ohhhkay, so, um, were you thinking this could be the kind of thing where you both went down on me at the same time, like switching off and then maybe kissing each other, and—"

He'd just barely begun to relax into it, letting his body sink into the rolls of fabric, Skyfox's talented mouth now wrapped around him, in truth hoping Haley and Mathias might walk into the garage at that moment so he could make them as jealous as they'd made him. He'd barely begun to have his own fun... when the Seventh-Minute Stop and its all-pervasive *tonggg* rang out.

It halted their moans and pierced the moment. At first Skyfox just froze with her head in David's lap, his cock in her now-still mouth. It was funny at first. But a minute is a long time. Soon, David began to lose his gumption. And his hard-on. And as he grew less and less impressive, he heard the girls start to snicker, probably at the ridiculousness of the situation in general, but David took it more personally. Soon, Skyfox let his shrinking prick slip from her mouth. When the *tonggg* rang them back into motion, the moment was gone, and the disappointment and frustration was palpable. David slid himself back into his shorts, climbed out of the fabric mound, and bowed.

"I hope you see: this just isn't who I am," he said, as if his resistance were voluntary.

—Ø—

David still didn't know who he was, so he convinced himself he could be many things: a leader, a follower, a student, a teacher, a hands-dirty DIYer, an above-the-fray manager, a radical activist, a corporate suit, a caped crusader, a businessman. He could be everything.

All the heroes, they each contained multitudes, didn't they? Owen was a jock, invested in his own physicality and the protection of the USV, but when David asked him for an update on their basement Electrocycle power system, he responded *off the top of his head*, "We need 50 kilowatt-hours to power the home on a normal day when the grid is up, but grid down, we can cut out HVAC entirely and focus on powering the fridge and freezers, Lee's lab, minimal radio equipment, a few computers, and our LEDs, so with 40 watt-hours produced in each half-hour workout, times forty-eight workouts per day if we max out, times five Electrocycles, we're looking at about 9.5 kilowatt-hours, minus fifteen percent transfer loss, so about 8 kilowatt-hours, times thirty days average, that's about 245 kilowatt-hours per month, and added to the solar—"

"Are we *good* on energy?!" David interrupted, the numbers hurting his head.

"We're not great. We're *good* on energy," Owen said. "For now."

Good for now. David knew the variables would continue to change.

The key was constant improvisation.

But while the USV was constantly evolving, the deadline for the PEN Startup Competition was fixed and had arrived. So David put the finishing touches on his file, printed and slipped it into a nondescript folder. He told the guys he was going to pick up more PVC for their Aquaponics system, jumped in the MaxMobile, and headed for campus.

Arriving at Princeton, his first time there in weeks, David was unable to park close to campus. It was pouring, and portions of Washington Road were underwater or blocked off, while University Place was packed with service vehicles and work crews. Most of the nearby parking lots—the ones that were still dry enough—served as staging areas. David ultimately parked at the Institute for Advanced Study, still a quiet haven away from campus. He slid the business plan folder under his shirt to keep it semidry and hoofed it across the golf course toward Forbes.

The course had gone to shit, obviously. The greens and fairways, unmowed and overgrown, had transformed into a lush and fertile pasture, while the bunkers and water hazards had overflowed and mixed together into a soupy quicksand. Forbes, too, was roped off with yellow police tape, the parking lot saturated and sandbags forming an inadequate barricade around the front door. Clearly, they'd evacuated his old dorm. But David saw activity up ahead on higher ground.

The fountain outside of Lewis Arts Complex had become a harbor for canoes and kayaks, and some enterprising or drunk students were staging a raucous water-joust, tipping each other over amid rebel yells.

They'd consolidated students into upper-campus housing, the rooms on the higher floors. Courtyards were now strung with a labyrinthine cat's cradle of clotheslines stretching between dorms, with waterlogged and abandoned laundry hanging like tattered prayer flags. Feeling sentimental and curious, David jogged toward Blair Arch, spotting an encircled crowd in the tunnel underneath. At first he thought they were just huddled under cover to get out of the rain, but they were watching some kind of whooping activity, and it sounded like a Brazilian capoeira demonstration, the kind of multicultural offering once commonplace on campus, but as he got closer and pushed through the pile, David realized it was just two assholes fighting.

Finally, David arrived at Alexander Hall. It sat on a small hill and was therefore serving as a common meeting place for numerous classes and administrative offices. The auditorium inside, once accustomed to singular events like orchestra performances or poetry readings by Nobel laureates, was packed to the brim, the seating sectioned off with masking tape and poster board into loosely delineated classes. Candles illuminated each space. David thought it looked cool at first, a kind of teeming Socratic arena, but the cacophony was intense, and soon David hustled to find the drop-off box marked PEN COMPETITION so he could be on his way.

There were only six other submissions in the box, so David knew he had a decent shot. How many kids would jump through such hoops? There was no secretary or department head overseeing the submission, but David hoped it would get to the competition's lead judge, Professor Zhou.

On his way out of the auditorium, he spotted a sign for the Environmental Studies 215 course in which he was enrolled, about ten students clustered around an exhausted-looking woman with glasses and flyaway hairs pouring out of a ponytail. She was lecturing on the topic of resilience.

"Of course, Frankl writes that *trauma,*" she read aloud from her notes, "a particularly difficult situation, is what 'gives man the opportunity to grow spiritually beyond himself.' Who disagrees?"

David found a dry seat and sat down to be a student.

iii.

The red was thick and dark on his hands like slasher-movie blood when David's parents called The Egg on their recently installed landline. Tiny hairs littered the kitchen sink. Remnants from his latest head-shave. He'd just finished dyeing his Mohawk again, but at a glance you'd think he'd slaughtered a lamb. David Fuffman: Demon Barber of Woosamonsa Court.

The power had been off for three days and David's cell phone was dead. When he rinsed a palm and lifted the kitchen receiver, his parents were there crying, "Hi, honey!" in unison. Squinting at himself in the mirror, half bald and slathered in crimson goo, David thought, *That's so wrong: I am a badass vigilante. I am dirty, raw, and radical. I am nobody's honey.*

"We haven't talked since my birthday!" yelped Mom. David vaguely remembered the evening in early March. He'd called just before midnight to wish her things.

"How about this Time Crisis!" said Mom. "I read about your friend in the newspaper."

They were excited, albeit concerned, about the USV. They knew their son was at the center of it. Maybe, in the same way that David was focusing on the USV to distract him from the reality that lay ahead, his parents were focusing on David, their own work in progress, to distract themselves from the same impending fear.

"Hey," David said absently to his mother. "Can I talk to Beth?"

When his little sister got on the phone, at first David thought Beth was crying or had a cold, but then he realized her voice had simply changed since they'd last spoken. It had been that long.

"Heya, kiddo, how's your bluegrass mandolin working out?" David asked her.

"I play old-time music, not bluegrass," she said. "They're completely different things."

"What's wrong?" he asked.

"Nothing."

"C'mon."

"You told me I could come visit you at college," she said. "But you never invited me."

"Beth, see, you're still really young and it's a little too dangerous for you here right now."

She sighed long into the receiver. "Yeah, well, I'm *twelve* now. Almost a teenager. And you didn't call." She dropped the phone and the line went quiet, muffled voices in the distance.

Oh fuck. He'd missed her birthday. He felt like such a shit. Hurting Beth was just too evil.

What was happening with him?

"You should have called," Mom confirmed when she got back on the phone. "But she'll understand about not visiting. Sometimes... you're just too young to be exposed to certain things."

"So... it's March 30," Dad interjected. And at first David thought he was again highlighting the fact that it had been weeks since their last call—an eternity in Fuffman time— but then his father clarified: "We're worried about your, uh, plan. For tomorrow. The Day of the Hero?"

"Oh," David said. Out the window it was still raining like mad. A group gathered round a reliquary mound of stolen clocks. They might've been praying, who knows.

This is so right, David thought. *Our Manifest Destiny.*

"We're concerned about the possibility of expulsion," his father said. "Or jail, by the way, mister. That letter from the president seemed serious and—"

"Don't worry," David snapped. "I'm protected."

"Protected how?"

"I'm the secret king."

After a pause, David's mother began speaking again—something about balancing the responsibility of the adult with the freedom of the child—but David wasn't listening. He was staring at a tiny head-shaving worming its way into one of the phone's mouthpiece holes. Using a dry knuckle, he pressed the hair all the way in, until it disappeared down there.

This will be your new home, little hair, forever and ever.

"We're just concerned that instead of studying you're spending *so* much time—"

"Look," David said, growing bold. "The work I'm doing with the USV is going to serve me better in whatever future than meaningless tests and grades ever will. This is the best way I can use my God-given gifts and my work ethic to do something real and important and create an organized container that might just save some lives and—"

"But are you really safe?" Mom asked.

"What is safe?! There's a war on, for chrissakes, and the campus is flooded and—"

"We have half a damn roof right now," Dad said. "We realize nobody's safe from weather. What your mother is asking is whether you're doing anything *illegal*, David. Your altruistic intentions are well and good, but if you wind up in jail? Not a very fun place to ride out a storm, buddy."

"If things ever go back to normal, I'm making connections," David lied. "I'm organizing, impressing people, being an important person. That's what you've always wanted, isn't it? For me to be *important*? Well, now I'm important. I'm the chief, kept separate from the action on the ground."

"Wow, you *must* be important," said Mom. "Better than getting dragged off by your hair."

"So don't worry. I'm doing *exactly* what I should be doing right now. And if you're so worried," David continued. "You should come up here and join us."

"Yeah, right," scoffed his father.

"Bring your camera, Dad. We could use the coverage. Something waterproof in case they use fire hoses again. Mom, you, too. Help us rally people like it's the Women's Marches all over again."

They were silent for a moment. Their own personal *tonggg*.

And then Mom asked, "Do we need costumes?"

iv.

David had to order the telephone booth special from a rec-room supply catalog. Up in the Frist Campus Center, he stood at a bay window, wearing his three-piece suit and wireless headset mic. He stared down at the old-time phone booth on the Princeton campus, his arms crossed, like a foreman surveying his factory floor. He was Business-Man.

Mentally, he did a quick accounting. The telephone booth had cost $1,560 plus tax. Typically chump change for Mathias, but lately funds were running low. The USV's primary expenses were the three mortgages, Lee's chemicals, costuming, food, and printing/marketing costs, in that order, and had grown to about $26,000 over the past month. That left a $4,000 monthly budget to plan the USV's intermittent public spectacles, since the revenue from pharmaceutical sales, Mathias's trust, and membership dues had generally exceeded costs.

But over the last two weeks, expenses had overtaken revenues, and David was reasonably sure it was Mathias's own side projects that had sent them into the red. Maybe this was just the nature of growth, a slow and steady expansion, a little here, a little there, until pennies equaled thousands. Like climate change—an incremental creep of degrees, too slow and subtle to notice when you're right there in it—the old yarn about the frog in the pot, water temperature rising from tepid to boiling, and the little amphibian doesn't realize he's being cooked alive. David resolved to recruit more quants—econ and math majors—and do a full audit, just as soon as time allowed.

David had confronted Mathias about the financial issue: "If you want me managing all of this, we need to trust each other, and I need to know what you're working on."

"Absolutely," Mathias had said. "You drive."

—Ø—

They flew across Jersey, David driving to who knows where, Mathias next to him, manic, speaking fast between short bursts of silence, gripping his axe. Christopher Walken's backseat was filled with shovels and rakes and other implements of mass destruction. David tried not to be frightened—was there blood on that axe?—but here was Mathias, babbling about some comic book called *ABC Warriors*, about Joe Pineapples and Happy Shrapnel and the Volgan War, and everything was somehow related to a song by the Jam called "Going Underground."

They were near Kingwood, a few miles north of Rosemont. Thinking it might give him strength, David stuck his nose onto the shoulder of László's blazer and took a deep sniff.

"I'm wondering now about your grandfather, David, about how he died."

See? He did it again. David hated when Mathias pulled that psychic shit and told him so.

"You were snorting your lapel. I figured you were summoning him. Doesn't take a genius."

"He was kind of messed up at the end, I'm told," David said.

"Did he have some kind of addiction?"

"Is there blood on that axe?"

"Some," he said.

"Where are we going, man?"

"We're burying something that's in the trunk!"

David pulled over. "I'm not driving any farther until you tell me what's in there."

Mathias swiveled his head. "Actually, this is perfect. Grab the shovels and follow me."

They'd arrived in the middle of nowhere. David felt even more vulnerable and wondered if maybe Mathias had brought him out here to do away with him. At first, David had been excited for this impromptu field trip with the Übermensch. But had he just chauffeured himself to his own end?

He took a breath and joined Mathias by the trunk, where he was now buckling under the weight of an enormous duffel bag slung over his shoulder. It was just big enough to hold a human.

Was this a dream? A joke?

"Is this a joke?" David asked.

"Right now," Mathias said, "I'm serious as a German."

They walked through a fallow field toward a copse of trees. The only other things in sight were skeletal towers holding power lines. David followed Mathias. He kept following. Why did he keep following, exactly? Curiosity maybe? Fear? After the Big Bang, it felt like there was no other choice but to follow this shaman, the only mouse who knew the way out of the maze.

By the woods Mathias doubled over, the duffel bag flopping to the ground with a cold *thud*.

"Here is good," he said, and reached for David to hand him a shovel. Mathias bent down to unzip the duffel. David steeled himself for dead elbows.

When the bag opened, all David could see was red and black.

Shiny orbs. Uniform and massive.

David bent in for a closer look, readying for the recoil, for the smell of death.

Inside the bag were four giant plastic eggs—two red and two black—each the size of a human torso. David reached in and touched them. They were smooth, seamless, hermetically sealed. He needed two hands to lift them an inch.

"Are they bombs?"

"No, man. They're time capsules. Black are machine. Red are meat. It's my thesis. Lee has his capsules. And I..."—he slapped the skin of a giant egg—"I have *my* capsules, too."

He kept digging while he explained:

"Our core biological instinct is to propagate ourselves, right? We want *immortality*. Women want to have babies. Men want to *fuck*. We both really just want to create ourselves over and over again. Grab that rake and clear some leaves, will you, I can barely see the ground..."

David let Mathias lead the conversation and did his best to follow.

"Now, the problem is you make a baby and fifty percent of it comes from a totally different person, so you're only really passing on *half* your genome. We try our best to make our children into identical versions of ourselves, but they're just *not*. They become separate beings, right? And this is where all the *pain* comes in. On a visceral or subconscious level, parents are disappointed with their kids, because they're ultimately not just *another yourself*, right? Keep raking."

"No, I don't know about that."

Mathias bent down and unscrewed one of his giant crimson eggs. The contents were packed tight, but he opened it enough for David to see inside. Affixed in meticulous rows were prescription bottles, Ziploc baggies, mason jars labeled in a loving hand.

"My red capsules are filled with organic matter. That's my hair, blood, tears... um... sweat, fingernails, skin cells, splooj, spit, I think some snot, too. This is the *meat*."

He closed it up.

"The black capsules are inorganic matter. Twenty or thirty terabytes of digital information in each egg: the hard drives of all my computers, copies of every book and article I've read, every movie I've seen. Blueprints of every place I've lived. Crazy-awesome neuroimaging—aha!—compilations of my daily to-do lists from the past ten years, plus some extensive personality tests I had done in Japan. I used to track the data manually, but now you can get pretty much everything through Google's or social media data, which becomes a closer approximation of my *consciousness* than anything found in my genes, so..."

"When did you start doing this?"

"I bury about twenty-five a year, for the last eight years. On four different continents. Each with directions on how to re-create Mathias Blues using the material provided. When the End comes and we turn to ash, *something* is going to take our place. The planet will survive even though humans probably won't. With a few hundred capsules buried, whatever comes next will eventually find one of my eggs and go through the steps to re-create me, even if it's centuries from now."

"Why would they do that?"

"Why do we study dinosaurs? They'll have advanced technology, either the ability to clone or else highly advanced artificial intelligence. Either way, I'm covered. They clone me with the meat or else upload the machine me into AI cyborgs."

"It's like Superman," David said. "Jor-El sent him into space when his home world was about to be destroyed. That spaceship is like a Superman time capsule."

Mathias let out a deep sigh. "Superman is a faggot," he said. David felt a sting.

"Wow," David said, letting it all hit home. "So then you're *completely* insane. You actually believe this is going to happen? The meat and the—"

"No, let me back up. It's an elaborate experiment. A piece of social theater, if you will."

"Yeah, I'm not sure I believe that. And I'm not sure *you* believe that. Burying capsules isn't your shadow. It's not a way of showing *weakness*. You're elevating yourself. Right?"

David turned to digging, letting his seed sink in and take root in Mathias's ego. David knew how to play the game, too. He remembered back to his first time on DMT, in that river, with countless beings pouring out of him. Maybe they were both destined to cultivate the masses.

Suddenly, Mathias smiled and lunged at David, who recoiled and tried to lift his shovel to protect himself from this onslaught, but then Mathias was hugging him like a brother. It was a strong, long hug. David wasn't sure why this was happening.

"So you won't leave?" Mathias asked, almost shaking. "Even when it gets scary?"

"No, dude," he said. "I'm not going anywhere." Mathias was still squeezing David tight.

"Promise me," he said. "I can't hold it all by myself. You're my best friend."

David promised, but soon he found himself laughing. And he couldn't stop. He thought of those orbs and doubled over, laughing at the ground. He reared back, cackling to the morning sky.

"Are you laughing at me?" Mathias's face had suddenly turned serious. "Don't laugh at me."

"No, man. I... oh god! I thought you'd *murdered* someone! I thought it was a fucking person! In the duffel bag! Fuck! I thought your fridge was full of hacked-off body parts wrapped in plastic!"

"No, David," Mathias said, blank-faced. "That would be ridiculous."

—Ø—

Blink. As David thought of Mathias's capsules and his questionable theories on procreation, he considered his own mom and dad. How David was similar and how he was different from them. How had he made them proud? How had he disappointed them?

Their latest spectacle was set, and David searched the courtyard below for his parents. Earlier that morning, after he gave them a tour of The Egg (skipping Lee's lab, obviously), his dad and Haley hit it off, comparing cameras and spouting film theory to each other: art vs. artifice, vérité truth, the uncosmeticized human landscape.

"The camera is the modern means of *bearing witness*," she'd said, glancing sidelong at David.

Yup. Haley still had a lot of rage about Halloween.

Beth was mad at David, too, or maybe at their parents. Mom and Dad had left her with Aunt Abby in Bethlehem, Pennsylvania. It was for her own good, but she didn't see it that way.

This campus was no place for her right now, David told her.

But nowhere was any place for anybody anymore.

The single best video clip of the day's spectacle was filmed by Channel 12's traffic copter—Ultraviolet on the roof of the Scheide Music Building, the campus revolving around him. The still photos, the ones that wound up in *Time* and *Newsweek*, those shots belonged to David's dear old dad. The local news arrived late to the scene, in time to catch a few final heroes getting shuttled away in a paddy wagon, but most of the video coverage from the Day of the Hero came courtesy of cell phone cameras and Cap'n Cunt's DSLR, which she then sold to CNN for a pretty penny.

Flipping through the footage you'd first find Ultraviolet's striptease: on the roof of Scheide he rips off his collared shirt, swings a cape over his head. He lifts a gallon of Benjamin Moore's Mystical Grape latex paint, displays it like an infant heir to the throne. Douses himself in purple.

Next: costumed heroes do the old Superman quick-change, entering and bursting from the phone booth like hornets from a hive. They head straight for the Scheide Music Building, where the plan is for these heroes to commandeer as many percussion instruments as possible. All but one of the members of Princeton's African Drumming Ensemble were now part of the USV and wanted their *djembes*, *dunun*, congas, and talking drums—which would be a useful, uniting force for Echo's Human DJ experiences.

It also served as a decoy, diverting the attention of campus police from the real heists going on all across campus, where a bunch of non-costumed USVers were pilfering fabrication materials from the architecture building, film equipment from the arts center, bedframes and mattresses and other furniture from the dorms, clothes and groceries from the U-Store, and all manner of mechanical and electrical components from the facilities warehouse. Three goofball heroes even scaled Nassau Hall and stole the clapper from the cupola bell that rang the hours.

For good measure, Ultraviolet initially shouted insanities from the roof about being able to fly, being ready to jump, an added wrinkle that forced the police into more of a crisis negotiation mode as opposed to offensive crowd control. Between his threats to jump, Ultraviolet orated to the USV below:

"Back in the sixties, there was a popular nonviolent response to police action they called 'going limp.' It's exactly what it sounds like. Do we want to be like bags of trash hauled to the curb for disposal? When the police try to move you today, tense your muscles. Make your body rigid, rooted to the ground. Be still. When they cart us away, they will loft our taut limbs wide as a soaring superhero! Stay stiff! Put the 'rigor' in rigor mortis! Evolve or perish!"

Business-Man watched about thirty costumed USVers get carried away in this fashion before a horde of heroes gathered at the door of Scheide, linking arms, an immovable clump. Cops realized this crowd was primed to riot, so they went after the leader instead, tiptoeing their way across the roof, nervously wielding the kind of pool-skimmer implements used to corral suicidal jumpers.

"How do you feel?" Business-Man asked into his headset as the cops got their bearings.

"Like a cold, sassy tree," said his fearless leader. "How 'bout you?"

"Like the fucking Wizard of Oz."

Ultraviolet laughed and said, "Pay *lots* of attention to the Man Behind the Curtain."

"Look alive, U.V. They're coming up behind you. Stay stiff."

And he did look alive. So stately up there, one foot raised on the roof's peak like a big game hunter resting a boot on a prized boar. Most of the USVers down below—with their costumes and tights and gadgets—they looked a bit silly. Haley'd done yeoman's work on fashion design, but superhero garb never looks as good on real humans as it does on illustrated ones. Real people lack idealized musculature. Costumes lack tightness. You can always find a wrinkle. But Ultraviolet somehow maintained the alien bravado of Superman, the litheness of Spider-Man, the millionaire swagger only Bruce Wayne could pull off. It briefly occurred to Business-Man, as the cops closed in, that Ultraviolet might fall. But no. Look at him. Balanced on the peak of a roof and yet this was the most stable he'd ever been. Mathias Blue was beyond clumsy accidents. He was unimpressed with gravity.

Complete equilibrium.

And here David was, pacing in his hidden skybox observatory. There was something so lonely about being him, he thought. All honor, no glamour. And, actually, not much honor, either. He was sick of being cloistered, separate from the action. Why not cast his lot with the rest of them doing battle down there? Was this the work of the Anointed, his shadow, who hadn't paid enough dues to deserve this current station? Was Mathias keeping him away from the spotlight on purpose? No, he didn't want the spotlight. He wanted the trenches, the dirt, the danger! Fuck it.He was sick of

Business-Man made an executive decision. He needed to be part of the game, duking it out down there on the board with all the other chess pieces. He sprinted from the study carrel. Braked hard as he emerged into the March air. Across the courtyard, by the door of the Scheide Music Building, in a human barricade of heroes, one arm locked with Sergeant Drill and the other pointing a video camera, there was Cap'n Cunt. She spotted Business-Man and lifted her mask. He slipped his goggles on, as if going to work. The Cap'n, in spite of herself, smirked. She pointed her camera Business-Man's way. David wondered how he'd look on film. How was his posture? His hair?

Quiet, vain shadow.

Business-Man worried he'd be snatched by cops before he could make it to the safe mass standing by the Scheide doorway. Cops would take him away along with Ultraviolet and the others they'd already loaded into the vans, and though Business-Man would have nobly sacrificed his freedom—something real—for the cause he'd created, it would really suck.

Because then he wouldn't get to stand next to the girl he loved.

Closer now. He spotted his father, crouched like a frog with cameras dangling from his neck, snapping shots. But he never took his eyes off Cap'n Cunt, even when his father got right in front and placed his lens inches from Business-Man's nose. Staring through it, he relaxed his eyes, and now there was only a dark blur in front of him. He walked into this black hole.

And he was feet away from her now and felt a magnetic energy pulling him, the pull of all those bodies, all those cells, like water droplets drawing one another in. Business-Man backed slowly into Cap'n Cunt, close enough to feel her breath against his neck. She slipped her hand inside the pocket of his blazer and gave his ribs a little squeeze. And then she slid aside, allowing him to take his place in the group beside her. They did not speak. But their arms touched and her arm moved upward with each inhale and he loved the way it rubbed. He synced his breath to hers, their limbs rising and falling in unison, and my god this felt exactly like what he should be doing right now.

APRIL

i.

On April 1, it rained birds. Three thousand ravens nose-dived into a Walmart parking lot in Utah, maybe mistaking it for a pond. Next morning, Coast Guard found two million fish floating on the surface of the Chesapeake. Was biology falling behind? Was this preemptive mass suicide?

David wondered which species was next.

A week after they released Mathias Blue from jail, he lined the back of the MaxMobile in mattresses, new and clean. He instructed them all to get into character, then drove to a cornfield, pulled over, and Cap'n Cunt slid into the back, turning on the dome light. She told them how she loved them, how they were locked into something special, the core of revolution, and how being a revolutionary meant living a revolutionary lifestyle.

Business-Man was dressed in character, and his mind wandered. He saw the crew reflected in Cap'n Cunt's oversized sunglasses: Golden Echo in his speaker-covered parka could have been an extra from *Starlight Express*—something part human, part machine, part homosexual. Peacemaker was armored like a self-defense training dummy but more imposing. He must've been so sweaty in that riot suit. Next to him was It Girl, who looked like a chic hobo. She pulled sunglasses from her massive canvas purse filled with outfits and accessories, augmenting herself with flapper gloves, a peek-a-boo hat, a mink stole, dirty pearls. This was one of more than a dozen personalities she could affect. It made David wonder which one was her truest secret identity. And beside her was SuperVisor, whose conservative surgeon's scrubs had recently devolved into a naughtier pants-less version, descending down to thigh-highs and high heels.

It Girl lit a Virginia Slim, nodded at SuperVisor and purred, "Swell stems, Doc."

"In the sixties they had these 'smash monogamy' campaigns," Cap'n continued. "I feel guilty. Blue and I have been off in our own world downstairs. We need to be working like a *single* unit..."

She spoke fast, as if she'd practiced this speech for hours and was trying to get it all out.

"Are you guys breaking up?" asked Golden Echo. He sounded like he might cry.

"We care for each other. We're just not going to be hidden away anymore. Blue agrees."

"I agree," whispered Ultraviolet.

It struck David: *Mathias* wasn't delivering this speech. Had he planted this idea of branching out and tapped Haley as his spokesperson? Or was Haley, in fact, *cutting herself loose*? Something wild brewed inside David. He felt the familiar first rush of a drug taking hold.

"So... some ground rules," Cap'n Cunt said. "Let's aim for connection more than like mind-blowing performance. We're here until sunrise. So take your time and enjoy each other. Cool?"

"Cool," they echoed. Business-Man's chest jumped into his jaw.

Dr. Ugs shook a bottle of pills. This was their new formula, the stuff they were going to start selling. Business-Man was hesitant to turn the USV into lifestyle-drug peddlers, but cash flow was dwindling—due to a major withdrawal by Mathias that he refused to explain, reminding David who was bankrolling this thing in the first place—and they urgently needed revenue. Besides, drug dealing was Cap'n Cunt's old domain. And Dr. Ugs's new pill was but a subtle molecular adaptation from the legal Zeronal pills that were making Pfizer plenty rich. Why not steal some market share?

"These are tweaked with lithium," said Ugs. "Plus a microdose of psilocybin and some sildenafil, the active ingredient in Viagra."

Sergeant Drill was always hesitant about taking something new. After a lifetime of sobriety she now approached drugs like a vendetta, but still, she had reservations about the path she was leading her body down. Dressed in black lace-up boots and her camo jumpsuit unzipped to her navel, she dipped Peacemaker's ROTC hat over her mirrored shades and played with her power drill. But Ugs placed a pill in everyone's palm and said, *"Kezepel,"* and, sure enough, everyone swallowed, except Ultraviolet who'd already taken his pill, and Dr. Ugs, who wanted to stay sober and observe the effects of his new recipe, lest any further tweaking be necessary.

It occurred to Business-Man what was happening. He tried not to say anything stupid. Inside his infrared goggles, his eyes drifted over It Girl's spandexed ass, over SuperVisor's tan thighs...

"Also," Cap'n continued, "we remain unprotected. Time is running out and so we shan't fear STDs or anything else, right? This is a *rawther* natural thing to do when Armageddon is in sight."

"At the End," Ultraviolet clarified, "humans need to fuck."

"Still," Cap'n Cunt added, "no activity without consent. Is this absolutely clear?"

They nodded profusely. Respect.

"How about this," Cap'n Cunt offered. "Consent equals a soft ear tug, like so." She leaned in and hovered her mouth over It Girl's, then thumbed her earlobe, gave it a pinch, and they kissed.

"If you cum, if you need a break, if you get weirded out, bored, overstimulated, whatever, jump up front and take a turn driving. This will be more fun if the car is in motion... Sound okay?"

They raised their eyebrows high. They nodded yes. It Girl said, "Oh, I'm just spiffy, sugar."

Cap'n Cunt walked on her knees toward the center of the pack and turned off the dome light. They all waddled into a circle. They giggled. None of them actually knew how to begin an orgy. Like, was there supposed to be a starter pistol? Should someone drop a scarf?

Then SuperVisor yipped, "Somebody kiss somebody!"

Right on cue, It Girl inched herself into the center of the circle and lifted up Echo's motorcycle helmet. Exposing his delicate mouth, she placed her own full lips on his. He was tense at first, but they all watched as she coaxed his tongue out of his mouth and into hers. It was an innocent, awkward, sweet kiss. It might have been sexier, but neither of them could stop smiling.

It Girl took off her glasses. Echo lifted his dark face shield. His eyes were welling up. He received a round of applause from those who'd assumed this moment between them *must* have already happened and realized it hadn't; this was their first kiss. Business-Man was thrilled for them.

"Okay," said Cap'n Cunt. "Somebody kiss somebody they wouldn't *normally* kiss."

Fired up, Echo leaned across the circle and planted his happy mouth on the purple lips of Ultraviolet. This was a newly empowered Echo, made strong by the love of a good woman. He went back to It Girl, who ran her tongue along his neck and then tapped his RacketJacket, asking for tunes. Echo obliged. Fiddling inside his parka, he produced a perfect blend of bass-heavy ambience.

Golden Echo's *Music for Orgies, Volume 1.*

Meanwhile, Ultraviolet went right for SuperVisor, and when they kissed there was nothing sweet about it. They ravaged each other's mouths, biting tongues, wet and hungry. She'd clearly been angling for this, for him, and she clawed at his taut, wiry chest as he pulled up her long shirt and squeezed her ass in his hands, covering both cheeks with streaks of violet.

David looked at Haley. She didn't even look jealous. With those big eyes, she held his gaze and sent David a hint of something hot. She covered her mouth daintily as if to say, *Oh dear...*

Cap'n Cunt skirted around the group. Business-Man thought maybe she was heading for him but she passed to Sergeant Drill—he would not be the chosen one in her game of Duck, Duck, Goose—and cajoled her into comfort, pressing the butt of the Sergeant's power drill between her legs, letting it vibrate against her as she shrieked at first and then settled in, her hips rolling and mouth opening in low moans. Cap'n smooched her and left her to Peacemaker's cautious advances.

So that was Haley's game, David thought. She wasn't aiming to smash monogamy. She was playing matchmaker. Sacrificing her relationship to foster the coupledom of half a dozen others.

Maybe?

Echo+It Girl crawled over to Sergeant Drill+Peacemaker, while Ultraviolet+SuperVisor were now jawing eagerly at each other's crotch, but, oh, Dr. Ugs. Poor, awkward, chemistry-grad-student, skinny-legged Dr. Ugs. He tried to make his way to the pileup in the back, but his path was cut off by Ultraviolet and SuperVisor, who was now cumming. Hard. She groped at Ultraviolet, shaking wildly, scratching lines into his scalp. It was the first of her many blistering orgasms that night (her body was an extremely easy math equation, which nearly all would succeed in solving). Business-Man knew that Dr. Ugs wished he were the one solving her. Ugs made a half-hearted effort toward the grouping in the back, then pantomimed a driving motion at Business-Man.

Ugs would take the first shift at the wheel.

Shift. Shifting. Something shifts.

And this is when David realizes Haley is finally looking at him. She's not in character anymore. She has no more work to do, no more social lubricating. It's been weeks. They owe each other some face time. He has waited patiently for this come-to-Jesus they're about to have.

They jolt as the van bounces from the field back onto the paved road. The bump sends David flying onto his elbows toward Haley, half by accident. There she is: his captain. Hovering over him, hair waterfalling. She's not smiling anymore and neither is he. She motions him to the side of the van and they lie down together, heads against metal, David's Mohawk spikes bending. It's then, with Haley's face only inches from David's, that they both notice how hard he is. They laugh at the pointy thing poking its way into space, amusingly smushed against his dress pants. She rests her hand on his stomach. He runs his knuckle against the felt of her captain's jacket and undershirt and bra and all those layers, but whatever; it's still *her boob* under there.

The music is hot and deep. He's thought nonstop of that one and only time in the backyard and now it's happening again, and he wishes he'd gotten more practice, learned some new and better tricks since the first time. Haley pulls at David's pants, skilled at operating the hidden clasps and zippers of the modern man's slacks. But when she tries to take off his blazer David stops her. He knows it's kind of twisted, but he wants to leave this amulet on. It's the magic that got him here.

When she grabs at his lapels he whispers, "No, stop..."

And then Haley's face turns. It's as if she's just tripped and fallen on her face and is now looking around, embarrassed and injured.

"No," he whispers. "I mean totally keep going. I just want to leave *this* on."

And maybe it's because he spoke, breaking the mood.

Or because Echo's music has just intensified, growing more frenetic, like an orgasm itself.

Maybe it's because they're on drugs, and everything is weird.

Or maybe it's because he said *"No. Stop."* David has triggered something. Something bad.

She hops off him. Puts on her sunglasses. And she's pulling at David's side, rolling him over onto his stomach—it's so fast—his face now pressed into the cold wall of the van. She thrusts her hand down the back of his loosened pants and in one motion pulls them down to his knees. David tries to crane his head back to her and he can almost see her face, her eyes obscured by those bug glasses, but instead she grabs his Mohawk and pulls tight, pressing his face into the wall, and he really doesn't know what she's about to do to him but he can take a guess and then it happens.

David knows in his mind that he is stronger than she is. But somehow he can't get his body to remember. And so he lies there, prone, pressed into the mattress as Haley shoves what feels like three fingers inside his asshole. David doesn't know what to do because this is the first time anything like this has ever happened to him. He cries out into the mattress—the pain odd and all-consuming, one of nature's processes in reverse—but she keeps shoving her hand in there, jamming him in place against the van wall. And maybe you'd think that something kinky and exciting takes hold. That pain becomes pleasure. That he relaxes into it. That it starts to feel good. But it does not feel good for him. It doesn't ever feel even a little good. It feels like ripping and degradation. Like the only thing he can do to aid his body is to leave it completely.

She pulls out, pulls back. But something is still inside David and won't go away.

He flips over quickly. Scrambling to pull up his boxers, he scrambles away from Haley, her body now slumped in on itself like a wilted daisy. She's still staring at him with those bug eyes. David hops to standing, accidentally banging his head on the ceiling of the van. Everyone else is so involved in each other's junk that they've completely missed what just happened. Which, for David, is a blessing and a curse.

He sees Ultraviolet, who's now pumping back and forth into SuperVisor, her ankles over his shoulders and her hips bucking back against him. Ultraviolet smiles at David, and somehow it feels like *he* was the one who just violated David along with Haley, instead of just Haley, kneeling there with strange and sweaty smiles on both their colluding faces. Haley pulls down her glasses so David can see her wet eyes. She's not crying, he realizes. That's rage. He stares back at her with the same fury.

David needs to go somewhere, but there is nowhere to go.

So he collects his clothes and jumps into the front seat.

"I'll drive," he barks at Dr. Ugs.

Ugs tries to say that he's fine, that he's the sober one, but when Business-Man grabs his lab coat and rips him from the seat, Ugs swings the van to the roadside and gives up the wheel.

Okay, David will drive.

Oncoming headlights leave wicked trails. David blinks and sees Japanese calligraphy. The sign for hope. Blink. The sign for machine. Blink. The sign for meat. Blink. David drives fast. Sixty, seventy miles per hour on dark back roads, speeding into turns and running stop signs. He knows he was recently in pain, and knows he's supposed to be mad about something. But who cares? The new Party Zero is amazing.

"How long does this stuff stay in your system?" David asks Lee.

"Who knows?" Lee responds. "We didn't exactly have proper clinical trials. Mathias is making me help with his shit for Fu's radio, this earworm idea, a piece of music that gets stuck in your head. I swear, the complexity of the brain compared with the body is insane. We don't know the mechanism faction of lithium, but we give it to tons of people. It's trial and error. The brain is a complete fucking asshole. At least the body's honest about what it wants."

"Well, this new stuff is genius. It'll make us a fortune. If we shorten Party Zeronal to PZ, the street name can be Pez, and we'll sell it in Pez dispensers made to look like the nine of us and—"

"You're good with words," Lee interjects. "What's the opposite of 'fear'?" Lighting a cigarette, he stares into the Bic's flame, drawing it ever closer to his face.

"I don't know," David says. "'Bravery'?"

"I think it's 'faith.'"

"Okay."

"Like, we fear our shadows, but if we only had faith to let them come out. One trip on DMT and you have faith the End is nigh, but that same faith *cures the fear of death*, right?"

"What's the difference between losing one's fear of death," David asks, "and a drug whose side effects include suicidal thoughts?"

Lee ignores the question and tilts the rearview. "Fucking whore," he says. "She knows exactly what she's doing. Told her not to fuck him and she's all over him right from the start."

"Who, Zoe?"

Lee shrugs. He's carried a torch for Zoe since the night of the bonfire, David's sure of it. He looks right and suddenly sees Lee anew. Bald and shivering like a little boy, like Owen cowering in the shower that day back in Forbes. Lee's heart is breaking and David isn't sure why, but he's in no mood to play therapist this time. David's got his own shit to deal with.

Eyes on the road, he reaches out his hand to try to pat Lee's bald skull, implying everything is going to be just fine.

"Uh-huh... I see," David says, groping. And he never feels it coming, but suddenly the smack of a knuckle catches David in the right eye. It isn't a solid punch, just a dismissive swipe.

"No," Lee says, "you're fucking blind."

Before he can retaliate, David feels lips on the nape of his neck. He knows this is pleasure, and that he's supposed to be turned on. And he is. And who cares? A tongue laps his mouth and he licks it back, sucking this foreign maw like it's his last chance to quench a thirst. There are hands on David's chest, maybe two of them, on his legs, maybe four of them, unbuckling him and pulling his cock from its hiding place, stroking it back to life. David looks down and sees It Girl's head in his lap. She pulls his cock from her mouth with a loud pop and asks, "Are you bleeding?"

Meanwhile, in the back, Ultraviolet is an absolute machine. He dominates the women, twisting their legs like bendy straws, plowing into them with some untapped power David assumed but didn't fully realize. David watches the girls' faces contort, their eyes rolling back.

They look scared and saved all at once.

He's cum three or four times now, but rather than pull out he finishes inside them, holding their heads close to his as he empties himself, making fierce eye contact the whole time, and then he brings them back down to earth, seals each intense physical climax with an emotional bond—a kiss on the nose, his palms cupping a breast, softly thumbing a nipple—something to make each girl feel special and chosen by him, but then when he's done with a given girl, when he's cum and he decides she's cum enough, too, and is curled up in a panting heap, he nudges her aside and kneels there glistening, waiting for the next one. It's hot to watch at first. But as the minutes or hours drag on, he's kind of a dick about it.

David grows weary of the whole thing. David grows weary in general, exhausted, spent. The action in the van becomes fogged, smudged. There are no couples back there. Only a writhing mass of humans. Blink. David wants to keep going but he can't keep his eyes open. Blink. The others are slowing down, too. They love each other and collapse and blink themselves to sleep.

ii.

And just like that. It's light outside but that's not what wakes them. Lee is bounding at Mathias, slamming him against the back of the driver's seat *(thudd!)*. Mathias ricochets into the metal wall *(claink!)*, sending vibrations across the cabin *(gagoosh!)*. And they're all groggy from sleep and think this is just a funny dream, but then it's not funny anymore. Shit gets serious. They're grunting and angry. Mathias grabs his side and there's blood on his hand.

"See? There you go, sweetheart! Come at me." Mathias taunts him and then somersaults out of the corner and he's on Lee in a flash. Fists swing at naked ribs. Mathias wails away on Lee's stomach and chest. Lee punches back, and a right cross staggers Mathias up toward the front seat and David doesn't even see him go for the glove compartment. When Mathias swings back around, he's holding his grandfather's antique axe, the one with the purple metallic handle.

"Tell them," says Lee.

They stand off. Then Peacemaker crawls over to break it up. He tells them that's enough, it's too late for this, or too early, who knows, but let's not ruin a perfectly wonderful, sexified evening.

"Eff that," says Mathias, grabbing SuperVisor's scrubs V-neck. They all wonder what he possibly has left to prove. Still holding the axe, he jumps into the front seat, wearing only the shirt, and takes the wheel. And now people are looking at Business-Man.

Like *he's* supposed to do something.

They're close to home and the crew in the back shakes off the sleep and gets dressed. Lee sulks behind the driver's seat but then inexplicably joins Mathias up front. David thinks he even overhears him say, "I'm sorry," and Mathias eventually reaches out a hand in acceptance.

It's pouring outside. A trio of early-bird initiates greet the vanguard, covering them in evolution capes as they trudge silently toward the front door of The Egg. They look like first-time skiers, bodies destroyed by the impossible physicality of the night. Mathias and Lee are first inside, Mathias slamming the door like a child. Britt rolls her eyes. Owen shrugs. They all feel the post-drug exhaustion, like after a night on Ecstasy, desperately wanting to melt into a hoodie.

"Who wants French toast?" asks Fu. As he and Britt and Nyla and Owen head in to crack eggs, Haley tugs David's sleeve and whispers, "Stay here."

Memories flood in. David doesn't know how to feel, whether to trust her. But he follows her to the van anyway, preparing for another torrent of assaults upon his backside.

"Get in," she says, sliding open the door. "It's pouring. *MaxMobiles make good umbrellas.*"

"Please... just don't do anything else to me," he pleads. She nods shamefully.

They get in and face each other in the front-seat captain's chairs. David isn't going to speak first, and he makes that perfectly clear.

"We slept so hard," she says, trying to break the ice. "Where did all the time go?"

"Nice weather we're having," he retorts, making fun of her stupid small talk. He isn't planning on forgiving her, but when she pulls his head and kisses him, he can't stop her. He pinches her earlobe. She undresses, pulling off her white tights. In the dawn light, this is the first time David sees her clearly.

She's bald. It's all gone.

Her vagina has been stripped and waxed bare, and though he wasn't exactly hoping for that same mound of curls, he's always envisioned her with *something*, some soft patch to run his fingers through if this moment ever came again. He wonders if Mathias made her wax it all off. She reads David's mind: she brings his hand between her thighs and says, "It's okay. It's okay."

He climbs between her legs, her feet on the dashboard. They make love like tired giants, hearts beating hard. But the slowness forces them to savor everything. The feel of her slickness. The rub of his belly. Hands on her scalp. Teeth on his ear. "It's okay," she whispers. "It's okay..."

And he whispers it back. "Yes. It's okay." Neither apologizing. Both forgiving.

David wants to swim in that absolution. He opens the van windows and lets the rain pour in, and soon it's rising round their legs, drenching their waists, lapping between their chests, overtaking the dashboard, the windshield, their necks, chins, up to the brim, one last gasp, until they submerge completely, drowning like the *Titanic*'s elderly aristocrats, wrestling like horny teenagers, playing like kids in a pool, entangled like twins in a womb, ready to begin again.

—Ø—

"Happy birthday, David," Haley says.

"Wow," David says. "Is it April 4?" He'd honestly lost track.

"I've honestly lost track," she says. "I think it's a few days after, but happy birthday anyway."

They stare at the van ceiling, heads down between the front seats. Her scalp smells terrible, either from the events of the past evening or her shampoo or just their general lack of showering amid all the power outages. She pops up, flips the radio past an emergency NOAA weather bulletin, and lands on the Doobie Brothers.

"What are you going to tell him?" asks David. "Like, where will you sleep after this?"

"It doesn't matter where I sleep anymore. Because this"—she places a hand over his heart—"*this right here* is where I live now." He dresses her, like in that other lifetime back in Pikesville. Pulls the tights up her legs. Holds her boots as she presses her heels into them with a satisfying *thump*.

David feels suddenly restless. "We're going to have certain responsibilities, you and me."

"People depend on us," she says, mostly to herself. "And I depend on them."

David understands. "The more good people I meet, the more I fall in love with them."

Haley begins to cry and says, "Then why do I feel like *we're* becoming more and more bad?"

David doesn't know how to answer her, because he wants to ask the same question.

"What if we go to Canada together? They're better equipped for environmental breakdown."

"You need to have more faith, David."

"In what?" David scoffs. "That *he* can save us?"

"That we can save us all," she says. "Don't you still believe that?"

David doesn't know what he believes. He believes he loves her, and that any day, hour, second away from her is one less they'll have together on Earth.

In the driveway, Haley and David fall asleep again, lulled by the wafting smell of syrup.

iii.

Blink.

David's parents met in ninth grade trig class. Gil had asked Eileen if he could cheat off her. Eileen said no, but he tried anyway and she let him. That became the catchphrase of their relationship: *He cheated off me*. They both wore it like a badge of dishonor.

While their friends got pregnant, Gil and Eileen missed the early boat to Parentland. Gil wanted to be a famous portrait photographer—the next Avedon or Arbus—but his desire for fortune outweighed his craving for fame. Dreams dissolved into reality, art into business. He sired Fuffman Foto, specializing in weddings and other lovely affairs. He helped Eileen open her private acupuncture practice, and she built her reputation as she-shaman of Pikesville, Maryland.

When they finally decided to have a kid, they read every bit of research on cognitive development, environmental determinism, nature vs. nurture. Eileen dove deep into brain science, studying Western diagrams of basal ganglia, cross-referencing Eastern Ayurvedic texts. Prenatal yoga happened each morning, accompanied by a comprehensive vitamin regimen; each night she lulled her gelatinous embryo to sleep with Mozart sonatas from Baby Einstein CDs. A team of doctors, osteopaths, midwives, and musicians ushered their child into the world via Jacuzzi birth, and when he popped out, a Navajo chief—yes, seriously—chanted a prayer of thanksgiving, his eternal voice wavering over primordial infant squeals.

His nursery was a multisensory play experience, an explosion of color and hanging mobiles. It's a wonder he didn't turn out epileptic. With activity gyms and phonics galore, they worked on David's hearing and vision, his fine motor skills, his emotional quotient. Sign language flash cards let him communicate early. David was weeks ahead on the charts, routing all infant rivals. He walked at nine months, was out of diapers before turning two. By age three he could read, kind of.

And he desperately wanted to read about superheroes.

But David's parents insisted *real* books were far superior to comics, those orgies of violence, those cheap vehicles for beasts, biceps, and huge bazooms. And they never bought into the educational potential of screens, but they knew entertainment was a healthy balance. So the compromise was as long as a *real* book dwelled nearby, he could watch the iPad on low volume.

David found a loophole.

He jumped around in cartoon series like *Teen Titans, X-Men: Evolution,* and *The Spectacular Spider-Man,* and then, when his parents decided the screen time was getting excessive, Dad diverted David's attention from thirty-minute shows down to eight-minute episodes of *The All-New Super Friends Hour,* a Hanna-Barbera classic from the 1970s available online, depicting the most powerful forces of good ever assembled: Superman, Batman and Robin, Wonder Woman, Aquaman, plus the largely ineffectual Wonder Twins and their space monkey, Gleek.

In one early episode called "The Brain Machine," an evil genius—Doctor Cranum—builds a device that advances man's mental evolution a million years into the future.

"The rest of the world must have these magnificent powers of mine!" Cranum cackles. Even Wonder Woman gets zapped and becomes his yellow-eyed convert. But Batman captures Cranum and hands him over to the authorities, and at the end Wonder Woman makes the moral clear:

"No man has a right to enforce his will on others, no matter how good his intentions may be!"

Cue the triumphant horn section.

David dug Wonder Woman. Something about the mysterious look on her face after she got saved and whispered breathlessly, "Wow. Thanks, Batman." Yet she was the only superhero girl—a strong, important, wonderful girl—and when the guys rescued her from Doctor Cranum, David saw the powerful profit of restoring a great girl to safety.

That's how heroism works, he thought. *You take back what the villain steals, and someone beautiful thanks you for it.*

David told his parents this newest prophecy, wondering aloud if it might be possible for *him* to someday save Claire from her leukemia.

They managed his expectations, but in *Super Friends* they realized there was morality to be learned. The accolades given to the good. The dangers of being bad. But as they grew more tolerant of superheroes, a new restlessness birthed inside David.

His fifth birthday was coming up, and David knew he was supposed to be getting older, more mature. But two months prior to his party, during a tense game of hide-and-seek, he'd accidentally found his big present. Squirming beneath the slate sanctuary of Dad's basement pool table,

David spotted a shopping bag. Peeking from inside was a sliver of the telltale *S* insignia. It was a reversible Superman cape, blue on one side, red on the other, which Mom had sewn herself. He dug his tiny fists into the fabric. He'd found a mystery, meant only for him. He put it on.

David assumed his parents would say, "Not yet, not till your birthday," or worse, they'd scold him for snooping. But by the time Dad's brown-slippered feet arrived on the carpet next to the pool table and asked, "Now where can David be?" David was already long gone. A new creature lurked on the floor. Waiting for the brown slippers to walk away, David took off the cape and promised to steal more time with this secret treasure as soon as the grown-ups weren't watching.

Until this deception, he'd known himself only as a good boy, the best boy, smart and brave, honest, caring, well behaved, a plate-cleaner, a colorer of complex squiggle-worlds on the backs of Chili's placemats, a hero in training. But now, hiding from his father's brown slippers, David faced the startling possibility that he was becoming a petty thief. A bad guy.

He'd never really known any bad guys. The only ones he could think of were on TV, thieves and scoundrels like Dr. Cranum. But the more he thought of it, Cranum wanted only to *share* his magnificent powers with the rest of the world. He seemed well intentioned enough.

In the days leading up to his birthday, David stole his cape for longer and longer periods, wrapping the cape around his face like a bandit mask, whispering villainous threats to the dark.

"You'll never stop me!" he'd cackle quietly. "I am David's evil twin: *David Instead*."

His secret minutes of capeness grew insufficient, and oh, how he longed for April, for his birthday party, when he could wear his cape unleashed from guilt and the limits of time. The big day was around the corner. RSVPs were being collected. There was to be a cookie cake.

He'd wait until April 4.

When it mercifully arrived, David spent the morning of his fifth birthday capeless. Hunkered by the front window, he kept vigil, listening for the first car to arrive, hoping it might be his best friend, Claire. But he soon grew bored and went trolling around.

The house looked impressive. His mom had laced the dining room with crepe paper and Mylar balloons boasting the emblems of caped crusaders. She placed hero-themed tablecloths, paper cups, and plates on a long party table where goodie bags lined up like good soldiers. And in a feat of majestic overkill, they'd transformed the exercise room into the Hall of Justice—old computers along the room's perimeter, and hanging behind the party table was a map of Earth with Christmas lights poking out from behind it, marking the world's major metropolises with yellow blinks.

Waiting for the party to start, David snuck into Mom and Dad's room to squeeze in one more training session. More flips off his parents' headboard—*jump, bounce, flip, land.*

"David! You're gonna give me myocardial infarction!" his mom screamed from the living room. "You remember what *that* is?"

"A hard attack!" he yelled back.

"Heart!" she said. He tried to fly quieter.

His guests arrived, dressed in capes and masks. Claire showed up in Supergirl garb, complete with a cool red-and-blue headscarf to cover her smooth skull. Soon, the dining room filled with activities. And after mask decorating and Pin the *W* on Wonder Woman, David finally got to open his Superman cape. His mom latched the Velcro around his neck, and as David merged into David Instead, she unveiled the final surprise.

The children screamed when Spider-Man appeared at the front door.

Claire ran crying to her protective parents. Most of the boys went mute. The neighbors' granddaughter wet herself. David felt conflicted. On one hand, he was pumped. Spider-Man had somehow gotten wind of his party and here he was, miming his red palms against Mom's freshly Windex'd French doors. David worried that evil lurked close by. After all, Spider-Man usually appeared in proximity to villains. Or, wait, maybe David Instead was himself that evildoer and here was a hero to deal with him accordingly.

Alas, he, too, had wet himself.

The center of the room cleared, parents lifting and rushing and patting their children to the far corners, trying to calm them down and help them face the fear. Scrambling to detach David's cape and refashion it into a kilt around his waist, Eileen positioned the Superman insignia in front to hide his urine stains. David might have been embarrassed—his honor besmirched and pants bepee-peed—but in point of fact, David failed to notice. Because *there he was.*

Spider-Man's Harlequin body tiptoe-danced onto the carpet, flicking his wrists into space, approaching with the grace of a cat burglar. Staring at his feet, David tried to imitate this animal-ninja walk, the subtle touch of Spider-Man's brown-tipped toes upon the carpet, peeking out from his leggings. Silently, Spider-Man motioned to David's kilt-cape, to the *S* insignia. His body language gave off an air of hurt: *Why Superman?* he seemed to ask. *What's so great about* him?

No, no, Spidey, David thought. *I have eyes for you, too.*

Then Spider-Man poked David in the tummy, shook his hand: he was only joshing.

But before Eileen could stop him, Spider-Man knelt down and unfastened the cape from David's waist, replacing it around his neck. When the Velcro was fixed Spider-Man saw the puddle on David's pants. He looked at David, then at Eileen. David couldn't think of what to say, so he made a desperate attempt to relate to the famous superhero.

"Hey, Spider-Man," he said. "My dad has those slippers, too."

Spider-Man hugged David. Which seemed to David, even then, unprofessional.

Still, he knew this was what adults meant when they talked about the best day of your life.

Newly emboldened, David grabbed Spider-Man's hand and dragged him to his parents' bedroom to show off his super-abilities. An audition of sorts. Maybe, if he proved himself worthy—if he could fly—and Spider-Man welcomed him into the ranks of the world's superheroes, that might mean David could save Claire from the evil attacking her.

As an audience gathered behind Spider-Man, David climbed to the headboard. Like an Olympic diver, he nudged his toes to the edge of this platform and held out his arms. He glanced at Claire, who looked up at him with red post-cry eyes. David took a breath. *Watch this,* he thought.

High in the air David flew, his fingers nearly scraping the blades of the ceiling fan.

His feet bounced onto the mattress, ricocheting him back into the sky.

At the zenith of his flight, he tucked up his legs the way he'd done a billion times before, and he went into his patented Fuffman Flip, the climax of this momentary aerial show, curling over himself, a perfect sphere in space, and just before David landed on his neck and the world went black, he thought, *I am flying I am flying I am flying.*

—Ø—

Guests trickled from the party, offering support and abandoning their goodie bags. Even Claire left, back to the hospital. This would be the last time David would see her and he didn't even get to say anything. He just lay on his parents' mattress, right where he'd landed, quiet, still, breathing steadily. Mom sat behind David and, placing light fingers on his skull, she checked his cranial rhythms. David could wiggle his fingers, so at first Eileen and Spider-Man thought this was another of his weird games. But then David peed himself again.

They feared him paralyzed.

David's parents think he doesn't remember any of this. But he remembers.

He remembers they put the TV on, or maybe not.

He remembers Krypton exploding.

He remembers Earth breaking.

Blue flames.

Rocks tumbling, the ground splitting as if sliced by a great cosmic knife. The dam breaks and water swallows the bridge.

All fall down.

So much dust and sand and dryness, but then no light, no power, no water to quench the trapped and fallen, the dark-haired women entombed in their cars.

It had all gone wrong, and the only thing left for Superman to do was fly faster and faster and faster around Earth's oceans until time stopped and rewound and everything was good again.

Pretend it never happened.

When David came to, his dad was standing in the corner, wearing a white button-down. His mom patted David's forehead with something cold and wet, singing a soft rendition of "Row, Row, Row Your Boat," calling him her good boy, her perfect little boy. His pants were still wet. He felt suddenly restless. As if kicking his way out of a sleeping bag, David hopped up and over to his dad. Eileen cried while Gil knelt down and squeezed David's shoulders, not yet sure his son was okay.

"Dad," asked David. "When will this world be gone?"

"The world isn't going anywhere, buddy. It's right here! See?" He stomped his foot on the carpet for emphasis, trying to make life tangible again.

"What if it blows up?" David asked. "Like Krypton."

"It won't," Dad said. "But even if it does, there's nothing to worry about. You know why?"

David shook his head no.

"Because even if the world explodes, *you'll* be okay. You remember how Superman's parents took care of him when Krypton blew up? Well, as long as we're good and we follow the rules and remember what Mom says and never ever *ever* flip off the goddamn headboard again..." He winked at David and unbuttoned the top of his collared shirt, exposing the red-and-blue Spider-Man spandex beneath. David's eyes widened. His dad pinched his costume, then tugged David's own Superman cape, held the soft fabric to David's face, and whispered, "Superheroes never die."

In time, David would resent his dad for making that promise, for telling the sweet lie fathers tell, for forcing him to see the great gulf between the damned and the saved.

But for the time being, David asked if his father was really Spider-Man and his father asked if David was really Superman, and they both said yes.

9
MAY

i.

Three thousand had now died in the Texas oil fires, with a million evacuated. Worlds away, the Maldives and Tuvalu islands were sinking fast, creating 350,000 new refugees. Closer to home, the water supply around the Chesapeake Bay watershed had either been polluted or, some thought, poisoned by the Chinese, and much of northern Virginia's intelligence community was relocated.

David's parents and sister left Maryland and moved in with Aunt Abby in Bethlehem. The news talked of diaspora, the latest exchange of people exiled by their environment.

The USV, too, had splintered and shuffled. It had grown too big for one roof. The Egg's basement remained its headquarters, its Hall of Justice. Taped over the tool bench was a map with tiny red dots marking all the satellite USV enclaves. David knew of chapters at a dozen colleges along the East Coast, plus the huge one at the University of Wisconsin. Other large collectives in San Francisco, Denver, Austin, and Chicago. Similar groups had cropped up in Canada, the UK, Japan, and even Australia, they'd heard. Factions and subfactions ready to face the future their own way.

There were the SuperJews, the Wakandans, the XX-Women, but these were social affinity groups more than silo'd operational divisions. Matters of race, class, gender, sexual orientation—the weather had worn down these historically ghettoizing barriers—but religion and spiritual ideologies still stood strong. There were the Sons of Ultraviolet, a more militant, anarchist crew destroying corporate property and picking fights with neo-Nazis; the Bearded Ladies, hippies preaching sustainable living; and the Black Holes, whose main mission was to break into pharmacies and steal Zeronal, antiparasitics, and water purifiers like iodine, stockpiling for the End. Now that their movement was connected to B&E charges, vandalism, and theft of Schedule II narcotics, David figured it was only a matter of time before the authorities descended.

The Egg pulled together. Lee and Mathias seemed to have squashed their beef from that night in the van. But the honeymoon period of the USV was done. Sinister elements threatened to emerge. Now more than ever, it was incumbent upon leadership to recommit to utopian ideals and stay true to the mission.

David and Nyla updated *The Superhero's Journey* with an official rulebook, a code of conduct for new converts, lest they poison The Egg. In addition to the smaller rules and regulations that helped them run a tight ship, a few big ones were added to David's original Code of the USV.

Following on #5, a tenet clearly referencing Batman—*You are not entitled. You're flawed—mortally—and must sacrifice and work like mad. If destiny fails, use your smoke pellets*—It Girl and her confidantes drew up a commandment inspired by Wonder Woman, applicable to all: *You are not yet free. You're chained—eternally—and must pull yourself from bondage and XplO. No man has a right to enforce his will on another.*

Nyla wrote a piece of doctrine inspired by Black Panther, also universally relevant: *You will keep your mask on, but you must not hide yourself. Our mystery is our power, but the world needs you to reveal your will. We cannot wait.*

And as a reminder, the final addition to the bylaws—rounding it out to an even ten—was from Ultraviolet: *You will zero in and emerge from the dark neck of time luminous without end.*

They played up the idea of Ultraviolet being able to envision what lay ahead and retitled these commandments "The Ten Assured Futures of the USV." But David felt the most prescient law was the one about freedom, chains, and men enforcing their will on others. With the incredible influx of great new arrivals, there were a bad handful looking to prey on the lowered inhibitions presented by drug use and communal living. So, among other things, that new measure was clearly intended to curb and correct any such nonconsensual activity.

Meanwhile, in those post-orgy days, Mathias only expanded and deepened his sexual curb appeal to the newly minted lady-heroes at The

Egg. The rest of the League of Nine had enjoyed their naked time in the MaxMobile together but organically fell back into the habits of mostly monogamous coupling (Nyla+Owen, Britt+Fu, and even Haley+David, kind of). Mathias, on the other hand, became the superstud, organizing regular field trips in the MaxMobile consisting of himself and up to six ladies (Zoe was a regular attendee). David was conflicted about this. He knew it was base and sophomoric, but Mathias was, well, a sophomore, and he could pull it off, so who could blame him? Above all, David felt Mathias was playing his part, and so long as things were consensual and of age and otherwise legal, it kind of helped the overall USV narrative David was cultivating.

There were transgressions, however, and this also fit well into their legend. For months, the USV had been practicing civil disobedience and nonviolent strategies of working through aggression; it'd been fighting invisible enemies—weather systems and cosmic funnels—and now it occasionally had to combat something solid. A cancer to be excised out. A shitty person.

It couldn't send lawless USVers to the cops, of course. And it was clear to David: fists felt wrong. Too brutal and premeditated. It's so weird to punch a face. And Haley wouldn't have it.

So, yes, the fire was initially David's idea. But others threw the gas on it.

—Ø—

Haley held the colored markers, waited for them to quiet down.

She figured they'd now covered the checklist for any good spiritual movement: they had a charismatic leader; a gateway drug; an initiatory vision; a promise of a new era on Earth and salvation beyond; a strict set of rules by which to become spiritually worthy; a comprehensive set of practical skills and cottage industries to generate revenue and to practice in the mundane hours; and a mealtime means of social gathering and fellowship.

What Haley insisted they lacked was *liturgy*: the regularly scheduled ritual worship that could elevate daily life in The Egg to a place both structured and sacred. And that's what the fire provided.

"Chainsaw, LumberJill, and the Inhuman Torch will be designated Fire Keepers," said Haley to the League of Nine, gathered in the basement of The Egg for their nightly planning session. The core USV heroes sat around a new circular table while Haley worked the whiteboard, scrawling a fire with red and orange dry-erase markers.

"Everyone who comes will be encouraged to bring combustible offerings," she said.

And so their heroes built a blaze in the center of the Woosamonsa cul-de-sac, which soon became a permanent fire pit ringed by large rocks.

"The first inner ring around the fire will be the dancers," said Haley, "wearing capes and masks and constantly moving clockwise to symbolize time."

"What about counterclockwise?" offered Owen. "Like time going backward?"

"Perfect. Love it," said Haley, changing the direction of the circular arrow around the fire.

And so the dancers and Hula-Hoopers and spinners gathered and spun slowly around the fire.

"The next ring is the drummers"—she drew another circle—"and the outer ring will be the chorus," Haley said. "Golden Echo's Human DJ musicians, split into his four-part harmony, soprano down to bass, arrayed in the four cardinal directions—north, south, east, and west."

And so the masses gathered in the outer orbit according to the timbre of their voices.

Mathias looked up. "Call it something insane. Like the Super Fucking Fire Circle."

"Wait, it's not a *circle*, it's a *zero*," said Haley, drawing a thick diagonal across the concentric rings. "This is the zip line, stretching from the top of The Egg to the far corner of the Pink House. Forget walking across hot coals. Our heroes will fly through fire."

"Badass," said Britt, pounding her fists on the table. "When do we get to do this?"

"Fridays," said Haley, tossing her markers on the table. "It's the best day to *fire* someone."

And so the Super Fucking Fire Zero was set.

Every Friday, the fire grew, the drums beat their unmistakably tribal rhythms, and the League of Nine took their place on top of The Egg, playing their executive parts while ushering new initiates into the zip-line harness. Echo was maestro, calling musical instructions into his ham setup, with the chorus below and their wireless earbuds tuned to four radio frequencies: four vocal parts.

By the third week, they'd added a new sacrificial component.

A set of heroes would offer to the flames some symbol of the old world—prepackaged supermarket meat, for instance—while demonstrating the new world SITS equivalent—field dressing a deer, maybe. A ritualized death and rebirth. The Kali Yuga followed by the Satya Yuga.

When the rains came, they still kept the fire going, even if one superhero had to take a piece of it into a steel bucket and keep the flames going, feeding it with scraps of newspaper. The fire was important. It was a forum for all to be exorcised. And to see justice done.

They wanted to ward against complex bureaucracy, but the USV had grown too big. They needed a way to establish and enforce law and order. So mediation was the first step. Then the duels returned. For minor disagreements where both parties were amenable, the paintball pistols were put back into service. A quick-and-dirty justice, once the province of daytime court TV.

Bonfire backdrop. Ten steps, turn, fire. Case closed.

For bigger issues, it was the League of Nine that served as judge and jury, there in the basement lair. And if a guilty verdict was reached, the sentence was always the same.

—Ø—

She sits beside him on the roof, this purple god.

Haley knows Ultraviolet's not a god. Nor even a man. Just a boy like all other boys.

He's smart and driven and sexy and powerful, but a boy still.

When she'd had her first Big Bang, she saw Mathias in that hyperspace. She'd discerned there something about his persona or character or soul. Whatever psychedelic tea leaves she could read and decode. That Nyla was meant to wield a tool or weapon, or that Britt was meant to morph into a hundred different beings. For Mathias, though, all she'd seen was purple, a kind of viscous lavender smoke, some kind of glittery goo curling around itself like a child's science experiment. She thought this was normal, at the time, or as normal as an abnormal drug experience can be. She thought she'd seen purple because David said to make him purple, the power of suggestion. But when she saw everyone else in such anthropomorphic forms she'd still seen Mathias as this formless smoke.

She tried getting closer to it, this second time. Millions of tiny beings were swimming in this whirlpool, or maybe drowning, she couldn't be sure. She remembers wondering, at the time and still, if this meant maybe Mathias was a god.

Or maybe he was nothing. Just smoke.

Haley likes to stay seated as he stands and holds court over his flock. He's got a great sense of humor and keeps it light amid all the serious darkness. He says something about the rain, the wind, the hot, hot heat of the fire. She has faith in everything he says, and yet she doesn't believe a word. All at the same time. It makes her feel insane.

When she got to college, she imagined she'd fall into what people refer to as a normal, long-term relationship. High school had been lots of short flings and hookups, even dabbling a bit with girls. She never wanted to commit. She knew she was smarter than most of the others in Pikesville, destined for big things, and the horror story of teen pregnancy had been drilled into her like one of those torture film screenings from *A Clockwork Orange*.

In college, when most people were finally off the leash and going nuts, *that's* when she'd settle down. She'd meet someone in her History of Jews in Hollywood class, and they'd flirt during precept, share some inside joke about the kid who pronounced "Warner" like "Wawner." Then they'd see each other out one night and it would be stupid drunk perfection and that would be that.

He'd be good in bed—her equal—and they'd hole up in his dorm room for the first few weeks, and then vacation in her dorm for a while, before she eventually abandoned her sad, involuntary roommate and moved into his room permanently. They'd start wearing sweat suits all the time because they were past that steamy first phase and were now in love.

They'd stay together all through college, one of those rare couples. Maybe they'd break up briefly and dramatically, in a way that made their mutual friends question the very nature of existence. And then they'd get back together, just as dramatically. And that'd be it.

They'd graduate. Marriage. Kids. She'd be a fine arts professor somewhere cool and edgy, and he'd be something noble and high-minded, too.

Instead, Halloween happened. And now it was the end of the world.

This was certainly a different way to go.

Mathias had been the perfect self-defense teacher in that month afterward. He was unassuming at the time, teaching the fundamentals and occasionally listening quietly when some poor girl broke down. He never got fresh, not with her and not with anyone else, to her knowledge. He didn't need some shitty springboard to meet girls. Still, Mathias let them kick the shit out of him in that padded dummy suit. He was plain. Not particularly funny or exciting. He was just exactly what they all needed him to be. And that made him beautiful to her.

She found out, of course, about his off-campus living, his money. She doesn't want to think about that, whether it swayed anything. It did and it didn't, but of course it did.

And then came the opportunity to dress him up any way she wanted. The paper doll with infinite costumes. Of course, it had been David dictating the first set of costumes, but still, she could take his suggestions and fashion them into her fantasy. Not that a guy wearing purple body paint and a straitjacket was her fantasy. Or maybe it was, who even knew anymore.

Mathias was a tremendous dancer. That much was incontrovertible. Masculine and soft and goofy simultaneously. As the drums pound, he moves like he's fucking her, like he's fucking them all. And it's pretty okay to watch and feel like his queen, like she's the one everyone is jealous of right now. Not so long ago she was the one everyone was pitying.

But it's not his magnetism. After she broke through the veil, and then broke through with him, he told her his secrets. She saw his burdens—something beyond privilege, like where privilege is pushed so far that it cycles all the way around back to abuse and pain.

His brother. His father. His pills.

She'd decided she had to save him. And save him she would.

David is up here, too, on the roof of The Egg. She knows *he* wants to save *her*. Haley has no desire to save him, the way she feels for Mathias. David will be fine. His is regular old privilege. He's young and stupid, but he's a rock, the kind of boy she might've worn sweats with in another lifetime, if he were a little bit taller.

Maybe Mathias wants to complete the Photoshop polygon tool and save David, or maybe he actually wants to save all of them, play his part in this big show and hope it becomes a self-fulfilling circus, where he can be ringleader and the acrobats all do their jobs. They've reached well more than critical mass by this point. There are capable lieutenants and teams working autonomously, improvising and evolving the USV the way good movements do. They look to him, but, hopefully, they're all really looking to themselves. The fundamental truth is that all of this could be gone at any moment. The chief virtue is independence, self-sufficiency. Mathias is powerful—he is power incarnate—but he is not the entire grid.

Or if he is, then like the grid, he cannot be relied on.

Haley knows that. She wonders if the rest of them do.

A new anger rushes over her. A familiar energy by this point. She's started to think of it like a drug wave, or the transformation the Hulk goes through. The Hulk used to scare her when she was little—one of the few superheroes she remembers viscerally because she remembers not understanding why he was called a good guy when he looked like a complete nightmare.

Right now, her anger is due to Stockman, who needs to be punished.

They bring him up to the roof. Below, the drums and dancing cease, but the fire's flames are still high. The USV initiates gaze up to hear the sentence and witness his penance.

Stockman had served as Cap'n Cunt's trusted assistant. But he'd only *posed* as gay in order to ogle and grope women as they moved through the costuming workshop in various states of undress. Held there on the roof, as they harness him up to the zip line, he screams a bizarre defense. Venemous attacks on Ultraviolet and Cap'n Cunt and Dr. Ugs and Business-Man devolving into crazier shit about the Illuminati and Metallica and Beyoncé and cloning farms and the prehistoric Vril Lizards and god knows what else. Haley had heard about psychotic breaks brought on by DMT, but until now she'd thankfully never seen one occur at The Egg.

Cap'n Cunt ties Stockman's hands behind his back using a handcuff knot and throws a purple evolution cape over his shoulders. As the congregation grows quieter below, she takes the strings of the cape and ties it around his neck. A double half hitch with a quick-release loop on the tag end.

Ultraviolet lights a candle and brings it to the hem of Stockman's cape. The flames grow from blue to orange. Then they push Stockman off the roof and he soars through the air, over the fire, trailing a wild cape ablaze. It's kind of gorgeous, actually.

When he gets to the other side, heroes are on hand to tamp out the flames. It is more scary than painful. Still, SuperVisor bundles him up and drives him to the hospital.

After this, a moment of silence. This is their typical end to the Super Fucking Fire Zero, and then the heroes travel inside or stay in their spots, meditating, or reconvene for all manner of impromptu talent show in The Shack, elevating the music or literature or theater that makes humanity worth saving.

As the crowd disperses, Haley climbs down from the roof and makes her way to the other side of the circle to retrieve Stockman's burned cape. She brings it to the cul-de-sac and tamps out the last of its embers, ash disappearing into asphalt.

Part of it is still good and can be salvaged.

She looks up at Mathias, stoic on the roof, nodding down at her and everyone else. This punishment might seem evil to some, but she knows this is Mathias protecting her, protecting all of them. The fervor is intensifying, and they need to hold the space, the structure, the Ten Assured Futures, for when the shit really hits the fan.

Leadership. Power. Safety. Evolution.

She looks up at him.

Ultraviolet sneezes, grossly, then smiles and shrugs and wipes his purple face with the sleeve of his straitjacket.

He is not a god.

But maybe he could be a hero.

ii.

David snapped back the neck of his plastic likeness, the face atop the Pez dispenser molded to look like Business-Man with his signature goggles and sideways Mohawk. Two of their heroes—Ninja King Pirate and Compass Rose—made it with the architecture department's 3-D printer. David accepted a Party Zero poking out from his own severed throat. He felt famous.

This was a dangerous feeling, a clear shadow moment—at odds with everything they were doing—but it was secretly thrilling to be recognized like this, his persona made plastic. And it wasn't just within the USV. He'd received an email, the "We are pleased to inform you" variety: David had won the PEN Startup Competition. Actually won the thing. When it rains, it pours.

David kept the accolade secret—to brag about his win would have been to admit fundamental disbelief in the entire mission of the USV in favor of the exact kind of capitalist careerism they were supposed to shun. But still. After some phone tag, he finally reached Zhou.

"I will say, it was the most comprehensive entry, extremely well written," said Professor Zhou. "And it certainly has its heart in the right place, so the team wanted to recognize that."

When David asked about the financial prizes, the possibility of funding, Zhou laughed:

"No, you didn't win because of the investment opportunity. Your plan doesn't have 10X potential, so I'm afraid it's not the kind of thing that'll garner even seed-round VC consideration," he explained. "But we were sufficiently impressed with the thought behind it and would be pleased to offer you a paid summer internship with Randolph-Forrestal Ventures. You'd gain some valuable and necessary experience."

"With all due respect, sir," said David, "have you looked outside lately? I'm not sure we'll all still be here this summer."

Again, Zhou laughed.

"You're still young," he said. "You haven't lived through enough of these so-called apocalypses. Once you're ancient like me and you've been through five or six of them—political, nuclear, weather-related, epidemics—but... no. There's plenty of future to be had. There always is."

David was taken aback. At first he wanted to hang up on Zhou, call him a name that young people call old people. He'd had such negligible mentorship from the elder generation since arriving at Princeton, despite his parents' best efforts. But maybe Zhou was right. Maybe every generation feels the threat of the End and simultaneously cultivates the people who ensure it doesn't happen.

Maybe David was one of them. And there was indeed plenty of future to be had.

"Are you available this summer?" Zhou asked.

"I think so," David said. "Any time after June 6."

The USV's entire modus operandi was all about cultivating these multitudes. Two dozen initiates now camped in the backyard of The Egg. The overflow moved back to campus, some of them into the safe-ish confines of the dorms, and others formed a tent city in the valley around Spinoza Field House, awaiting instructions.

June 6 was on the horizon. David figured they needed one more interim spectacle before this D-Day. By now there were teams responsible for executing the nuts and bolts of David's ultimate vision. He only had to plan the big picture.

But he couldn't plan. His mind was stuck on Haley Roth.

David stared at her across their circular table, trying to oonch out a wink, a smile, or some invisible pheromone to let him know she was thinking of him, too. But her poker face stayed strong.

Although she was also battling a virus, so maybe she was just trying to not vomit.

"Try again," Haley said to Britt, then burped. "I swear I'm listening this time."

"Okay. So how much do you all know about psychoacoustic weaponry?" Britt asked.

"Some," Haley said, burping. "Sorry. What I mean is: *What the fuck are you talking about?*"

"Transmission of sound directly to the subconscious without affecting other brain function." She spread a bunch of psychology articles on the table, pointing at pages like a quarterback drawing up plays in the mud. She and Fu explained: to the ear, psychoacoustics sound like white noise. But subliminal sounds are overdubbed and encoded into the lower frequencies. The sound doesn't hit the outer eardrum mechanically, but it's processed by the inner ear the same way.

Your *brain* hears it.

Echo had his trio of laptops open, layers of audio files stacked on a musical timeline.

"The KGB has used this stuff since the seventies," Mathias said. "FBI used it in Waco. And in Afghanistan, look"—he flipped pages—"'used psychoacoustic frequencies to engage the neural networks of the enemy's brain' blah blah... here! Quote! 'ONE soldier talked 450 enemy troops into surrendering.'"

"I thought we were after nonviolence," David said.

"No, *ours* isn't a weapon," Britt said. "It's for post-disaster communication. It's my thesis!"

Owen's headset crackled. He mumbled a few words into it and then sprinted upstairs.

Mathias sat. "When I was a kid they used psychoacoustic correction in the hospital," he said. "They take pictures of your brain with electroencephalographs, which are totally rad, actually. Once they map the different areas, they can physically affect the mental landscape with psychoacoustic messages. Like terraforming the brain. Commercials used this as subliminal advertising for aeons."

"A Colorado professor found a psychoacoustic that makes people shit themselves," said Fu.

"Ours will pipe in Fu's Human DJ tunes," Britt said. "And any encrypted instructions."

Under the articles was a schematic drawing of what looked a little like a gramophone, that big bell-horn at one end, leading to a small black box. Mathias's plan was for a new spectacle—one where they'd transmit music directly to the USV and be able to start and stop it at will, creating a sort of coordinated freeze dance. David wasn't sold yet on the new idea, which Mathias had dubbed "the Silent Dance." David owed a new communiqué to the USV outposts and he needed to get his head fully around the concept before writing and disseminating clear instructions. He pretended to pore over the articles and schematics, but the words went through him without catching hold.

Haley looked sad. Why was she sad? he wondered.

"This must've cost a fortune," David finally said, sifting aimlessly through the ledgers. Accounting was becoming his province by default. And he kind of sucked at numbers.

"You can actually do it for less than ten grand," said Fu.

David's head shot up at Fu. This number he understood. Because it was massive.

"Okay, everyone," David said. "We are literally hemorrhaging money right now. Mathias, dude, what do we need more technology for? We're already toying with drugs and, you know, the fabric of time and stuff. *Now*, you... you're always coming up with this half-baked—"

"*This* has always been the next logical step," Mathias shot back. "*This* is what zeroes us in and connects the collective consciousness needed to enter the Null Point. *This* is Echo's thesis."

"His thesis is a musical flash mob?"

"This is *his* hour. *This* needs to happen so the next thing can happen. Stay positive!"

This was Mathias's power—always nine steps ahead and beckoning everyone else to catch up. Had he told David about the psychoacoustic noise machine last year when they met in that river, or during winter break, or *any time* before now, David probably would have laughed and walked away forever. But on the heels of their latest ante-upper, anything was possible. Everything was necessary.

If you're not growing, you're dying. Business 101.

Just then, Peacemaker bustled down the stairs. He looked uncharacteristically frazzled.

"Someone's here," he said.

"We're all here," It Girl said, stretching like a cat in the sun.

"I think it's, um, your dad," he said. He was staring at Mathias.

Their leader pursed his lips. They waited for him to speak, but he looked spaced, paralyzed.

"Hide him in the lab," Owen said, and they all kicked into gear. "Nyla, stay with Mathias. Take the map and hard drives and turn on the incinerator, just in case. David, come with me?"

"You want *me* to go?" He wasn't used to being the public face of anything.

"He asked for whoever was in charge," Owen whispered. "What else could I say?"

—Ø—

In Woosamonsa Court were two black town cars filled with men in suits. Only Colonel Nathan Blue stood outside. He was examining the dormant fire pit and the circle of pavement surrounding it that had been hammered up to create a trench for floodwaters during a particularly bad Friday night storm. The colonel wore a midnight-blue military uniform, a trivet-sized block of decorations pinned to its breast. The man's balding head was buttressed by dark hair, and he was entirely unsmiling. His unimposing body seemed to disguise an ability to do great, terrible things.

He removed his sunglasses. Business-Man took off his own goggles and approached.

"Colonel," Business-Man said, voice shaky, trying his best to steady an outstretched hand.

"I'm told my son is in Altoona," he said. "Which one are you?"

Again offering a hand to shake, he proudly said, "I am Business-Man."

"No," said Mathias's father. "You're David Fuffman from Pikesville, Maryland. Your parents are Gil and Eileen and they're in Pennsylvania right now with your sister, Elizabeth, who's an absolute bluegrass prodigy, by the way. You, however, are enrolled in three classes"—Peacemaker shot a surprised glance at David—"two of which you're failing."

David swallowed and sized up this formidable opponent. It felt so nice to have a human adversary for a change. Hating the weather and cosmic phenomena was so impersonal.

"She plays old-time music," David said. "Not bluegrass. There's a big difference."

Colonel Blue now leaned in to whisper in David's ear: "If you don't want me to tell your little revolutionary cadre here that you've secretly landed a summer internship at a venture capital firm, I'd ask that you bring me to my son's room very quickly."

David did as he was told.

When the colonel and his two FBI types entered The Egg, they found about thirty superheroes sewing costumes, painting signs, cooking vats of penne. The heroes might not have noticed the officers had the *tonggg* not chimed right then.

The USV ant farm went still, frozen. Including David.

Though he was ushering a serious threat into the belly of the beast, the Seventh-Minute Stop was sacred. Disregarding it would break a covenant with those he sought to lead and protect.

Colonel Blue and his two suited associates kept moving, of course. In a roomful of frozen offenders, they took the chance to slalom among the still bodies, the colonel eyeballing each USVer carefully as if he were inspecting uniforms and footlockers for punishable defects. He halted briefly beside two freshman initiates wearing sandwich boards that read WAR WASTES TIME!! and PREPARE TO KILL YOUR DARLINGS. David couldn't help but notice the jacket bulge under the colonel's armpit with what could only be a pistol.

"Check upstairs," Blue said to one of the suits. And to the other, "Check the basement."

David wanted to respond and ask about warrants, but piercing The Egg's hallowed silence felt more invasive than the illegal search being conducted. From his peripherals, David saw one of the suits hop up the stairs toward the training rooms, while the other circled the kitchen, opening pantry doors until he found the locked basement door. USVers tilted their eyes toward *him,* the living room's ranking officer. Owen subtly shook his head, but what was that supposed to mean?

"You've got nice furniture," the colonel said, running his hand over a teak table covered in red T-shirts screen-printed with Øs and the phrase

WE CAN SAVE US ALL. "This one used to be in my dining room. It was Matt's grandpa's."

David stared straight, trying his best to stay calm and leaderly.

"What's your water capacity for this many kids?" Silence. "Whatever it is, it's not enough."

Just then the intruders succeeded in opening the basement door with some kind of lockpick and Colonel Blue went for the stairs. And David awkwardly exploded with sound and motion.

"Sir!" he yelled. "Colonel! I'll escort you down if you'd like!" David tripped over an ottoman and chased them downstairs, his ears pelted by a collective tsk of disappointment from the USV.

As they tromped the steps, David weaseled his way in front of Mathias's father, wondering if the man might push him down the staircase. Once downstairs, he saw Fu, Britt, and Haley frozen near David's bedroom as Business-Man accompanied the father of their leader to his son's humble abode on the other side of the basement. Maps and other incriminating evidence had been hidden in Lee's lab under the stairs, but the two suits poked around, examining Owen's array of batteries on the tool bench. David glanced at the vise, the secret trigger. He imagined Mathias, Lee, and Nyla hiding inside the lab, staying the stiffest they'd ever been.

"He's really not here," David admitted loudly. "My guess is he'll be back in a week, but..."

The colonel walked to Mathias's door and said, "Open it, please."

Together, they entered. Everything looked sticky. David had never seen the inside of this room for more than a few seconds. It smelled like cinnamon and turpentine and Haley. David tried not to picture every sex dream / nightmare he'd had for the past two months. Meanwhile, Colonel Blue inspected the strewn bedsheets, picked some peanut butter off the wall with his fingernail. He scanned the floor and seemed to be searching for a clue, or maybe a trace of Mathias himself.

"Your son is a great guy. A leader," David offered. "Everyone thinks he's a genius."

The colonel shut the door to Mathias's room. "What do you think?"

David was legitimately nervous now, being alone with this man.

"I think he's scared. Like all of us," David said. "But somehow less so. Like this is simply the natural order of things, and what comes next will be perfect. He's a man of vision. He sees things. The world needs a hero like him, with so little time left."

"It's over," Colonel Blue said. David assumed he was referring to the universe. "You seem smart enough, and if you're really in charge then you can stop this USV before people get hurt."

"Sir, I don't think it's possible to stop it. Not without people getting hurt."

"Young people do stupid things when they gather in times of crisis."

"Or we'll do *transformative* things that older people simply don't understand or don't have the... I guess you have too much to lose. We see what's possible and we're not tired or trapped yet."

Mathias's father began to speak again but David cut him off.

"With all due respect, do you know what we're *doing* here, sir?" David asked. "We're not mutant, alien superheroes pretending to save the day. We're *protecting* each other, our communities. And we *are* willing to get our hands dirty and assist with whatever kind of relief effort you might—"

"What's in that refrigerator?" he asked.

"I wish I knew. Nobody has the key." David shook the padlock as if that proved his point.

It happened quickly. Colonel Blue moving David aside, reaching into his jacket, pulling out his gun, and firing point-blank at the padlock. It exploded into brilliant metal shards. David found himself on the floor, wedged beside Mathias's bed. He'd never seen someone fire a gun outside a shooting range, with intent to actually destroy something. It was insanely loud and every cell in David's body felt infuriated. The colonel cleared debris from the fridge door. He opened it.

The gun went to his side and his body suddenly slumped out of its officious posture.

Convinced the firing was over, David yelled assurances to the USVers outside and joined Colonel Blue by the fridge. It was colder inside than David imagined, no light. The upper shelves, as he'd suspected, were Mathias's genetics: blood, semen, stool, a half-full mason jar of toenails. But the bottom shelves were his medicines. And these were news to David. Row after row of prescription bottles. Stuff that definitely didn't come from Lee but from real doctors. They were alphabetized.

Jesus, he thought.

Colonel Blue examined them and picked out a handful of bottles, maybe six of them. These, he explained, were the most important ones. The ones that kept Mathias even. The rest he'd never heard of, which, to him, meant they were probably doing more harm than good.

The bevy of pills suddenly made sense. David knew something was slipping inside Mathias. Maybe it was simply misdosages or unintended interactions? The new Zeronal?

"Did my son tell you about his brother?"

"Sure," David said. "Everyone knows. Edison is part of Ultraviolet's origin story."

"What has he told you all about Edison?"

"Not a lot, quite honestly," said David. "I know about the Derecho and the tree, how your other son survived but then fell into a kind of coma and passed away. But he doesn't—"

"My other son?"

"Sure, Mathias's twin."

Colonel Blue scowled. "People always say how *twins* have such distinct personalities. This one's the quiet one. That one's the life of the party. But Matty and Eddie were exactly the same. Perfect clones, do you understand? Their mom even dressed them alike for a while. I couldn't stand it. I insisted they wear different colors. Matty was red, and Eddie always wore purple. Always."

"So Mathias took his brother's color!" offered David. "A way of keeping his memory alive."

David loved this new detail. He considered how to work it into an upcoming comic book.

The colonel's voice descended to a whisper. "When we were all in the hospital, Mathias—they caught him doing it. There was no storm, no tree, that's all just his fabrication, but Edison *was* in a coma. A nurse caught Mathias, right after. After he'd finished smothering Edison with a pillow."

David sat down on the bed next to Colonel Blue, taking this in. Was this real? Or just a ploy?

"They tried to revive him, but... We buried it," the man said. "Nobody had to know. They still don't need to know, all the kids out there. But someone should know. *You* should probably know. He's a... a lost person."

"Maybe," David mumbled, "with all due respect, sir, maybe he felt his twin's pain so strongly—they say that happens, right?—maybe he was helping him, y'know, die the right way?"

"It wasn't his *twin*," said the colonel. "It was his exact replica."

"Right, spitting image."

"No, wrong. Edison was the first successful case in DARPA's ST13B project, Advanced Mammalian Genome Engineering. I'm telling you Edison was his *clone*, David, a flesh-and-blood person made from his DNA. And he was perfect for... four years or so. When he started to fail, Matty saw it. And he decided that it was time for Edison to die. But we don't get to decide when and how people live or die, do we?"

"Not unless you work for the Department of Defense, I guess." David shrugged. "Do you have any proof of this? Any of this? Video? Classified documents or something?"

The man sniffed once at the air.

David wasn't sure if the colonel was messing with him. He was talking about human cloning, which was objectively insane, but David also knew they'd cloned a sheep back in the 1990s, so was it really so unbelievable that maybe they'd been doing humans for decades and just not talking about it? Everything in him wanted to ask the obvious questions, to respond as a little kid, screaming, "No, it can't be!" Awestruck and incredulous. But David realized this was exactly what the man expected. So he tried to project the opposite response instead. Unimpressed. Credulous.

He wanted the colonel to know whom he was dealing with.

"He's sick, David," said the colonel, his face shifting. "I'm his father. You don't know what that's like, but it supersedes everything. You don't have to want to help *me*, but if you want to help *him*, if you want to help yourself and all these kids out there, if you want to help *Haley*—your... the... she's the captain girl, right?—then help us bring *just him* in quietly. Help us take care of him. The weather is only going to get worse for the foreseeable future and it's safer if he's—"

"He's right, isn't he?" David said. "The gods are putting us out of our misery."

"There's just too many of us," said Mathias's dad. "Overpopulation."

David remembered a tale from the Problem of Evil class. He told Colonel Blue the story of how there was once two levels of gods: the minor gods had to do all the work for the bigger, important gods, until one of the lesser ones got the idea to create humans to help with the grunt work.

"They just didn't realize how fast we'd procreate and how much noise we'd all make, and pretty soon the gods, especially Enlil, who was something of a whiner, couldn't sleep for all the racket. So they figured out ways to lower the population. Mathias thinks that's what's happening again. Maybe the gods can't hear themselves think. When earthquakes and disease and the war don't do the trick, they'll unleash the supercell, which catalyzes the flood, and we won't know how to live together when the power goes out and the population will decline. Right?"

"I'm hoping science will intervene before God," Colonel Blue said. "Okay, listen. I won't ask you to surrender this operation, and I don't want to put my son in jail. But we're out of time. He's *dangerous*. He's messing with things you don't understand. So here's my deal, my offer to you. First, I'll need you to hit me in the face."

—Ø—

She'd been standing beside Owen, ready, straining to make out the mumbles inside Mathias's room. Haley jumped when she heard the crash. Colonel Blue spilled out of Mathias's room. David was holding the man's pistol firmly, keeping it trained on the colonel's head. When the FBI lackeys reached for their pieces, Owen pulled an AR-15 from below the tool bench and locked on.

The colonel halted his minions, swiped a trail of blood from his mouth.

"For smart kids, you're extremely stupid," he said. "*Now* we know you have guns. *Now* you're a violent threat. *Now* we have cause. Haven't you heard? Guns are *dangerous*." He looked at Owen. "And you're now in the unenviable position of having to figure out whether you want to shoot three decorated military officers in this sweaty basement. I hope your aim is true."

Haley stepped in front of Owen, who kept the rifle aimed at Colonel Blue, never breaking his eyes from his target. Haley stepped closer.

"You say 'decorated military officers' as if you're good guys. You've directly threatened us, illegally searched our house, and your generation and government are responsible for the evils of the world that have put us in this situation. So, *now*, you need to understand that you're in our basement, where *we* are the good guys."

Blue moved toward the stairs and smiled, the blood between his teeth. He turned to David.

"You've made a massive mistake, son," he said. "A stupid, stupid mistake. You shut this down or we come in and round up all of you savages ourselves, understand? One week!"

"Time is irrelevant," David said, pointing the pistol at Colonel Blue's head. "It's a new era."

Colonel Nathan Blue laughed a condescending laugh and stomped up the stairs.

When they were out of sight, Haley glanced over at David, still holding his stance. She'd never seen him like this, in full protector mode—not protecting *her*, but protecting all of them. As soon as the colonel was clear and his tiny motorcade gone from Woosamonsa, the call rang out and The Egg erupted. Haley strode over to David and gripped his neck and put her forehead against his.

"You were so fucking good!" she said.

"Will you go to the Silent Dance with me?" David asked, holding her, holding the moment.

She said yes.

—Ø—

There was aripiprazole to decrease hallucinations. Codeine for pain. Depakote for migraines. Levoxyl for his thyroid. Detrol for his bladder. But then there was Propecia for hair loss caused by the Levoxyl and Depakote. Flexeril for the muscle spasms caused by the aripiprazole. Aricept for the memory loss caused by Detrol. Cialis for the stagnant libido caused by the Propecia.

And even all of that didn't worry David. What worried David were the amphetamines.

After Mathias and the others had emerged from their hiding spots, David admitted quietly to him: the fridge had been breached. So Mathias offered David the tour. Just David, though.

"I'll give you the dosages and frequencies tomorrow," Mathias said once they were alone, "but Dad's right, I could use your help. If I stray too far I can become a real mess and a half."

David stared at the bottles. Almost nobody else—maybe Haley and probably Lee, he now realized—had seen inside this fridge. Mathias aimed to keep it that way.

"Lee has kept me even, but I need to distance myself a little bit there. He's been in love with me from the beginning, which is flattering. I kissed him a few weeks ago—I wanted to give him that much—but I can't swing all the way. We've come to an understanding. Some distance until he gets his head straight. Which is to say I can't totally trust him right now. This isn't easy to admit, but I need *you* to protect *me*. Keep this a secret. Doctor-patient confidentiality."

David wasn't sure which new piece of information to tackle first. He chose the obvious one:

"Your dad also dropped some pretty intense shit on me about human cloning," David said. "Care to comment?'

"It's sad," said Mathias. "Dad's convinced himself that Edison's death was part of an elaborate DARPA experiment. There is an experiment—that part is real, I've seen aspects of it—but it was only funded and launched about ten years ago, well after Eddie's death, and it's not really focused on cloning, per se; it's about engineering artificial chromosomes as a platform for introducing large DNA vectors into human cell lines to engineer more complex functionalities. Shit, it's basically creating superhumans, now that I think of it. But it's not *cloning*. I worry about Dad."

"I worry about you," said David.

"That's kind."

"I just committed a federal offense, I think," said David. "I pointed a pistol at him, okay? Please do me a solid and tell me I'm not doing all this to protect a crazy person."

"You want me to be Superman, David. But what defines Superman? Seriously, I'm asking."

"He's strong, he can fly, saves lives, does good. Truth, justice, American way, all that crap."

"Do you have a pen?"

"Why would I have a fucking pen?"

Mathias took from his fridge a jar of blood. "I know you're still skeptical," he said. "But the rest have crossed that threshold and I need you here with us." He unscrewed the top and dipped his fingers into the red goo. "The Silent Dance will be your revelation. I can see it. You'll feel us zero in, and we will move like birds together, a single strong unit." He grabbed a piece of paper and fingerpainted. "Surrender to it, zero in, and you will see with your own eyes a hero that can fly, that saves lives." He handed David the bloody paper. It looked like a shield, with words that read: DEI SUB NUMINE VIGET.

David gingerly gripped the corner of the gross thing. "What does that mean?" he asked.

"I have no idea. It's just what I see. It's what you'll see when your hero flies. You know?"

David knew what he knew. He knew what he believed. He knew what he had to do. He was terrified, but he smiled and clapped Mathias on the back. "I'll take care of you."

David retired to his room to think, to work, to google Mathias's nonsense. *Dei sub numine viget* meant, roughly, "Under God's Protection She Flourishes," Princeton's official school motto. David was sick of riddles and koans. USV enclaves were waiting for a communiqué. Concrete instructions on next steps. So he and Haley recorded an encoded video message, uploaded via Fu's crazy system of rerouted IP addresses. He detailed the Silent Dance, all the particulars.

But once the USV settled down for the night, David walked outside, snuck into the tool shed, and dialed the secure number Colonel Blue had given him.

Mathias's father answered the phone by saying, "If you decide not to take my job offers with DARPA, Booz Allen, or the agency, you've got a future in acting, Business-Man."

David again detailed the Silent Dance, all the particulars. And where exactly Mathias would be stationed. He reminded himself: the mission was more important than the man.

"University chapel courtyard," he concluded. "Probably only two bodyguards. He'll be in the exterior pulpit on the south wall, Friday night at eight o'clock is when it starts."

"I thought time was irrelevant," the colonel scoffed.

"Occasionally it's important."

"I trust you, David, to do what you have to do. You'll rise to the occasion. This is the best thing you can do to protect them."

"I'm a man of my word," David replied. "But if I'm selling out Mathias, just promise me—"

"We have a deal," said the elder Blue. "You and your girlfriend will be protected."

iii.

Costumes again. This time: suits, ties, tails.

"You look dashing," Haley told him, flowers in hand. Did he? David thought he looked just okay. He'd left László's blazer at The Egg—it would be a messy night—and instead wore an awful fire-sale tux. It fit well at the store but had somehow grown too big since then. Was he shrinking?

Blink. A bowling alley. Blink. Claire Shiller on lane six getting smaller in the distance. Blink.

"You're sure it doesn't look like I'm shrinking?" David asked.

"Dude, you've gotta stop asking me that," Haley said.

David scanned Haley's body with upturned palms. A tribute to her.

She liked the way she looked, too. Feeling glam in a French-blue dress with a formfitting bodice, delicate spaghetti straps, her breasts looking firm and shiny and fantastic. Her silver hair was pulled up, defying gravity. She let David take a deep breath of her head and whisper, "Vanilla."

She slipped her hand into his.

David squeezed.

She squeezed.

They played like this. Pulsing back and forth in rhythm.

"Stay close to me tonight," he said. "Whatever happens, I'll protect you."

She batted her lashes and said, "My hero." But what she meant was *I will protect myself.*

Protection was now key. After Colonel Blue's visit, SITS had doubled down on security.

When they try to shove you—and they always open with a shove—move like a matador. Get them off-balance. Swing down to control their arms, then up to strike the nasal septum, delivering a shock to the cervical spine. Bring his face to the ground. End it quickly. Move on.

This was Self-Defense 101, as taught by Peacemaker and Sergeant Drill.

With the entitled grace of tomorrow's elite, David and Haley strolled toward the chapel, toward McCosh Courtyard, the venue for Princeton's official spring formal, which the USV was about to ruin. David found it exceptionally silly for Princeton to plan an outdoor dance at this moment in history, what with the world exploding outside their bubble. But it was a Princeton tradition, one of many taken too seriously.

"We'll rebuild stronger than ever before" was everyone's line.

What they meant was *We're being destroyed.*

Somewhere around Monday, the American Evangelical Alliance suicide-bombed the Wailing Wall—claiming preordained, noble sacrifice—and most thought Jerusalem wouldn't last the month. *Fundamentalists are doomed,* David thought. *For those who can't see the comic within the cosmic, everything will burn.* But here in this funny place called college, David still had a chance to protect his followers.

That's all that mattered anymore. Taking care of his flock. Protecting and providing for. That's why Mathias had to go, David told himself. Not because David was power-hungry, ready to elevate from number two to head honcho. And not because he wanted Haley's former lover out of the way. No, Mathias was sick. Possibly a sick*ness*. You have to cut out the cancer before it spreads.

The last Super Fucking Fire Zero had more exiles than initiations. Mathias was growing more paranoid and quick-triggered, ready to remove anyone deemed weak. He said he needed to purify the pack before they all arrived at the Null Point, that this was the time to separate the men from the heroes.

"What about the women?" Haley had asked him, quite publicly. "Do we threaten you?"

"I'm not threatened by you," Mathias said. "I'm *thrilled* by you."

Zoe didn't make the cut, however. And this was Haley's call. David thought it was due to Zoe's new role as one of Mathias's preferred lovers—"His fucktoy," Haley called her.

But no, it was something else.

"You whine too much," Haley said to her. "We're all scared—you'd be crazy not to be—but that doesn't mean we act like victims. More importantly, *you* can't be trusted. You were there on Halloween, Boo Berry, you were supposed to be my sister. Can't blame you, but can't trust you."

Haley mercifully gave Zoe the option to leave quietly, voluntarily, rather than suffer the public humiliation of exile by fire. Which she did. Mathias remained the singular chieftain, with many left in his rotating harem.

Leading the pack to McCosh was the power couple of this particular night: Britt and Fu, arms linked. She'd helped with the psychological rationale for the Noise Machine, but this was Fu's night to shine. He'd built the thing and composed the music, and all the USV heroes would be his instruments. David loved seeing Echo in a tux. It Girl looked red-carpet-worthy in a slinky white number by Someone Important. Haley and David wandered over to schmooze.

"Let's see the backyard," Britt sang as they approached. Haley twirled. "Ugh!" Britt said. "My kingdom for an ass like that."

"Are you in charge tonight?" asked a mild-mannered Fu to David.

"No," he said to Fu. "You are."

"Business-Man's here on pleasure?" drawled Britt, puffing a cigarette.

David opened his mouth to display a Pez pill dissolving on his tongue. The stress of the preceding week had ground him down. He knew he'd narced on the USV, or at least Mathias, but he was doing the right thing. Any minute now, Navy SEALs might rappel from stealth choppers to vaporize them all. He tried to put it out of his mind. David needed a night off. He was sick of being in charge, the secret king, holed up in some turret. He was sick of the USV machine. It was mid-May, probably. After tonight, they'd either be free of Mathias or all go to jail. If tonight was to be their last dance, their last free day on earth, David wanted to be a beast.

He waved in Fu to tell him a secret and whispered, "I'm shrinking!"

—Ø—

McCosh Courtyard was a long lawn walled in on three sides by Gothic architecture. In the lawn's center stood the towering Mather Sundial: a twenty-foot tall limestone column holding some astronomical sphere and a symbol of Christ's sacrifice, a pelican—the bird once believed to nourish its young using its own blood. On sunny days, the tower cast its clockwise shadow around the lawn, a favorite landmark, a perennial stop on campus tours.

This was the USV's target.

Haley had handed off much of the filmmaking for the night to two of her assistant directors, OS Infinity and Stanley Jewbrick, who'd affixed bodycams to a dozen heroes and arrayed tripod cams to capture and distribute their spectacle widely. It was only spitting tonight, but weeks of rain meant Haley's heels sank into the soft ground. Under the event tent, USVers disguised as cumberbunded catering staff passed their trays, briskly plucked of grilled vegetables, seasonal fruit, carved beef, pills. Blink. David saw the bar mitzvahs of his thirteenth year. He saw vague outlines of orthodontured middle school BFFs lip-syncing in oversized Elton John sunglasses. Blink. Blink. Blink. Tracing paper on top of reality.

A fake waiter skipped over to David and Haley, eager to please. He brushed his shaggy hair aside and displayed a tattooed zero, right there on his forehead. David believed his name was Ted.

"Cocktail, sir?" said Maybe Ted. "Cigar? Cigarette? Pez?"

"Don't forget these, sir." Another pseudo-waiter had sidled up and handed them wireless earbuds, packaged in a self-charging white case that looked like a thing of dental floss. Fu's factory of electrical engineers had completed their massive effort to install miniature receivers in hundreds of pairs of earbuds. Soon, all of them would be dialed into Fu's ham radio frequencies.

Haley and David each popped another pill, accepted a cocktail, put in their wireless earbuds.

They mingled. A few hundred kids in tuxes or dresses. Many USVers. Normal students just here to party. Plenty of faces David didn't recognize one way or the other.

The night slowly began to speed up.

The dance floor was being rocked by Party Shooz, an eleven-piece wedding band in red sequined vests. They played all the Motown favorites. Once the USV cut the band's power, Peacemaker's generators would become the USV's power source for the night and help transmit Golden Echo's improvised opus—the *real* music for the event—via wireless earbuds. No amps. No noise complaint.

David glanced skyward. Echo was now in costume, setting up his transmitters in the south pulpit attached to the chapel exterior, as they'd planned. Ultraviolet stood in the shadows behind him, looking darkly heroic. He was exactly where David told the colonel he'd be.

Party Shooz's searing rendition of "Love Shack" suddenly cut off.

Echo's music took its place in the USV's ears.

Only the deep bass drum at first, the central metronome they'd all lock into. The pulse.

Echo's musical-industrial complex was impossible to explain. He'd load something here, twist that dial, press buttons with the meticulousness of a master chef. He was the king of multitasking, always stirring two pots, two turntables. David really did love Fu Schroeder. Underneath Golden Echo's beats were sets of psychoacoustic instructions, looped into the fabric of the sound. Echo Music. Haley and David turned from the pulpit and joined the mass under the tent. Once aboard the dance floor, Haley said, "Let's dance like old people."

She grabbed his shoulder and palm, attempting a proper waltz. David placed a hand on her exquisite hip. She pressed herself against him. The top of her chest plumped, as if holding back some delicious juice. At once,

David felt the rush of blood. He blinked. An image flashed again. Haley's face blurring into Madeline's face at homecoming that time.

"Are you getting lots of superimposition, too?" David asked her, trying to shake it off.

"Yeah," said Haley. "I'm feeling it really strong. You were just my dad for a second."

"Gross," said David, hard as a rock. They parted momentarily, focused on their pulse beats.

It was getting a little weird.

Every so often, the pulse stopped and a *tonggg* sounded bright and clear in their ears.

The Seventh-Minute Stop.

Silence and stillness. Catch your breath. Okay.

Then things grew deeper and dirtier.

Haley accompanied David arm in arm to a grassy patch against the chapel. She spun and kissed him hard on the mouth and he kissed her back, hard, wanting to press his face right through hers until it came out the back end and she sprang from the back of his head till they were Janus, god of beginnings and ends and end and end and end and end and—

"I'm kind of freaking out," Haley said, her voice shaking a bit. "This is really intense."

"Are you okay?" David tried to ask, exhaling audibly. He was kind of freaking out, too.

"I think this batch of Pez is bad. I feel like something else is in control."

And suddenly, shifting, David softened. He smiled at her eyes and said, "Something else *is*."

And she softened, too. "I can hear you inside me," she said, and giggled. She asked him if he'd hold her hand and he said yes, and he squeezed, and she squeezed back, pulsing in rhythm.

—Ø—

Haley's ears are not David's. They're a different one of Echo's frequencies.

His is this:

... BOOM.... . . BAP... BOOM-BAP... BOOM.... . . BAP... BOOM-BAP...

He vocalizes along with dozens of others. Hers fits the silences. Hers is this:

Tik... . . . . . *ta-ka*... . . . *ta-ka*...... . ... *Tik*... ..... *ta-ka*... . . . *ta-ka*... . . . .
Tik . . . .

She hears other parts throughout the courtyard. Echo likes to play with contrasts. Bass and treble. One rhythm is intricate and fast, the other simple and thick. One staccato melody, the other a single extended drone. It all blends perfectly. The USV becomes unified, one record turning, and Echo is their Human DJ, twisting the center spindle.

But they are not alone this time.

From outside their earbuds they hear other audio—arrhythmic, unmixed. Screeching brakes of armored vehicles pulling to the far edge of the courtyard. Shouted commands. Feet on pavement.

Riot cops are here.

They pour from tanklike trucks and squad cars. They rise up on roofs. They hover in helicopters, penning the naughty children into the courtyard.

There is another group alongside them. Baseball helmets and ski goggles, carrying their own shields and guns, waving flags bearing the insane emblems of monsters. They carry torches.

What is happening?

It is daytime again. And it's then—*when?!*—for just one brief blip that David realizes he has no idea how long they've been doing this psychotic shit. He finds Haley again, grabs her wrist, and she grabs his.

"Stay close to me," he says. "Whatever you do."

"We are sharing the same face," she says. "I can't get any closer."

The USV comes together, forming a huge clump of humanity around the sundial, as per their doctrine: the best offense is a strong defense. Zero in. Pull together. Lock arms. Stay stiff.

Machines begin their work, but it's too late. An array of circular saws with diamond blades goes to town on the base of the stone pillar. Heroes pour constant streams of water over the stone, keeping the dust to a minimum while they tear down this monument to time.

David looks up at the chapel pulpit. Where is Mathias? Has he been captured already?

And now he looks across the lawn at these people amassed against them. What has the USV done so wrong? Is it the fear of property damage, somehow more important than human life? The vague religiousness of this statue? Who has called the cops? Who has leaked to the neo-Nazis?

"Throw down your firearms," comes the call from across the field.

Oh, right, David remembers. *The USV has guns now.* They have invited this trouble and have no moral high ground to escape their own flood.

The opposition is dressed in its own costumes. Uniformed riot police and, separately, an uninvited third party of self-uniformed militia, armed to the teeth.

The cops back off, regroup. Peacemaker's crew establishes a barricade—upturned tables from the event tent, crisscrossed chairs, metal trash bins—like that giant French wall of garbage from *Les Misérables*. They wear masks covered in vinegar to help when the tear gas comes. Each side shouts epithets across the field:

"Liberal elite cucks!"

"White Nazi fascists!"

"Pussies!"

"Virgins!"

The USV faces off against the other side. Haley wonders if maybe those toxic men arrayed against them have their own double-headed Januses, just like she and David do.

Facing one way are the cops, who are not playing dress-up and do not appreciate the USV very much at all. They wear black uniforms they call blue and carry functional utility belts with actual tools of protection, apprehension, detection, and violence. They still have the haircuts they made them get when they enlisted. This is what they trained for. To protect and serve the community.

They were meant to be heroes.

Facing the other way is a different Janus face, begging for a fight. Maybe these are the guys who were not focused or stable enough to become cops, so instead they found alienated brethren on the internet and formed themselves a militia. This is the moment to show these Ivy League fucks who've had every privilege, every resource, every gentle parental push in the right direction, rather than a pounding shove down the stairs, and still they've chosen to squander it. This is the wrong kind of freedom that threatens the right kind of freedom. And it must be stopped. So they will stop it.

Because they, too, were always meant to be heroes.

They advance.

Black boots enter the mud and rain of the courtyard, soiling themselves.

Peacemaker raises both arms, fists clenched, like a superhero about to take flight.

His voice caroms off the echoing stone, and the others chant with him:

BOOM…. . BAP… BOOM-BAP… BOOM…. . . . BAP… BOOM-BAP…

From the sidelines, David and Haley watch the USV march toward cop shields and militia torches. And for a moment, David and Haley both believe peace is possible and that this thing they are doing is too big to fail. The skies will open and an angora blanket of hope will billow down and cradle them all. Along with the rain, there will be revelation.

Haley points to the sky. She spots a deus ex machina coming toward them! David sees it, too. It is small and blinking. Propellers buzzing, some kind of alien craft, maybe. It opens. And some billowing cloud issues forth over dozens of torches, dispersing down onto their would-be attackers.

For a moment, they believe that peace blanket has come to save them.

But it is actually a dragon, breathing deathfire.

Or, no, it's just a small remote-controlled drone, the thesis of one of their heroes, no doubt, Junior Pez or maybe Mind Boggle. Their drone is dropping flammable kerosene spray onto the Nazi torchbearers. Not a direct hit, but flames engulf a pack of them, and the screams go up as they roll in the mud or sprint wildly in full retreat. The ones spared by the fire run to the police, pointing fingers at the USV, at the sky, at anything to be blamed, demanding arrests and retribution. As the Nazis lick their wounds, the cops advance.

So this is it. The two sides rush at each other. The melee is on.

This is David's cue. He's got a predetermined spot by the chapel wall, behind some bushes. His home base where he won't be beaten or arrested—only corralled later—all according to his deal with Colonel Blue.

"Come with me," he says to Haley. "To the bushes!"

"No, are you crazy?!" she screams. "We have to stay all together, zeroed in."

"Trust me! You and I, we keep going."

She is too confused to fight him.

She sprints with him to the outskirts of this spectacle and slips or keels over backward, splashing the mud, making a mess of her clothes. David joins her down there.

Sludge makes a good traitor's costume. A full-body mask.

He protects her, laying his body atop hers as he watches the scrum commence in the middle of the field, too busy and muddy to know who is who anymore. They are all mud.

Finally, a grave still point. David stares up at the sky, stuck mid-snow-angel. The Big Bang is happening again, constantly, up there in space, down here inside him. A billion revolutions every second. Every cell in transition. Perfect blissful constant conversion forever...

Tonggg. They hear it in their ears, in their brains.

They are still stuck to the ground when the tent comes down and the media moves in. Haley pulls out her cell phone to film, to have some objective record she can return to when the psychedelics wear off. She sees pocket universes of USVers locked in the same act, the same rhythm. It's like watching a clock, inner gears moving at different speeds but all ultimately working in harmony. This group sprays yellow puffs of mace. That group squirts milk at burning eyes. A group of masked heroes abandons its work at the stone pillar and wields its circular saws overhead like crazed horror movie villains.

We are this mechanical wonder, David thinks. *This machine.*

Cells look uniform from far away, but magnify further and you see all the ganglia and pock marks that shape an organism.

We are a machine in beast mode.

Haley sees the barricade break. Superheroes swarm the police, jumping on their backs and biting their legs like bratty toddlers. Cops are wary at first, scared of accidentally clubbing a senator's son, and they focus on their normal targets—the women, the smaller statured, the people of color. But soon, tuxedoed kids are bleeding. Skulls cracking. Peacemaker has procured a long pole. He swings it in an arc around him, cutting a wide circular berth. No one wants to fuck with that.

David darts his head around and spots Ultraviolet behind a wall of protectors—*There he is! What the fuck?*—waving a Ø flag until Nyla and a pack of bodyguards swarm and shuttle him away.

But Golden Echo stays. He is a triumph. He jumps from his pulpit and hops on his Yamaha, driving doughnuts around Peacemaker's nucleus, around the makeshift barricade, round and round he goes, wheels kicking up a spray of soil, engraving a brown circle into the lawn.

Cops chase him, but they're hopeless. They're on foot. There's too much mud. The USV is too coordinated, or too reckless and frightening, completely in and completely fucking out of control. When the tear gas comes, the kids are ready for it. They have giant fans and gas masks galore to scatter the smoke and survive it. Some throw up or lose motor control, but the vinegar helps. For every USVer who goes down, there are plenty more to fill the void.

But everyone whoops for Echo. He is a rock star. He is Golden.

He dodges more cops on his dirt bike as they try to cut off his path. An officer in a Dodge Challenger pulls onto the McCosh lawn, trying to scatter this pack of wild animals. It skids and turns, headed back for another pass. David sees headlights pointed at him now and burrows into the mud. He closes his eyes and listens. In his ears, a heartbeat.

Tik... . . . . . ta-ka...

Tick... Tock...

Tick.

Tock.

But when David opens his eyes, the headlights are even closer.

Unless they turn, these wheels will bear down on David and Haley and run them over deep into the ground. He sees it happening, but thinks, *We are ready to make this sacrifice, to give ourselves to the mud and the wheels and the rain and the brothers and sisters around us and the USV movement on high. We are ready to be killed by cops and sent to the annals of student protest, the newest heroic martyrs for a growing youth tide that will never subside, never shrink, only grow bigger and bigger and bigger until the End. The Luminous Ones are the next wave, and the Normals primed for extinction can't do a thing to stop this sea. We are ready. We are pelicans.*

But then another set of wheels cuts through the headlights. A silhouetted motorcycle flies in front of David's eyes. The police car tries to bail. Its wheels swerve. Now, with the high beams out of his eyes, David sees everything. He snaps his head back to the moment and watches it unfold.

He sees Golden Echo drive right into the car's path.

Mud flies.

Another day.

Metal crunches metal.

Another night.

And now Golden Echo, he is soaring, body bereft of bike.

Fu is soaring, arms outstretched in front of him, and when his body slams into the stone wall of the chapel and hits the ground in a heap of twisted leather limbs, David sees it a thousand times, a body in its last dance, a superhero flying through the air.

10
JUNE

i.

For a day, it is big news. An ambulance scattering color into the sepia courtyard. The USV exploding in all directions, cloaked by the crash. Peacemaker dragging away It Girl, who's begging to stay and sob to the cops, her limbs flailing into space. Her Fu Schroeder is gone.

Neck broken.

Dead on impact.

The key camera shot, though, the one that plays over and over on social media and the twenty-four-hour news cycle, is of the exact spot where Fu's helmet struck the chapel's stone wall. A grisly gash is carved into a stone relief of the Princeton University crest.

It's a shield with Latin words: DEI SUB NUMINE VIGET.

"The school motto translates as 'Under God's Protection They Flourish,'" says the CBS anchor. She uses the phrase "tragic irony." David stares at Mathias, a different revelation in mind:

He sees everything. Mathias is for real. A prophet. David finally fully believes.

And he almost ruined it all.

Then the news switches to weather. There are typhoons in Texas.

—ø—

They spread themselves around the pews, trying not to cluster or draw attention.

The reverend Dr. Anthony East addressed the university chapel, and the USV mourned through all the usual turns of phrase: "It fills my heart with sadness." "A bright future." "A lesser community without his presence."

But the good reverend understood his audience. He thought he understood.

He chose his Scripture carefully:

"'Be not overcome of evil, but overcome evil with good,'" he quoted. "Romans, chapter twelve, verse twenty-one. Twelve: twenty-one. I do not think it's an accident that these numbers are a palindrome. A mirror image. For in every action, in every human being, there is possibility for evil and potential for good. Some claim evil is always on the verge of triumph. That there are demons everywhere, and good souls must attempt to walk the narrow moral line between two massive walls of treachery.

"I do not hesitate to call the death of Fu Schroeder 'tragic.' In examining the events surrounding Fu's demise, however, I do hesitate to call his death 'accidental' or 'senseless' or 'heroic,' as others have. Those of us who watched those frightening and heartbreaking events transpire on Livestream are aware that Fu Schroeder was a member of an underground organization linked to domestic terrorism and public acts of disruption and that he was instrumental and highly visible in the activities of May 20.

"I do not say this to trample a young man's memory or to provoke animosity toward those boys and girls of the USV who are undoubtedly in attendance here today. I assure you, the police presence you see within and outside the chapel walls is strictly for peacekeeping. No arrests will be made in this time and place of mourning. You are safe in your grief.

"I will not speculate on the USV's spiritual merit—Christ himself was seen by many in his time as a dangerous cult leader—but I would be remiss not to ask students lucky enough to escape real harm to take note of this truth: despite the trendy seduction of the USV, the organization fosters recklessness. Death is no passing fad. I encourage students to move forward with appropriate levels of trepidation and to choose life instead. And let us say, amen."

—Ø—

But they were not safe in their grief. Not at all.

While the mourners crowded the chapel, standing room only, evil attacked.

The Egg went up in flames.

Fire was a lot like grief, Haley decided, in that there are different sorts of fire. There was the kind that started small, almost a secret, little embers kissing a sisal rug, maybe, turning the fibers brown, then black, then that hint of orange that catches a breeze, spreads slowly, and the smell is what tips you off, sends you sprinting to stamp it out and say, *Wow. That was close*. But then there are also the fierce explosions. They boom out of nowhere. They're hard, maybe impossible, to fight. You just have to let them run their course. Fu's death was like this.

Haley had sat in that pew, having found an empty spot next to her old roommate Jessica. She hadn't seen or talked to Jessica since just before winter break, but there was something so familiar about her in that moment. A neutral space. A thigh she could press hers against and cry. There was no small talk—no talk at all, actually—but as Haley's body rocked with sobs, nauseous dread coursing through her body, Jessica's hand on her back felt like a perfect piece of protection. Haley peeked around her hanging hair and spotted David standing behind one of those tall candles marking the outer aisle of the church. He was looking at her, too. She felt so unbelievably, endlessly guilty, wondering if this fire would ever go out. Fu had saved them, her and David. He'd given everything for them, and she was entirely sure they did not deserve it. They'd been cowering on the outskirts of that skirmish as their brothers and sisters took flagpole stabs to their necks, mace to their eyes, boots to their backs—so many twisted into the mud and hogtied with plastic cuffs. They'd hidden. They were too goddamn high to do anything else. And, as if to make that point completely clear, for the rest of their lives, Fu had given himself to them. He was the ultimate hero, would always be so. She looked up at the pastor, waxing on.

Fuck that, she thought.

They dispersed after the service, taking long, meandering routes back to The Egg to ensure they weren't being followed, which gave the fire plenty of time to establish itself and spread to Fred's House and the Pink House as well. By the time Haley arrived at Woosamonsa Court, USV members and middle-aged neighborhood allies were standing back, just watching the blaze. There was plenty of wailing, but not enough frantic motion for there to be people stuck in there. This was pure property destruction, but obviously it was more than that, too. Haley found a storm drain to puke into, having held back this bile feeling for hours now. When she was done, she could finally survey the scene clearly. Some elders laid hands on the shoulders of these newly exiled youth, like parents might. A fire truck was doing a half-assed job of spraying the conflagration, and Haley wondered what had shifted, how the USV had fallen so hard, from being darlings of Pennington to outcast pests needing to be fumigated. Superhero personas non grata. She took video with her cell phone, not knowing what else to do. Her lens captured some USVers near Main Street, peeking out from behind trees like refugees, and she spotted David among them. She went to him.

"My grandfather's blazer is in there," he said to her, eyes wet with tears, "turning to ash. Like, it survived revolution and exile from Hungary to Austria to America, decades of time, but I somehow let it be defeated by the Jersey suburbs. I let it happen. I destroyed it. It's my fault."

"*They* did this," Haley said, motioning to firefighters loafing at the far end of Woosamonsa Court. David wasn't sure whether she meant them specifically or "adults" in general.

"I love you," David said to her. "I mean, not the way we all love each other. I mean I'm in love with you. If something happens I want to make sure you know that." He engulfed her in his arms, or he let himself be subsumed by her hug, one or the other. He told her again that he loved her, that he wanted very much to protect her, send her away somewhere that no bad guys could find her, and at the same time he needed her to promise that she'd stay close to him, that they could be together in whatever came next. Haley held him and looked at the fire curling from the windows, wrapping around the curvature of that dome. The Egg was gone. It was going. Getting eaten away.

Even the rainstorm was no match for this inferno.

Haley stared at the flames and thought, *God, why is tragedy so fucking romantic?*

"I'm sorry," he said, kissing her forehead. "I didn't expect to fall so hard in love with you."

"I did," she said.

—Ø—

There were rumors. Owen heard The Egg's wood gasifier blew up. Nyla said it was something having to do with all the kerosene-laden innovations—the Dragon Drone they'd used on the Nazis, for instance. Lee worried it was a chemical fire, some lab substance made incendiary.

But it didn't matter what the USV thought.

When the FBI called it "arson" and found the remnants of Lee's drug lab and the weather got even worse, the USV went into lockdown. On Mathias's instructions, the USV issued a press release propagating the narrative that it was the government who'd set the fire. Haley read it aloud, her voice filtered through one of Fu's machines—a last tribute—and they posted the audio online:

> This is the eighth communiqué from the Unnamed Supersquadron of Vigilantes.
>
> Your methods of subliminal and overt suppression have failed. When we followed your rules quietly, you piled on the work. When we attempted independent thought, you suspended and expelled us. When we tried to live quietly, you murdered us and burned our home. We now bow out of your game and commence to finishing our own.
>
> The fire originated from a projectile fired from outside The Egg. The fact that none were hurt in the blaze is a miracle. Our legend will prove this preordained.The gods have chosen us as their survivors.They have opened the skies for rains to quench the fire you set.The disasters are responses to humanity's actions and inactions.The gods are upset.
>
> All we are are superheroes. We have succeeded in locating the best parts of ourselves and we now choose to wear these on our sleeves. This is who we are, who we wish to be.The villain is you, the scared and faceless that stand in the way of our Final Protection. Let this message be a warning: we intend to protect ourselves at all costs.
>
> You say we are embarrassments to the great institution of Princeton, we are dangers to America's youth. You call us irresponsible and savage. Let this message be a warning: we intend to show you just how savage we can be.
>
> —The Unnamed Supersquadron of Vigilantes

They all needed to be alone at first. They needed time to think. Time to mourn. Time to squirrel away time, minutes, like walnuts.

But the core League of Nine—no, seven, they were a League of *Seven* now without Fu and Zoe, weren't they?—had to protect themselves. Beaches were good for this.

They set up in a condo called the Calypso, far enough from the ocean and fifty miles from campus, in a Jersey Shore town called Neptune City. The shore regulars were gone, and local lawmen were too busy with hurricane prep and cleanup to worry about some spoiled college kids.

Mathias's moratorium on clocks was still in effect, and when they first got to Neptune City David thought the days were speeding up, but then he realized it wasn't the days, it was his body. He'd exhaust himself so quickly. Circadian rhythms out of whack. His beautiful and vibrant Haley became sluggish. David did some googling and found they were lacking *zeitgebers* (German for "time givers"), the external stimuli that tell us what time it should be. He once fell asleep while shitting.

They'd boarded the big windows and kept the blinds closed for security and also because Mathias said the sky was another irrelevant timepiece they needed to relinquish. Didn't matter, since it was always raining. Every noon looked like night. Death by darkness. The ninth plague.

—Ø—

Mathias was comatose on the couch, his drugs worn off or waiting to work. He was officially wanted now, in hiding. He had to stay inside, just in case. Kill the head and the body will die.

David let him sleep and headed for the door, shushing the TV. He wanted to go for a walk by himself. It was the easiest way to keep a low profile. Rolling solo.

Venturing outside, he saw a middle-aged lady wobbling down the sidewalk, shirt soaked with rain. She carried a crystal highball glass filled with dark liquor. She had no pants on, and her angry-looking bush poked out from under her tank top. Spotting David, she stopped and reached her arms up to the sky.

"You feel that stretch?" she called to him. "The sky is pulling us—uh!—I friggin' love it!"

See, *she* felt it. And David's commitment to Mathias was stronger than ever. He was the mouse who knew the way out of the maze. David felt it, too.

—Ø—

They had this jar of coins back in the room, and if David took about four dollars in loose change he could buy himself dinner from the condo vending machine, plus an evening of swirly entertainment. Each snack was a choice, a chance to watch the spiral spin. When foodstuffs dropped he let them collect down there, forgetting what he'd bought. The fun part was when they got stuck. Because then he could wail on that fucker and nobody would wonder why.

This is another way of saying he still had a lot of mourning to do.

They got Fu's helmet back. It sat atop the Calypso's fireplace mantel. David hated looking at it. Those brown and white scrapes down the side from where his head hit the wall. You'd think he'd been mauled by a jaguar. Britt kept hiding the helmet in the condo closet, but Owen kept exhuming it and placing it back on the mantel. They waged this silent war until Britt gave in and let it stay.

Once, David broke his sorry silence, but before he could say a full sentence, Britt jumped from the couch, grabbed Fu's helmet, and hurled it hard at David's head. He ducked just in time.

"It's *your* fucking fault!" David wasn't going to fight her on this. She was right. "*You* were lying in the fucking dirt while *we* were fighting with cops!"

That's not why it was his fault, though.

The truth, via endless news coverage: the Silent Dance, which seemed to David like it took days and days, actually lasted a grand total of eighty minutes, from the time Party Shooz stopped until Golden Echo sacrificed his noble life for David's worthless one. Sure, he'd avoided the battle, but he'd also caused it. He was the leak. He'd told Colonel Blue, who'd told the police, who'd certainly tipped off their white supremacist pals, and all of it caused Fu to die. David knew it was cosmic punishment. This was what happened when you betrayed those you were supposed to protect.

—Ø—

The news branded it Superstorm Phil, which seemed silly and anticlimactic considering this was the end of things. They should have chosen a name with an *X*, *Y*, or *Z*. Superstorm Xerxes, Yastrzemski, Zeus. Still, Phil was formidable. A combination of jet streams and pressure systems ganging up on the Western Hemisphere. Hail like grapefruits.

Newscasters started signing off. The most familiar faces stayed on the air to calm the world through this final tragedy, as they had during so many dark moments before, but they excused off-camera employees to be with their families, whittling down to a skeleton crew. People had to decide where they wanted to be, where they were needed, whose faces they wanted to see last.

Power was unreliable as ever, but a mobile generator running on biodiesel gave them plenty of juice to keep their phones on, and video clips filtered to them in fits and spurts. The news highlighted Princeton as one of the iconic hubs where humans were gathering for the end times. Jerusalem and Mecca were in shambles. But Trafalgar Square, Stonehenge, Alcatraz, Princeton, these were the magnets. City folks created underground communities in subway tubes, and after The Egg burned down, students gathered in the dorms close to Nassau Street, on higher ground. They did their best to expel all the administrators and adults from campus, who clearly couldn't be trusted anymore. Most were all too happy to leave, but the ones who'd converted and joined the USV and developed their own superhero personas, some of them had to be forcibly removed.

Still, the USV didn't implode, the way some assumed it might. It simply relocated and banded together, tying tight to itself like the logs of a life raft. Some gathered around Spinoza Field House, which was situated on low ground but had nice natural protection from the worst winds. News anchors referred to it as the "Superdome," a throwback to New Orleans during Hurricane Katrina maybe, or a nod to the costumes and capes that made them who they were. A mass of young humanity orbited the arena's exterior like some new-fangled Kaaba, paying homage and waiting for their masked messiah to return.

—Ø—

David needed to come clean. He needed to apologize. He needed to admit to Mathias that he was now a full believer. How could he have known the exact spot? *Dei sub numine viget* written in blood? It's not something Mathias could have premeditatedly orchestrated, not in a million years. Mathias had *seen* it. He was real. And David almost ruined everything.

He wanted to tell Mathias of his betrayal and he was about to, really, when they were by the vending machine together one night, but then Mathias beat him to the punch. He told David the most important revelation that ever came from his mouth. David's face went hot, ears cold.

"Haley is pregnant," said Mathias.

Something cosmic flipped back on itself.

Early signs of total molecular collapse, perhaps.

Hurtling toward that black hole in the center of the wishing well.

About to become a perfect blur.

David knew he needed to ask a question, but all he could say was "Haley who?"

"She's early still." David couldn't tell if Mathias was excited or fuming mad.

"How long... when did you find this out? I mean... how far along is... when did... ?"

"*When? How long?* Who fucking knows, David."

"Are you sure... I mean, are you definitely sure it's... ?"

"We're definitely pregnant."

"Wait. You think it's *yours*?"

Mathias scratched at his beard and then stared at David. His face was an empty vessel.

"Yes," he said, "we're definitely sure. *Under the Gods' Power She Flourishes*. Some other heroes are also with child—lots of little eggs growing—but I know they mean less to you than Haley does."

David turned away, afraid to let Mathias see his eyes.

"I'm sorry, Dave, but I see right through you. I see everything. And you are my nemesis!"

David hated him in that moment, but he yelled back, "I'm not your enemy, dude."

"No, no, no! Nemesis doesn't mean *enemy*, the way everyone thinks. Nemesis is the Greek god of *payback*! And that's *you*, thank the heavens. You're the one who gives me my due."

—Ø—

Maybe he was right. Maybe Mathias was the flesh and blood David had been waiting for. He'd been fighting invisible enemies most of his life. Those evil cells in Claire's blood, the good ones that had accidentally turned bad. Cold fronts and barometric pressure, they were faceless, too. Invisible enemies were David's favorite.

Because when the *real* enemies are right there in front of your face?

By David's calculation, if you tracked back to the homecoming bonfire, conception could have coincided with either David or Mathias. She was maybe fifteen weeks, barely beginning to show. If anything, she looked skinnier. But everyone found out. It gave their meetings a new weight. When they'd lost Fu, they'd gained a new, tinier member. Cap'n Cunt's tummy became the new USV figurehead, this child to be born under the flag of revolution. They all operated as expectant parents.

Still, Haley and David hadn't really spoken about it. He'd been waiting for her to apologize, to divulge a secret, to confess her love anew. To tell David it was his. But she steered clear of the topic and they were never alone in that crowded condo. He was forced to confront Haley in the bathroom while the others were sleeping. She was running her fingers through a rising bath.

"I can't really think about that right now," she said, eyes focused on the ripples.

"Well, I can't really think about anything else," David shot back.

"There are bigger things at stake."

And this was kind of true. When one thing felt huge it would soon give way to something so crushingly overwhelming that the previous thing would crumble and dissolve. When he thought about school, his career, his friends, his love life, those notions were washed away by the threat of war, the flood, and the end of time itself.

But no, wait! A month ago David might've agreed with her. But now? From here on out? He really couldn't think of a single bigger thing in the world than that goodness growing inside her. She told him it wasn't the right time for a DNA paternity test. And ultimately he acquiesced. Either answer might've destroyed him. Neither father was good enough. Case in point:

"Mathias thinks someone tipped off the cops about the Silent Dance," Haley told him. "He says they reacted too fast. They were in perfect position to trap us. He thinks there's a leak."

"I bet it was Lee," David whispered, adding another shitty silk to his web of lies.

Owen took ownership of Fu's helmet, co-opting it into his own Peacemaker costume. Personally, David thought he ruined the thing. But it was Owen's now, so whatever.

Also, Owen began fashioning a sword/staff/pole weapon comprising all the nightsticks he'd ripped away from various riot cops, attaching them end to end through some fusing process David didn't understand. What *did* he understand anymore?

One night, Owen told David the tenets of the samurai code: honor, honesty, respect, kindness, courage, righteousness, and, above all, loyalty. He said he wished to be "a good retainer." David touched Owen's shoulder, thanked him for his service. Owen made a face and said, "*You're* not my master."

Britt fell apart. Which, somehow, only strengthened her persona. It Girl became a hot mess, a once-great starlet fallen from grace. Her weight dipped and her ribs rose. She wore less clothing but adopted a huge furry hunter's cap with earflaps. This was her new thing. This and melancholy. And having sex with Mathias Blue.

David wondered if that was Mathias's ultimate superpower: fucking broken people to make them whole again. Whatever he'd done to Lee had made that shithead much more centered lately, David thought. But no. Britt was getting worse. One time he asked how her day was going and she said, "The entire right side of my head and body is ringing." What do you say to that?

—Ø—

Tactical nuclear strikes on Iran were said to be precise, targeted, of generally low radioactivity. The nukes hit Iran's underground sites and uranium-enrichment plants, but a goodly number of civilians were also wiped off the map. Nobody knew what China would do.

David fled to Google, reading about Ragnarök this time. A Norse legend. The gods fight the evil giants of chaos and destruction. The *Naglfar,* a ship made from the fingernails of the dead, sails to the battlefield to strike the final blow against Odin's army.

And then, when all seems lost, a Golden Age rises from the sea.

Getting up his confidence, David finished drafting the USV's final spectacle. He made his presentation to the group, and they unanimously approved it. He then recommended everyone call their parents to say goodbye. Poor moms and dads who'd coached their kids so far only to watch them sit down in the middle of the race and marvel at the stars.

David went to 7-Eleven and bought a burner. He dialed from a windy beach, hoping the signal might get lost in the surf. His mom sounded as if she'd been through the more hysterical stages of the grieving process and was now residing in quiet anger. He asked them to get Beth.

"I might be going away for a while," David said to her. He'd kind of always wanted to say something like that, and he'd kind of never wanted to say anything like that.

"The news said that USV leaders have abandoned their followers," said Beth. She sounded about thirty-five years old. "I told my friends that's probably true since you already abandoned your family."

"Jesus," David said.

"I have to help bail water from Uncle Marc's basement. We can just say goodbye now."

With that, she dropped the phone. And it was true, he couldn't argue. He'd gone to college, grown into a new family, left his old one behind. Was he doing it again to the USV?

"We understand," said Dad when he got back on the phone. "It's safer to stay put, David."

"No, Gil," said Mom. "Nothing is so important. Come home. We'll protect you."

"You can't protect me anymore."

"Sorry, we can't just say goodbye," Dad said. "You're our son."

It suddenly hit David that *he* might have a son, or a daughter, and there was nothing much he could do to protect it from the inevitable, and that feeling crushed him into the sand. He caught his breath and told his parents what he wished his own child might say to him someday.

"Hey, guys," David said, finally crying. "I need you to know I've really loved being your son."

"Please come home?" Mom asked.

He considered saying something dark and cinematic, like "I *am* home." But instead he just said, "I've really loved you." And they said it back. And then he threw his phone into the sea.

—Ø—

Mathias and Britt stayed home, but the rest went scavenging.

Nyla scrounged up a cooler full of live lobsters to steam in the kitchenette.

"Where did you find these?" David asked.

"Jailbroke them from an abandoned Chinese restaurant aquarium. They smell okay."

Then Lee and Owen returned with a duffel full of guns. They unzipped it, and there on the floral condo bedspread was a shotgun and a 9 mm..

Nyla left momentarily and came back with her AR-15.

"This one is my father's," she announced. David was still freaked out by firearms and said as much and asked if they'd stolen them, wondering if someone was now looking for them. Mathias, however, was boundless energy. He threw in his grandfather's axe, adding to the pile.

That night, when the winds picked up, Mathias and Britt moved all the beds from their respective rooms to form a communal sleeping space in the living area. It felt like a family beach vacation. From a Calypso closet they'd foraged an ancient DVD player, and the only DVD they could find in the house was *Miss Congeniality* with Sandra Bullock, but they watched it three times through, stupidly eating into their limited generator supply, but they didn't care, they needed a laugh.

After ripping Nyla's crustaceans apart, the gills and mustardy intestines flying helter-skelter across the table, they created their own carnage in the living room, making love again as if the world might end at any moment, as if they were still ripping shells apart to suck out morsels of meat.

And, in that way, it actually wasn't very much like a family beach vacation.

—Ø—

"It's time," David said to Mathias. "Storm cell just passed. Let's move before the next hits."

The power was back and the news showed two massive high-precipitation supercells on their way to Jersey, white humps rising from Doppler radar like twin sharks cresting from the ocean.

Mathias stared at the condo vending machine. "Famous Amos or honey roasted nuts?"

"Peanuts are more substantial, but cookies are more fun," David counseled. "Depends which is more important to you at a time like this. Survival or indulgence?"

"Evolve or perish," he said. "I do like honey. When I die, I'd like my body to be mellified. Embalmed in honey. It preserves the tissue for centuries. Turkish kings used to do it."

"So..." David continued. "We should probably hit the riggity-road, yeah?"

"I guess my time capsules achieve the same effect. Still, it's an interesting way to die."

"Well, we don't always get to choose how we die."

"Do you feel like you've *grown* since meeting me, David? Evolved a little?"

"If life were a video game I would've leveled-up like six times since meeting you."

"I've treated you well? Gave you a place to live. Funded your thesis. Helped get you laid."

"Sure."

"And you still believe in what we're doing, yeah?"

"Yes," David answered. "Completely. More than ever." It was the absolute truth.

"And you'd never abandon me or hand me to the cops, just as we're reaching the End?"

Stop. Stay stiff. Don't move.

"Of course not. I won't abandon you, and you won't abandon the USV. *I am another yourself.*"

He smiled. "We *do* get to decide how we die. Once you realize how much power we have, anything's possible. Some people seem like nice, law-abiding citizens. Then they put on a mask and rape girls on Halloween. Others subvert obsolete laws. We put on a mask and save the world."

"Are you okay?" David asked. Just then, the vending machine's lights and electronics went black, the power gone again. And they didn't know it yet, but this time, the power wouldn't return.

"I think I'm just hungry," Mathias said. Then he reached for the fire extinguisher on the wall and handed it to David. Another koan.

It happened quickly. Without thinking, David smashed the red canister through the vending machine window. It exploded into jagged plastic slivers. Mathias picked out a few bags of chips, some gum, a Snickers. David stole both the cookies and the nuts. They agreed: it was time.

—Ø—

She was sitting on the edge of the tub when David walked in on Haley in the bathroom. In one hand was a length of cord twisted around itself. In the other was some metal implement catching candlelight.

His heart shook.

"Christ, Haley, is that a fucking noose? What are you—"

"Chill your bones, Business-Man." The metal was a pair of nail clippers—she was working on her toenails—and she held up her knot, shook it out, which David now saw wasn't a noose but something more benign—Mickey Mouse ears surrounding a lovely figure eight.

"Handcuff knot," she said, then undid the rope and started over. "You make two identical loops, lay them on top of each other like a Venn diagram or like tying a clove hitch, then pull each loop through the other until it looks like a butterfly. Like this. You can put an arm or ankle through each loop and apply traction to the tag end, like this, and the little twisty bobcat pretzel in the center cinches up. But if you cross up and pull back on these two outliers, like this, it adjusts out and loosens, like a Chinese finger trap. Voilà."

She looked up at him with those eyes.

"Bondage 101," David said. "As taught by Cap'n Cunt."

David felt himself stirring. He stepped close. She exhaled, resting her head on his thigh.

"It's funny, everyone loves Wonder Woman so much, like she's this feminist icon, and I guess she is, but she was also created by a dirty old polygamist guy with a bondage fetish. In all the early comic books she's always bound or shackled, just another sexy gal tied to the railroad tracks."

Just then she moaned, put a hand to her belly. She burped. The moment passed.

David wasn't sure whether chronostrictesis was accelerating her baby's growth or slowing it down. She looked calm, resigned. Small tasks were becoming more difficult, though. David told her the plan, that he and Mathias were aligned on heading back to campus in the morning.

"That sounds exhausting," she said. "I'm having trouble managing basic grooming tasks."

So David offered to cut her toenails. She smiled, handed him the clippers. He wondered how long it might take to collect enough nail clippings to build a Norse ship.

David got down on one knee in front of her. He wanted to propose.

"Haley?" *Clip.*

"Cap'n Cunt, if you please." *Clip-clip.*

"I have a question to ask you." *Clip.*

"Ask away." *Clip.*

"Would you like to take a shower with me?"

"Mmm," she said. "I'd give that idea a solid nine and a half."

David put down the clippers. He reached past her and turned the faucet, afraid she might change her mind if they didn't just get in there. When he peeked outside the door, Mathias had his back to the bathroom, tweaking wires and tubes on Fu's ham radio machine. The rest of them were on the bed gathered around a single cell phone. A video was saying something about the supercell, the flood, the End. The twenty-four-hour news cycle had identified its final all-encompassing story.

"I have to warn you," Haley whispered, "my nipples are getting *raw-ther* huge these days."

He locked the door and they climbed into the water. David got down to his knees again, soaping her toes, her ankles, her knees, her thighs—all the places that would soon be hard for her to reach. Her skin grew slick under his hands. He kissed her belly button, on the cusp of becoming an outtie. Her nipples were, indeed, very large. When he stood up she backed into him and took his cock in her hand. David put his hand between her legs, too, wrapping his arm around her gorgeous belly. And though there was water everywhere, when he reached that different sort of wetness below it was like swimming for the first time. She craned her neck back, resting her head on his shoulder, and she cried or moaned, he couldn't be sure.

But then they heard thunderous slams against the bathroom door and were sure the SWAT or FBI had come to collect them. They said silent prayers. Held each other tight.

"Listen," she said, eyes urgent and speech quick. "I want it to be yours, I need it to be, but I don't know. And I need to be honest because I don't ever want to lie to you, David, okay? Okay?!"

"Okay."

"And we need Mathias to think what he thinks. He's got too much and... Wherever they're taking us, for however long, I don't know what will happen to him, but you and I will find—"

Something shattered. David tried to shield her, to get in between her body and the shower curtain and the bathroom door, but the police battering ram made so much noise. David's body, too, was about to split at the seams. The doorjamb exploded, and David prepared for the onslaught.

But it was only Mathias.

"Goodness!" Mathias bellowed when he saw them. Then he headed for the medicine chest. "Sorry to crap on your moment," he said. "It's time for my meds."

He uncapped, swallowed, pissed, flushed, left. A wake of detritus littered the floor.

They breathed there together, freedom restored. David thought he might throw up.

"I need to go lie down," Haley said. "Wake me when the sky starts falling."

David turned off the water and watched the last of it whirlpool down the drain.

—Ø—

Blink. Start with a black hole. Float upward and there's the thick beige doughnut surrounding it.

Soar even higher and there's David and little Beth, leaning over the rim of this vortex, pouring quarters into the side of a spiral wishing well. They are trying to cure cancer.

When Beth was still tiny and David was just getting big, the family took a trip to Ocean City on Maryland's Eastern Shore. They spent every night at the boardwalk—playing games, riding rides, eating funnel cakes, and pouring change into the plastic funnel wishing well. Load a quarter in the launch ramp and watch it spiral in ever smaller circles down the vortex, spinning so fast it blurs the eye, finally dropping and disappearing into the dark hole at the center with a satisfying *plink*.

The sign said SPIRAL WISHING WELL—HELP FIGHT CHILDREN'S LEUKEMIA. So when Beth watched that first quarter go and then asked for another one and another, David couldn't say no. He wanted to fight leukemia, too. For Claire. Forget the arcade, this funnel was clearly the appropriate receptacle for quarters. Once David was tapped out, they launched Mom and Dad's quarters and got demoted to nickels and dimes, which didn't roll well, but it was fun to watch them spin and fall anyway.

"Why does it do that?" asked Beth, watching a coin whirl and vanish.

"Because that's how the ramp is shaped."

"But why doesn't it spin the other way?"

David was confused. "You mean, why doesn't it spin *up* instead of down?"

"Yeah."

"I, well, because of gravity, I guess."

"What's grabbity?"

"There's something big underground, at the center of the Earth, that's always pulling us downward. That's what makes the quarters spin down. And that's what keeps us on the ground."

"Is that why we can't fly?" she asked.

"Yes," David said, "that's exactly why we can't fly."

Beth thought a moment. "I hate grabbity," she said.

"Me, too," said David. "Grabbity sucks."

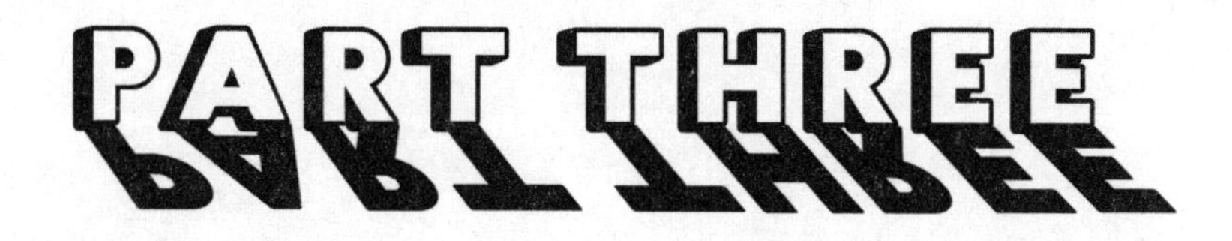
PART THREE

11
COMMENCEMENT

i.

"It's too deep," says Sergeant Drill, knee-deep in sludge. "Back up. To the left."

Business-Man is carrying a rowboat on his head. Sergeant Drill is steering, and he's got the back end, balancing a bench seat on top of his noggin while gripping the sides. They look like one of those two-person donkey costumes. Business-Man can't see but he knows they're in lower campus, somewhere near the tennis courts probably, still a good few hundred yards from Spinoza. Ultraviolet is up ahead. They follow his voice. It's hard to hear over the sound of rain beating against the hull.

Rowboats make good umbrellas.

"Your turn," Sergeant Drill says.

"Air travel," Business-Man says.

"Okay. I'm gonna say all of Cincinnati. Fuck that place."

This was the game. They each picked what they wouldn't miss. It wasn't wishing death on anyone or anything, not exactly. Life would simply be easier once these things didn't exist.

"Bicyclists," he says.

"Shit, all outdoor sports types," she says. "All of Colorado."

"Those little fucking gnats that fly right into your eyeballs all the time," he says.

"The president," she says.

"Snow."

"Wind."

Superstorm Phil had arrived. Everywhere coastal, every lakeside spot, it was all flooding. Wind and rain and hail. It was enough to set off seismic sensors, with tremors felt across twenty-nine states.

First, the dams broke. Levees, too. Fire hoses in Boise tried to edge out lava from Yellowstone, but the city was evacuated anyway, after nineteen deaths. They were prepared. Nineteen was a good number and better than expected.

This was it: the Null Point.

They unleashed hoses at Princeton, too, as Business-Man instructed. Plugging the drains in Spinoza Field House, they initiated the built-in system for turning a basketball court into a hockey rink. But the USV didn't need ice. It needed fresh water. Only the hydrated survive.

The sky is purple. The air is purple. Everyone is purple. The rains wouldn't stop and the USVers got sick of their costumes drooping like dishrags. So they adapted, evolved. They donned their mouthless gray masks and looted Home Depots across Jersey. Along with other provisions, they stole every can of Mystical Grape latex paint. A fraction of a gallon made a cheap, formfitting superhero costume.

From his hair to his feet, Business-Man, too, is purple. László's blazer, his magic talisman, is gone, so he's co-opted this new costume. Bare except for boxer briefs, his skin feels snug inside the latex. He can't tell whether he loves or hates the feeling. The look suits Sergeant Drill, though. She's wearing something like bike shorts, and he watches her ass muscles flex against the purple, powering through space. She looks like a medieval candle dripping wax.

Here was Business-Man's plan, originally.

First, uniting their legions, they'd take Nassau Hall. They'd gather things to eat and drink. They'd support Ultraviolet and let him lead. They'd survive the storm. They'd emerge evolved.

It didn't happen that way.

Nassau Hall proved simple to occupy but difficult to sustain. Too many doors and windows. Business-Man worried they'd be easy pickings for snipers and assumed cops had set up a perimeter, like in the movies. In the president's office, they got a great photo—Ultraviolet sitting at Graynor's wide mahogany desk, cigar in his mouth and the love of Business-Man's life on his lap—to post and prove that the USV leaders were back on campus. When the cell towers finally shut down, the untethered feeling hit home. Some kept their phones just for the flashlight. Others needed the security blanket. Plenty of kids smashed their useless devices in cathartic panic, relying on ham radio from now on, tuning in only at the top of the hour, only every three hours, only for three minutes, to conserve power. But nobody knew whether clocks made sense anymore. When gale-force winds blew an uprooted telephone pole through a window, this was their cue to abandon Nassau Hall.

Now, the Superdome is their ark, capacity 4,500, and the USV will fill it to the brim.

They shoulder-press the rowboat over their heads. Fuck, it's heavy.

"I'll say working out in general," Business-Man says. "Won't miss it, nor the impetus."

"Fat dudes," Sergeant Drill counters. No judgments or retorts. Just pure, unbridled honesty.

"The woman who makes the announcements at the Baltimore train station. I hate her face."

"Old people," she says.

"All the Real Housewives of Wherever," he says.

"Christians," she says. "The self-righteous proselytizing churchy ones, at least."

"Loud, annoying Jews," he says.

"My dad," she says, straining against the boat's weight. "No. Yes. Yes, fuck it: my dad."

And it's not that he can't think of anything to top her admission—he can—but he can't focus on anything besides this bulky lard-ass sonuvabitch boat. "You win," Business-Man says.

"Put some back into it, you pussy!" growls Sergeant Drill, shifting more firmly into her persona. Her deltoids put Business-Man's to shame.

"I'm trying, Sarge." He loves it when she disciplines him like this.

Up ahead in a low valley is Spinoza Field House. The disk-shaped stadium is their bunker, situated like a flying saucer come to rest in a crater of its own creation. Their Superdome.

The roof has a circular skylight in its center, maybe thirty feet across. The flooding is bad around the foundation of the venue—two feet of water and only getting worse—but the valley protects the Superdome, a natural windbreak.

Ultraviolet, their charismatic Noah, is also up ahead. He's got his grandpa's axe raised high. He sits Indian-style atop another overturned rowboat carried by ten USVers. Heroes stretch to place their palms on his hull, paying respects as if to a Torah coming down the aisle. *Hands on a Hard Body.* Business-Man blinks. *Hands Across Princeton on a Rowboat for Please God Don't Fucking Kill Us.*

He can't help it anymore. He believes in Mathias, who sees things. In every age, when apocalypse is imminent, there are still the chosen ones, the survivors. This is the point of everything.

We are the future, he thinks.

Now down a quick hill, the boats pick up speed. The whooping crowd parts way, slapping their hull then curling back around it as in a ship's wake. They all push toward the Superdome door.

Somebody moos like a cow.

It takes some maneuvering to get the boat inside the glass atrium entrance, but a team of USV underlings is on hand to take the heavy thing from Business-Man and Sergeant Drill. The duo high-fives, shakes out their arms. They watch a sweaty horde of USVers spirit this ship up a ramp that leads from the entrance to the arena above. It'll join the other nine or ten dinghies pillaged from the Princeton crew team's boathouse. Sergeant Drill is fired up, her muscles craving more. She salutes him and joins a team running canned goods to the commissary.

Business-Man needs a breather. He hugs the wall, slowly following their boat up the ramp's incline. It looks like the gangway to an alien craft. He reaches the crest and the cavernous rink comes into view, this temple to collegiate team sports, walls made of dark natural stone that you'd find in a wine cellar.

Along the ceiling is a catwalk spanning the length of the building, skirting the giant circular skylight. Aside from the skylight there are no windows, which is part of why he chose this spot.

Less glass for flying telephone poles to shatter.

The USV crew's been working hard in here. About a thousand of the early recruits went above and beyond to prep the space for the several thousand now arriving. For the past three days, they've been filling the rink with water. Powerful sprays still shoot from the four corners enclosed by sideboards. The water has by now filled the rink space and overtaken the towering hockey Plexiglas. They've formed a manmade lake, maybe seven feet deep and rising. Their reservoir for when the pipes go dry. A fleet of boats is tied off by the far scoreboard. It's coming along nicely, according to Business-Man's plan.

—Ø—

Cap'n Cunt can feel it: the quickening.

Not just inside but all around. She sees the clock ticking, knows her powers and weaknesses. She has overcome her various selves, has always seen her way past the mild-mannered nerd, always known she was entitled, and never believed she was free. Until now.

It is time to evolve or perish, to shore up this house.

She powerwalks the Spinoza concourse, eyes darting, analyzing, judging. The urge for nesting is strong—that shit is no joke—and she recognizes that in a different dimension she'd be buying the type of gear she bought for her cousin Julie's baby shower—the Bumbo and Boppy and other silly-named things—ensuring her life and space were ready for a baby. But instead of a sensible two-bedroom apartment in Park Slope, here they are in this flooded college hockey arena, provisions and preparations both a foregone conclusion and a massive uncertainty. It makes her head hurt.

There's only one way to ensure safety and protection against all of this.

Cap'n Cunt knows that now. She's seen it.

She will zero in and emerge from the dark neck of time luminous without end.

Cap'n Cunt steps into the arena space, looking down on this bowl filling with water. She associates arenas more with concerts than with sports. Still, when she scans the ceiling of Spinoza, it's sports that are on display. Thick blankets hang, each ten feet tall, each boasting some serious accolade that she can't help but find funny. PRINCETON MEN'S HOCKEY QUADRANGULAR CHAMPION 1941.

Good for you guys! she thinks. *Some eighty years later, we still pay tribute to your mighty quadrangle!*

There are other big blankets showing off single uniforms, too. One for KAZMAIER '86 and another for BAKER '14 with the subhead MAKE HOBEY PROUD. She'd laughed at this one initially, until she found an exhibit case in the concourse extolling the virtues of Hobey Baker. Before building Spinoza, they'd named the old hockey rink after him. He'd done lots of great football and hockey sports stuff and he'd also written for the *New York Times*, worked for J.P. Morgan, and been a fighter pilot in World War I, and he'd died in a plane crash. An anonymous poem on his tombstone inscription read:

You who seemed winged, even as a lad,
With that swift look of those who know the sky,
It was no blundering fate that stooped and bade
You break your wings, and fall to earth and die,
I think some day you may have flown too high,
So that immortals saw you and were glad,
Watching the beauty of your spirits flame,
Until they loved and called you, and you came.

Cap'n Cunt considered sports and business and war—these things that men believed themselves called to—and saw that they were all the same. Or at least poured from the same wellspring of toxic male bloodlust. We'd grown more civilized since the days of gladiator death matches as a form of entertainment, or even dueling with swords or pistols, and had tempered this need into swooshing on ice skates, tickling a puck with a stick, only occasionally smashing or punching each other in the face. Sports were a release valve, she got that, even if she didn't totally get the emotion they were meant to release. Even war was more civil these days. Computer hackers attacking power grids were marginally better than barbarians impaling each other with metal spears.

Right?

She spots Business-Man over there. He's been gone for hours, it seems, and now here he is directing the deployment of rowboats. Before they left the Calypso, David had pitched them about ancient Rome, where Julius Caesar staged naval reenactments. *Naumachia,* they were called. Caesar dug mile-wide basins in the earth and filled them with water and brought in ships for battle. It was a spectator sport, crazy expensive. A crew of POWs manned each boat, prisoners whose death was a foregone conclusion in these gladiator games. David envisioned something like this as a final USV spectacle—but with effigies, with symbolism. Filling the stadium with water was a way of neutralizing the fear of the rising tides. Another release valve substituting for violent battle.

But now there are women on the battlefield, Cap'n Cunt reminds herself. This was the difference. She answers only to herself. To the Egg inside. She has no need to "Make Hobey Proud."

It's true that she microdosed with Ultraviolet, just one more time—her last trip ever, she promised herself. It was over a month ago, at the tail end of the first trimester, when a part of her—a part that scared her—whispered dark possibilities of losing the baby, of being rid of this anxiety, once the wrenching grief was over. But no, the trip only made clear the gift of this baby. It only solidified her love into something simultaneously unbreakable and horribly fragile.

She'd seen Ultraviolet's vision, and he'd confirmed it afterward. So she knows what must happen. David's plan is decidedly different from Mathias's. She knows, finally, there's only one way out. It's the end of the game, and humans are losing, and you have to do something big and bold to win. A Hail Mary, they call it. She believes she's ready. She will be when the time comes.

Until then, she will keep her mask on.

Her mystery is her power.

"It still smells fresh," Cap'n Cunt says, sidling up next to Business-Man. "What happens if it gets contaminated?"

"We have filtration and purification systems at the ready. Charcoal, sand, iodine. Lots of water is better than none, and we'll just do our best to keep it clean and use the gray water for—"

"No, we're building a lake within our bounds," she says. "As the end comes, we'll all pay the ferryman and sail together across the great river dividing living from dead." She blows him a kiss.

"Well, that's a less practical-sounding plan, but sure!" he says. "If it gets really bad, we'll climb into the rowboats and hold on tight."

"And if the water reaches the ceiling?" she says. "Do we smash that glass skylight, pour out the top through the Null Point window, overflowing like champagne bubbles, and emerge evolved?"

"Or we just wait till the weather's better, pull the plugs, and walk down the ramp, back into the world outside," he says, finding a smile for her.

"I got you something," she says. "A little end-of-the-world gift." And she hands him a pink iPhone with a cracked screen, plus a set of earbuds tucked in their white charging cube. She tells him she'd found a hard drive when cleaning out Fu's room, before the fire: an archive of sorts with hours' worth of original compositions, solo experiments, live recordings of Human DJ sessions from The Egg. A sonic diary of Echo's last year of life. "Some of it is batshit crazy," she says, "but a lot is *rawther* genius. I loaded everything on to this phone for you. If you keep the antenna off, you've probably got a good ten hours of charge. Thought it might keep you centered."

He feels bad and he's touched. He didn't realize they were exchanging gifts. Business-Man thanks her, kisses her, tells her he loves her forever.

She says, "You're my bitch."

Business-Man takes a breath. He feels clear, cool, collected. In a state of preparing. He feels a cosmic pull with every human body in this great space, like a murder of crows. As if silently summoned, he looks up and finds Ultraviolet at the top of section 124. With a quick head nod Ultraviolet motions David up to the upper deck announcer's booth they've reserved for the League of Seven. Business-Man heads that way. Cap'n Cunt joins him, belly growing bigger by the second.

"How do you feel?" David asks, pointing at her midsection.

"Distended, tight, incredibly pressure-filled," she says. "Like it's pulling my back forward where I can't correct it and the bottom is pulling up tight, and the sides are tight when I breathe, but above all"—she squeezes his hand and he squeezes back—"I feel ready."

Then her face perks up, like she's just remembered the answer to a nagging question. She takes his palm and places it on the side of her belly.

Tonggg!

The sound booms through the Superdome, which means they've succeeded in powering and patching into the arena's PA usually reserved for announcers' voices and jock jams. It echoes.

They hold still, that's the rule. But then, good god, David feels it moving, the only thing still moving in this whole huge place, just a tiny flutter, barely perceptible, but he imagines a small knee, maybe, or elbow, or hand waving hi, or maybe a butt rolling to find a more comfortable position, but whatever it is, something's magically *alive* in there. He wants to see it, to see through her belly skin with X-ray vision and know exactly what body part of the baby he's touching right now, what it looks like, what shape is its nose, is it a boy or girl. Feeling it writhe, he imagines it looks like a little alien, this thing roiling beneath her skin, but why does it automatically conjure *alien* when it's the most *human* thing of all?

David once read that when people get closer to something awful—death, for instance—they become better able to look away and pretend it's not there. The closer to disaster, the easier to deny. But not for David. He feels the baby moving and silently promises it that he'll stare straight ahead and let the brightness blind him and pray the oncoming train is really a light at the end of a tunnel.

—Ø—

They step out into the narrow concessions concourse. Above them is the underside of the stadium seats, an Escher-like upside-down staircase. Blink. Business-Man remembers the first time he saw the stairwell open wide in The Egg, those unnatural ridges beneath. Here, hanging low from the steel girders, are some of the USV's provisions—mostly smoked and dried meats dangling down like some massive Chinatown butcher shop—venison and duck and ham hocks and clusters of dried sausages bunched thick like the bristles of a giant broom. With the power off, the hanging light fixtures are useless, but some enterprising soul has dangled mason jars from each one and filled these with candles, lending a soft Renaissance light to the hundreds of humans below.

Business-Man can't be sure whether this infrastructure extends around the entire circumference of the stadium, but this section 121–125 stretch right here has been transformed into a kind of shopping mall of USV merchants and service providers. The concessions have been largely gutted of electric appliances, but the ventilation hoods still work well enough, so small fire pits in metal trash cans serve as cooktops, and an extensive team of chefs and servers are working hard to rough out the night's dinner. The concourse concrete has become the USV's Shakedown Street, the kind of pop-up parking-lot-style commerce he remembers from music festivals. It's lined on both sides with purple craftspeople—woodworkers, metallurgists, glassblowers—all plying their wares from makeshift workshops behind makeshift storefronts, plus musicians and massage therapists, commodities traders and preachers, scavengers and superheroes, pitching their unique skill sets via cardboard signs, the last sort of CV these Ivy Leaguers ever expected to present to the world.

There are buyers, too. Heroes with signs scrawled ISO: DEPACON/ANY MIGRAINE RX and the like. Dr. Ugs is holed up in the arena's Lost & Found with his cadre of chemists, doing his best to help the many kids who are off their meds. Beyond the recreational stuff and performance enhancers and world-openers, some of their heroes need daily synthetic thyroid medication, insulin, and asthma inhalers and will be in serious danger soon. They've stockpiled and scavenged from pharmacies, but that won't help if they're stuck in this place indefinitely.

Beside a first aid station, Business-Man notices a tent marked D-DAY DOULAS. A team of hippieish midwives in white sarongs holds court for a dozen or so girls sitting cross-legged before them. The girls don't appear overly pregnant, but each caresses her midsection, practicing some kind of slow, circular motion, so perhaps they're just not yet showing. Business-Man realizes Cap'n Cunt is merely the furthest along of the USV's many expectant mothers.

A throng of underlings has formed a tighter corridor for the League of Seven to walk through. There's Ultraviolet up front, Cap'n Cunt now right behind him, Sergeant Drill marching with purpose, while It Girl gets derailed every few steps to give hugs. Business-Man pulls up the rear with Peacemaker and his newly expanded task force of enforcers, all of them strutting like a tight and important entourage. Which is, after all, exactly what they are.

Business-Man feels like an NBA all-star, dropping low fives along a gauntlet of teammates.

"Business-Man!"

"How are you?" David says, shaking hands. "What a pleasure to see you, Mayline Ranger."

"The water level is at the top of the hockey boards, starting to run over the Plexi."

"Keep it coming until it fills the lobby, then seal off the west entrance. Only the west. Go."

"Business-Man," says Johnny Pockets, a human Swiss army knife. "Where do you want—?"

"Firewood in the boiler room," he says. "Cans in concessions. And send Savage Horrorshow and DJ Jigglepuss to siphon more gas from the cars in the parking lot before they all float away. Go."

It's been like this for days. Everyone's so intimidated and awed by Ultraviolet, and Business-Man has de facto and by definition become the guy who gets it done. He suddenly realizes he's very good at his job. He sees Ultraviolet's theoretical vision but is the one who can communicate it in practical fashion. He understands the nuance of numerous choices but makes executive decisions quickly, projecting confidence and certainty. He is scared but is excellent at pretending otherwise.

He's like a dad, maybe.

The Schirminator says, "Business-Man, which cape do you like from these three?"

"The one on the left." He couldn't give a shit, but it's better to be decisive.

Yes-Man says, "Business-Man, I brought you a Diet Sierra Mist. Maybe the last one ever!"

"Delightful," Business-Man says, accepting the offering, shaking his hand. "Excuse me."

When he's out of range, Business-Man leaves the can on the concrete. He's got things to do. He cares much more about water, pure hydration, or maybe it's better to abstain from all public displays of ingestion and appear ascetic at a time like this.

Cosmik Debris says, "Business-Man, I was awake all night, saw the sun and all of space-time. I understand now. Can you get me ten minutes with Ultraviolet so I can explain? He'll understand."

"Minutes don't exist, my hero." David pivots, bobs, weaves.

He tries to get stealthy, but immediately a new trio of heroes, two girls and a guy, accost him, looping arms around his neck. It's hard to keep the faces straight, especially now that most of the costumes have been replaced with paint, but David does his best to remember. He never was great with names, but he's found himself to be pretty solid with personas. One of them, buff and gender neutral, is Androgenius, and David remembers the girl—she calls herself Serious Miss Givings—because she's blown him twice, and the other girl he's never seen before but she can barely keep her eyes open because of drugs.

"We're having a *thing* tonight, section 110," Androgenius says. "Anything goes."

"I appreciate the offer," Business-Man says.

"David!" says another voice. And this time Business-Man does a double take.

"It's Esteban. From Forbes," the guy says. "I mean, I'm Steel Wool now, uh, my thesis—"

"Yes, I realize. I know who you are. But your name is terrible. That's a name for a punk rocker or someone with a good Jew 'fro. C'mon, Esteban. You have like two days to figure out who you are before you are no more. So who are you? *Why* are you?"

Esteban nods. Business-Man can see he's scared. "I was going to be a lawyer." His voice quivers when he says it. "I don't know what I am or how to help anymore."

"It's okay," Business-Man says, putting a hand on his shoulder. "The good news is that you're strong. Physically and mentally, my friend. You have arms and legs and can help us haul. You have goodness in you, a sense of right and wrong. It's what drew you to law, right, and it's what makes you a valued hero in the Satya Yuga, after we pass through the dark neck of time. We have no idea how long we'll be buried in this human time capsule before we emerge evolved. I'll guarantee we will need law and order inside this sacred space. Find Sergeant Drill, up there. She knows our laws and you can learn them the way you've studied the ones of this dying world. We need your help, Esteban. And incidentally, as long as you're offering to help, I'd kill for a Diet Sierra Mist."

Esteban wipes his eyes, gives him a hug, and runs off to make himself useful. Business-Man watches him run, scans the gathered crowd. He can see it all. *He* did this. He knows what he is here to do next. He will gather the masses, guide them through, and save them all.

—Ø—

The announcer's booth is windowed along one side looking down on the arena below.

Peacemaker is continuing to tweak Ultraviolet's ham radio setup with the arena's PA system, trying to get the timbre of their Seventh-Minute Stop's *tonggg* just right, removing the static. This tech stuff would've been Fu's job. But Peacemaker has his solar panels and Electrocycles, while H-Bomb and TarHero brought their biodiesel-powered generator, too, for later. On the audio front, he's really stepped up since Fu died. David is so proud of him. That broken boy from last semester—the roommate who'd screamed and cried and smashed trash cans and fallen apart after Soccer Bob's rightful expulsion—has picked himself up off the Forbes shower floor and learned to fly.

Ultraviolet sits at the head of a long wooden table, the remainder of the core USV scattered around him. Security stands guard along the walls and windows of this press box, trying to stay out of the way while looking generally imposing. The League is gathered to give and get final instructions. Business-Man paces a slow circle around the table, arms crossed.

He feels powerful, yet maybe a little self-conscious in his skintight suit. He glances down at his package to see how it looks in these boxer briefs. Just okay.

"Get some food, take your moments alone, whatever you need to do, do it now," David says. "Intelligence says we've got about an hour of power left."

He's making this stuff up, but he must project confidence.

Ultraviolet lays his hand in Cap'n Cunt's lap. "Feel this palm," he says, totally calm. "It's so phantom-y, right? Maybe it's the latex, but somehow I can't believe these things *belong to me*."

Business-Man continues: "My guess is they've set up a perimeter around us."

"Or what if they haven't?" asks Haley, breaking character. David hates it when she challenges him like this. He ignores her, tries his best to command the room. But nobody's listening.

"Seriously," says Ultraviolet, directing his voice at It Girl this time. "Something is *disappearing* me like Marty McFly. The End is under way. We're stretching upward. I mean, just *feel* these things."

"Feel *this*," Cap'n Cunt says, bringing Ultraviolet's hand to her belly. David suddenly wants to disappear Mathias himself. He stares at his stupid purple hand lovingly stroking her.

"It's a boy," Ultraviolet says. "I can see it."

"I think I'm ready," Cap'n Cunt suddenly announces, more to Ultraviolet than to the room.

Business-Man continues: "They've probably sent state police plus SWAT, and maybe—"

"We're on our own, David, now shush!" Ultraviolet snaps at him, swiping his hand to sever his speech. Everyone gets quiet. "What does that mean?" he says to Cap'n Cunt. "Either you *know* or else you're not ready."

"I'm ready," she says immediately. "I see the clock ticking."

Ultraviolet nods. He motions to the security detail by the door and they gingerly move to escort her from the room. She rises, slowly, with the extra weight of a child and something even more than a child that David doesn't yet understand. She stops beside Business-Man and kisses him on the cheek. He can't tell whether she's mad or horny, or maybe this is some kind of new emotion that has no particular name except in German. She smiles, and before he can ask where she's going, the rest of the League lines up along the windows, standing at attention.

Ultraviolet approaches each hero individually, leans in, whispers. Then, each time, he says, "Do you know what you have to do?" And each one nods. And then each one leaves.

He's moving down the line like this so, okay, Business-Man joins the row, playing along. But he honestly has no fucking clue what he has to do. Has he missed a meeting? When the rest have scattered and only Business-Man is left, last in line, Ultraviolet bellows to him, "Join us up on the roof, won't you?" And suddenly USV security is headed his way. They don't give him a choice.

ii.

David never assumed Mathias Blue was real—real meaning unenhanced, unadulterated—but he believed in him. From the roof of Spinoza Field House, they see the gray swell on the horizon. They see more grids going in the distance, browning out one by one, disappearing in the evening, bequeathing a gray and choppy sea. David looks to him, the Übermensch, Mathias Blue.

"That giant anvil thing is beautiful," says Ultraviolet, staring at the massive cloud.

He's right. It curls and gathers everything to itself. A cloud magnet. Growing denser and darker until nothing can escape. Standing beside his leader, Business-Man watches the supercell coming at them like a movie giant, stepping over towns. He can feel its pull. It has its own gravity. It spins howling wind and rain and hail at them, coming in sideways, pelting their purple skin like hundreds of paintballs. They stand there shoulder to shoulder and take it.

They're strong enough to withstand this squall.

"That's the supercell," Business-Man says. "Insane thunderstorm with a cyclone inside, constantly spinning up and out."

"Ascension," says Ultraviolet. "Perfect. The gods will elevate us all."

"That's not the plan, dude. The plan is not to elevate. It is to hunker down and survive."

Ultraviolet puts a finger in his ear and scratches. He turns away from the far-off storm, looping casually around the circular glass skylight in the stadium's roof. Business-Man follows. He is second-in-command. He is nineteen years old. Blink.

It is the fifth of June, probably. The sun is rising and setting faster than ever. The adults have left. The Princeton campus belongs to the USV, and with the electricity gone the students will look for Ultraviolet to glow in the dark. They're downstairs, the student body, just babies really. There are a handful of heroes here on the roof of Spinoza. They seem like good soldiers, but Ultraviolet can see it: man is weak and known to fall apart. He tells them to keep their masks on, no matter what, keep them on. "Like all leaders," he says, "our mystery is our power."

If the water inside the arena keeps rising and reaches this high, Business-Man's plan is to break through this glass and pour out the top, but now that he sees the skylight glass from the outside, there's a kind of chicken-wire mesh inside that'll make it tough to fight through from below. Maybe he should gather a crew to cut through the mesh now. Where is Peacemaker?

"Where is Peacemaker?" Ultraviolet asks, reading his mind again. "And Dr. Ugs?

Where are *you*, Business-Man?"

He is here. And now it's his turn to ask questions.

"Where is Haley?" David retorts, breaking character. "What are you going to do to her?"

"Your darling is right here," he says, tapping his breastplate. "This is where she lives."

David wants to punch him, but instead he spits off the edge of the roof. His loogie plummets with the rain.

"We need them to be strong," Mathias says. "I'm going to caution them about Nietzsche's concept of the Last Man. Cut off, apathetic, weak. Lacking a certain imagination."

David's read some of what Mathias told him to read, and so he says, "Right: nihilism."

"Listen," Ultraviolet says, "here is your job." He pulls from his pocket an orange bottle of pills. Mathias's pills for energy, pills for strength, pills for connection: his charisma.

"They're not going to last." He's right. "Some days, you're going to administer a placebo."

David hates to state the obvious, but: "I don't actually know how to make placebo pills."

"It's in your hands now. It's up to you," Ultraviolet says. "Use your imagination."

He hands the bottle to David. Then the grid goes down and the world is blind.

"Hold them quietly," Ultraviolet says. "Our mystery is our power."

Ultraviolet lights a candle. He turns from the flood and walks downstairs to orate, to lead, maybe to drown. David squeezes the pill bottle, opens the childproof cap, and pours two white capsules into his palm. He looks at them, these babies, these tiny, smooth secrets.

By the time they run out, maybe Mathias will be real.

—Ø—

Business-Man knows he has a choice: he can hold Mathias's pills quietly, tightly, figure out a way to keep him at his best for as long as the drugs will allow. He can be the best number two on the planet. Or, instead, Business-Man can take the pills himself. See where they take him.

He swallows one.

Inside, Ultraviolet orates. A commencement address. All day and night. Endless streams of prophecy, poetry, mad genius. He sits at the controls of the announcer's booth, a microphone at his mouth. It's working, but there's tremendous static, an ambient chorus of shushing behind Ultraviolet's vocal solo. He lays out the path of the USV's mass purification:

"Return to the Stop, my heroes, to the stillness... When there's no time, do not pine for busyness... When food is scarce, do not pine for fullness. Appreciate the fast, the cleansing... Keep these waters clean. This lake is our salvation..."

Like this. He jumps from topic to topic. Nietzsche to chronostrictesis to education to moral determinism to his own disappearing hands.

"... Drink with moderation. Prepare yourselves... Only then will our silence carry the necessary weight to appease the gods and usher in a new Satya Yuga..."

First, it's annoying. But then it melts into the aural fabric of this place and becomes music.

"This lake is our salvation our sea some rye red yes but why is emblem emblem 'Cask of Amontillado' ice helado drowning in underground oil black to the reddest core of earth set to XplO it rumbles red the trees red the grass red the flood red beneath red above it all bursts into flames at once and becomes the sun exploding..."

The only sound is Ultraviolet's incessant announcement. Business-Man pops in Haley's earbuds to enjoy Echo's music.

Much of the Superdome is asleep, bodies passed out on bleachers like fallen knights. Some who cannot sleep venture to the concrete concourse, having their final alone moments. Their eyes are wide and dark. They rock back and forth on their heels. They are praying, perhaps. Or preparing. Reading aloud from *Tales of the USV* comics like it is scripture. *"But that's not the fucking moon,"* they say. "That's *the fucking moon."* Others go to town on each other, bend each other over concourse trash cans, a tremendous amount of sucking and fucking. A silent line forms at the concession stand, USVers reverently receiving whatever canned goods are left.

Nobody notices Business-Man. He is invisible. A new superpower.

On the other side of the stadium, the concourse is more alive. A wedding in progress, although surely not legally binding, depending on whose laws matter anymore. Two superheroes in love—Zorro Astor and Cadmium Cobalt—speak their quiet vows and kiss as a small congregation showers them with white rice kernels. Or maybe those are pills. David wonders which is scarcest.

Before Mathias's pilfered amphetamine pill kicks in, he lies down for some final moments of sleep. One last dream before reality hits. From the bleacher planks, he looks up at the rafters.

A central catwalk runs down the length of the ceiling, like a spine.

Why do they call it a "catwalk"? he wonders. Whose job was it to man that catwalk, to manage the building's electricity from such a high place, staring down at athletes and crowds?

Velvet banners hang—the retired jersey numbers of Princeton athletes. *They were the original supermen of this campus,* he thinks. He pictures their stadium crumbling, exposing the sky. Business-Man lets Echo's music take him, a call-and-response from beyond the grave. He inhales, feels the supercell filling him, charging his body with energy. Or maybe that's Mathias's pill he feels. He can see his synapses firing.

Welded sparks. Hot white light.

A statue is being cut down, iron toppling from a stone pedestal. The Mather Sundial, maybe.

When it's gone, millions of purple beings climb up to the plinth, their faces amorphous. They keep climbing, scurrying over one another like noble roaches, building a tower of humans taller and taller. The tower rises up into the sky, beyond clouds, beyond sound, and when it reaches the silent ceiling of the world, the heavens burst forth, sun spreading outward like sideways lightning, and—*XplO!*—a beam shoots down, blasting this tower of heroes, bodies falling like firework ash.

David is watching from afar. From on high. From pure omnipotence.

And then he's one of the bodies, falling.

He feels the pull of gravity.

The plummet.

The speed.

—Ø—

"Slowly," a whisper says. "Pull it. Pull!"

"It's too full," says another voice. "I don't want to touch it."

"Do it for fuck's sake. Hurry, he's moving!"

Eyes closed, Business-Man feels hands fumbling around his crotch. He must've fallen asleep in Miss Givings's section 110, inadvertently signed up for one last end-of-days orgy. But when he opens his eyes, ready to make a polite exit, he sees familiar faces arrayed over him kaleidoscopically. Dr. Ugs and Peacemaker and Sergeant Drill and even Esteban, staring down at him with wide eyes.

Zoom and he's awake.

"Now! Do it!" Ugs screams.

Water pours down on Business-Man's face, and he gasps at hands raking at his eyes and fumbling his mouth, prying open his jaw and pouring water in from the bottle that was in his pants. They're force-feeding him, and though at first he's convinced this is still his dream, when his arms flail against his quartet of attackers, he can immediately guess what substance is in that bottle.

Lunging forward, wet, Business-Man weasels out of Sergeant Drill's grasp. "Don't touch him!" they say, giving him a wide berth.

"What the fuck?!" he says.

"We know what we have to do, Business-Man."

He can taste in the water that metallic trace of Liquid Zero.

He knows what's going to happen but he has no idea why.

David spots a fire extinguisher fixed on the wall near the concourse opening, pulls the pin, and unleashes a flurry of white on these heroes, then turns and runs like mad. He bursts from the bleachered section, sprinting, sprinting through the concourse, thankful for his legs. He hears footsteps behind him.

The chase is on.

Blood pounds in David's ears. He needs his arms to run, to sprint, to find a way out of this nightmare. Busting through a doorway he hits a cinder block stairwell and bounds down the steps three at a time and almost eats it on the concrete.

At the bottom, the floor is filled with water. Up to his knees. It's dark, but he must be in a basement, somewhere underground. Shafts of moonlight pour through windows near the ceiling, and David hears fast footsteps coming for him. He's in a locker room, part submerged. Slogging through water-filled aisles, he blinks and sees a supermarket, the frozen food section. Blink. He sees Haley emerging from a phone booth, naked. Blink. He spots another phone booth. This one is real, it's here, not a superimposition. And it's more a phone *closet*, the kind with a glass-pane door. An old cubby built for college athletes to phone home. Maybe it still works.

He heads for the booth, falling face forward into the water. He can almost feel the floor moving on this sinking *Titanic*. Behind him David hears the muffled pop of another door opening.

They are coming.

He dives forward and reaches the booth. It takes great strength to pull open the glass door against the water, which rushes around as David sloshes into the phone booth and pulls the door shut and thinks, *Please, gods, please, ghosts, please, Grandpa László, dear Claire, give me a dial tone.*

The receiver is cold against his ear and it sings the sweetest hum David's ever known. Cold age of cell phones! The dial tone has been brought out of retirement to fight this one last battle.

Voices bark outside the booth. Metal lockers open and close. They're here now, searching for him. David huddles into the water, only his head and hands above the surface.

C'mon, push those three square buttons.

His hand is going numb. He strains to hit the 9, the 1, once more, but his elbow can barely lift itself. No no no, god no, this is not happening, why, shit, how long does he have—

"911," a voice says. "How is your emergency different than everyone else's emergency?"

"This is Business-Man, uh, David Fuffman," he hisses into the speaker. "At Princeton University. I'm under attack, I repeat, under attack. Send in SWAT now, goddamn it, *now*!"

Why can't he stop speaking like this?

"Calm down, sir."

"Send in reinforcements from the perimeter!"

"The *what*?"

"The *perimeter*. Don't you guys have a goddamn perimeter set up?"

She sighs deeply. "You listen to me," she says. "Last time a squad went to that campus some kid broke my husband's collarbone. So tell me one good—"

But David doesn't get to tell her one good anything.

Because suddenly a trash can smashes through the glass above him and shards of window pour down on his face. And David plops into the water, like an idiot, because now he can't get up.

He looks up and there is Sergeant Drill. She's got Peacemaker behind her plus a small army of his goons. David can't sink any deeper into the water or his face will be submerged, drowning. He has nowhere to go, nowhere to hide. They open the door and yank him up by his armpits. He tries kicking their knees, but it's no use. Something slams David's forehead and then his neck and he's in the water again, probably bleeding. He can't see anything. And that's the thing about getting the shit beat out of you—it's impossible to find a still point. You're constantly upside down.

Being dragged up a flight of stairs now. Once his eyes come back David sees a single blurry face bouncing up above him. It's Cap'n Cunt. His Haley. At the top of the stairway. Thank the gods. But no, her eyes are wide and dark and everything good is washed away from them.

David is about to say something, some explanation, some warning, but she beats him to it.

"Any minute now," she says catatonically. And then she's gone from his vision.

He feels himself being raised up, and for a moment he believes it's finally happening. The End. The Ascension. But no. This is weirder. His body feels tight and numb, like Novocain or a slept-on arm. When he tries to shake the sleep from his limbs and regain feeling, David knows he's stuck inside himself again. The feeling that only comes with Liquid Zero.

David is paralyzed.

But Mathias's speedier pill is kicking in hard, a million pinballs rattling around his rib cage.

And, also, he's flying. A security team of USV heroes holds him aloft by his outstretched limbs—their standard-issue "airplane," just like move-in day at The Egg—and they're flying him up a set of stairs.

He can't lock his core, find balance, find equilibrium.

He's just a stupid rag of a man, a prisoner.

From below, David hears a familiar voice. It's Dr. Ugs. He sounds a little drunk.

"Y'know, I tried to rat on Mathias one time, too," he says. "Got as far as the precinct, but then I looked around at those fat asshole cops scurrying with paperwork, trash everywhere, drinking shit-colored coffee out of Styrofoam cups, some handcuffed crack head calling everyone faggots, and it's like I was looking at dinosaurs. Like the *T-rex*, with those tiny arms. It was like, oh, of course that experiment was flawed and they didn't survive, right? Just look at those stupid fucking arms!"

They fly David into the USV skybox, onto the conference table.

Ugs is over him now, staring down at David's still body.

"Help. Me." David can barely speak.

"You still think he's Noah, like I once thought. The practical savior gathering and preparing us for survival and repopulation. But soon you'll see." Ugs leans in. "He's Abraham. Father of all."

Then they are gone. David is in the skybox, Ultraviolet's lair. He hears his leader breathing.

Sometimes it takes a loud sound to wake one from slumber. Sometimes it takes a good slap in the face. Sometimes all it takes is a startling image. So when David's head lolls to the side and his eyes focus in on a blurry figure, another himself, something shifts. Because here is what he sees: Ultraviolet in profile. His pants are off. There's an axe in his hands.

He is leaning over himself, slicing a delicate cut into his penis with the razor-sharp axe blade.

Blood drips darkly down his hand. He flips his grandfather's axe onto a desk in front of him, blood spattering like swirl art, and then grabs a mason jar to collect the blood from his member.

For David, *this* is what breaks the spell, the glitch that gives it all away.

David stays stiff, still, body frozen with fear and also drugs. Once Mathias has collected a centimeter of blood from his own cock, he patches himself up with gauze. He screws a lid on the mason jar of redness. Then he pulls up his pants and hits Record on his radio.

"Watch this," he says to David.

He speaks softly, all in a steady monotone, different from his melodic oration: *She must be sacrificed the only way to salvation kill the queen and her child please quench me the only way to salvation she must be sacrificed to swim in her waters the only way to salvation she must be sacrificed listen to the gods please quench me...*

He goes on like this. Who knows for how long? Minutes don't exist.

Once he is done chanting, he goes to his controls. Echo's radio has many dials and buttons. The recording plays quietly—. . . *Kill the queen and her child please quench me the only way to salvation...*

"If I twist *this* knob here, the bass drops out of the voice," Mathias says.

And it's true, his vocal recording loses its low-end timbre, becomes tinny.

"Then *here* goes the treble," he says. And with a turn of some knob, more of Mathias's voice gets swallowed up into nothing. But it's still there, mostly muffled.

"And then all we do is introduce the noise-masking signal at 1,500 Hz. And my instructions become inaudible! See, the slope control accommodates variation in the frequency response and—"

David stops listening. White noise engulfs Mathias's overdubbed words. Static. All shushing.

But the voice! It continues in David's brain, like a song lyric stuck in his head...

Kill the queen and her child... please quench me... only way to salvation... please... His brain hears this earworm over and over. A loop of instructions. A call to madness. A voice in his head.

"Please..." is what David mumbles. "Please, man. Please..." He doesn't know why he says this. Maybe because it's the noise in his head—*please quench me.* Or maybe he's saying *please* because he's experiencing the wrong kind of revelation. Witnessing the ultimate destruction of your hero.

It's suddenly so clear: the USV is being hypnotized, encoded, conditioned.

Like Dr. Cranum, Mathias Blue has built himself a Brain Machine.

"Plee..." David says. His jaw is tightening up.

Mathias turns slowly and looks David in the eyes. Undaunted, he recites:

"Quetzalcoatl gathered them all. He bathed them in a green bowl. Quetzalcoatl bled his penis on them. Then all the gods in that place gave him merit."

He says this like it's so obvious.

"You're brainwashing them."

"What do you think we've created?" Mathias asks. "These heroes! The water below!"

"Iz for drinking, azzhole."

"You still think that's a *well.* For survival. But no, that's a sinkhole, a cenote, a passage to the underworld. When we offer ourselves to Chaac, the water god, he will stop the floods and usher in the Golden Age. The Satya Yuga. But if we don't quench his thirst, that's the end, dude. So we'll call our heroes up to the altar to receive their medicine. Cap'n Cunt will bleed the water. And the earth's elite will pass through the dark neck of time and emerge luminous without end."

"That's mass murder." Now it's David's turn to quote. The ancient wisdom of the Super Friends. "'No man has a right to enforce his will on others, no matter how good his intentions may be!'"

Mathias laughs, "You're a fucking Boy Scout!"

"You're fucking crazy!"

"I'M RUNNING THIS MONKEY FARM NOW, FRANKENSTEIN! AND I WANNA KNOW WHAT THE FUCK YOU'RE DOING WITH MY TIME!"

David is truly frightened now, because it's clear he's gone. And it's David's fault. All of it. He instigated this. He planned the spectacles. David is Dr. Frankenstein and this is *his* monster.

"Sorry, that's a line from *Day of the Dead,*" Mathias explains, calm now. "It felt a propos. Truth is I am doing exactly what I'm supposed to be doing right now."

"Whuriz she?" David's losing his tongue fast.

"Or," says Mathias. "If you don't believe the shaman stuff? Maybe chronostrictesis is fake. Maybe I made it up. You know business, right, so do you know what 'condition branding' is?"

David knows what it is, from his Viral Marketing class. It's when pharmaceutical companies coin phrases like "restless leg syndrome" and get people all worried. First, they sell the disease. Then they sell the cure. But David's mouth is getting stuck. So he just nods.

"Right! So maybe that's what Business-Man can believe. Maybe I've been working with SCISM, with Pfizer, DARPA, NIST, and we've branded the idea of chronostrictesis in order to launch the most lucrative blockbuster drug in history. Is that plausible?"

David doesn't know anything anymore.

"What about this? Maybe dear old Dad was telling you the truth. Maybe mononuclear reproduction has been available for decades, to those of us with access to the right government facilities. You know those advertisements in the back of the *Princeton Alumni Weekly*, where Ivy League women offer up their unfertilized eggs to couples who can't have babies of their own? Elite genomes available for like $25K apiece? Well, you can also harvest those eggs for free—if the donors are willing, if they *believe*, David. I've paid for the lab time, but the eggs were all free, the most perfect time capsules money can't buy. Because you can either *use* those genetics or you can *destroy* the egg nucleus, all of its genes and chromosomes, using ultraviolet light so that none of its genetic makeup is left over, and *then* you simply do a microinjection—"

"Whur iz Haley?"

"—adding *my* DNA to that nucleus, which can be taken from skin scrapings, blood, semen, whatever one might have lying around in a refrigerator, for instance, and, well, I guess what I'm saying, David, is that *I'm smarter than you*. I'm more zeroed in. I've seen things you haven't seen, so I know you think I'm nuts, but I think *you're* nuts, okay, *you're* the crazy one, because *you* don't have the first goddamn clue what's going on, yet you pretend like you know what's good and what's evil."

"Whur iz Haley? The baby..."

"Ha! Full savage truth, man: I tried to implant her the old-fashioned way, same as you did, and it's anyone's guess which of our seedlings took hold. But it's not *yours* and not *mine* and not even *hers*. It belongs to the gods." He seesaws his palms like balancing scales. "There are many possible narratives. Ascribe to the one you prefer. *That's* belief. I *believe* what I *believe* because I *see* it. Like I *saw* that you'd take those pills I gave you."

"Why?" David mumbles.

"Because you're fucking selfish," he says. "And because you *told on me* to my daddy, David."

The arena shakes. Wind so strong David can hear layers of roof being ripped off.

"Golden Echo is dead because of *you*," Mathias continues. "You'll die a traitor."

"Whur iz Haley?"

"Oy vey, she's right here, buddy." Mathias tilts David's head. He can see her behind him. "I told you: this is where she lives."

Haley is naked, smiling down like a mother. She pets his bald head around his Mohawk.

"We are not yet free, David," she says. "But we are so close. Seven days, times seven weeks, equals forty-nine days. On the forty-ninth day, the baby's pineal gland is fully formed. The gender becomes clear. The soul transmigrates. The power is pulled into the womb. For us, for this baby, that was April, do you remember? Your birthday, maybe, in the back of the van when we all came together? The forty-ninth day. I didn't even know yet. You fell asleep, the drug's sedative was too strong for most of you. But Ultraviolet drove us to the lab. And he showed me—I could see it, it was so beautiful, these pure magic eggs that could be carried in any of us! Birthed to the world! I was ready to give mine over to the gods, but then they tested me and I was already pregnant. Do you understand?"

David didn't understand a fucking thing.

"But the other girls? They wanted to give themselves, and I explained to them what I'd seen at the center, how quick and painless the procedure, and they all gave their eggs so the USV will live on. We can save us all. Don't worry, the women will carry on and take care of everything. The mothers. We can save us all. Do you understand what I'm telling you? We can—"

"SuperVisor was the first successful egg," Mathias says, "but then she got cold feet and terminated. She threatened our group, David, so she had to leave. Now, you have to leave, too. Tie him up, please, my Cap'n."

"I'm going to bind your hands now, David. I'm sorry, baby, I'm going to put you in this handcuff knot for when the Liquid wears off, do you understand, David?"

"I'm not. The bad guy," David says.

"Oh, I heard the recording of you and Mathias's dad. It was *rawther* gallant of you to try to protect me. It's just... you want so bad to *survive*," she says. "You think we're too important to die. You think we'll live and help people after the storm, deliver canned goods to kids in Trenton or something. But we won't, David, and that won't save anyone. Only sacrifice saves us. *That's* our value. That's our power."

David's mind is aflame. And here she sounds calm and collected.

"You can believe one of Mathias's stories," she says. "Or you can believe what you already know: that time is running out and the world *is* going to end. Unless we make a sacrifice."

"Haley," David implored. "Nobody haz to scrifice anythng."

She smiles and begins to tear up. "That's always been your motto, hasn't it? The Anointed!"

"Pluhz." David's eyelids can't move. "I had. A plan."

"This has always been the plan," Mathias says. "You've always known it, and you've helped make it so. *This* is how we pass through the Null Point. You're frightened, is all. But push through that veil and find faith. Find peace. And by the time you can move again, it'll be time."

"Any minute now." Haley kisses David's face and says, "It's okay. It's okay."

And it is not okay. It is not even a little bit okay. So David brings out the final piece of artillery. The nuke. The only trigger word that might possibly snap her out of it.

David manages to say to her, "He's. Raping. You."

"Come here, David," Mathias says. "I want you to feel my palms."

One minute the world is there, but crumbling, and the next, there's a pure purple planet hurtling through space, Mathias's fist flying, exploding into David's eye socket, turning his sight red, darkening his sight the way that apocalyptic asteroid darkened the dinosaurs' sky, and in the blink before David loses consciousness, he considers not just the awesome weight of that astral body crashing to earth but also its aftermath; not one cataclysmic crash turning the planet to ash in the blink of an eye, but the massive dust cloud that followed, cutting off the sun, choking the plants, claiming the world's inhabitants one by one as they trudged along the wasteland looking for water but finding none, finally collapsing with the slow and painful realization that this was fucking *it*.

iii.

First, he smells it—a mass of humanity, animalistic. Ash and body odor and semen and ass. It's how ancient caves must have smelled, David thinks. Where cavemen hid from paralyzing ice.

Fire turns ice to water.

Man turns water to blood.

Is this death he's feeling? Or do the gentle rocking, the scent of his own sweat, the weightlessness, do they all mean he's coming to?

He chokes awake. Eyes swollen, dried shut. Skull heavy. David thinks he's still dosed on Liquid, but no, he can move his arms again.

His infrared goggles are on his eyes. He tries to lift his head. But something is wrapped tight round his throat, digging into his neck flesh.

Frogs, insects, livestock. Fiery hail. Were these biblical plagues inexplicable God-magic, David wonders, or just some very reasonable bioscience? Red algae in the Nile? Bacteria from the algae killing all those fish and frogs? Then the insects—without frogs there to eat them—they swarm the land, feast on cows and pigs, spread their pestilence? Plus, just tons of shitty weather? An unhinged and misguided ruler. A perfect storm.

"Awake, awake!" thunders a voice from above. "Stay stiff!" It is Ultraviolet's, of course.

David draws heavy hands up to his gullet and paws around. His wrists are lashed together with Haley's rope, and his fingers find metal pulled tight against his Adam's apple. It's thick like a wire hanger, and it squeezes tighter when he swallows.

Inside the silence, David still hears energy. He assumed that once the power grids failed, the familiar hum of electricity would fall dormant. But no. Power lines still buzz. It sounds like locusts, the ones that only show up every seventeen years. The eighth plague.

He closes his eyes again.

The ninth would be darkness, which is already here, right on schedule.

But even in the dark everything is wobbly. He opens his eyes again. Tries to focus.

Up above is the skylight, the dome gone dark, except when the lightning strikes illuminate its hub-and-spoke structure. It's night outside, and in all ways terrible sounding. Inside, he can't hear the rush of the water pipes filling the arena anymore. Aside from the lightning, the only color is an orange flicker tickling the ceiling—a fire most likely—so the power must be dead.

But David's still alive.

He is in a rowboat. Drifting in their manmade lake. Above, hailstones have smashed the skylight, and a driving rain falls through this hole. David drifts into a column of rain. He looks up into the downpour, droplets coming fast like *Star Wars* hyperdrive. A fat one nails him in the eye.

Blink.

But what of the tenth plague? That last awful one that broke the Pharaoh. There's no greater pain than the death of a child. He searches his cloudy mind for some indication of Mathias's plan—he's got some Passover sacrifice in mind, smearing blood over Earth's doorframe in hopes the gods will pass them by.

A new call goes out over the PA, loud and clear, bursting through the cracks of David's fingers. But it's David's voice this time. And the voice of Mathias's father:

David: *"... He'll be in the exterior pulpit on the south wall, Friday night at eight o'clock is when it starts."*

Oh fuck.

David's wearing a blazer, not László's but something close, he can feel that much. He can't stand. That wire is pulling at his jugular. Underneath his body he strokes a bed of velvet. At first he thinks this is just some royal vestment, but when he cranes his neck he finds orange and black and the tip of a number, 2. One of the massive arena banners from up in the rafters has been tied to David. Some athlete's retired jersey number locked with twisted wire around his neck, draping off his shoulders.

A cape. Ten feet long and heavy as fuck.

Colonel Blue's voice: *"... If you decide not to take my job offers with DARPA, Booz Allen, or the agency, you've got a future in acting, Business-Man."*

David eyes the stands. Holy shit, everyone's here. Collected, lined up on the bleachers, lit by the dim dance of a fire. Their masks are on. Their heads are bowed forward. Totally silent. All of them. David opens his mouth to call out to them, but it's sealed shut with layers of duct tape.

David is a POW, the newest convicted felon of the USV. Which means he's in trouble.

David's voice: *"I'm a man of my word. But if I'm selling out Mathias just promise me—"*

On the far end of the stadium, under the scoreboard, a fire blazes, fueled by wooden chairs and library books. A makeshift pulpit has been erected from a bookcase and Mathias stands behind it, wearing a purple graduation robe, a mortarboard and tassel. He's the valedictorian of this ceremony, and he holds court above the rising waterline. The basketball nets are nearly sunk by now.

Behind Ultraviolet is a long table lined with cups, almost definitely filled with paralyzing Liquid Zero masquerading as DMT. The high priests of the USV—Dr. Ugs, It Girl, Sergeant Drill, Peacemaker with his army creating a perimeter(!)—are arrayed around Ultraviolet, ready to divvy out this incapacitating Kool-Aid.

Lined in the bleachers beside Ultraviolet, each wearing a purple robe like a gospel choir, are seven masked women with hands folded on their stomachs—all the surrogate mothers carrying Mathias's fertilized eggs, David's betting.

And seated below Ultraviolet, by herself on a bleacher bench, is Cap'n Cunt. She is naked, seated like some throned Anubis statue, with one hand on her stomach and the other gripping Ultraviolet's axe like a scepter.

Her back straight and eyes wide. Weirdly so.

Something is wrong, David can see it. She's not really there.

Colonel Blue: *"We have a deal. You and your girlfriend will be protected."*

As the call audio loops over again, David scans the arena. Angry masks everywhere.

"There before you," calls Mathias to his minions, "is the last vestige of the old order! The Kali Yuga. The corporate suit. The Business-Man. The *busyness,* man! Selfish and self-serving. A villain. The last shred of evil to be purged before evolution can happen."

David knows what's coming, of course. It's the Super Fucking Fire Zero.

"The time of the Business-Man has come and gone. The corporate drone, the white-collared capitalist slave. We are done with his way of life. He is primed for extinction. He must be destroyed so that the new leap in evolution may begin. This, my heroes, is our Commencement Ceremony!"

Howls spring forth from the stands, a volume so great it stirs the boat beneath David.

"Hope and the future are not in lawns and cultivated fields, not in towns and cities, but in the impervious and quaking swamps!" A Thoreau quote, a final dickish wink from Mathias. Maybe it was that time on the roof, or wearing Haley's earbuds during his nap, that saved David's brain from total annihilation.

Wait.

He looks down at his wrists locked together in Haley's handcuff knot, the one that hid an escape route like a Chinese finger trap. A secret message? Is that why she shared the knot's trick? He looks at Haley and her eyes are wide and shiny but give him nothing else.

"So what will we do with him, my heroes? Will we let him ruin our purity? Chance our salvation? Will we let this rat loose outdoors, exiling him to his rotting way of life?"

"NO!"

"Superheroes uphold justice, protect the universe. So I challenge you: save us all!"

With a sweep of his hand and a hearty "XplO!" Sergeant Drill fires a rifle shot into the air, and suddenly the crowd breaks from their poses and rushes to the water. Some dive directly in, splashing toward David. Others go for the boats moored to disappearing basketball hoops and paddle toward David, looking like furious purple Vikings.

He crosses his wrists together and grabs the two tag ends, like Haley showed him, squeezes and loosens them. The loops widen and he can jimmy his hands, stretching the rope wider and wider until, just like that, his hands are free. Voilà.

David claws at the tape around his mouth, pantomiming to them, *Cover your ears, cover your ears!* But it's too late. Ultraviolet has unleashed them and there is nothing rational David can say that will stop this onslaught. The hunt is already on. The USV has fully fallen into the deep well of Mathias's mouth, and David has no bucket with which to pull them back up.

An oar rests in David's rowboat—a weapon left to give the illusion of a fair fight? He picks it up and paddles like mad, heading away from Ultraviolet's pulpit, to the back edge of the lake. But he doesn't get far before the enemy rowboats close in. Purple heroes stand like bears, claws out, ready to feed. When they get close, David grips his oar like a baseball bat, knees quaking as if preparing for a fastball straight at his head. But there are other heads in range now. Dirty minds. Tainted by Mathias's insidious evil.

David rears back, takes a swing. He lands his shot directly across some hero's head and he goes down, but David topples as well, thrown off by the weight and by the creepy feeling of hitting a fragile skull with this blunt weapon. He has no balance, strangled by the banner-cape, and as he's about to pick himself up, dust himself off, and take another shot, praying his oar will knock some sense into these zombies, David looks up to find flaming bottles flying through the air.

They twirl end over end like batons. Some splash, but one of these Molotov cocktails comes crashing down in the bow of his boat. Exploding, the bottle sprays flames across David, along his boat and cape. For a second he can't believe it: he's actually on fire. His exile is here.

The flames move fast, scampering up his cape and heading toward his face. He closes his eyes, the heat all around him now, and there's nowhere else to go but down.

He jumps off the rowboat into the water below. The cape is too unwieldy, too heavy. David's limbs get tangled, and the cape just sucks up water and grows heavier, pulling him down below. He is carrying a billion pounds around his throat.

Trying to swim to the surface is pointless. All he can do is dive deeper.

And then, in the depths of this manmade lake, David bumps into another body.

At first he tries to fight it, to claw its eyes out with everything he's got. But the body doesn't fight back. It just hovers there, in front of David, arms outstretched. A frozen marionette.

It's lifeless. Dead. A body in the water.

A superimposition. *Another yourself.* Blink.

Jesus Christ, it's Esteban. An earlier prisoner, perhaps, another alleged evil purged. Maybe he figured out their plans for Business-Man and tried to stop them, tried to uphold justice and got trampled by his own goodness, another boy who gave his noble life to save David's unworthy one.

He yanks the goggles from his head and wraps them around the dead boy's face. *Please be my decoy,* David thinks. *Buy me some time.*

Underwater, time moves fastest. David's breath is running out.

He keeps breaststroking down into this gateway to the afterlife, dragging the tremendous weight of the cape behind him. David needs to be rid of it or it will be the End. He's losing breath.

Panic sets in.

Searching his body in vain for a tool, a weapon, a gadget that will loose him from this noose round his neck, David knows he has nothing.

So he uses the only thing this poor excuse for a superhero has left: his own brute strength.

Stretching out his neck, David finds an opening between skin and wire. He slides his fingers in there. And then David goes still. But he's not dead yet. He's staying stiff, building energy, preparing to XplO, harder, stronger, faster, more, now, do it you fucker get this thing off just pull you fucker pull goddamn it because this is the time where heroes are made when you've got nothing left in the tank and need to dig deep so pull like Superman in Lex Luthor's blue pool wrapped in Kryptonite chains glowing green be the man you are and remember that power lies not in your muscles but in your guts so find it you fucker pull and scream that you still have work to do and people to save your life your love your child maybe in there about to be sacrificed to this madman unless you do something about it so just pull you hero pull you fucker pull!

XplO!

All that tension spent in the bliss of release, and when the wire busts loose it's like David's life has just found its spot. This is who he is now. He is David fucking FuffMan.

To the shore! He sees all those kicking legs above him. They're headed the opposite direction, splashing a frothy brew lit by the orange flicker of a boat on fire. They're headed to Esteban's body, a gift from the imperfect gods.

David's legs kick Plexiglas. He guides himself to the surface. And thank god his mouth is covered with tape, because he can't swallow much water or make much noise when he emerges. Water spews from inside of him, filling his eyes and skull and purging from his nose. No one sees or hears him yet. They're howling to the ceiling, gathered round the dead goggled body found next to that cape. It's too dark to see. They know nothing but wrath now.

David pulls himself up onto the bleachered shore like the first fish crawling from the water. He rips the duct tape from his face and bails out water from his insides, the vomit burning him all the way through. But no time to recover. Staying low along the concrete stairs, David makes his way up the aisle, heading for the concourse. He ditches the blazer, back to purple, blending in. If he moves slowly enough, maybe the crowd won't spot him. Up he goes, slithering one step at a time. But when he gets to the top of the section and looks toward the pulpit, the fear in Ultraviolet's eyes belies his confidence. This is no half-assed villain. Not one to be satisfied until the body is verified. He's going to push forth. Time is running out.

As David bolts into the concourse, he finds a gray mask on the floor and puts it on, a bit of camouflage. But he still has no weapon. No easy access to the pulpit without first breaking through all of Peacemaker's bodyguards. David is full of power, but he can't singlehandedly take out an army.

He needs the element of surprise.

Then David finds a door marked CATWALK.

It's unlocked.

Taking the stairs three at a time, the latex suit pulls at his skin. The purple paint is shredded from the underwater struggle, so David claws at his breastbone and splits a vertical seam and pulls outward, exposing his bare chest and its zero tattoo, like Clark Kent tearing off a dress shirt.

Every cell is on fire as David reaches the top of the stairwell.

The catwalk. It lies before David, high above Mathias's lost followers. He climbs up into it, the grated metal cold on his bare feet. The ceiling smells like smoke from Mathias's pulpit-fire on the opposite side of Spinoza. David's eyes are blurry, but he can make out Mathias standing behind Haley and keeping a low crouch, David heads toward the space above the two of them.

Storms smack the roof above his head, the kind of tempest that exists only in movies where people are lost at sea. He hears Mathias orating again. He can't catch everything because the acoustics are weird and his heart is running hard, but snippets of speech waft up to the rafters.

"Woman's womb," he yells, "is our final pill! A final Big Bang as the gods come to collect!"

David's at half-court, directly over the center of the lake, his rowboat still ablaze below. Outside, the supercell must be directly over the arena. A piece of roof rips off, exposing sky.

"Break free from this egg. When *they* perish, *we* begin our silence! Her blood will prime the waters below! Then each of you will rise to receive your medication. We are pure or we are Nothings! Wade into the waters below. Stay stiff as you quench the gods."

Reaching the end of the catwalk, David is directly overtop of them, heat from the fire warming his feet and legs. On one side of this makeshift graduation stage, Dr. Ugs is pouring Liquid Zero into an endless grid of Dixie cups. A line forms on the other side, and heroes march single-file to receive their drink. The seven pregnant surrogates encircle Mathias with meticulous choreography and remove his robe. One raises a branch and the others rub oils into his purple skin.

"Droch, Mirroch, Esenaroth..." they chant.

"Our queen will quench the thirst of the great Timekeepers. Listen closely! You can hear their voices whistling around us now."

Indeed, David can hear voices. Over and over in his brain the mantra runs.

...Kill the queen and her child... please quench me... the only way to salvation... medication...

He shuts his ears and scans the catwalk for a tool, a rope, something to throw, anything to thwart this villain and save this day. But there's nothing up here besides smoke. Smoke and David.

And now Peacemaker, who has found him. He's on the far side of the catwalk, snarling for David to stop. David sees this juggernaut sprinting toward him, closing fast. More roof rips away.

Please, Grandpa. Please, Claire. Give me some sign here of what it is I'm meant to do.

"Let the countdown commence!" shouts Ultraviolet below. "TEN!"

David is above them. Mathias below, sizing up Haley. She raises Mathias's axe to the sky.

Swim in her waters. It's the only way to salvation...

"NINE!"

It's time, David.

"EIGHT!"

She must be sacrificed. Listen to the gods.

Bounding stomps on the catwalk. Shadows in David's periphery. Peacemaker getting closer.

"Betu, Baroch, Maaroth..." the surrogates chant.

"SEVEN!"

The path of heroics is long and winding. You may still exert influence on mankind, the way you've dreamed.

Staring straight down, he tries to block the noise.

Please quench me...

To whom do these voices belong?

"Holy Trinity, punish him who has done evil toward us..."

"SIX!"

Please quench me.

Blink. Batman. Blink. Superman. Blink. Golden Echo. Blink. Wonder Woman.

How can I put my faith in a higher power, ask it to give me guidance?

"FIVE!"

Only sacrifice saves us.

Metal bounces below David's feet. His old roommate, this samurai goliath, approaches fast.

"... and deliver us from this evil by thy great justice."

David's eyes find fire, dancing in its ancient glow. His skin flickers, alive and naked.

"FOUR!"

Dear ghosts, I am finally wearing the correct costume.

Peacemaker screams David's name.

FuffMan!

Below, Sergeant Drill points her rifle upward and takes aim at David.

"Elion, Elion, Esmaris. Amen."

Haley raises the axe from her waist, straight-armed, a firm gatepost. She curls the blade in front of her own throat, holding it there, poised and ready. David knows it's sharp enough to slice her jugular with one swift pull. A swift death. Their sacrificial offering.

"THREE!"

David throws his leg over the catwalk railing. He nudges his heels to the edge of the platform. He stares at Mathias's bare skull and lines up his shot as a bullet whizzes by.

David's hands find the railing. His heart finds a moment of silence. He fucking *has* him.

Just then, Mathias glances upward. His eyes are sad. He winks.

And I am you.

"TWO!"

And David launches himself.

Time falls apart in the air. History dying softly in David's ears. Future nowhere to be seen. Who knows what human bones can do? Speed and spirit and gravity, something drawing him back to itself, something good. The center of the earth, the electricity of it, the magnetism. He feels the air rushing through his hair, this good wind, and he looks down on Mathias's head, coming fast as a fist, and he sees that it is terrifying. So he looks away, up, up at the rain accelerating with him, reaching the same speed, droplets fixed like pixels in space, pushing him along, pulling him closer and connecting him to that same water rushing through time, the torrential superstorm above and sinkhole below, pulling or funneling down that vortex of declining time sinking the plague the flood of frogs finally feeling heat and hopping from that boiling pot pouring over her foraged tea leaves unfolding from a weightless womb an embryonic egg cracking the dam breaking and swallowing the bridge and Superman flying round Earth's oceans until time stops and rewinds and everything is good again.

He looks back down. There's nothing left to dream or imagine or hear or see. No sirens, no sea. There is only this mad final duel and the outcome will not be decided by David or Mathias, but by the physics of wind, the forces of gravity, their water all one and the same, and as his body comes crashing down, David feels that *pull*, his skin pulling, the earth pulling, and as he lands on bone and the world goes black, he thinks, *I am flying I am flying I am flying...*

12

THE SATYA YUGA

i.

Blink.

Bleep.

Bleep.

David saw a heartbeat.

He saw the monitor spiking with each *bleep*.

He saw everything again.

He saw his dad standing in the corner of the hospital room. His mom was combing David's hair, the tines massaging his head. She sang a soft song he recognized from somewhere, but he could not place the words. He felt an ungodly need to pee, but had no idea how to make that happen.

Blink. Tubes and wires circled his arms and chest, and he saw covers pulled taut across his legs, and with a sharp inhale David felt violently restless and tried kicking his way out of these sheets. Again, the message went nowhere. He lifted his neck, just barely, wanting to get a look down at himself. The effort was immense, as if that strong banner were still tied round his throat.

David's dad hopped up and over to him. Gil cried while Eileen squeezed him and shouted to God or nurses.

"Mom," David managed, his tongue thick and dry. "Is the world gone?"

"Nope, not yet," she said, laughing through her tears. "It's just a little different! Smaller."

"Jesus fucking Christ, buddy," said Dad. "We thought *you* were gone."

David shook his head no.

He tapped his chest, where the Æ tattoo would be. David whispered, "Superheroes never die."

His dad's face turned ghostly.

"Yes," he said. "Yes, they do. Plenty of them do."

—Ø—

A true blackout holds no dreamtime. No imagery. Only darkness. Three months of coma.

The fall had broken David's back. Cracked his T7 and T8 vertebrae. It took away his legs.

They call it paraplegia. Not a complete lesion of the spinal cord, so they're hopeful. Doctors say David may regain a high percentage of his motor function below the waist. They say they want to begin rehabilitation immediately, that there are some great new FDA-approved drugs and other experimental ones in late-stage trials.

When destiny fails, use your smoke pellets.

They're mobilizing his muscles. Functional electrical stimulation. Belly binders and neoprene shorts with electrodes built in. A new costume. He's watching for radioactive arachnids.

But David's in no rush to be rebuilt. As soon as he's well, he'll have to deal with the trial.

Because the end didn't come for David.

The world didn't come to its End, either.

But it did for Mathias Blue.

David's fall smashed Mathias's skull. It killed him instantly.

There were thousands of eyewitnesses—unreliable, sure—but enough consensus that a narrative could be formed. David was the one responsible for the final implosion of the USV, and the State of New Jersey charged him with assault, gross negligence, arson, theft, inciting riots, and second-degree murder. His lawyer thinks he can get that last onerous one dropped to voluntary manslaughter, a crime of passion. They're still discussing what plea to use. Self-defense? Diminished capacity? Insanity? Either way, he's guilty. But there's also no hard proof. Regardless of David's plummet from above, the autopsy discovered an insane amount of drugs in Mathias's system, including a possibly lethal dose of phenobarbital. David's lawyer thinks once Colonel Blue has exhausted the easy legal options he'll drop the charges against David, scared to publicly dredge up any details that could incriminate himself. Maybe they can settle. Only time will tell.

Until then, Mom and Dad come to visit him. They know all the cafeteria employees by name, and the grill cook, Moe, is always willing to make his mom eggs well after breakfast is technically over. Mom and Dad help David do the things he can't do for himself.

"You only lost three months," they say.

"You have your whole life ahead of you," they say.

"Your body will come back," they say. "All it takes is time and effort."

David tells them, "Time is irrelevant."

They rephrase. "Okay, all it takes is *the illusion of time*. Plus effort. Plus, the nurse said you—"

"Yes, I got a boner," David says. "She told me, too."

"See?! Time and effort!"

They are still so proud. Masters of denial, impervious to reality. That's their superpower.

And, somehow, David still feels strong and virile. After all, he's killed a person.

And he feels weak. After all, he's killed a person.

But he's created one, too.

"Buck up," Dad says, "you've got a baby on the way that you'll need to protect."

David is beginning to understand the craziness of bringing a new human into this world. The thrill. The horror. What if it's not even *his* child? And what will he do if it's a girl? Or a boy? What if something happens? What if it's blind or stillborn or contracts smallpox or leukemia at age four? David still fears the gods' awesome power to taketh away.

But lest he forget: he is not mild-mannered.

He will count his blessings, not whine. Shit could be worse.

Superstorm Phil lasted all summer and reportedly destroyed upward of 1.2 million lives—more than 120,000 in the United States alone—especially when factoring in not just the flood and heat waves, but also the resulting food shortages, the water contamination, the uptick in malaria and dengue fever caused by the massive increase in mosquitos. The NOAA called it the most extreme weather event in two centuries. David saw the peak storms at Spinoza, but the coma shielded him from the power drought and mini-disasters that followed. He woke during the rebuilding effort, $900 billion in damage. Maps altered. Populations dispersed. A global XplO.

And when David killed Mathias, the League of Seven—no, Six—had their own frantic XplO, scattering from the Superdome like fragments of fireworks.

It Girl / Britt Childress wound up in an in-patient psychiatric hospital in Tucson. They diagnosed her with anorexia and paranoid schizophrenia. They're rebuilding her from scratch.

Dr. Ugs / Lee Popkin quietly sought asylum at a few different pharmaceutical companies until AstraZeneca took the bait. With some shady plea-bargaining, Lee will serve six months house arrest for distributing counterfeit drugs before going to work full-time and forever for Big Pharma. It'll be a kind of lifelong indentured servitude, but hey, better than prison.

As for Peacemaker / Owen Surber, he was many kinds of men. Injured football star, would-be soldier, cheerleader, swing dancer, a gentle giant, a bodyguard, a good Christian, a badass motherfucker. He ended his life as a samurai. Noble protector of Mathias Blue, a.k.a. Ultraviolet, Supreme Leader of the USV. But he failed to save this leader from assassination, and when a retainer fails his master, there is only one thing a samurai can do. They found his body in the center of Woosamonsa Court. He'd knelt on the pavement near the fire pit and pulled off Golden Echo's old helmet. He'd Bic-ed himself bald again on the top, leaving tufts of hair around the back and sides. Opening a slit in his costume, he exposed his chest and positioned against it his staff of police nightsticks, with a butcher knife fixed to the tip like a bayonet.

Bowing forward, Owen impaled himself.

Samurais call it *seppuku*. A good death.

Beside Owen, they found a death poem, the kind all samurais compose at their end:

The lights, the lights are out again,
The power's dead and done.
The lights, the lights are out again
But the dark is much more fun.

He'd also been shot in the head with a rifle, so someone else must've been there to finish him off. Probably Sergeant Drill/Nyla White, who went on the run. David isn't sure where she ended up. He keeps his mouth shut. He hopes she'll build great things someday.

And Cap'n Cunt/Haley Roth.

She was alive. Naked, brainwashed, and prepped for ritual sacrifice. But alive. The world has once more cast her as the victim (which she hates) and David as the villain (which he hates). But he's happy to take another fall. David will play the bad guy and go to jail. She will play the victim and go free. The media thinks he's the evil mastermind of the USV, and she's some sad chick who stumbled into a cult and got herself knocked up, along with the other surrogates who've mostly returned to the comfort of their biological families. David tells her sometimes gender stereotypes work out for the best. Babies need their mothers.

The rest of the USV, all the students and converts at the Superdome who tried to throw away their bright futures in favor of a blinding present? Bereft of leadership and left to their own post-traumatic devices, they might have succumbed to some even more awful fate were it not for the saviors who arrived at Spinoza just outside the nick of time.

It wasn't police who came. The parents were the ones who saved the day.

Maybe three hundred Princeton moms and dads descended on the Superdome, broke through the glass entrance just after David had taken his leap and the other USV leaders had run.

Some superheroes were too far gone. When the cups of Liquid Zero didn't work to paralyze them, they weighed themselves down, stuffing canned goods into coat pockets, and wandered into the flooded arena, their bodies drowning, dying a stupid, unnecessary death. In the end, there were only six of these ritual suicides. The rest of the mass of thousands was saved. Parents discovered confused and exhausted kids coming down from otherworldly moments. They talked their children back into some semblance of reality, boys and girls flopping into parents' arms in tears. Most went willingly. Some got dragged away kicking and screaming. The parents did whatever had to be done.

There was Time. Which returned.

David's parents were there. His mom knew enough medicine to immobilize her son, keep him stable until the worst of the storm passed, and then got him to Capital Health Regional Medical Center. David's parents saved his life. They hunkered down in the Superdome and survived the worst of the storm and emerged evolved.

Mathias Blue's parents were not there. The colonel must have been busy with larger governmental and global concerns, so did not arrive in time to save his child from David, the way David saved *his* child from Mathias. Blue resigned from DARPA and landed at Google.

Every officer who comes to David's hospital room door he assumes is Colonel Blue arriving to exact revenge, or to ask the questions he should've asked when Mathias was alive, or to give David the answers to all that's haunted him since. Maybe he's digging up his son's time capsules, to either eliminate them from the earth or finally take the time to understand his flesh and blood, poring over Mathias's journals and to-do lists and hard drives as a kind of posthumous parenting. Maybe he's busy tracking down the babies Mathias placed into those genetically pure surrogate eggs, to either raise that first army of Mathias clones or else destroy them all before they grow up to be too powerful. Maybe that's the sequel, the next set of characters in the USV multiverse's unfolding.

But probably everyone will just move on. Grow up. With time.

David was waiting, at first, for the world to really end. When it didn't, he understood the reality of his situation: there was time. Plenty of time. Time to get better. Time to trudge and claw his way back to normalcy. He'd been given a second chance. And why?

David wonders: What actually happened? What does he believe about himself and Mathias and the almost end of the world? In his quieter moments, David believes Mathias was right. The gods were angry and required a sacrifice. Maybe Mathias was Abraham in this scenario, the true believer, the father they all needed. Maybe David was. Or was he Isaac, just barely saved by the grace of God? Maybe *Haley* was Isaac, and David the lamb or the ram or whatever it was that took Isaac's place. Either way, the gods were appeased, and they let the world live another cycle.

A second chance.

In the fall, most students returned to Princeton and began the tough transition back to normal lives of overachiever-hood. Even David was reinstated. Some dropped out, never to return. Some, like Bob Badalamenti ended up radicalized. He found refuge in dark corners of the internet, David had heard. Far-right men's-rights groups camouflaging a deeper-seated hatred—come for the misogyny, stay for the fascism. David wonders if they'll ever see him again, whether Haley will someday need to close that loop.

Retention rate took a nosedive in most liberal arts colleges' *U.S. News & World Report* rankings. Kids had learned enough. Trade school enrollment went up, though. For many, the USV was a blip, a quick foray into the world of radical college activism and cultish zealotry. For others, Mathias Blue was, and always will be, an honest-to-god savior. So David assumes there are many who would love to see Ultraviolet's murderer dead. David Fuffman is the USV's Benedict Arnold. Who *wouldn't* try to sneak into David's hospital room and smother him with pillows? But maybe the USV faithful will agree that the state of his being—the prison of walls and bars that he'll likely enter, and this other prison of flesh and bone—perhaps that's plenty punishment for evil old David Instead.

Besides police protection, David's sister is here to watch over him while he's confined to hospital beds, wheelchairs, and operating tables. Beth has built a tent in the corner of the room. She stays there as much as the orderlies will allow. She says she's keeping guard, making sure no one messes with her brother in his sleep. She is protecting him. And she knows everything about the USV. David answers whatever she asks about what he's done. It's *his* way of protecting *her*.

He remembers what she said to him, the first day she saw him: "I heard you flew!"

"I fell," he clarified. "Grabbity sucks."

She hugged him lightly. She promised she'd protect him.

"How do I look?" David asked, scared of the answer.

She shrugged and said, "You'll get there."

Even Thoreau was an outcast. Once, he accidentally burned down three hundred acres of forest while trying to make clam chowder. Neighbors called him a damned rascal. He did jail time, moved to the woods, and was the kind of guy who brought laundry home each week for Mom to wash. But every Tuesday he floated a rowboat out to the center of his watery backyard, carrying a compass and sounding line, to survey the bottom of Walden Pond. He needed to fathom how deep it went.

If you can divine your own backyard, David thinks, *you can rule a world.* This is David's new world. This family.

The best part of being in the hospital is that Haley Roth is only three floors away. They have her downstairs in the maternity ward. She almost lost the baby. All those drugs and lack of proper nutrition. Doctors put her on strict bed rest at first, but now she can move around freely. As freely as any other exhausted nine months pregnant woman ready to pop.

David still lies awake scared shitless that they'll lose the baby before it has a chance to fight its way into the world. After all of this. After he's finally learned the true nature of sacrifice.

But he still has a lot to learn. He understands this once Haley finally tells him the truth.

She wheeled into his room one day, or maybe it was night, with that giant fleshball exploding on her stomach. "Watch this, Business-Man," she said, and popped a little wheelie.

David responded with anger, masking his fatherly fear. He said something childish and self-righteous, something like "I didn't throw myself off the roof and save you both only to watch you accidentally kill yourself in a wheelchair."

Haley grimaced, and David knew her enough to see she was hiding something.

The truth: Haley had never been hypnotized or brainwashed, nor paralyzed. She'd never intended to slit her own throat with that axe—was he insane?

What she'd intended was to kill Mathias Blue.

And with his own weapon of choice. Once his countdown ended and he got close enough. She'd trained for the moment, knew exactly where to strike. She was fully prepared to save herself and her baby. To save them all.

Blink. David sees Cap'n Cunt's knuckles turning white, gripping that purple axe handle.

"I'm sorry, David, that you'd fashioned me into a maiden that needed saving from some dragon." She put a gentle hand on his legs, immobile in their hospital bed. "Because, buddy, *I am* the dragon."

He wanted to say "I'm sorry," but instead he let tears fill his eyes.

"It's okay," she said. "You're the fucking dragon, too."

"But you'd been dosed with Liquid," David said.

"I learned a little while ago not to drink just anything at parties."

Blink. Haley spits a stream of liquid through pursed lips. When Mathias turns to look at her, she pantomimes like she's blowing him a kiss.

She laughed at herself, or at life. There were other dragons, it turned out.

Dr. Ugs had not dosed her, nor poured hundreds of Dixie cups' worth of paralyzing Liquid Zero. His Kool-Aid was actual Kool-Aid, the placebo of the masses. He had, however, loaded up a syringe with a lethal dose of phenobarbital, telling Mathias he was administering the same intravenous cocktail Hitler once received: glucose and methamphetamines. The phenobarbital would've caused respiratory arrest if David had not beaten Lee and Haley to the punch.

Maybe this is what actually killed him.

Blink. A needle punctures skin, and that puff of blood clouds the syringe liquid, a tiny cenote.

"Even the other pregnant girls were trying to off him," Haley continued. "They had this whole witches' coven thing going on, Blue Star Wicca, really leaned into it at the end there. They claim it was the Black Book revenge spell they cast. They think that's what called you down from the sky."

Blink. David looks down from the Spinoza ceiling at surrogates arrayed in a seven-pointed star, a heptagram. The days of creation. A symbol to ward off evil. A sign of perfection.

"But Nyla wasn't in on it!" David insisted. "She was *shooting* at me, I remember!"

"Nyla could've hit a damn raisin if she wanted. She was shooting *near* you. To stall or keep you cowering on that catwalk, out of everyone's way."

Blink. An errant bullet pops a light fixture ten feet away.

"What about Owen?!" David was screaming now.

"I don't know why he killed himself," Haley said. "I'm fairly sure he ran up to that catwalk to stop you, to help you, but... he knew he'd failed both of you, failed everyone."

"And Britt?"

"Oh, she was just off her rocker," Haley said. "Totally gone."

"Haley, um, if you all were planning this... Why. Didn't. Anyone. Tell. Me?"

"Nobody knew about each other." Haley shrugged. "We all thought we were the only one that saw through Mathias, that *I'm* the one who has to take matters into my own hands. Somehow we were all too scared to be the only one challenging his authority. Like, assumed we'd be outted and exiled. I mean, by that point there were thousands of kids that would've died for him. Blindly."

"I'm so stupid," he said. "And here I thought we were all so zeroed in with each other."

"Maybe we were," she said.

Another sickening thought arrives.

"You were all going to let me burn," David said. "Exile by fire."

She went silent, and her stare stayed fixed. "I'm sorry, David," she said. "I…I guess, first of all, everyone else believed *you* were the bad guy, or at least just as dangerous as Mathias."

"What did you believe?"

"That you're good," she said, wiggling his toes. "Or you've got potential, at least."

"Then why didn't you help me?"

"I *did* help you, remember?" She wrapped her fingers around his wrists like a human handcuff. She thumbed his palms. "My job was to save this baby, and for that I had to be willing to sacrifice my own decency and be ready to murder someone. I saw it all playing out and I *believed* that if I could get rid of Mathias, we might all be okay. You and me and this baby and everyone else. But I also believed about *you* what you doubted about *me*," she said. "I knew you were strong enough to save yourself. I had *faith* that you were. And you were. You are. You've never needed someone else to save you. So I need you to promise me something."

She had asked if he believed that he'd walk again. He said he did. She asked him to promise.

And although, someday, a mixture of time and magic and science and drugs and love would eventually make it happen—this slow evolution from crawling on the shores of Spinoza to sitting to standing to actually walking upright again—David couldn't actually see this future when he told her yes.

"Yes, Haley, I promise I will walk again."

Sometimes we make promises only to force ourselves to keep them.

It's a promise for himself, and for Haley, and for the baby primed to arrive. David promises out of love and out of fear, because he fears what every expectant father fears: that it won't make it. Or that it'll just stop breathing one day. Maybe this fear never ends. Maybe it'll be born perfect but eighteen years from now be co-opted by some dangerous college cult that forces his child to take psychotropic drugs while zip-lining across fucking bonfires.

It never ends.

After David recovers from his final surgeries, all he does is ask the nurses and cops if he can visit Haley. Sometimes they say yes. When David finally arrives at her room she's usually sleeping. And he's still on so many drugs. He sleeps all the time, too.

Blink and it's day.

Blink and it's night.

Days pass like hours and they keep missing each other. Rowboats in the morning.

But David is there and awake for the baby's delivery.

He lets Haley squeeze his hand as hard as she can, digging in her nails, drawing blood. Watches her writhe and sway on a birthing ball; waddle around the delivery room, veins straining beneath her skin; hanging from a squat bar, her legs splayed like some Yoruban goddess so gravity can do its job. Haley lets him scream along with her. They both refuse to time her contractions, but David can't help but keep track of the dilation count from zero up to ten centimeters, praying for the numbers to keep climbing. When she gets stuck at eight, David worries that, after all they've been through, it's still possible to get stuck in the dark neck of time.

David says, "Remember when you once told me that you wished your superpower was to shrink really tiny so you could hide in small spaces and not take up too much space?"

"What?" she pants, another rush coming on strong.

"Well, now it's time for you to get as big as possible. To grow bigger and bigger and bigger."

Whether or not she hears him, she reaches full dilation after two more contractions and now it's time to push. When the baby starts to crown, they wheel David around to the other side to see. That white magic head coming out of nowhere, through a ring of fire, into the world. When the shoulders emerge, David hears the child's cry mixing with Haley's last push, and David realizes this thing Haley's doing is the first truly superhuman feat he's ever witnessed. She is divinity. Earth shifts on its axis and cycles back on itself at the sound of a primordial howl.

His *daughter's* howl.

Claire Eloise Roth was born November 1, the day after Halloween. For David and Haley, it was the day the clocks reset and time started over again.

And though David can't walk or stand, he's sure he can fly around that hospital room, high above the bed, out of his body, out of his mind, the obliterating miracle of the moment sending him into some stratosphere, imbuing him with the strength of some mighty god or demon. He's sure, absolutely sure, she's *his* daughter. She must be. The connection is too strong. They are zeroed in. She makes him move his toes. She is a new superpower running through him.

The nurses swaddle Claire in her first cape. Haley holds the baby girl, cradling her head, and raises her up toward the ceiling. A tiny human airplane.

The little one wobbles a bit at first, shifts her hips.

And then, just like that: equilibrium.

ACKNOWLEDGMENTS

Countless books, films, shows, articles, and comics mixed together to inspire this novel but I'd be remiss not to explicitly call out a few that directly influenced specific scenes. Consider this a list of Suggested Further Reading: Ursula K. Le Guin's short story "Some Approaches to the Problem of the Shortage of Time," my father Barry Nemett's novel, *Crooked Tracks*, Mark Rudd's *Underground: My Life with SDS and the Weathermen*, Samuel R. Delaney's *Heavenly Breakfast: An Essay on the Winter of Love*, Nathaniel Hawthorne's short story "Earth's Holocaust," Rick Strassman, M.D.'s *DMT: The Spirit Molecule*, and Rebecca Solnit's *A Paradise Built in Hell*.

The Human DJ ritual is based on a collaborative musical exercise developed by the innovative music education nonprofit, MIMA Music; aspects of Mathias's thesis are based on works by my grad school colleague Lee Pembleton, and the Princeton Dueling Society was an actual student organization cofounded by my friends Ari Samsky and Rafil Kroll-Zaidi.

Enormous thanks to my literary agent Noah Ballard at Curtis Brown, Ltd., who has an unparalleled passion for narrative and has been a tremendous editor, champion and friend throughout this entire process. My endless appreciation to you for getting this book out into the world. And hey, thanks to the agents that passed on the book, too, but still gave it a thorough read and offered helpful feedback. Thanks to everyone at The Unnamed Press, including Chris Heiser, Jaya Nicely, Nancy Tan and above all Olivia Taylor Smith, for saying Yes to this book and pushing it to be as risky and as real as it could be. Olivia, you have been a true partner from start to finish. Thanks also to Ryan Neuschafer, Laura Grafton and the team at Brilliance Audio for migrating the book to a new medium and for being so patient with me in the recording studio.

Thanks to all the folks who read drafts, provided feedback, blurbs and other helpful boosts, including Chris Beha, Clara Bingham, Mary Diaz, Tim Edmond, Eva Hagberg Fisher, Ann Garvin, Keith Gessen, Justin Goldberg, Zachary Phillips, Brian Sewell, Kayti Wingfield, Matthew Jent, Brian Deleeuw, Ann Marie Svilar Black, Liz Femiano, Virginia Wagner, and special thanks to Justin Taylor, whose body of work and whose kind decision to include my story "The Last Man," in his anthology *The Apocalypse Reader* gave me the confidence to turn a piece of flash fiction into this long-ass novel.

I had the unbelievable privilege to work with some awe-inspiring teachers and professors who pushed me along when they could've easily brushed me aside. Thanks specifically to Richard Kalter, Elden Schneider, Chris Mihavetz, Ned Sparrow, Joyce Carol Oates, Jeffrey Stout, Cornel West, Dale Peck, Sam Lipsyte, Tom Barbash, Holly Payne, John Laskey, Leslie Carol Roberts, Gabrielle Calvocoressi, Shoshana and David Cooper, and all the artists and pseudo-parents I've grown up with at Maryland Institute College of Art.

I've never found writing to be a *lonely* pursuit, but it's solitary by nature, so I consistently seek and find amazing crews of people who've expanded my understanding of creativity and influenced characters in this book: the guys I've known forever, especially Jesse, Ryan, Brooks, Andy and Greg; the characters of Terrace F. Club and *Nassau Weekly*; the cast and crew of *The Instrument*, especially Jamie and Macauley; my brothers at MIMA Music, especially Christoph, Caleb, and Trace; my brothers at the Zookjera flophouse in Pennington, especially Ajay, David, Peter, Andy, and Stu; the team at History Factory, especially Bruce and Rick; and the gentlemen of The Shack, especially Evan and Trent.

Finally, my family. Thank you, Abby Rosen, for always being there, and for introducing me to meditation, rites of passage, and the world behind the world. Thanks to Heather and Jason Dressel for taking care of me and for giving me the push I needed to get this book published. Thanks to Bruce and Geri Schirmer and Liza and Zachary Rubenoff for welcoming me into your families with so much love and support. Thanks to my grandparents, Rose and Daniel Rosen and Bobbi and Milton Nemett for defining what family should be. I still talk to you guys all the time and I'm pretty sure you're answering back.

Thank you to my parents, Diane and Barry Nemett. You sewed my first reversible Superman/Batman cape, made me fall in love with stories, pushed me to pursue every passion and project, gave me confidence, and kept me grounded. Above all, you've taught me how to be a loving and supportive partner and parent. Thank you for this life. I'm really enjoying it. Thanks to my sister, Laini Nemett, my first and forever sidekick. Your talent and work ethic astound me. Thanks for always being my best sounding board, my biggest fan and my coolest friend. And thanks for finding my future brother-in-law, David Leiberman, who is undoubtedly also a superhero.

To my incredible kids, Jack and Rose. I hope you wait a while to read this book and, when you do, I hope you don't think Daddy is insane. You're both so hilarious and sweet and curious and creative, and I love re-experiencing life and Batman through your eyes. Nothing will ever be as important and interesting as you two. Thanks for changing my life forever, in the best possible way.

And to Kate Lynn Nemett. Thank you. From the moment I first saw you in that poetry class where you were constantly brilliant, and I was constantly eating a large sandwich, I was fascinated by you. Thanks for being my muse, my motivator, my cheerleader, my challenger, my partner in time, my heroine, for keeping me honest and making me whole. Thank you for the home we've built, the kids we've made, and the history and future we're creating together. Thanks for being the person I think about when I'm writing. Most of all, thanks for loving me, and letting me love you. I'm so excited to discover what we do next. I'll meet you by the rowboats.